PASSION'S PRICE

"You scoff at my offers, Mr. Killeen, so why don't you tell me what you would need to take this job? Name your price and I'll see if I can match it." Jenna waited for his answer, her heart pounding with anticipation.

Chance smiled wryly. His thumb moved up to her lips and stroked them sensuously, as he gauged her reaction to his intimate touch. "I think you want me so bad that you'd offer me just about anything, wouldn't you?" he said in an alarmingly seductive voice. "Maybe you should offer me the last thing you have to give. It might just be the thing to make me say yes."

His eyes, as alert as a hawk's, focused on her mouth. She was not swift enough to elude the lips that came down on hers with ravishing boldness. Jenna pushed at his naked chest, but she was no match for his strength. When he had taken his pleasure, he pulled his lips from hers with deliberate slowness. With mocking eyes, he dared her to meet his price. . . .

LINDA P. SANDIFER
MIDNIGHT HEARTS

ZEBRA BOOKS
KENSINGTON PUBLISHING CORP.

To Janie Storck
Friend, fellow writer, kindred spirit.

ZEBRA BOOKS

are published by

Kensington Publishing Corp.
850 Third Avenue
New York, NY 10022

First printing: September, 1991

Printed in the United States of America

10 9 8 7 6 5 4 3 2

Prologue

1870

The street lamp cast a golden glow upon the snow and upon the gleaming black landau parked unashamedly in front of the New York tenement house. Chance Killeen's tired, cold feet slowed upon the snowy sidewalk as he neared the elaborate carriage. Upon its high seat the driver slept, emitting snores from deep within a heavy fur robe that he had pulled around him and over his head. Evidently, he was not lost.

With hunched shoulders against December's frigid breeze, his cap pulled snugly over his black hair, seventeen-year-old Chance curiously sidled up to the coach. Through the delicate silvery patterns Jack Frost had laid upon the window glass, he tried to see the landau's dark interior, wondering . . . just wondering what one looked like on the inside. Were they really lined with velvet and leather and enameled with silver and gold as he'd heard they were?

Suddenly, a girl's face sprang up from the other side of the glass. Startled, Chance inhaled sharply and leaped backward, nearly losing his footing in the slick snow. She frowned at him for a moment as though trying to identify him, then she rubbed some of the frost away from the inside with a gloved hand, but her breath immediately clouded her image again. All Chance could see of her were huge blue eyes, generous lips that turned down rather sadly, and a hat of gray fur that framed her small face from forehead to chin.

Embarrassed to have intruded upon her privacy, he managed a sheepish, lopsided grin and shrugged his shoulders while mouthing, "I'm sorry." He expected her to respond with the typical girlish reaction of sticking out her tongue or even screaming at the coachman to protect her from him, but she merely looked past him with disappointment and disinterest as her gaze traveled to the building. Then she shrank back into the huge, luxurious carriage and vanished from view.

What kind of person would bring her into this neighborhood at this late hour and then make her wait on the street where she could be molested or get frostbitten toes? And who inside this shabby tenement house knew someone as wealthy as the owner of that expensive landau?

He twisted his body and glanced upward at the dark, unlit windows that appeared as eyes closed in slumber. There was only one light on in the building, the usual one at this hour—his mother's. She always left a lamp burning for him until he got home. Oftentimes she waited up for him, using the late hours to sew on the dresses she made for others. Since he'd been working at the rail yards, she worried constantly about him, but it was no wonder after what had happened to his father just a year ago.

It had been difficult to take on the very job that had killed his father, but destitution and desperation had given him no choice. Being the oldest, it was his responsibility now to support his mother and two brothers. She'd begged him not to go to the rail yards, but she'd had to relent when she saw no other way to put food on the table.

The memory of his father's horrible accident erased the thoughts of the wealthy owner of the landau and the fact that he hadn't satisfied his curiosity about the carriage's interior. Weary from going to school all day then working at the rail yards until midnight, Chance opened the main door to the tenement house and started up the stairs to their second-floor apartment. He hoped it wouldn't be too cold in there tonight, but the wind coming out of the north could freeze a body to the bone this time of year.

He moved up the stairs with more urgency now, anxious to get inside, see what his mother had saved for him from supper, and then fall into bed. His two younger brothers would be asleep in the room the three of them shared. His mother laid out her own bed each night on the living room sofa and gathered it up each morning.

In the hall outside the apartment, his hand hesitated over the doorknob. He heard voices within . . . voices in low, frustrated tones, trying not to rise in anger. One was his mother's; the other was a man's.

"I never meant for him to be killed, Lily. You know that. You know it was just a freak accident that took his life. Why won't you believe me?"

A sound of anguish came from his mother's throat. Chance wanted to protect her from her apparent pain, but something kept him at the door, afraid to go inside, for he sensed her pain was not the physical kind.

"You don't understand and you never will," she said to the man. "All you've ever thought about is what you want and what you'll do to get it—no, what you'll do to *take* it. How can you expect me to forgive you? How can you expect me to go willingly to your bed? I'd rather die in squalor than become your wife now. You ruined Duke with your underhanded manipulations of the stock market. You're no better

7

than the thieves who hold up the trains with their guns. Now, get out of my home and my life, Sol. I never want to see you again!"

A long silence prevailed, and Chance unknowingly held his breath.

"I never meant for it to turn out this way, Lily," the man insisted.

His mother gave no response.

In a moment, Chance heard footsteps nearing the door. He glanced about anxiously for a place to hide, not wanting to be caught eavesdropping. But there was no shadow, no alcove; just a long, foot-worn hall. Boldly, he jerked his tired, lanky frame to proud attention just as the door swung inward and the golden light from the room angled across him.

Solomon Lee's crystal blue eyes pierced Chance for a moment in surprise, then unflinchingly met his gaze of silent hatred. He understood the look well and didn't begrudge the boy his feelings. For the first time in his life, he hated himself with the same degree of intensity reflected in those youthful eyes. Enemies were something he normally made with glee, but this time his heart ached so fiercely he felt it might fail him.

Releasing a weary sigh, Solomon Lee at last turned away from the boy who looked so disturbingly like his deceased father. Solomon's footsteps echoed in the corridor, haunting him with their aloneness. Perhaps it was merely guilt, but he felt Chance Killeen's green gaze burning into his back long after he rounded the corner.

Part I

The Alliance

Chapter One

March, 1886
Idaho-Montana Border

In the waning light, Chance Killeen grimly watched the mules and ore wagons disappearing into the mountains that towered over them like unsympathetic, omniscient sentinels. He hunched his shoulders against the cold and tried to wiggle his numb toes.

"Well, I guess we ought to feel lucky that bunch of damned hoodlums didn't take our boots, too," he said.

Bard Delaney, a short, stocky Irishman and Chance's partner in the Wapiti Silver Mine, apprehensively eyed the heavy snow clouds draped over the Bitterroots and their first flakes of snow vanishing into the icy current of the Clark Fork River.

"Shoor enough, and our lives," he replied in his thick brogue. "And if it wasn't enough that those thievin' rogues robbed us, they had to leave us stranded, too. I'd like y' to be knowin' that I came close to losin' me temper when they made us drive their booty halfway to Plains—and just fer the sole purpose o' puttin' them further from the law."

In a frustrated movement, Chance readjusted his Stetson. "They'll make good money off those mules for sure. But at least we got the ore on the train and headed for the smelter, so I guess the trip wasn't a total loss."

"God bless us. We were such an aisy mark." Delaney shook his big head disgustedly. "They must have sat and watched us unload the ore onto the train, all the while wantin' nothin' but the mules."

"You know these mountains are a haven and a heaven for bandits, Delaney. Besides, we were outnumbered. No sense in brooding about it."

"Nivertheless, I'll have me eyes open fer those mules. Those thieves will hang if I iver hear o' them, and I won't be havin' a hard time findin' a tree—y' can be sartin o' that."

Delaney clenched his meaty fists and continued to complain of their misfortune, his words drifting past the more important thoughts on Chance's mind. They both knew that the odds of ever seeing any of the mules again were minuscule. The brands would soon be altered and the proof gone.

It was a setback for their mining company that they didn't need. They were operating on a shoestring as it was. Not only did he and Delaney work the mine themselves with a small crew of men, but to save the expense of hiring outside freighters, they also hauled the ore over rugged Glidden Pass to the train at Thompson Falls, where it in turn was taken to the smelter at Wickes. If their profit margin became too small, they might be forced to sell to that big conglomerate that had had their eye on the Wapiti, as well as every other small privately owned silver mine in the Coeur d'Alenes. And, buying two new strings of mules and wagons was going to hurt the pocketbook tremendously.

Chance pulled his coat collar up to his ears. The wool scratched against the stubble on his jaw and somehow made the situation even more abrasive. To top it off, the wind cut through his pants and wool

12

long johns as though they were nothing more than a lady's silk pantalets.

The solemnity of evening and the stillness of the falling snow was beautiful but extremely dangerous for men with nothing but the clothes on their backs. The cold northern gale whispering through the valley and stirring the snow on the ground into small drifts suggested a blizzard might not be far behind. In the mountains, Winter didn't seem to know that March was supposed to belong to Spring.

Chance shifted his weight to keep the cold from seeping deeper into the leather soles of his boots. "We could toss a coin on which way to go, but I think Thompson Falls is closer than Plains and we know people there. Maybe we can find a place to stay for the night."

"And what would we be usin' fer money, me frind? Y' can be shoor that our good looks will open no doors today. Of coorse, now, if y' had shaved this morrow, it might have helped. But, then, how were y' to know we'd be robbed?"

"Maybe somebody will take pity on us or give us some credit. There's old Jerry Winthrop that runs the Gold Bar Saloon. God knows, we've contributed to his pocketbook from time to time."

Delaney grumbled some more and uselessly tried to brush aside the snow slapping his bearded face. "Freezin' to death offinds me, Keely. It shoorly does. So let's be on our way, whichever it might be."

Snowflakes drifted down thicker and faster as they started their journey back to Thompson Falls, following the Northern Pacific railroad tracks that skirted the river. Chance stepped up his pace, anxious to get to shelter and warmth. His feet felt like blocks of wood.

Delaney panted alongside him and tried to keep up. His breath drifted up from the obscure opening in his beard. "Oh, murther! Slow down, Keely! Me legs 'r' a mite shorter than yers and me stomach a mite heavier. Have some consideration fer yer dear frind—just a wee bit would be monstrous sweet. If it is me death ye're wantin', 'tis a wish ye'll soon be gettin'."

Chance didn't slow his pace; he knew Delaney was only griping, as usual.

The rush of the wind increased. The heavy, wet spring snow pelted and stung their faces with new determination. Chance pulled up his red bandana, positioning it just beneath his eyes. Delaney did the same. Too miserable to talk, they suffered in silence for at least a mile.

Then, to the south, as though a godsend, the long-drawn scream of a train whistle pierced the empty land and echoed against the silent, windblown mountains. Chance looked toward the sound and saw the single headlight of the locomotive and a bundle of black smoke rising into the white sky. Steam from the engine also rose in great white puffs before the wind snatched it and scattered it against the snow clouds. The black smoke from the smokestack took on the shape of a cone, its top seemingly spinning. He could hear the steady rhythm of the drivers now and could feel the distinctive vibration upon the rails beneath his feet.

Excited, he grabbed Delaney by the arm. "It's the Northern Pacific, heading for Spokane. We'll jump it and take it all the way to Rathdrum."

His words were muffled by the red bandana still over his face, but Delaney heard him well enough and his heart began to race. "Oh, murther! Ye'd be wantin' me to jump a movin' train at my age! The depot in Thompson Falls suits me better, Keely. And look at where we are—barely clingin' to the mountainside. The divil himself must be wantin' to distroy me today, and he's usin' you to do it!"

Chance glanced up and down the track. Delaney

14

was right, of course. There wasn't a level piece of ground anywhere except for the railroad bed itself. The mountains, purple-cast in the day's fading light, were nearly perpendicular and covered with pines, scrub brush, and rocks. From the mountains' sides, the roadbed for the railroad had been cut and laid. On the other side of the tracks, down a steep embankment, the Clark Fork River wound through the valley at the base of the mountains. In either direction, the naked and frosty steel rails found a course alongside the river, until the thin black stripes upon the earth's white expanse narrowed, ran together, and finally disappeared around the base of another mountain.

Stepping down off the track was necessary anyway to let the train pass by, but it would place the top of their heads just about level with the underside of the cars. Jumping onto it from this position would be no easy feat, especially for Delaney, a short-legged and heavy chested man of fifty. Still, if they didn't, they were likely to freeze to death before they ever reached town.

"Tell me, Keely," Delaney couldn't conceal his apprehension. "By the Murther Saint herself, do y' honestly think I can do this? I'm not exactly doubtin' yer judgment, but by the same token, these conditions 'r' not in our favor."

"The train won't be going too fast through here." Chance pointed up ahead to a spot where the ground widened out a bit next to the track. "We'll catch it there." At Delaney's skeptical expression, he tried to ease his friend's mind. "You want to get home to my mother's cooking, don't you?"

Delaney's face fell. "Curse yer bloody ancestors, Keely! Y' know where to hurt a man."

Chance grinned, his green eyes twinkling with excitement and mischievousness like a young boy. "You're the best blaster in the Coeur d'Alenes,

Delaney. If you're brave enough to handle dynamite, surely you can't be afraid to jump a train."

Delaney didn't like it when Chance got that unwavering look of determination, because he knew he didn't have any choice but to go along with him. A rescue of easier means was not likely to be forthcoming, and the storm was much worse than it had been when they'd started out. Visibility was fading swiftly, along with the day's light, and his feet were already so cold he could barely stand on them.

"Fer yer information, Keely," Delaney replied, "lightin' off dynamite is one thing. Jumpin' a movin' train is quite another. I hardly see how y' can compare the two."

They reached the wide spot next to the track. Delaney squinted through the blowing snow and wiped a nervous hand across the bandana covering his beard. The train was fast approaching.

"Ye've taken leave of yer sinses," he exclaimed. "That is, if y' iver had any, and I'm beginnin' to doubt it. It'll be slick as the floor o' hell on scrubbin' day. I tell y', me feet are so cold, Keely, they feel like pegs."

The train whistle screamed again and echoed down the dusky valley. Its black serpentine shape slid through some trees, bolted into the open, then disappeared again behind the protective evergreen foliage. Its headlight glared and shimmered like the eye of a monster. Chance wondered if the engineer had seen them, for there was no reason for him to blow his whistle way out here so far from a town or train stop.

Then the train burst into full view. The sight and sound of it stirred Chance's blood. Like a living thing, it panted exhaust, screamed its warning, and thundered ominously toward them. There was that old mysterious romance to it that he realized he missed, but that he had turned his back on years ago.

In the dusk everything was black and white. The

16

brush and trees, naked in winter's remaining grip, as well as the train's dark body, were highly visible against the snow-covered backdrop. A billowy plume of steam and exhaust mingled together and twisted out into the white sky. Like a lady's scarf whipping in the wind, it blew back along the length of the train, nearly concealing half of the cars from view in the white vapor.

With a roar, the train raced past them, blasting the air and shaking the ground. The huge wheels passed over the rail joints with a rhythmic "click-click, click-click," and its bottom side nearly brushed their shoulders, dwarfing their size. The noise was deafening. The train seemed almost rickety as the cars swayed back and forth, but Chance knew the instability was only an illusion. It wasn't going to topple over on them. Nor was it traveling as fast as it seemed.

Chance concentrated on its motion, its speed, and timed his own movements accordingly. The gleaming pistons, like gigantic arms bending at the elbow, propelled the mighty wheels with constant, unerring power. He counted the cars going past, then hollered to Delaney above the clatter and pointed down the circuitous side of the train. "Catch that car just before the caboose!"

Delaney's heart pounded in pure fear. He could only think of being crushed beneath the mighty wheels that were level with his eyes. But he had no time to dwell on it.

"I know the truth now, Keely, I surely do!" he hollered above the clattering of the iron wheels upon the track. "Ye're out to distroy me—you and the divil!"

Chance just laughed. "You can make it, Delaney! Here it comes!"

Chance set his eye on the designated passenger car, gauging the oncoming speed and ignoring the snow lashing his face. As it approached, he ran toward it

17

over the sloped, uneven ground. When the platform steps approached, he easily caught the hand rail and swung aboard. He then turned to help Delaney.

Delaney's short legs pumped powerfully while his arms worked in rhythm much the same way as the drivers on the train. Regardless of how fast he was traveling, he was losing ground and the train was getting past him. Chance moved to the top of the platform steps to make room for him, then reached out a hand while wrapping his other arm around the platform railing. "Get my hand, Delaney!"

With a surge of his short legs, Delaney got even with the metal platform. He reached out for Chance's hand, stumbled, and missed it. After several attempts he caught hold just as the ground went out from under him. The train passed swiftly around a bend with Delaney's legs dangling in midair.

Terrified, he made one last mighty effort and swung his bulky body across both the steps and the platform. Panting as hard as the train, he clung there for a moment to catch his breath. Finally, Chance hauled him onto the main platform, where they collapsed into a heap, shoulder to shoulder.

"Damn yer bloody ancestors—*again*." Delaney's head lolled against the solid wooden body of the passenger car. "If it warn't fer them, you wouldn't be here. Y' neerly got me torn to smithereens."

Chance leaned against the railing and caught his breath. "You need to lose some weight, Delaney. I damned near couldn't get you on."

"Is it the fault of me weight, Keely?" he demanded hoarsely. "No, I think instead yer brain is the root o' the problem. To be sartin, it's made o' mush—a worse kind than me dear murther used to force me to eat. And some of it must have wint to me own head, fer I'm as insane as you fer goin' along with yer blarney."

With the danger past, Chance allowed himself to

see the humor in the situation. Suddenly, he leaned his head back and laughed into the bandana. "Nearly doesn't count, Delaney, except maybe in dynamite."

Delaney glared at him, but Chance's dancing eyes held an infectious mirth. Delaney finally softened toward his friend, as he always did. "Ye're right, of coorse, but a bastard just the same."

Chance straightened and turned to the door that led to the rear of the passenger car. "Come on, let's get in out of the cold. We can slip into a back seat and maybe go unnoticed by the conductor."

Delaney gathered himself up and led the way, but just inside the door he stopped abruptly. From over the top of the Irishman's head, Chance immediately saw the reason for his friend's sudden paralysis.

Before them stood a tall, svelte woman, whose silk gown and huge eyes were both as blue as a hot September sky, and whose hair was as golden as the summer sun. She was truly a sight for a weary man's eyes. Unfortunately, her tiny pearl-handled derringer had a gleam all its own and was aimed directly—and quite steadily—at Delaney's heaving chest.

Solomon Lee leaned back in his velvet-tufted chair, puffed on his cigar, and scrutinized his opponent from across the small round table. The man hardly looked the sort to use violence in his quest for wealth, but Solomon supposed that when a man was lacking in intelligence, he had no alternative but to revert to physical force.

As Solomon blew smoke to the clerestory ceiling of the club room, he decided he would make no recriminations at this time. It might work more to his advantage if Ted Durfey believed he was not accused of any misdeed—namely, murder and attempted murder. Not only had Solomon's chief engineer recently been killed, but last fall while he and his granddaughter, Jenna, were floating down the Coeur d'Alene River on a preliminary trip to determine the feasibility of building a railroad through the mountains, shots had been fired on them. They'd been fortunate to walk away with their lives, but their boatman had been killed.

It was apparent that someone didn't want him building in the Coeur d'Alenes and was trying to scare him away. But the gold and silver had been found. There was money to be made here and everybody wanted in on it, including him.

"What a coincidence that you were on board this train, Durfey," Solomon said at last, breaking the moment that was obviously uncomfortable for his opponent. "It'll give us a chance to talk."

"I doubt it was a coincidence, Lee," Durfey responded with a feral snarl to his lips. "You've probably had my every move dogged since you found out I was going to build a railroad through the Coeur d'Alenes."

Solomon chuckled and puffed on his cigar again, seemingly impervious and utterly collected.

Ted Durfey couldn't deny that he was intimidated by Solomon Lee and maybe even a little afraid of him now that he was face to face with the man. After all, he didn't have much experience in the railroad world. He was just a small-timer who had ventured into incorporating a company for the first time. Even though his partners were seasoned railroad men, it was still a frightening undertaking with so much money involved. He didn't like sitting here talking to the infamous railroad baron who was known to demolish empires with nothing more than a signal to the big men at the New York Stock Exchange.

Durfey shifted restlessly in the chair, waiting for Lee to proceed. He was extremely uncomfortable in the elegance that surrounded him. This car, the

Crescent, was one of the two privately owned by Lee. The other was the *Marietta,* and both had been coupled to the Northern Pacific for this journey. Overhead a crystal chandelier added depth to the ornately designed clerestory ceiling and cast its light upon the white paneled walls, making the room appear larger than it was. Burgundy and gold velvet furnishings and matching burgundy carpet added to the blatant richness. Both walls of the small room were draped with gold brocade but drawn against any curious eyes outside in the twilight as the train rumbled its way slowly through the mountain snowstorm, determined to reach its destination.

He felt undeniably like a field clod placed in the center of a mound of gold nuggets.

"Well, Durfey," Lee said between puffs on his cigar. "What's your price? And don't tell me you don't have one, because every man does."

Durfey's throat constricted and he felt his face turning hot with outrage. The old geezer just sat there with legs crossed at the knee, waiting like a hawk, knowing with confidence that he could snare his prey. But he was mistaken this time. Little did he know that two could play his game.

"I won't be bought off, Lee. By you or anyone."

Solomon shrugged indifferently. "I'm going to build a railroad through the Coeur d'Alenes, Durfey, and what good will it do you with my line running parallel to yours in a canyon so narrow you can spit across it? I can run you out of business eventually, and you know it."

Durfey held his ground. "It won't be as easy to run me out of business as it has been your competitors in the past."

A chuckle gurgled in Solomon's throat. His eyes gleamed with the joy of a good challenge. "All right. So you can't be bought this time, but you need the money hauling the gold and silver from the mines to the smelters. I don't, but I want it. In other words, you're desperate and I'm not. Did you know that desperate people usually fail?"

Durfey tensed belligerently, gripping the chair's armrests until his knuckles turned white. He could handle the imperious Solomon Lee if his partners would only let him. A man didn't have to know how to manipulate stocks to eliminate an adversary.

"There will be profits enough to go around," he said hatefully. "There's always room for competition. Even as we speak, more railroads are in the planning stages. There will be a railroad up every canyon in those mountains."

"Yes, and I plan to see to it that they are all mine."

Durfey set his jaw stubbornly. "You won't have them all. This time you've met your match, old man."

Solomon considered his opponent. He knew he had more experience and more money than Durfey, but the man had an idiot's single-mindedness that clouded his judgment. He would have to be careful with Durfey. A cowardly dog was oftentimes the first to bite.

"Let's not squabble, Durfey. Figure out how much it will cost you to build your line and I'll write you out a bank draft in the same amount."

"And how about the profits I stand to gain over the life of the mines? That could go on for decades and be worth hundreds of thousands of dollars."

"Or it could all dry up before the tracks are even laid."

Suspicion leaped in Durfey's eyes. "You're willing to put out thousands and take the chance of that happening?"

Solomon shrugged. "I can afford to gamble. I doubt you can. If you sell out to me, you will be assured of coming out ahead. Sometimes—and especially in your case—it is better to get a little than to lose a lot."

Durfey stood up and walked to the door, but Solomon knew he'd set the man to thinking. He'd put some doubts in his mind about the possibility of loss as well as the prospect of profit.

"You haven't given me your answer," Solomon reminded him.

"I'll have to talk to the other incorporators, but I'm sure they'll agree with me that we won't be intimidated by you."

Solomon smiled. "Quitting while you're ahead would be the most profitable thing you've ever done in your life, Durfey. And if you were smart, you'd convince your incorporators of that, too."

"Oh, murther," Delaney groaned as he and Chance automatically raised their arms skyward. "This day has shoorly been the divil's own handiwork."

With a quick, sweeping glance, Chance absorbed the woman's surroundings. In that brief second of visual surveillance, he realized he and Delaney had blundered into a privately owned Pullman, replete with costly paintings, gaudy artistic gilding, expensive velvets and brocades, ornately carved furniture, and gleaming mahogany-paneled walls.

"We can explain, ma'am," he offered calmly, but was leery of the steely determination in her eyes and the stubborn set to her lovely jaw.

"I'll just bet you can," she said. "But first I'll relieve you of your weapons."

"I'm afraid that's already been done, ma'am," he replied. "You see, some road agents stole our mules and wagons and left us afoot. We had to jump the train or freeze to death. We're just wearing these bandanas to keep our faces from getting frostbitten, and I'll gladly remove mine if you'll promise not to shoot me."

Jenna Lee had learned long ago that power was taken, not given, and she could not afford to relinquish hers if these suspicious-looking men were here to kill her grandfather. And after what had happened last fall on the Coeur d'Alene River, that was foremost in her mind. She'd been at the observatory window when she'd seen the two of them, and it appeared that they had purposefully chosen to board the *Marietta*.

"I'll promise you nothing but a bullet if you don't do as I say."

Chance decided that if she was bluffing, she was doing an excellent job of it. There was no fear in her eyes, only the threat that her command be obeyed. Then, to his utter dismay, she moved her hand just enough to make him her target, as though she sensed more opposition from him than Delaney.

"All right, Shorty," she said to Delaney. "You go first. Remove your coat, hat, and boots. I want to make sure you're not concealing any weapons. Place everything right here in the center of the floor. One wrong move and I'll shoot your friend."

Delaney obeyed but had to grumble about it. "God forbid! 'Tis our clothes we must part with now, and to a fancy lady who would shoorly be havin' no way to use them—*and* who insults me by callin' me 'Shorty.'"

"You know what they say," Chance replied lightly. "First your money, and then your clothes."

"To be shoor," Delaney agreed. "But when she sees our fine male figures, what will she be wantin' then, Keely? It is afraid I am that me vartue could be in serious jeopardy."

Jenna ignored their rather ribald exchange, which might have embarrassed a less worldly woman. She

24

simply saw it as a clever trick to get the upper hand. As for that flirtatious little gleam in the tall one's eyes . . . it could be ignored, too.

He stood, even under her gun sight, with a confident ease that was almost annoying. And those startling emerald eyes peeking out between his red bandana and black Stetson hat raked her feminine proportions with a roguish regard, as if he considered her no real threat but rather a tasty peach ripe for the plucking.

Well, she would not be swayed by flirtatious eyes and polite words. Men would take what they could— if a lady was foolish enough to let them.

When Delaney was down to his holey stockings and hatless head, and his empty gun belt was at her feet, Jenna decided that maybe they *were* telling the truth. Still, she'd take no chances.

She shifted her gun back to Delaney and said sardonically to Chance, "Your turn. Same rules apply."

Unexpectedly, Chance felt an odd curling sensation inside him. There was something about her. . . . Had he seen her before? No, surely not, for if he had, he sincerely doubted he would have forgotten such a striking face and hourglass figure. He drew his bandana down, letting the cloth's cotton folds fall loosely at his neck, while his mind puzzled over that fleeting look in her blue eyes that had stirred the coals of some forgotten yesterday.

Suddenly, the palace car shook beneath them as though the ground itself was moving. Before they could understand what was happening, they heard the squeal of air brakes and the entire train lurched forward, coming to a grinding halt. They were hurtled toward the front of the small observatory room. Jenna was flung backward into the wall while Chance and Delaney were thrust forward, colliding with her. The chairs by the windows flipped over and skidded across the plush carpeting, becoming a tangle around the fallen three's flailing arms and legs.

In a chain reaction, like a spine being unkinked, the train settled back. The couplers connecting the cars strained from the unusual pressure and clanged the entire length of the train as though they might snap. The force of the backward shift now sent the occupants tumbling in the opposite direction. Together Jenna and Chance rolled upon the carpet, an entanglement of limbs, silk, and petticoats. Past them went Delaney, trying to catch himself and eventually toppling onto an overturned rococo chair.

The long train shuddered down its entire length, shook a few times, groaned, and was silent. It had all been like the forward and back lash of a whip, and it had happened almost that swiftly.

On her back on the floor, Jenna saw the chandelier swinging violently. Slowly, the light around it began to fade. She realized she was about to faint, but she couldn't pull in a breath, and she wondered dully if they'd had a train wreck like the one her parents, brothers, and grandmother had been killed in. The one from which only her grandfather and herself had survived.

In the increasingly dim light, she saw the tall stranger scramble to his feet. She knew in that moment that she had lost the battle of authority with them and he would surely overpower her now. To her amazement, he merely shifted to his knees and leaned over her, a worried look on his ruggedly handsome face.

Her head whirled, while everything before her went white. Suddenly, he pulled her to a sitting position and swatted her hard between the shoulder blades. She gasped and her lungs filled with air, but it seemed to be on fire. She began to cough until finally she was able to breathe again, although raggedly. Immediately, she tried to crawl away to the derringer lying on the floor a short distance away, but the stranger caught her by the shoulders and scowled at her.

"Stay still! You've had a bad fall."

She struggled against his insistent hands, ignoring the burning in her chest and the way his closeness made her much too aware of the dangerous quality of his virility. She had to get to the gun. Following her gaze, he saw the object of her interest and her hopes collapsed. Still holding her by the shoulders, their eyes locked in a tense exchange of angry wariness.

"Get the gun, Delaney," Chance commanded with clenched jaw, wondering why he was suddenly mad at a damned situation that had actually started out rather amusing. Maybe it was because she thought he was nothing but a low-life bastard. Did he honestly look like a criminal?

Delaney scooped the gun up from the floor and handed it to him. The woman watched the exchange with bold defiance.

Chance rose to his feet and hauled her up with him. Holding her captive with nothing more than his angry green eyes, he turned her hand palm up and slapped the offensive little weapon upon it.

"You won't have to shoot us, Blondie," he said tightly, then grabbed his hat from off the floor. "It appears as though this is where we get off."

Chapter Two

Moments later, Chance and Delaney hurried from the train, the latter with his boots pulled hastily on and the rest of his clothing in a bundle in his arms.

"What a she-divil!" he exclaimed. "Beautiful, yis, but meself was thinkin' she would be wantin' me underwear before her fancy was satisfied."

"Don't pretend innocence, Delaney. You would have loved every minute of it." Chance's long strides took him quickly through the snow and away from the privately owned car whose gilt-lettering identified it as the *Marietta*.

"Murther! Slow down, Keely," Delaney scrambled after him, at last getting both arms back into his coat. "Why have you gone so temperamental? 'Tis not a bloody fire we're runnin' from, just a small derringer!"

Chance pulled his collar up and shielded his face with his gloved hand. The driving snow bit into his skin like pellets of sand. "Do we really look like bandits, Delaney? Be honest."

From behind him, Delaney's bearded face twisted contemplatively. "So that's what's troublin' y'? Well, 'tis plain we're used to oursilves, Keely, but I'm sartin we don't look the sort that the darlin' would be wantin' to invite to tay. Now, if you had shaved this morrow, like I said earlier, then she could not have mistaken us for anything but the true gentlemen that we are."

Chance tried unsuccessfully to put the incident from his mind. "Well, it doesn't matter anyway, because I'm not exactly fond of tea. Now, let's go see what stopped the train."

The wind howled between the mountains and down the track, piling the snow to mid-knee and concealing the bulk of the Bitterroots. Chance and Delaney hurried alongside the panting train, at times nearly lost in the steam puffing from the engine as it drifted back along and beneath the cars. Men were everywhere, shouting above the gale, and concerned women and children watched it all from the passenger car windows.

As they reached the locomotive, they blended in with a pack of male passengers gathered around the willowy engineer, who was trying to project his voice above the keening wind.

"The snowslide went right over the tracks and down that slope to the river," he was saying, "but there's enough left on the tracks that we're going to have to clear it off. We could wait for a bucker from Spokane, but this snow is so wet and heavy that I imagine we'll have to dig most of it out anyway. We might as well get started. There's an emergency supply of shovels, lanterns, and axes in a corner of the baggage car. I'll need three men to keep snow shoveled into the boiler for water and three more to keep the fireboy in wood."

Not waiting to hear any arguments or refusals, he led the way to the baggage car and distributed the equipment.

Chance and Delaney were the last in line, and when they stepped forward, the engineer eyed them curiously through the increasing darkness. "You two picked a fine train to jump, didn't you?"

29

Chance explained what had forced him and Delaney to board the train, and when the engineer learned they were owners of the Wapiti Mine in the Coeur d'Alenes, he lightened considerably.

"All right," he said. "If you two will shovel along with the rest of them, I won't mention to the conductor that you don't have a ticket. I suppose we can find a cubbyhole somewhere to hide you, if and when we ever get moving again."

They thanked him, then trudged away to join the others.

Much of the way was lit by the glaring yellow headlight of the locomotive. Only those out of its reach needed the lanterns. Most of the snowslide had gone over the tracks. What remained was ten feet deep and packed solid. The recent warm trend had loosened it, and the shaking of the train on the track had been the impetus to bring it down.

Chance found a spot to work, pressing his lantern base into the snow until it sat upright by itself. The circle of light opened the darkness only a few feet, and even then the snowfall obscured it.

Delaney chose a position nearby and they worked together in silence. Several men selected the job of keeping the fresh snow off the cleared track, while the others continued moving the snowslide itself and all the debris that had tumbled down the mountain with it. It was going to be an all-night job, and there was no hoping otherwise.

Solomon gingerly pulled his derby hat down over his thinning, gray hair, mindful of the cut next to his hairline. The train had stopped so suddenly that he'd taken a nasty fall and hit the corner of the credenza in the *Crescent*'s club room. The cut had bled a little, but it would be all right.

Outside, he pulled his coat collar up higher as

protection from the wind and, with galoshes sinking into the snow, found a shovel and joined the others.

Immediately, silver-haired Henry Paterson, his construction boss, saw Solomon and rushed toward him, using his thick chest and six-foot frame to politely but effectively push several shovelers out of his path.

"Dammit, Solomon!" he snapped. "Nobody expects you to shovel snow."

"Why not?" Solomon tossed a shovelful nearly onto Henry's booted feet. "Because I'm Solomon Lee, or because I'm seventy years old?"

"Both, for Christ's sake."

"What are you worried about, Henry? Are you afraid I'll have a heart attack? I should think you'd be delighted to see me labor toward that outcome, because then you wouldn't have to build this railroad for me."

"Can you blame me for not wanting to build it? After you and Jenna were nearly killed last fall, and our surveyor *was* killed this spring, I think someone is trying to send you a message. Maybe you ought to take heed and give it some serious thought. I know you don't care what happens to yourself, but you should at least think of Jenna."

Solomon glared at him, unmindful of the snow hitting him in the face and collecting on his eyebrows and eyelashes. Henry had the gall to accuse him of not caring about Jenna. In truth, she was the only thing he *did* care about. The money games he played were now just a frivolous pastime performed in memory of days when he'd had the dream to be more than a poor emigrant boy.

Ever since she was five years old and he'd been called upon to raise her, Solomon had wanted to spare his granddaughter any kind of pain and sorrow, for he had considered losing her parents and brothers to be pain enough. But he could directly blame himself for the worst she had experienced in her adult life—namely, that bastard Philip Dresden she'd married and divorced eleven years ago.

God knows he should have recognized the man as a fortune hunter. But he had even encouraged the marriage, because he had thought Dresden would be an asset to the company. Dresden had fooled them both, as well as numerous women all over the world. They'd learned, shortly after the marriage, that for years he had made his living by preying on wealthy women. It had hurt Solomon nearly as much as it had hurt Jenna, when they came to realize she'd been used and manipulated in the worst way.

Since then, she had judged every man as if he were another Dresden. And most of them had been, to varying degrees. None had been able to separate her entirely from the potential of wealth and power associated with Solomon Enterprises, and so she had turned inward and closed herself off from all romantic involvements. The only man she had anything to do with on a regular basis was Henry, twenty-five years her senior. Of course, they were only friends, but she trusted him implicitly.

Although Jenna had never spoken of it, Solomon recognized the emptiness she felt in her life. Oh, she had her horses on her Connecticut farm—an enterprise she'd started and had run on her own since she was twenty-two. But for as much as she cherished those four-legged creatures, they could not entirely fill the void in her life. Nor could her friendship with Henry. She was no different from other women. She wanted to fall in love with a man who loved *her*, not the Lee money. And she wanted children. Jenna Lee just wanted nothing more than a normal life.

At last he spoke. "I've never forced Jenna to come with me out here. She knows the risks involved and she's thirty years old, so I think she can make her own decisions."

"And while you're ignoring these death threats, Solomon, I believe there's something else you've also failed to consider. You've provided well for Jenna, made her heiress to your fortune, but have you prepared her to deal with your counterparts who will most certainly try to take advantage of her when you die—or get killed? She's never run anything except her horse farm."

"Don't use Jenna as a ploy to get me to take to my bed for the next twenty years, Henry, or however long it takes for me to die." His eyes gleamed like frosty blue daggers. "You underestimate her. She can handle Solomon Enterprises. She knows things that I sincerely doubt even you are aware of. Now, let's drop this annoying subject, and why don't you tell me if you have those right-of-ways along the two rivers."

Henry's clenching jaw was the only outward evidence of his annoyance. "It's been slow. They're a bunch of stubborn damned fools. About as stubborn as you."

Solomon ignored the brash comment. "Stupid damned adventurers, you mean. Since they got wind of tracks coming through here, they've all run out and staked their claims on land bordering both the Coeur d'Alenes—the north and south forks. If they can't make their fortunes in gold and silver, they think they'll steal it from me. Their claims are undoubtedly illegitimate. I have never fallen for such tactics, and I don't intend to start now. Do they honestly think I made my fortune by being stupid?"

There was little to be said to that remark. Solomon Lee personally managed twenty-five thousand miles of railroad line in the United States and controlled another thirty thousand. The world had branded him a robber baron and contemptuously named him "King" Solomon Lee. He had made his fortune honestly at times, but on occasion—as was the custom for nearly everyone dabbling in the stock market—he had also made hundreds of thousands through undeniably unscrupulous methods. But they both knew he had never made a single dime by being stupid.

Unexpectedly, and much to Henry's relief, Jenna appeared before them in the blur of the storm, her gloved hands shielding her eyes from the vicious wet flakes. "Grandpa?" she queried, peering at him through the blinding snow. "Is that you?"

Solomon straightened his back with an obvious effort and leaned heavily on his shovel, trying to catch his breath. She stood in the falling snow wearing a lavish, full-length sealskin coat bordered with sable. The matching black hat framed her pretty face, making him proud that she was of his flesh and blood. For just a moment he felt a twinge of regret that her parents had not lived to see how beautiful she had become. There were times when certain expressions and certain little nuances of her personality reminded him of his own beloved wife, Marietta, who had died in the train crash with his son, daughter-in-law, and other grandchildren twenty-five years ago.

"You've found me," he said, short of breath. "Is something wrong?"

Jenna glanced over the edge of the railroad tracks, which barely hugged the steep slope that led down to the icy Clark Fork River some distance below. She found it difficult to stay upright on the slick slope and clutched at the mounds of snow for support.

"No, but don't you think you should come in now, Grandpa?" She elevated her voice above the howling wind and squinted against the snow stinging her face. "Why don't you let the younger men do the shoveling? That bump on your head was rather nasty."

A smile was difficult to form on his cold face, but Solomon managed it for Jenna. Her lovely face full of awareness and intelligence always dissipated the orneriness that Henry never failed to draw out in him, her sunny smile pulling him back down to earth and keeping him from becoming too heartless and too old in his thinking. He was sure that if he hadn't been put upon to raise her, he would have become like so many of his cohorts in the industry, who seemed to have acquired no healthy diversions in life to balance out their acts of avaricious plundering.

"Not bad enough to slow me down, my dear."

"Well, Charlotte has dinner on. Will you come and join me?"

He stood his shovel up in the snow. Where Henry had failed to get him to quit, Jenna easily succeeded. "That sounds excellent, my dear. Come on, Henry, if you've a notion."

"No, thank you," he replied testily. "I'll be in later."

Relieved that her grandfather had been easy to convince, Jenna started down the narrow path, holding her lantern high to light the way. She had gone some distance when, above the wind, she heard a peculiar muffled sound—a dull, quick popping noise.

She turned into the blowing snow, peering through its heavy mantle. She was able to see the light from her grandfather's lantern, but it was tipped nearly on its side in the snow, and Solomon was nowhere in sight. Wherever he was, the darkness and the storm had engulfed him.

She rushed back along the snow-laden trail, stopping short when she saw a long streak of blood upon the snow trailing down the steep slope toward the river. Panic and fear consumed her. Not knowing what had happened or what she should do, she raced frantically back to Henry.

Gasping for breath, she clutched his arm. "He's gone, Henry. I think Grandpa's been killed!"

35

Chapter Three

Everyone within earshot dropped their shovels and shouted the message on up the line. In seconds, men came running, sliding to a halt on the edge of the roadbed's steep embankment. Solomon Lee had literally vanished into thin air. Jenna knew he was surely being carried downstream by the water's deathly cold current. But what about the blood? Had the sound she'd heard over the roar of the storm been a gunshot? It was the only explanation.

Suddenly, unable to wait for the men to act, she started down the slope after him. Henry immediately took after her and hauled her back to the tracks. "You can't help him now!"

She struggled against him until they both fell into the snow. He grappled with her until he managed to get them both back to their feet, but she continued to wrestle against the constricting bands of his arms.

"There's nothing you can do!" he insisted. "He's probably been swept downriver by now."

"Let me go! I've got to try to save him!"

To her utter relief, she saw the dark shapes of two men sliding down the embankment while others ran to the train, hollering that they'd get some rope. The din rose around her, the men blocked her view, but Henry still held her tightly lest she try to go to the rescue again herself.

She caught snatches of the conversation as more men flew into action, getting ropes and then linking arms to form a human chain that extended from the tracks down to the river's icy edge. Finally, Jenna escaped Henry and shoved her way through the crowd.

At that moment a voice came from the darkness below. "We've spotted him! He's holding onto a rock not far from shore. We're tying the rope around him now."

Nearly blinded by the blowing snow, Jenna ran along the tracks to the spot downstream where many people had congregated. Henry was right behind her and tried to grab her again, but she successfully evaded him.

"Throw down those ropes!" somebody shouted. "And hurry, or all three of them are going to be frozen!"

The men pulled the dark, wet form of her grandfather up the hill through the snow. A rope was around his chest, but his arms were limp at his sides. Behind him the two men scaled the steep slope with some help from the others.

It seemed to take forever, but at last her grandfather was placed onto the snowy cross ties. She dropped to his side and pulled his head and shoulders onto her lap. His side was bloody and she couldn't tell if it was a gunshot wound, but the cold water seemed to have temporarily stopped the bleeding. She brushed the snow and water from his face, then breathed a sigh of relief when he opened his eyes. Sluggishly, his gaze shifted from her to the two rescuers who collapsed on the other side of him, out of breath, soaked to the skin, and shivering uncontrollably.

The men who had saved her grandfather's life were the two who had jumpd the train. But as Jenna looked up at the black-haired one, there was no mistaking the shock and the utter horror that twisted his handsome features as he stared down at her grandfather.

Others hoisted her grandfather into their arms and headed for the train, leaving the rescuers behind to tend to themselves. Jenna leaped up to go with her grandfather, whose eyes were still focused on the stranger with some degree of surprise. But although he moved his frozen lips, no words came out. The crowd closed in behind him, blocking his view of the two men, and the hand reaching toward them dropped limply to his side. Jenna hurried to catch up, frightened by the beseeching look he gave the two men. Why? Who were they? Did he know them? Or was he only trying to thank them for their bravery?

He was taken to his stateroom aboard the *Marietta*, and everyone went back to clearing the tracks. Jenna, with the help of her father's valet, Malcolm Reed, and his wife, Charlotte, the maid, got her grandfather out of his frozen, wet clothing and into warm blankets. They could see now that the wound was definitely from a bullet.

Malcolm, a frail Englishman, turned pale at the sight of it and quickly excused himself to discard the ruined clothing and get bandages and antiseptic. Solomon appeared to be in shock while Jenna and Charlotte worked over him. He stared at the ceiling with a faraway look, not reacting to anything, not even pain.

Unexpectedly, a man in his upper forties appeared at Solomon's stateroom door. "I heard what happened," he said. "My name is Louis Wood and I own a lumber company in Coeur d'Alene, but I'm about as close to a doctor as you're going to get on this train. I had the misfortune of being forced to remove scores of bullets from wounded men during the war. Would you like me to take a look at him?"

Jenna was greatly relieved. "Oh, yes. Please come

in." She moved aside to make room.

Solomon remained detached while Wood examined the wound. "The bullet passed through," he finally announced. "And it appears to have been a small caliber—something from a derringer perhaps. But from the looks of the powder burns, it was fired at close range."

Jenna leaned over her grandfather. "Did you see who did this, Grandpa?"

He kept his eyes focused on that distant spot and replied weakly, "No. Whoever it was came up behind me."

Malcolm returned with the antiseptic and bandages. He, Jenna, and Charlotte crowded into the small stateroom and watched Wood complete the doctoring. When he was done, Solomon fell asleep.

While Wood cleaned up, he worriedly scanned Solomon's ashen face. "The bullet wound shouldn't kill him unless infection sets in. That dousing in the river could harm him worse. I don't see signs of frostbite, but keep him warm and get him to eat some broth as soon as possible. Let him sleep for now, and make sure you take him to a doctor as soon as you reach Coeur d'Alene."

Jenna followed Wood into the narrow hall and saw him to the sitting room, where she tried to pay him for his work.

"No, Miss Lee. I'm not a doctor and legally can't accept your money. I'm just happy to have been of assistance."

He touched the brim of his derby hat in a gesture of farewell. When he was gone, Jenna hurried back to her grandfather's side.

His hands were finally warm and color was returning to his face. Now that the incident was over, the crux of the situation weighed heavily upon her. There was no doubt in her mind anymore that someone wanted him dead.

She needed to talk to Henry. Charlotte volunteered to sit with him while he slept, and Jenna left the stateroom.

She found Henry in the sitting room, deep in thought and holding a glass of brandy in his hand. He came hastily to his feet when he saw her. "How's Solomon?"

Suddenly weak from the aftermath of the emotional trauma, Jenna groped for a chair and sat down, then relayed all the information Wood had given her. "I just hope we get out of this storm soon so we can get him to a doctor," she concluded on a worried note.

Henry went to the mahogany sideboard and topped his glass off with another brandy. "Dammit! I told him to leave these mountains alone before he got himself killed, but isn't it just like him to put business over the importance of his own life? Jenna, we've got to talk him into abandoning this project," Henry insisted. "There are others more lucrative and less of a gamble. Don't you agree with me?"

Jenna's natural reaction was the same as her grandfather's would be. If they were frightened out of the Coeur d'Alenes, then who would try to scare them away on the next railroad, or the next? Perhaps Henry was being the most practical, but she knew that power and strength had to be asserted to be maintained. To retreat meant ultimate doom. Unfortunately, their enemy was one who chose ambush over confrontation, so how could even the bravest person fight such an underhanded adversary?

"I'll discuss it with him," Jenna replied, offering no more of her personal thoughts because she knew Henry would not approve of her opinion. "I'm afraid no one has much influence over grandfather, not even I. You know when he wants something, he doesn't give up until he has it."

Henry polished off another glass of brandy. "Yes,

unfortunately. I just wonder what it is about this particular road that's making him so damned determined to go on with it even at the risk of his life."

"I'm afraid I don't have an answer for that, Henry. He's never really said, except that there's money to be made here."

"As if he needs more."

"You know it's the challenge more than anything."

"Yes, I suppose you're right. A challenge has always been as necessary to Solomon as air is to the rest of us."

Jenna anxiously parted the gold drapes near her chair to see how things were progressing outside on the snowslide. Just being able to see lantern light dotting the drifts was a good indication that the storm was abating.

In the passenger cars, the women and children had turned out most of the lights and were trying to sleep. Everything was quiet, except for the wind. She strained her eyes in order to see through the darkness to the shovelers.

Abruptly, Jenna dropped the curtain, realizing with a startling jolt that she had been searching for the green-eyed stranger. What was it about him that had made her yearn for a second look?

Henry left his glass on the sideboard and crossed the short distance to her side, misunderstanding her thoughts and actions. "Don't worry. Your grandfather will be all right."

He pulled her to her feet and into his brotherly embrace. She placed her head on his strong shoulder, feeling so tired. What would she ever do without Henry? He was always there when she needed him the most.

"Let me fix you a drink," he offered. "It'll help you relax and get some sleep."

Jenna didn't really care for liquor, but this was one time she felt it might be beneficial. She nodded her agreement.

Shortly, he handed her a brandy and she lifted it upward, the golden light from the chandeliers dancing off the glass and the rich liquid inside. "A toast," she suggested, hoping to lighten the dark mood. "To Grandpa's health and future success."

Henry's lips suddenly thinned to a hard, surly line. He tossed his brandy down his throat without accepting her toast.

"Henry, what is it?"

"Dammit, Jenna. Does everything have to be centered around him? What about *your* success? And *mine?* Why do you think of no one but that old man? You don't even think of yourself." She was astonished by the bitterness of his words, but Jenna had to admit it wasn't the first time he'd spoken of her grandfather with an underlying resentment. And, in all truth, she supposed his attitude was understandable. After all, while everything Solomon Lee touched turned to gold, Henry's one big venture in life had failed because of a panic on Wall Street—or so she'd heard. She'd been just a child at the time.

Henry had never recouped his fortune nor recovered from the mental devastation, although most people, including her grandfather, thought he had. His wife had divorced him and had taken his children. When he had nearly touched bottom, her grandfather had hired him as a construction contractor, something Henry was highly qualified at. He had good organizational abilities and handled large groups of men successfully. He'd been involved in railroad construction before he'd gotten involved in the lofty speculation that had ruined him.

Jenna had asked him once, about five years ago, why he had never remarried. "Sometimes it is simply best to dream, Jenna," he had said. "Dreaming brings no disappointments and no pain."

Henry fingered his empty glass and didn't look at her. "I'm sorry, Jenna," he managed apologetically. "I suppose your success and mine is—and always has been—contingent upon his. It bothers me sometimes, that's all. I just wish we could convince him to step out of this thing. You've got to talk to him. All of our lives could be at stake, not just his."

Jenna didn't know why her grandfather wielded such power over her, but he always had. He was a dear, and she loved him more than anything in the world, but she also knew him well enough to know that it was useless to try and change his mind once it was set. And it was always set—on something. And because of that fact, she couldn't help but feel that if he were willing to die rather than to back down to the enemy, then the least she could do was to stand by him.

He had no one else to take over for him but her. There was no one who cared if all his life's work merely vanished like snow in the river. His only son was dead. And having lost his only sibling, a sister, decades ago, he now had only distant relatives on his mother's side. They were all in Europe and knew nothing of him and the things he'd accomplished, let alone those things he held deep conviction for. He needed someone to fight *for* him and *with* him, to preserve all he'd accomplished in his life.

If her grandfather couldn't complete his work now, then she would do it for him until he was well again. She had gone through life in a tight and safe cocoon of dreams, which she had never actively set forth to fulfill. She had stayed in his shadow, ridden his coattails, and allowed him to manage everything, even her thoughts. Her horse farm in Connecticut was the boldest endeavor she had ever undertaken, the only thing she'd ever done solely by herself.

Henry wanted her to go against her grandfather,

but she couldn't. She wouldn't.

She laid her brandy aside. "I need to check on him again, Henry." She hesitated in the narrow hall that led to the staterooms. "And would you happen to know where the men are who rescued Grandpa? I'd like to thank them and make sure they're all right, too."

Henry now seemed preoccupied and obviously more concerned with putting some sense into Solomon's head than with thanking strangers for their good deeds. "I offered them the use of the *Crescent*'s parlor and two staterooms for the night. I also gave them some dry clothes."

"I'm so glad you thought of it, Henry. I surely wasn't thinking about anything but Grandpa. Please finish your drink. I won't be long."

Chapter Four

Chance fingered the shot glass, amber with whiskey, and stared out of the *Crescent*'s frosty windows at the storm. By morning, as was the nature of spring storms, its passing would be evident only by the devastation it had left behind. Much like the morning after his father's death, seventeen years ago.

He hadn't relived that tragic night for years, but seeing Solomon Lee again had triggered many things from the past that he had wanted to put behind him forever.

He lifted the glass to his lips and tossed its contents down his throat in one swallow. The fiery liquid warmed him. He had some dry clothing on, offered by Henry Paterson, and the room was warm, too. But the comforts and the relief from the icy, paralyzing water did not help to ease the turmoil that coiled like a snake inside him, ready to strike out at any second and at any thing.

God Almighty! He'd saved the life of Solomon Lee! That was a hard truth to swallow. He would have gladly let the old bastard die if he'd only known who he was. He and Delaney could have perished in that damned river, and for what? The likes of a thieving, murdering son of a bitch who had taken Duke Killeen to his knees and then to his grave.

And, as if adding insult to injury, the beautiful woman he'd met today was none other than Lee's granddaughter. If that was justice, then his had been served royally and upon a silver platter. He'd actually harbored the romantic notion of seeing her again, in that instant before the snowslide, but he wanted nothing to do with anyone who carried the tainted blood of King Solomon Lee.

Even though he hadn't purposefully summoned the recollection, his mind leaped back easily to another night many years ago in New York. He put past to present and knew without a doubt that the young girl in the carriage that night in front of his tenement house had been the woman he'd met today. That girl's forlorn face, in pathetic contrast to the wealth that had surrounded her, had never really left his memory. It had only faded a bit, blurred, then moved into sharp clarity tonight.

A rustle of silk alarmed him. He whirled about with a scowl on his face. She stood there as beautiful now as she had been before he had known who she was. She appeared weary and worried, vulnerable without her pearl-handled derringer. In the soft light from the gas chandelier, he saw shadows beneath her large eyes. He could comfort her, if it wasn't for who she was.

His hatred for Solomon Lee sprang up to encompass her, as though the past were as much her fault as her grandfather's. He was judging her guilty, simply by association, and he knew he shouldn't. Still, he could not manage even a polite hello, or give his appreciation for the warm room and dry clothing. His tongue felt swollen, his vocal cords severed.

She nodded acknowledgment of his presence with a simple "Hello," then attempted casual conversation, although her tone was laced with worry. "This is a terrible storm, isn't it? I hope we make it out by morning. Grandpa needs to see a doctor."

46

Chance poured himself another whiskey, foolishly thinking it might help him hack through the jungle of emotions growing rampantly inside him. Why did he have to find her so attractive?

"This is nothing," he said coldly. "We always have storms like this in the Bitterroots."

Jenna had hoped it would be easier to talk to him. He had been friendly, of a bantering nature, when he had first come on board the train, even flirtatious. But now she felt tangible insolence as his gaze raked her, and she wondered if the change in his attitude possibly had something to do with his friend's absence. Immediately, she became concerned.

"Is your friend all right?"

"He's fine. He just went to the dining car for something to eat."

Jenna released a sigh of relief. "Since I didn't see him, I was afraid something had happened to him. We're very grateful for what you both did."

"I hear your grandfather was shot," he said rather disdainfully. "Is he still alive?"

"Yes," she replied pensively. "He's resting now and seems to be stable at the moment. An ex-army man with some doctoring experience was kind enough to tend to him."

For some reason she felt as if she might cry, just thinking how close she had come to losing her grandfather. But she struggled to keep her composure in front of this man who appeared ominous and completely hard-hearted in his intensive scrutiny of her. He seemed not at all the man she'd met earlier.

An intense, uncomfortable silence yawned between them. The stranger merely stood there and glared at her, apparently willing her to leave. For twelve years, ever since Philip, she hadn't cared what a man's opinion of her might be, so it was a new and startling realization that she did not want this man to dislike her, and yet was painfully certain that he did. The

47

emotion made no sense in light of the fact that he was being plainly rude.

Her hope of having a pleasant conversation with him had vanished, as well as the tiny hope that she might see him again under more pleasant circumstances. But it was plain to see by the almost hateful glow in his eyes that there was no need to prolong the meeting.

"Well, I must get back to my grandfather. I just can't tell you how grateful I am for what you and your friend did. Words are hardly sufficient weighed against the cost of a man's life, so if there is anything I can do for you, now or in the future, please do not hesitate to ask."

Chance's jaw clenched at the memory of his father's death. "You're right, ma'am," he replied bitterly. "Words *aren't* sufficient when weighed against the value of a man's life."

For the space of several seconds, their gazes locked in a silent duel of sorts. Then, all purpose of the meeting over, Jenna bid him good day and departed back down the hall.

Despite her rigidly erect posture and controlled steps, Chance knew she was running from him and his unfriendly behavior. The courageous woman with the derringer had vanished. It didn't give him any satisfaction to have alienated her. On the contrary. It only brought him more anger and anguish. He could call her back and apologize, but it was best to let it end here. Now.

Briefly, he was haunted by the earnest, sad eyes of the young girl in the carriage all those years ago. She'd suffered in the cold that night, waiting for Solomon Lee, and Chance guessed her devotion to him had not changed or lessened.

Over the years, he'd heard and read about the two of them. The society pages liked to follow their lives and their loves, but he had usually avoided reading about them. He hadn't wanted to know about Lee—unless it was to learn that he'd died. He knew, though, that Lee's granddaughter was a divorcée. Her former husband had been a fortune hunter, which wasn't terribly surprising. It would be hard for a man to separate her from all that money—that is, if money is what a man wanted. But what was her name? Why did it persist in escaping him?

The most puzzling thing about her, though, was that she seemed to be an honest, sincere, moral person, so how in the name of God could she love a man as immoral as Solomon Lee? And love him she did. It had been plainly written in her eyes when they'd dragged him out of the river and she had taken him into her arms.

He lifted his eyes to the dark windows that reflected his angry image. But it was neither his image nor the blizzard that he saw, but rather the wintry night in New York when his father had been crushed to death between two freight cars, and he had stood helplessly by, unable to prevent it.

Over the many years he had come to blame himself for his father's death nearly as much as he had blamed Solomon Lee. But nothing, not even self-inflicted guilt, could erase his hatred for the Wall Street corsair. The truth came home to him again, as it always did. Duke Killeen's fate could not be transferred from—nor denied by—the man who had set out to destroy him from the very beginning . . . and had succeeded.

Long purple shadows of twilight stretched across the snow when the train pulled into Rathdrum the next day. The winding trip along the Clark Fork River and around Lake Pend Oreille had been slow. They had gotten a late start waiting for the plow to back up to a side track, and then there had been stops at Thompson Falls and Sandpoint.

From the observatory window, Jenna watched the green-eyed stranger and his short friend leave the town's livery stable on horseback. They headed across the snowy prairie that rambled southward away toward the Coeur d'Alene Mountains, serrating the distant horizon.

So he was going to Coeur d'Alene, too. But there would be no reason for her and her grandfather to ever cross his path again. And that was just as well, except that there had been something about him undeniably appealing. If nothing else, she had to respect him for not fawning all over her on bended knee, as every man she'd ever met was prone to do in their obvious and clumsy attempts to court the Lee fortune. But intuition told her this man was different. He was his own man. Unlike the others, he would never be a puppet to Solomon Lee.

She turned down the hall toward her grandfather's stateroom, only to find him wrestling with Malcolm in a scene that would have been comical if he hadn't been wounded.

"Lie down, sir, please," the skinny manservant begged as he tried to press Solomon back onto the pillows. "You are in no condition whatsoever to be sitting up and looking out that window."

"I'll be the judge of my condition!"

"Grandpa!"

At the sound of her voice, the struggle ended. Malcolm moved aside as Jenna came forward into the narrow little stateroom that hardly offered the space to turn around in. Solomon laid back against the pillows, out of breath.

She pulled aside the covers and saw fresh blood on his bandages. "Look what you've done. You've opened the wound again. Are you trying to kill yourself?" she demanded.

"My dear, if I wanted to kill myself, I'd have laid

50

back without a struggle and let that miserable river carry me away to purgatory. I've got a railroad to build, and we've been sitting on this damned piece of track so long I have the infernal scenery memorized. Where is Henry, anyway? What's he doing?"

"He's supervising the uncoupling of our cars to a side track. Now, lie back down, Grandpa."

"I want to go to Coeur d'Alene tonight."

"It's thirteen miles by stage," she objected heatedly. "It would be much too rough of a journey for you right now. We'll get a doctor to come here."

Solomon snorted. "Doctor! I'm not sitting here waiting for some silly doctor to tell me I've been shot! I know I've been shot!" His blue gaze darted about the small room, seeing it as little more than a prison cell. "The bullet didn't hit anything I can't live without, Jenna, and there's nothing a doctor can do now for this hole in my side. It will simply have to heal on its own. Besides, Ives and Leaman are waiting for me in Coeur d'Alene."

"They can come here."

He waved his weathered hand impatiently and glared at the snowy window, where he could catch a partial glimpse of the little town that had become a jumping off place for miners en route to the riches of the Coeur d'Alenes. "I can't conduct business from here! I'll rest when I get to Coeur d'Alene."

"You're starting to run a fever." Jenna laid her hand upon his wrinkled forehead, hoping to verify her statement. "Yes, you're hotter than you were earlier."

"Wood looked in on me again before he left the train. He warned me of that. Said it's normal. Now"—he gently but firmly removed her hand from his face and gave her a tolerant smile—"I know you're afraid I'll die, but quit worrying. I have too much to do to die. Ives and Leaman are probably already in Coeur d'Alene. Have Henry arrange for a

51

wagon I can lie down in. We'll tie the saddle horses behind and leave first thing in the morning. Will that be good enough to suit you?"

"No, but you're so damned mulish, I doubt I could stop you short of tying you up."

Solomon's eyes suddenly glinted with glee. "When did you start swearing, my dear?"

"At this precise moment, and don't tell me to stop because I can be as stubborn as you."

"Good. You'll need to be before this road is built."

His expression suddenly took on a pained look. Feeling guilty for being harsh with him, Jenna spoke in a gentler tone. "Get some rest tonight, Grandpa. We'll go tomorrow."

Solomon sighed, feeling completely thwarted by the wound that had sapped his strength. He'd never been down more than a few days in his life, and he didn't like it. He had to work to survive. If he laid around he *would* die. He had a lot of enemies so it didn't surprise him that someone wanted him dead, but he refused to go back to New York unless it was on a funeral train. As for who had done it, that troubled him a bit—not for his own life, but for the others who worked for him and especially for Jenna. He would send out word to his men to set up armed guards and be wary of trouble.

As for conserving his strength, perhaps Jenna was right. He did feel a mite puny. Slowly, he laid back on his bed, trying to ignore the pain in his side. He closed his eyes and suddenly saw those green eyes that hated him so. Had he imagined them? He had known for over a year now that Chance Killeen was here in the Coeur d'Alenes, but surely it would have been too much of a coincidence for him to have been on the train. When he'd come out of that river, he hadn't been sure of anything. It wouldn't be the first time he'd been haunted by faces from the past.

But mostly it was Lily's face that haunted his

dreams. He saw her so clearly. The long hair falling into his hands like a length of black silk; the green eyes just like Chance's, but hers always so full of wonder and innocence; and her skin as perfect as porcelain and as soft beneath his lips as a rose petal.

She was here—in the Coeur d'Alenes. His enchantress from a fairy tale. Always just out of reach, like an ethereal goddess appearing and fading into the haze. And like a hypnotized fool, he had tried to possess her, tried to buy her love. But how could anyone have blamed him for wanting her back then? And how could anyone blame him for wanting her still?

Chapter Five

Clouds the size of dreams, and surely as illimitable, seemed painted on the azure sky. On Lake Coeur d'Alene the paddle wheel steamers ran placidly to and fro, carrying their cargoes of miners and materials from Coeur d'Alene City to the inland canyons, via the St. Joe River and the South Fork of the Coeur d'Alene.

From the hotel's second-story window, Jenna watched the activity on the elongated lake nestled in the forested mountains. The town itself, or "city," as its inhabitants preferred to call it, lay in the curve of the heavily timbered shoreline, growing rapidly and bawdily as mining towns usually do. And yet, for all the bustle, there was a serenity here, making it easy to forget the thousands of hard-rock miners hidden deep in the canyons, eviscerating the earth in search of fortune and empires—a fabulous wealth that would soon be divided with the railroaders who had come to claim their share.

"Get on with business," she heard her grandfather say from his bed in the adjoining room. The door between the rooms was open, and from her peripheral vision she saw his men gathered about him.

"Enough about my health," he continued irascibly. "I'm alive for now. The sun is out and spring is on its way. Has the frost left the ground, Ives?"

Jenna pretended no interest in the conversation, but she heard her grandfather fidget with the sheets. She heard the creak of the bedboard as he propped himself more firmly against it. She heard the little cough in his throat, which he tried to suppress. All the while, she waited impatiently for Owen Ives's response, which was slow in coming.

"Not entirely, Solomon," he finally said. "There's still a lot of snow in the passes and on northerly slopes."

Jenna sensed Solomon's frustration at the delay. He coughed again, this time a torturous sound from deep in his chest. It sounded worse than it had this morning. Seven days in bed had done wonders for the bullet wound, but a cold had set in. He was still feverish from his ordeal, and he needed his rest. She wished the men would leave.

It was Henry who spoke first when Solomon had quit coughing. "We have some more bad news, Solomon. Just last night our chief engineer was found dead in his tent."

"What!"

The explosive rejoinder brought on a full-scale coughing attack. The hacking sound gave flight to Jenna's feet, and she rushed into his room, past the men, and grabbed the cough syrup from off the night table. Solomon's face was bright red. He was coughing so badly that it appeared he might collapse from lack of air. Jenna hastily removed the cork and shoved the bottle at him. He accepted it without embarrassment and guzzled a healthy portion right from the bottle, screwing up his face after the nasty liquid was down his throat. He exhibited one last disapproving shudder before handing the medicine back to her.

"And what was he dead of?" he finally demanded, his voice still weak from the coughing, his eyes watery but steely bright and glaring. He appeared to hold them personally responsible for the death of yet another crucial man in their team.

"Gunshot wound to the head," Ives replied dispassionately. "Nobody heard it. It must have happened while we were blasting for the roadbed."

Solomon's gaze traveled over his hired men as he silently digested that bit of information. Owen Ives was a burly man whose disposition, as well as his eyes, burned black and fierce. He was a good grading foreman and made sure that the blasting, the removal of mountains, and the hauling of dirt and gravel was done to the exact specifications. He was also a damned tough boss, hard-nosed and unsympathetic, but he knew his job, and his authority was seldom questioned by the men who worked for him. But a wise man did not make enemies with Owen Ives.

In contrast to him was timid John Leaman, purchasing agent for the construction of every railroad Solomon had built over the past twenty years. Leaman knew where to get the best materials as well as the best deals. He wasn't timid when it came to the bargaining table, but physically he was stoop-shouldered and so slight he had to hold onto something solid when the wind blew. Solomon often wondered if shaving his heavy white beard might relieve him of some unnecessary weight and allow him to stand straighter. He appeared to be an artless man, and perhaps he was, but in all his years he had never compromised his integrity.

Between these two men in both appearance and disposition was Henry. He had a rugged appearance from his life outdoors but maintained an air of smooth sophistication. His diplomacy won him respect with the men. Basically, he was a private man—perhaps too private—for although Solomon had known him for nearly three decades, he felt at times that he didn't know him at all.

Regardless of having these three highly qualified men, Solomon could hardly afford the loss of Westbrook, his chief engineer and superintendent. Westbrook had known everything about every job, from surveyor to treasurer, and had overseen the entire operation. He'd had an uncanny talent with grades and curves. To hire someone of lesser ability could be disastrous.

"Did you hear from Durfey on my offer?" he asked, still silently pondering the problem of replacing Westbrook.

"It's a no go," Henry replied. "He's not interested."

Solomon had expected as much and accepted the news calmly.

"We can proceed without Westbrook," Ives said, pulling them back to a matter he obviously felt was more important. "I know the course he planned to take. We discussed the trouble spots and what would have to be done to handle them. There's no reason to find someone else to take his place. You know Durfey will get well ahead of us if we delay. There's going to be a race out of this whether we like it or not, Solomon, and the winner of the race will be the winner in everyone's eyes, and they'll get the monopoly of all the Coeur d'Alene shipping and traffic business."

"Maybe at first," Solomon said. "But the mine owners will soon go to the company that offers the lowest price to haul their ore. As for the passengers, they'll take the train that gives them the cheapest and most comfortable ride. I can afford to do that. I doubt that Durfey can. To hell with a race, Ives. I want a railroad that's built right and will be profitable . . . one that won't be obsolete a year from now."

Henry began pacing the floor. Perhaps *stalking* would be a better word. "I don't believe you, Solomon. Our surveyor was murdered just a few weeks ago, you were nearly killed—*twice*—and now our engineer is dead and you act like nothing's happened. Aren't you going to think about the consequences of your decisions, and whether this miserable track through these godforsaken mountains is really worth dying for?"

"I have thought about it," Solomon snapped. "For the space of about ten seconds. You know, Henry, you're about as bothersome as a damned deer fly buzzing around my head. I'm building this road. Now, you can stay or you can go. It doesn't really matter to me. I can always get someone who will be more than willing to take your place."

Henry grabbed his hat and left the room, but not before having a last word. "You're a stubborn old fool, Solomon Lee. And I daresay you'll die one, too."

Solomon waved an irritated hand at the slamming door. "Bosh! He doesn't care if I get killed. He's just afraid if I do, he'll be out of a job. Now, Owen, I want you to arm your men. Put somebody on Durfey's tail. Infiltrate his camp with spies. Do what you have to do, but watch every move he makes. If he's behind this, we'll stop him—one way or the other."

Ives was always in favor of using force. He nodded agreeably. Knowing the discussion was over, he and Leaman left.

Solomon suddenly felt very tired. The deep, sharp pain in his chest was getting worse, making it more difficult for him to breathe.

"Can I get you something, Grandpa?" Jenna asked, still sitting on the edge of his bed.

Solomon tried to look perky, although he felt as though he barely had the strength to hold his head up. His throat hurt, and he felt feverish. He didn't have time to be sick, and now everything seemed to be going wrong. It was difficult not to brood, but Jenna's presence was as uplifting as a ray of sunshine and always helped to make him more jovial.

"Nothing at the moment, dear." He squeezed her hand fondly and managed to smile. "But tell me, I want your opinion now. Do you think Henry is right? Do you, too, think I should walk away from this one?"

How she'd love to tell him, "Yes, walk away before it's too late," but she couldn't because she knew he didn't want to, and because she couldn't bear to see the disappointment he would surely feel with himself and with all of them if they succeeded in forcing him to give up.

"Well, while I was standing there looking out the window," she said, "it did occur to me that it might be a shame to disturb this lovely place with the clatter of trains. It really is a paradise right here on earth."

Solomon mused over his granddaughter's idyllic picture of the world. Normally, she was not a dreamer of sorts, but he supposed even a woman of thirty had occasional lapses into girlhood's romantic notions of the world and of life. Sometimes, even old men of seventy tried to remember what it was like to dream dreams that had no place in reality. But pragmatism had ruled him for so many years that now it was impossible for him to be idealistic for more than a moment or two.

He decided to humor her. "Don't ever let your emotions rule your judgment, Jenna. There's money to be made here."

"I believe you have quite enough." She laughed.

He didn't care about the money, and she knew it. He was a millionaire now, but as a child he had lived in virtual poverty. Because of that experience, he'd acquired a restless ambition to become rich. In his prime, that goal had been achieved. Now, in his waning years, the challenge of difficult tasks and monumental undertakings were the things that motivated him and thrilled him. These mountains, so long avoided because of their ruggedness and remoteness, might very well present him with his last and greatest accomplishment.

"Worlds are not conquered by men with a conscience, my dear."

"And this is another world you must conquer?"

"You know it is."

"Then I can't tell you what to do, but I'll stand behind whatever decision you make."

She was the only person who had ever been completely loyal to him. "Yes, I thought you would agree with me, but it doesn't make the decision any easier. I *am* worried about you, Jenna. It's just that I don't believe your life is in danger even if mine might be. And this could be my last railroad. I can't give this up, not even for the life of me. Can you understand that?"

She was glad to see him still dreaming. She put her arms around him and felt the body that now contained only a fading memory of youth. "Yes, of course I understand."

He rested a tired hand on her shoulder and she snuggled up to him, almost as if she were a child again, and laid her head on his thin chest. But slowly she drew away, troubled by the rattling sound in his lungs.

"I've got just the thing for that cold," Jenna said, hoping not to alarm him with her new concern over his health. She went to the bureau where the liquor bottles stood all clumped together in their rich shades of amber and red. Without hesitation, she selected the bottle of whiskey and tried to sound cheerful. "A hot toddy will fix you up in no time. I'll have them heat some water in the kitchen."

"Jenna."

The tone of his voice drew her around with bottle still in hand. His mood had shifted again to absolute seriousness, and the weariness had returned to his eyes.

"Jenna, I have a couple of things I want you to do for me. Put the bottles down and come sit next to me again." His voice was weak and breathy. "I need your help until I get on my feet again. Owen thinks he and Henry can engineer the railroad, but there's more to it than meets the eye. I need a man to replace Westbrook. A man with complete integrity and the knowledge to do the job."

She waited for him to catch his breath, painfully realizing that he was not invincible, that—like them all—he was quite mortal, and that truth frightened her in a way it never had before.

It was getting very difficult for him to talk. "The man I want is here in the Coeur d'Alenes, Jenna. He'll be stubborn because he turned his back on building railroads some years ago, but do whatever you have to do to get him here. Pay him whatever he wants. I don't know where he's at, but find him. His name is Chance Killeen.

"Don't tell the others," he said after a few moments. "They'll only try to talk you out of it, and I'm not up to opposition right now."

"Yes, I understand."

"Jenna," he said, much too somberly. "You'll need this railroad for your future. To prove to yourself and to others that you can run Solomon Enterprises without me."

She started to protest, but the flare of warning in his eyes effectively silenced her as well as any word could have done.

"Finish it no matter what happens to me. Promise me you will. Promise me, Jenna."

His grip tightened painfully on her hand. A desperate look surfaced in his eyes.

"I've never been able to refuse you anything,

61

Grandpa," she said reassuringly. "Don't worry. I'll do it for you."

"Do it for yourself, Jenna. I mean it."

She nodded, troubled by the direction of the conversation that too boldly spoke of a not-too-distant future when he would no longer be with her.

"Now, get me the toddy." He closed his eyes and relaxed against the pillow. "Then go for the doctor. I think I've got pneumonia."

Chance sat with his booted feet propped up on the corner of the desk, a whiskey bottle in his lap and his black record book right next to it. In contemplation of the Wapiti's financial situation, he tilted the whiskey bottle to his lips. Just then the door to his office opened and Delaney popped in, as sprightly as a small leprechaun.

"Keely, you've got to come and see our new string of mules. I wouldn't be braggin' to say that they're better than the last ones."

Delaney's enthusiasm failed to rub off on Chance. "Good, Delaney. Any leads on the stolen ones?"

"I'm afraid there's none." Delaney's gaze fell upon the ledger book and the bottle of whiskey. "Fine companions you have to entertain you, Keely. No wonder there's the hole we cannot get out of, as you proclaim. Would it iver have come to your thinkin' that maybe the whiskey is makin' you put the wrong numbers there in the columns and we're doin' much better than we think we are?"

Chance handed the bottle to Delaney, who readily lifted it to his beard-encircled mouth and poured a considerable amount down his throat. He immediately screwed up his face and wiped his lips with the back of his hairy hand. "Murther! 'Tis rotgut, Keely! Would you be tryin' to kill yerself?"

Chance looked at the books, but his mind was on

Solomon Lee and his granddaughter, as it had been for days. "It helps to have a few drinks when I'm doing this, Delaney. Otherwise, I could see no humor in it at all. As for the whiskey, we can't seem to get anything better up here in Bayard."

Delaney came to look over Chance's shoulder. "So what would be the problem, me frind?"

"We've got three thousand tons of ore waiting to be hauled out. It'll cost us too much to hire freighters, and you and I will never be able to do it in a coon's age with our two wagons unless we shut down the mine until we can get caught up. But that loses us money, too, and maybe even our crew. That conglomerate is still trying to hound us out of the Wapiti, and the loss of the mules and wagons set us back a couple of thousand. The bank will give us an extension on that last loan, but the president—that Tucker son of a bitch—is beginning to have his doubts about our abilities as miners. He's encouraging us to sell to the conglomerate."

"To be sartin, you were never one to put sugar on the truth, Keely." Delaney frowned. "I said to meself often, 'Why mightn't it be yer good fortune, Delaney, to be the man that the gold was laid out fer to find?' And, shoor enough, you and I found the pot o' gold at the end o' the rainbow. Only the faeries played a trick on us and turned it into silver, a substance, which to my deepest regret, clings to the insides of the mountains like a frightened child clings to her dear murther's hand. Now, why could it not be as simple as gold nuggets that can be picked from the ground and laid in a pouch?"

Chance stared solemnly at his babbling friend, whom he suspected to have already had his share of whiskey on his way over here. "Does your story have a point, Delaney?"

Delaney sighed with exaggerated frustration. "Did not a word of what I said reach yer ears, Keely? Then

63

it is into words you can understand that I will put it. Patience we must have. To be shoor, we would be foolish to throw away the gift o' the faeries, even if they did play a trick on us. And it wouldn't hurt if you would build yer own railroad. By the Murther Saint herself, I cannot see the sinse in givin' to yer dear frind Solomon Lee our hard-earned money to haul our ore. And, it would seem to me that our fellow mine owners here in Bayard would be over-joyed indeed to allow us to haul their ore, too, on our line—for a wee price that would be fair, of coorse."

"I'm through building railroads, Delaney, and you know it."

"That's undeniable, but by the same token, it is to the man who distroyed yer father that we will be forced to be forever beholden."

Chance looked out the window, listening for a moment to the piano music coming from down the street. Things would be picking up over at the Widowmaker Saloon soon. "We might be able to come up with the financing, but I'm not sure I want to get into that again. I'll have to think on it."

Delaney knew all the reasons why Chance had turned his back on engineering railroads. A shame it was, what with all the schoolin' he'd had and the experience, but the business had brought him too many unhappy memories about his father's death. The grief and loneliness in his eyes right now made Delaney wonder if the memories had returned, as sometimes they did.

Delaney conceded the argument and moved to the coffeepot sitting on the potbellied wood stove. He poured each of them a cup, hoping he could get Chance to put the whiskey away. "Durfey's talkin' o' runnin' a line 'round the lake through Fourth of July Canyon," he announced. "To say the least, the steamboat owners are not happy with that."

Chance nodded. "Yes, so I've heard. If he did that,

the line would bypass the lake completely and put the steamers out of business. Actually, a line from Coeur d'Alene to Rathdrum would be more beneficial, or a line over Lookout Pass to Missoula. No matter which one is eventually built, the steamers lose."

"They could be the ones tryin' to scare old Solomon out of here. It would be wise, indeed, for both him and Durfey to walk with eyes in the backs of their heads if it's not dead they hope to find themselves."

Chance considered the many factions against the railroad. Each one could create opposition and strife for the railroad companies if they chose to. But no matter what anyone did, they would never succeed, for once plans were laid, it was nearly impossible to turn the steel rails away forever.

Because of their mine's location, he and Delaney took their ore over Glidden Pass to Thompson Falls. But other mines to the west—the Bunker Hill, for example—had to take their ore to the Old Mission Landing, then across the lake by steamer to Coeur d'Alene City, where it was loaded back into wagons, hauled the thirteen miles to the tracks at Rathdrum, and finally transported to a smelter.

The ore was being shipped without concentration, making it even more expensive. The railroad would make it possible to get the piles of ore shipped out easier and quicker, and thus make the mining more profitable. In addition, the railroad would make it more feasible to build concentrators and mills near the mines. But of all the people to come to the Coeur d'Alenes to lay track, why did it have to be Solomon Lee?

"Then there haven't been any leads on who tried to kill old Solomon?" Chance queried.

Delaney gingerly put his lips to the cup and sipped the hot liquid, shaking his bushy-faced head negatively. "I can't deny some admiration fer Solomon," he said. "He seems afraid o' nothin'. 'Twould not come as a surprise to larn that 'tis 'ell he's lookin' fer to outbid the divil on, so he can lay some forty thousand miles of track down there. There's no knowin', but the souls down there would shoorly benefit by havin' a railroad to transport them from one fire to another a wee bit quicker."

Chance smiled. "Yes, and Solomon would be there now if you and I hadn't interfered." He lifted the bottle to his lips again, ignoring the coffee.

"Don't trouble yerself with that, Keely. We couldn't have been fer knowin'." Delaney stood up and gently pulled the bottle from his friend's hands. Their gazes locked. Chance's was militant, but Delaney's was adamant. "Let it go, Keely, and come with me to the Widowmaker. The music is playin' and darlin' Faye is there waitin' fer you to dance with her. If i' 'tis whiskey you must be drinkin', then take it with some company."

The blond-haired Miss Lee flashed across Chance's mind again and made him feel empty inside, dissatisfied with everything that had been fine just a few weeks ago. Suddenly, he set the record book aside and came to his feet. "Come on, then. If what you say is true, I'd best not keep darlin' Faye waiting."

Coeur d'Alene City came alive with the setting of the sun. Suggestive female laughter, husky from too much whiskey, filtered from the saloons along with the low rumble of the hundreds of male voices. Each establishment would not be worthy of its name if it didn't have a piano, but unfortunately no two pianos played the same tune at the same time, and the songs ran together into an annoying cacophony of notes and rhythms.

Dogs that apparently slept all day came alert now,

66

so they could bark all night in time to the men fighting and the pistol shots that occasionally ended the fights. The haunting whistles of the steamers could be heard across the lake, echoing against the mountains. But the loudest and most annoying noise of all was the slurping of the parrot-nosed, unkempt man sitting across the small restaurant table from Jenna, sifting soup through a drooping black moustache that desperately needed a trim.

"Yeah, I've heard of him," Jethro Ritchy said through slurps. "Him and another feller own the Wapiti Mine up in Canyon Creek. I can take you there . . . but it'll cost you." He didn't look up, but just kept slurping his way to the bottom of the bowl as though he didn't really care one way or the other whether she accepted his offer or not.

Jenna decided it would be hard to trust a man like this Jethro Ritchy if one were inclined to judge character by personal appearance, but Louis Wood had recommended him as a private detective and a general source of information. He'd been doing some trapping in the Coeur d'Alenes when the rush for the gold and silver had begun, and Louis assured her that he knew more about this area, and everybody in it, than anyone else around.

He certainly looked the sort to have his nose in everybody's business, and God knows the appendage was big enough for the task. But those shifty eyes in that narrow face appeared in continual pursuit of something, suggesting he might also be the sort who might tell secrets, who might be tempted by easy money, and who would do just about anything— short of hard physical labor—to get it.

Unfortunately, she didn't have time to get a detective from New York. And as much as she hated to admit it, Jethro Ritchy was known in Coeur d'Alene and no one would be suspicious of him roaming around asking nosy questions. A detective from New

67

York would be sure to have her grandfather's assailant on the alert. It helped to know that Ritchy had been with the intelligence branch of the army during the war. As a matter of fact, several of his missions had involved investigating sabotage of the Union's railroad equipment by Southern sympathizers.

He had the credentials, but she wasn't sure she wanted to be alone with him out in the wilderness. Still, time was of the essence. Her grandfather had been diagnosed as having pneumonia, just as he'd suspected, and she was reluctant to leave him for long should his condition worsen.

Jenna had always traveled with an entourage and had gone in safety and comfort everywhere. This wild country filled with hard, seasoned men was a new and frightening experience, but if she was going to take responsibility during her grandfather's illness, then she had to start strengthening her backbone.

If cleanliness was not one of Ritchy's virtues, then hopefully honesty was. "All right then," she said, deciding she had no choice but to turn to him for help. "Will you take me to the Wapiti Mine? I can leave first thing in the morning."

"It's a four-day round trip," he said, tearing his bread into two chunks and dipping one into the bottom of his bowl to sop up the last drop of soup. "Bring a good horse, 'cause I ain't gonna supply you with one."

"Don't worry, Mr. Ritchy. I brought one of my own animals from my farm in Connecticut to ride while I was here."

"Good. Good." Suddenly, he glanced about the room surreptitiously. Then he whispered, "Still want me to sleuth around for the person who's trying to kill your grandfather?"

Jenna was anxious to get this deal wrapped up and

68

go back to the hotel. "Yes, please proceed. But a word of warning. I may look naive, but I want something for my money, so don't try to trick me."

His eyes shifted over the room again. Apparently satisfied that no one was within earshot, he leaned across the table, smiled confidentially, and whispered, "If I don't find the culprit, Miss Lee, you don't even need to pay me. You have my word on that, and I always keep my word. You just ask anybody in this town, any time, and they'll testify to that."

Jenna was forced to stand up to avoid the strong odor of his breath. "I must go now," she kept her voice low. "If anyone questions you about this conversation, you tell them I hired you to escort me to the various mines to determine the feasibility of building branch lines for the railroad."

"You have my word, Miss Lee." He slid a scrutinizing glance over her. "But I have a feeling you'll wish you was back here in your easy chair before this trip is over. This ain't a trip for a woman who's used to silk and fancy Pullman cars."

"The silk isn't important, Mr. Ritchy. It's the fiber it conceals that really matters. Now, I'll be on the *Amelia Wheaton* when it pulls out in the morning. What about you?"

He grinned. "Yes, ma'am. I'll be there, too."

Chapter Six

At Old Mission Landing, the river was wide and deep, and marked the farthest point to which the steamers could travel upriver when the water was low. It was a busy place. Along the river, men for hire waited with wagons and pack animals to escort travelers to the mines or the inland mining towns if they had no transportation. There were also scores of ore wagons, coming from the mines, waiting to board the steamers and their barges and make their journey across the lake en route to the railhead at Rathdrum.

Jenna and Ritchy unloaded their horses and were soon on their way. The Mullan Road, even with the stage running to Wardner, was no pleasure ride. The road had been left to nature, and every man who traveled it was left to his own devices to get over it. The arduous twenty-mile trip from Kingston to Wallace, and the additional six-odd miles up Canyon Creek to Bayard, not only required two days, but also required fording the South Fork of the Coeur d'Alene River numerous times, for seldom had bridges been built past Wardner where the stage service stopped. The road was full of deep ruts, boggy in some places from the spring run-off, and still covered with banks of snow in others.

The first night Jenna collapsed in a shabby little hotel in Georgetown, then laid awake for hours wondering if someone would slip down to the livery and steal Tia's Fortune. Upriver and overland both, the horse had brought covetous stares from hundreds of men and even several bold offers to buy her. One man had wanted her for a race horse so badly that Jethro had finally had to use the persuasion of his Remington to get the man to accept the fact that the mare was not for sale.

When morning dawned at last, every muscle in Jenna's body ached and she had become extremely aware of saddle sores where she thought they weren't possible. Ritchy was right. She did wish she was back in Coeur d'Alene in her easy chair. Riding horses back on the farm was nothing compared to riding over this rough terrain—on a sidesaddle no less.

She hurried to the livery and found with relief that the mare was still there. She then met Jethro at the restaurant as planned, and by seven they were on their way.

The road that led up Canyon Creek was worse than the Mullan Road. It wound along the creek, which in turn cut a serpentine course between high, forested mountains. There was barely room for a trail in places, but one had been hacked out of the brush and the rock and occasionally sliced from the hem of the mountains. Numerous times, she and Jethro had to force their mounts off the narrow roadway into brush, and on occasion even into the creek, to let freight and ore wagons pass by.

Most of the time they rode through the quiet, looming mountains without speaking. At the end of the second day, some of Jenna's fatigue was replaced by nervous anticipation at meeting Killeen.

Near Bayard, the mountains had been relieved of much of their timber for lumber, and it was easy to

71

see the mines dug into the slopes. Jethro told Jenna that some of the earliest discoveries two years ago had been in Canyon Creek: the Ore-or-no-go Mine, Tiger, Poorman, Black Bear, San Francisco, Gem of the Mountains, and the Wapiti.

Jenna was surprised to see that Bayard was a community consisting of forty or fifty wooden structures stretching in three rows along the canyon's floor, two of which bordered the creek. There was no room to expand except lengthwise along the canyon floor, for the small town was pressed up against the base of the mountains on either side as far as it could go.

Jenna needed no mirror to know that the journey had taken its toll on her appearance. A dusty film coated her face, and dried mud was spattered on her skirt and boots. Even though she wore a hat, strands of hair had escaped the pins and now hung raggedly about her face. The lacy cuffs of her white blouse were dirty and tattered.

She could never recall having been so dirty and tired, but there was a certain inner satisfaction at having something important to do and not just standing on the sidelines watching others. Much could be said for the adventure of it.

Immediately, she sought a hotel in which she could bathe and change. Jethro looked only to the nearest saloon for refreshment and left her on the steps of the hotel, telling her he'd return in two hours with information on Killeen's whereabouts.

He nudged his dun cayuse, and Tia's Fortune trotted along behind to the livery stable. Jenna forgot her weariness. Apprehension descended upon her at this important business meeting with a man her grandfather had already warned would not be easily persuaded to take the job. She had never handled any business dealings for her grandfather, only those involving her horse farm. But she could not fail in this one.

When she joined Jethro later, he had learned that Killeen was working late at his mine. Jenna didn't have the patience to wait him out, so dressed in her clean black riding habit, she put Tia on the trail to the mine, high up on the mountainside.

The trail zigzagged in an obvious attempt to keep the traveler on relatively level ground, but it was still a challenge for Jenna to stay on the sidesaddle even though she was an excellent horsewoman. She saw right away that ore wasn't hauled down from the mines by wagon, but rather sent down through huge metal chutes to the canyon floor below.

When at last she reached trail's end, she found a plot of flat ground that prefaced the mine opening. She dismounted and tied Tia to a bush, all the while searching the approaching twilight for any sign of Killeen. The mine area was quiet, appearing deserted for the day.

Nervously, Jenna removed her riding gloves and readjusted the pink gauze veil that wound around the crown of her black silk riding hat. She wondered again just how adamant this man would be. This job would have been made considerably easier if her grandfather's condition had held up long enough for him to discuss with her just what she should offer and how far she should go before she gave up. But that was not to be. He had lost his strength and had been unable to discuss it further.

On the journey here with Jethro, she had silently rehearsed the different propositions she could offer based on deals her grandfather had made in the past, and what she felt he might make if he were doing the bargaining. She felt she was relatively prepared unless Killeen was completely unreasonable.

From far back in the mine she heard a scraping sound, like someone shoveling rock. She took a deep breath and moved hesitantly toward the mine's gaping black entrance, positive she didn't want to go

73

inside. But soon the sun would set, and she wanted to get the mare back to the canyon floor before darkness made the descent too treacherous.

There were both candles and lanterns at the mine's entrance, and she chose a lantern. She found matches in a tightly sealed metal container next to them. After lighting it, she held it high and stepped into the yawning dark tunnel. The wavering light cast eerie shadows upon the rock walls and along the floor. An occasional creaking of the brace timbers, along with the moaning shift of rock overhead, caused her to pause and hold her breath, but the distant scraping encouraged her onward.

She hadn't gone far when her lantern light joined the circle of light from Killeen's numerous candles. Stripped to the waist and with a revolver hanging at his slim hips, the golden glow of the candles bronzed his hard body and put glistening highlights to the sweat that beaded on his bulging muscles. His black hair curved onto the back of his neck in wet curls. He was at least six foot four, and there was something disturbingly familiar about him, but she couldn't quite put a finger on what it was.

She shifted her weight and a rock crunched beneath her boot. Killeen whirled. His shovel dropped to the mine's floor and his revolver appeared in his palm, cocked and ready to fire as if by magic. A stifled scream erupted from her throat. She closed her eyes, bracing herself for the impact of a bullet. He swore. She opened her eyes, just a fraction, and saw the revolver slip back into its holster.

Even in the dim light of the silent mine, and even minus the Stetson, heavy coat, and black stubble, she recognized him. "Oh, my God." Her whisper of utter dismay echoed in the empty drift. "It's you."

His green eyes blazed. His chest, broad and hairy, heaved as erratically as her own. "What in the hell are you doing here?" he snapped. "You damned near

74

got yourself killed sneaking up on me like that."

Dear God, why of all people did Chance Killeen have to be this man who already seemed to detest her before even knowing her? She had envisioned herself coming up to the mine and finding a kind but stubborn man in his fifties or sixties. But she remembered now that the Irishman had called this man Keely, obviously a nickname for Killeen. She had been correct when she'd sensed that he and her grandfather had recognized each other in those dreadful moments on the Clark Fork. But if so, why hadn't her grandfather simply told her who he was? Whatever his reasons had been for not mentioning the incident, she knew there was bad blood between the two of them.

He waited for her explanation. By the hostility in his eyes and because of that earlier meeting on the train, she knew she was stepping onto a battleground. "Are you Chance Killeen?"

"Yes. And you must be lost."

"No, actually I'm here because my grandfather sent me, Mr. Killeen, to discuss a business proposition. He would have come himself but he's still not feeling well from that bullet wound." She decided it would be best not to mention the pneumonia, for if Killeen thought her grandfather might die, she would lose her bargaining ground.

Instant wariness leaped into his eyes. "I wouldn't do business with the devil, Miss Lee, and Solomon sits by his right hand. Save your breath and go back home. And tell Solomon to do his own dirty work in the future."

He waited for her to go, cold unfriendliness in his eyes. But she held her ground, wondering if, at this very moment, her grandfather might be dead. The thought made her feel small and alone, but she managed to conceal her worry and fear. She met Killeen's brazen look with one of her own.

"He wants to hire you as chief engineer for the Bitterroot Railroad, Mr. Killeen."

Jenna saw his mind working rapidly, but his lips quickly curled derisively. "And what happened to your old engineer, Blondie?"

Jenna forced herself to ignore his insolent green eyes and the disrespectful nickname he insisted on using. She was beginning to wonder why she had ever thought he was attractive. At the moment, she didn't even like him.

She strolled a few feet to where she could touch the mine's wall and the rich galena belt. She knew nothing about silver, but even a fool could see that here was the mother lode that every miner dreamed of. "Our engineer is dead. But you know that, don't you?"

"Yeah, he's the one who got the bullet in his head."

Jenna had her limitations, and one was having no tolerance for disrespectful people. Even Jethro Ritchy had treated her like a lady, but she also realized that at this moment her role was not to be a lady, but to be Solomon Lee. Many men might be charmed by a woman's sweet smile and wiles, but she sensed by the hard, no-nonsense look of Chance Killeen that if she intended to do business with him, she must gain his respect, and pretending to be a helpless woman would not work.

"That's correct, Mr. Killeen," she replied flatly, offering no explanations that would lessen the severity of Westbrook's death or shed light upon it. "And we're offering the position to you. We know you have the qualifications."

He went back to shoveling rock. "Find somebody else who wants a bullet in his head, Blondie. I've got silver to mine."

Having anticipated his refusal, she was prepared. "Yes, you do have silver to mine, Mr. Killeen. I see

76

you have a great deal of silver, and much more in the canyon waiting to be hauled to smelters. You don't make any money until it gets there, and you and all the other mine owners in these mountains can't make a profit without a more efficient way to get your ore out."

He tossed a chunk of ore into one of the hopper cars that tomorrow would be hitched to mules, pulled outside, and dumped down the chute with the rest of the ore.

"Have you got a point to make?"

Jenna curbed a deep burning desire to slap his face, but she knew she must remain cool at all costs. She could not afford to walk away from the table until all her cards had been played. "If you take this job, we'll haul your ore on the railroad for free."

Chance knew good deals invariably had strings attached, and especially those where Solomon Lee was involved. "Sure, Blondie. But for how long?"

"For as long as we own the railroad."

His interest vanished as quickly as it had been aroused. "You've probably already signed papers turning it over to the Northern Pacific or the Union Pacific. Don't waste any more of my time."

"My grandfather is in the habit of buying railroads, Mr. Killeen, not selling them. We don't plan to turn the Bitterroot over to anyone, now or ever. But we could incorporate measures into an agreement to protect you. Perhaps we could agree on a specified number of years for this agreement. Say ten."

"Say twenty. Say fifty. I don't give a damn, Blondie. With Solomon Lee, even signed agreements are worthless. He takes what he wants and does whatever it takes to destroy his competitors and all the inconsequential people standing in his way. I wouldn't even be surprised if he's cooking up some deal to steal the Wapiti right from beneath my nose."

"We don't want your mine or anyone else's. We're

77

only here to build a railroad that will hopefully make us a profit."

Chance shoveled with a rancor that threatened to consume him. He remembered how cleverly Solomon Lee had manipulated the stock market until he had destroyed his father's new but prosperous railroad company. Had he come once again to interfere with their lives and to destroy their small acccomplishments?

"Exactly what would it take to get you to accept this position, Mr. Killeen?"

His silence was lengthy, and Jenna wondered if he'd heard her question or if he simply chose to ignore it. She had the feeling that no matter what she offered, he would refuse. If only she knew what had caused his antipathy toward her and her grandfather, then maybe she could deal with him more effectively. But she sensed that if she stirred those mysterious waters, she might bring so much mud to the surface that hiring him would be hopeless.

Slowly, Killeen straightened and rested his work-roughened hands atop the shovel. Like emeralds in the dim light of the semi-dark mine, his eyes gleamed in harsh scrutiny of her. "You're right about a couple of things. I need to get this ore out and we need the railroad, but I'll pay the freighting price like everybody else. You can't offer me anything to convince me to work for Solomon Lee."

Jenna swallowed hard and frantically racked her brain. Every man had a price. God knows, she'd heard that plenty of times. "Please give this more thought, Mr. Killeen. I'm sure there's some agreement we could come up with that would be suitable to both of us."

"Listen to me, Blondie, and listen real good. You just lost your engineer and before that your surveyor. There's been two attempts on your grandfather's life.

I'd be a fool to accept your offer, even if I had the slightest interest in it. If I'm going to risk my life, I'll do it for myself, right here in this mine. I won't do it for something as flimsy as free freight . . . a deal that may not even last until the tracks are laid."

Jenna watched him fill the hopper car in a steady, angry rhythm. What could she do next? What could she offer him?

"Isn't that about all, Blondie?" He didn't halt in his work, nor did he look up at her.

"No, Mr. Killeen." She hoped her voice wouldn't reveal her nervousness. "I'm not one to quit. Once a person starts running from something, he can never stop. You ought to know that."

The shovel halted in mid-arc. His eyes narrowed, stabbing her mercilessly. "What exactly do you mean by that?"

"I don't know why you've taken on the role of a hard-rock miner when you have the education and qualifications to engineer roads and railroads all over this country. My guess is that you're running from something, hiding here in this hole in the ground. I'm just curious to know what it is that put your tail between your legs like a yellow-bellied dog."

He set his shovel aside. Immediately, she regretted her attempt to shame him into doing her bidding. When he took a stalking step toward her, she took a frightened one back. But he kept coming, until he had forced her up against the cool rock wall. He splayed his hands against the wall on either side of her head, just above her shoulders, and leaned his broad, hairy chest threateningly toward her.

She pressed her shoulder blades harder against the tunnel's rough sides, but what little distance the movement put between her and his ominous body was inconsequential. His naked muscles bulged with each little shift of his arms and with the flexing of his hands against the rock walls behind her. He had the strength to snap her in two if he chose to, and she wasn't sure that he wouldn't.

"You'd better quit while you're ahead, Blondie. That kind of tactic won't work with me. I'm here for reasons that I don't care to discuss with you. All I will say is that hard-rock miners are honest men doing an honest day's work. That's more than I can say for entrepreneurs such as yourself and your grandfather, who live off the labors of men like me. Go back to Solomon and tell him I said no."

If she thought it would do any good to beg, she would try that, too. "You scoff at my offers, Mr. Killeen, so why don't you tell me what you would need to take this job. Name your price and I'll see if I can match it."

He smiled wryly. His lips were too close, too strangely distracting. They were tempting even now in this horrible moment when they shouldn't be. Even his male smell was oddly tantalizing. He shook his head in disbelief at her persistence. His mood seemed to shift unexpectedly to a level of tolerance. Had he realized that she was like a pesky little tick that would not let go of his hide until it had had its portion of blood or was literally jerked off against its will?

"Come on, Blondie. I don't own a suit of armor, and money can't give me back my life if somebody decides they don't like me replacing Westbrook. Tell Solomon to hire someone else."

His breath was disturbingly hot upon her lips. He was far from repulsive, even though he was trying hard to be unreasonable and rude. But she had seen him in a lighter moment when he had been friendly and flirtatious, and that was the man she hoped to find again.

"We don't have time to get anyone else," she said,

"and possibly have to wait until they can finish another project."

"What's the rush?"

"We need to complete the line before winter, but we also stand to lose a lot of business if Durfey gets his line to Silver Bend first."

"Yes, you'd lose the monopoly of the Coeur d'Alenes and 'King' Solomon would have to take a second seat to somebody. I suppose that would kill him quicker than any bullet. But what's he worried about? He can always pull the rug out from under Durfey. Isn't that his usual procedure?"

She ignored his taunting remarks and refused to let him upset her. He was at least talking and he hadn't run her off yet. Something in those arresting eyes suggested that he was interested, despite what he claimed.

"Durfey's plans do not include branch lines to all the mines—or didn't you know that?" It was her turn to taunt him. "He doesn't have the money. He'll have to wait until he earns something off the main line or can get more financing. That delay will undoubtedly hold you up. Your ore is just going to keep piling up out there, Mr. Killeen, until someone builds a branch line up Canyon Creek."

"I can build my own line if I have to."

Jenna kept badgering him. "I've offered you free freight for a period of years that we can agree upon— perhaps indefinitely—and all you have to do is take a job that will last six months at the most. I can offer you one more thing. On top of a handsome salary for those six months, I'll offer you ten percent of the profits that this railroad pulls in for the next ten years. In a sense, I'm offering you a partnership in this railroad, and all you have to do is oversee the work on it."

His amused smile was an improvement over the previous snarl, but she automatically tensed when he

81

took her chin in his hand, all the while marveling at how the coarse surface of his fingertips could be so frighteningly provocative.

"It sounds more like a bribe to me, Blondie. Now, wouldn't you say so?"

His thumb moved up to her lips and stroked them rather sensuously, purposefully gauging her reaction to his intimate touch. Her heart hammered so hard against her chest she thought it might burst the fragile walls that confined it, and she was sure he saw the erratic rise and fall of her bosom. His touch was relatively gentle, but he was surely only planning to humiliate her in some way in order to get her to leave. As for a rebuttal, all words fled her mind.

"I think you want me so bad that you'd offer me just about anything, wouldn't you?" he continued in a voice that had suddenly gone alarmingly seductive. "Maybe you should offer me the last thing you have to offer, Blondie. It might just be the thing to make me say yes."

His eyes, as alert as a hawk's, focused upon her mouth. She was not swift enough to elude the lips that came down on hers with ravishing boldness. She pushed at his naked chest, but it was as effective as pushing against the sides of the mine. When he had taken his pleasure, he pulled his lips from hers with purposeful slowness. With mocking eyes, he dared her to meet his price.

Her lungs seemed to contain no air, as if he had sucked it all from her and into himself. "I'm no whore, Killeen," she hissed. "I'll find someone who isn't such a proud fool."

His smile held a smug victory. "And I'm no whore-monger, Blondie. I just wanted to see how far you'd go to give that old man what he wants. And now I know."

She shoved at him again. Amazingly, he stepped back, but not without chuckling at her discomfiture.

"You're not worth two cents," she managed, "let alone an engineer's job. And I'll have you know my name isn't Blondie."

She stalked away, her boot heels creating loud, hollow echoes in the mine. Dusk's light touching the mine's entrance was only five feet away when his voice echoed down the long drift and caught up with her.

"Maybe you'd better tell me what your name is," he said. "I'll need to know if we're going to talk business."

Her breath caught in her throat and her heart fluttered wildly. Extremely leery of him now, and of the touch that had so thoroughly disarmed her, she turned once again. He was now only a dark shape silhouetted by the light of the many candles. Jenna didn't want to sound relieved; she wondered if he was only planning one last final nasty skirmish. If her grandfather's orders hadn't been so explicit, she wouldn't have wasted her time with him.

"All right, Killeen. Name your price."

There seemed to be some consideration on his part as he censured her from the distance. Finally, he said, "Fifty percent of the Bitterroot Railroad, and no money out of my pocket to get it *or* to build it."

The look on his face was serious, but she laughed anyway. "That's absurd, and you know it."

He shrugged. "Maybe it is, but that's my price. I can't see risking my life for something that isn't mine—or at least part mine."

The man was impossible. "Don't toy with me, Killeen. Even if I was foolish enough to go along with such an insane idea, it would take too long to prepare the necessary paperwork on such a deal. I need someone now."

"It would only take the stroke of a pen," he said. "I already know that the Bitterroot Railroad is independent of Solomon Enterprises. It's your grand-

83

father's personal baby. He's financing the entire thing himself."

"I'm surprised you didn't ask for one hundred percent," she added dryly.

"What?" He lifted his brows in mock surprise. "And be totally unreasonable? Besides, one hundred percent would mean I'd have to foot the bill, Blondie."

Those naked, muscular shoulders and furred chest nudged at a basic, primitive need she'd nearly forgotten she possessed. It had been eleven years since she'd lain with a man. Her gaze slid to his lips. His kiss had not been revolting, even if she had pretended it was. If she walked out now, she might never have the opportunity to sample it under less hostile circumstances.

Why that point came to mind was beyond her, because the man was probably nothing *but* hostile. But he was good-looking in a wild, rugged way that was sure to arouse any woman.

"I guess it just depends on how bad you need me, Blondie," he continued. "And from the way you put on, I'd say you need me pretty bad." He went back to his work.

Jenna stood in the entrance to the mine for a few moments longer, then slowly retraced her steps down the long drift. She stood about fifteen feet from him and watched him scoop a dozen shovelfuls of ore into the hopper.

"I'll give you thirty percent," she offered.

He didn't seem to hear her.

"Forty percent."

"I need this road, just like you said," he replied. "As for you and your grandfather, you're likely to dispense with it at a whim. But my life is here. It's not a game, not a pastime for me. Besides, I'd be putting my life on the line for you and that old man. Give me something to make it worth my time. It's fifty percent

84

or nothing, honey. That's my final word."

Silence filled the mine. Timbers creaked overhead, as though restless in waiting for her response.

He was too damned sure of himself. She sensed that he had knowingly put the price up so high that there would be no way she could go along with it. But what if she called his bluff? What would he do? What would her grandfather do?

Do whatever you have to do to get him here.

Yes, those had been her grandfather's words, precisely.

"All right, Killeen. I'll have the contract drawn up. Can you be in Coeur d'Alene in seven days to go over it with my grandfather and sign it?"

If she wasn't mistaken, he paled considerably, or was it just the dim light that rendered his face suddenly colorless? His brows shot together in a scowl.

A smile crept onto her lips.

The muscles in his strong jaws leaped, flexed. His eyes blazed. She'd duped him and he knew it, but he'd stated his price, and she was almost proud of him for not trying to wiggle out of it.

"All right, Blondie," he spoke grudgingly, "but make it ten days. And I'll tell you right now that I won't work with—or for—Solomon Lee. From here on out, I do business with you."

Her smugness wilted. Kissing him might be one thing; working with him was another matter entirely. She balked. "But the other fifty percent isn't mine. That isn't possible."

"It will be yours if he dies. In the meantime, you're doing a great job as liaison. I prefer working with a person who has a few moral limitations. Of course, maybe I didn't push you hard enough to see just what yours were."

"Maybe you didn't . . . but you'll never know that now."

"There are some more conditions," he said, sauntering toward her. She tensed at his nearness, but he didn't come as close as he had before. "I won't fire your men, but the decisions I make on the railroad will not be put up for argument among your people. Not even your grandfather. And I want the first branch line built to be up Canyon Creek to my mine."

"All right. That sounds reasonable."

"A couple more things. I want the first option to buy the line if your grandfather sells out, and I want a clause to protect my position if he dies either before or after the line is finished."

Jenna nodded, deciding that this was his game all the way. She had to give him what he wanted, and he knew it.

"If that's all, then I'll be leaving." She turned to go, when the import of it all struck her. Suddenly, she broke into a cold sweat. Had she made the worst mistake of her life? What would her grandfather say to her bartering away half of the line?

"There's one more thing, Blondie."

That nickname suddenly became the last straw. She whirled about, her eyes flashing. "My name isn't Blondie, damn you!"

He smiled sardonically. His eyes flirted over her, the way they had when she'd seen him that first time, stirring the embers of wanton desire all over again. He seemed to know she was vulnerable to his virility.

"That was the one more thing I wanted," he said calmly. "Your name."

A warm flush rose into her face at the tone of his voice. She knew, no matter how slight, that at least one obstacle between them had been hurdled. She wondered if the absurdity of the deal had been broached because of the invisible force between them that seemed so potent. Did he feel it, too?

"My name is Jenna," she said, forcing herself from the peculiar trancelike state she had seemed to fall

86

into under the intense perusal of his eyes. She offered him her hand. "I need to be on my way. Let's shake on the deal."

He kept his hands wrapped around the shovel handle, eyeing her outstretched palm contemplatively. "A handshake wouldn't mean a thing to Solomon Lee," he said. "I doubt it will you, either. Just have the agreement drawn up. I'll be there in ten days. You'll get my message of expected arrival."

He went back to work, dismissing her—and for all she knew, the deal as well. Having no choice but to trust his word, she lowered her proffered hand and left the mine.

Chapter Seven

"I say we just go up there to his room and put a bullet in his head while he's asleep," Durfey declared. "It worked well enough on Westbrook and Bartlet, and we wouldn't have to sit and wonder if he's going to die. All our problems would be solved, once and for all."

Henry Paterson sauntered from his spot by the hotel window to the table where Durfey, Ives, and Leaman sat drinking, smoking, and feigning interest in a game of poker. With cool viciousness, he grabbed Durfey by the shirtfront and hauled him half out of his chair.

"We don't want him dead, you fool. We only want to scare him enough so he'll drop this project. How many times have I told you that? You damned near killed him with that derringer and that dousing in the river. Who in the hell told you to do that, anyway?"

He released Durfey, shoving him backward so hard that both he and the chair nearly toppled over. Henry glared down at him, still holding his whiskey glass in one hand as if nothing had happened to upset him. "If you don't follow my orders, Durfey, you'll be the dead one. Remember who brought you in on this road and remember who's paying your way."

"But he made me mad, coming off so high and mighty in his fancy Pullman car, figuring all he had to do was offer some piddlin' amount of money and I'd cave into him."

"You're already the prime suspect in the murders," Henry reminded him. "You've got to be careful where Solomon is concerned. He's an important man in this country. If he's murdered, there'll be pressure from high places to find his killer. We could all be implicated."

"Nobody questioned me about those other two murders, and I had an alibi during that storm." He was whining now. "People just think some freighter or steamboat owner wants to stop him. I could go up to his room and shoot him, and nobody would be wiser."

"Not unless somebody sees you in the hotel. He has servants. There are people in the halls. Think, man!"

Sheepishness washed over Durfey's face like melted butter over hot bread. Henry repeated the plan to him, as if he were a child who couldn't get directions right the first time. "Ives, Leaman, and I will be out of a job if you kill Solomon. If we're out of a job, you're out of a job. We can't afford for that to happen now, can we, until this railroad is laid and the money starts rolling in? We can't let Solomon know we're trying to get out from under his thumb because he'll fire us for not being loyal to Solomon Enterprises. Then he'll snuff this company. His decision to build definitely ruins our plans for the monopoly of the Coeur d'Alenes, but making hasty decisions out of anger will accomplish nothing. Am I making myself perfectly clear?"

Durfey nodded, squirming.

Owen Ives slowly drew the fat cigar from his mouth and, fingering the cards, said, "In my opinion, everything is falling right into place. Looks like he's going to die of pneumonia. And even if he doesn't, he might be sufficiently cowed that he'll go back to New York and stay there. All of you just calm down. Let's wait a few days and see what happens."

"Could he know about our company?" Leaman asked worriedly. "It would be just like Solomon to try and teach us a lesson in his own conniving way."

Henry returned to the window and pulled back the chintz curtain. The dark town was lit by candles and lanterns and was noisy with drunken miners, but he gazed at it only absently. There were things his men didn't know, things he didn't want to tell them. For one, he hadn't told them of his desire to marry Jenna. When they did find out, they'd think it had come about naturally, not that he'd had the idea for over a year. Perhaps that plan really had nothing to do with this one, but he didn't want either to jeopardize the success of the other. But if one failed, then he still had the other as a safeguard for his future.

He knew Jenna was reluctant to marry again, but she trusted him and never dreamed he might want her money. If he kept playing on her emotions and their friendship, she might eventually see him in a different light. With Solomon dead, she would be more likely to turn to him, but as he'd told Durfey, the timing wasn't right.

His partners thought he merely wanted the monopoly of the Coeur d'Alenes with his own railroad company, but little did they know that for him this railroad was just a small coup before the final victory: Solomon Enterprises.

At last he spoke. "I don't think there's any way he could suspect us, John, and he'll never be able to tie us in with the Coeur d'Alene Central."

Ives leaned back on his wooden chair, pushing its front legs off the floor. He puffed thoughtfully on his cigar and scrutinized Durfey through the thick smoke dispersing along the cheap hotel's yellowed ceiling. "Unless Durfey spills his guts. And you aren't going to do that, *are* you, Durfey?"

The cold threat in Ives's black eyes unnerved Ted Durfey, for he knew that Owen Ives could kill with no qualms. Durfey didn't mind shooting someone from a distance or in the back, but he'd balked about having to put that bullet in Westbrook's head at close range, so Ives had taken up the gun himself, walked into the tent, and done it without even flinching.

"Don't worry," Durfey replied quietly. "I won't say anything, and I won't do anything else on my own again. I just got mad at that old bastard. You can't blame me."

A knock at the door turned all their heads in that direction.

Ives nonchalantly dropped his chair back to the floor and tossed his cards aside. "The girls are right on time, boys. Let's have some fun."

Leaman stood up, straightening his suit and gathering his satchel. He opened the door and quickly slipped past the painted women standing there. He never participated in women sport; that was understood and accepted.

The women strolled into the room and each took the arm of the man they had previously arranged to meet. Each couple then departed to separate rooms, leaving Henry with the voluptuous redhead named Claudine. She wasn't pretty, but she was painted sufficiently enough so that no one really noticed. With hips swaying provocatively, she stepped toward him and pressed her heavy breasts against his chest. Immediately, she slid her hands inside his open jacket and around to his back.

"I'm glad you're back in town, Henry honey. I hope this railroad business won't keep you out in the field too much."

He smiled while sliding the straps of her green satin gown down off her shoulders. His lips touched the curve of her neck as he spoke. "I'm sure you keep busy in my absence, Claudine."

She pressed her hips against the hardness now forcing an obvious bulge in his pants. "Sure I do, Henry, but none of these men around this place have your sophistication."

Smiling, he put an arm over her shoulder and turned her toward the bed. With no prelude, he removed her clothes and she his. With a hunger born of the thrill of power and lust, he laid her back against the pillows.

Delaney rolled to his side and propped himself up on his elbow. He fingered a tendril of Lily's black hair, which had fallen across one creamy white breast after their lovemaking. Her green eyes sought the shadows on the ceiling, etched there by the lamp, and he was certain that somewhere in those flickering shadows she saw something that did not include him.

"What would it be, me darlin' Lily, that keeps yer mind so far away?" he whispered. "Did I fall short of yer expectations tonight?"

A throaty chuckle escaped her and she slid her fingers into the heavy mat of hair on his powerful chest. She gave him her best smile and another kiss. "Never, Bard. Don't be silly."

He pulled her against his thick torso, only slightly hairier than the rest of his body. He was a brute of a man—barrel-chested, muscular, and big-boned. Heavy he was, and solid, but he couldn't be called fat. He faced the world with the charm and wit of a leprechaun, but was a passionate and considerate lover to this small and seemingly fragile woman who had stolen his heart. He enclosed her in his massive arms, cradling her tenderly and placing kisses upon her fragrant, ruffled hair.

He had never dared speak of his fear that she might

not love him the way she had Duke Killeen. She *did* love him, but however deep, he couldn't be knowing. But he'd be wantin' fer brains to deny himself any amount she had the goodness to allot.

He had never loved anyone the way he had her. It was why he had never married; why he had spent his life rambling and roving, carefree and careless—lonely until the day he'd made her his own nearly six months ago. There was no denying he'd been touched by the faeries, and it was not in his ability to imagine losing her now. All comfort and meaning would vanish from the world, like a horde of the devil's demons before the face of God. To the life, he would take to his grave if it was away from him she walked.

"Then what would it be that keeps yer mind so distant?"

Her forehead creased like the furrows of a farmer's field. "I was thinking about Chance and what he plans to do about Solomon's offer."

"He's thinkin' only of you and me and the Wapiti. To be sartin, I'm surprised by it all, but there's no denyin' that it's a profitable venture. How he came about it, I would like to be knowin'. 'Tis as if good fortune was placed right in our laps."

"But he hates Solomon. And it's dangerous. He could be next for that sniper's bullet."

"Aye, 'tis true, but there's risk in everything, Lily. Could it be that he's decided he'd be cracked mad to let his emotions get in the way of a profit? And, fer the other point, it's with Solomon's granddaughter he's makin' the deal, not Solomon himself. Don't be worryin' yerself. Your son is smart, he is."

Still, she brooded, and while she brooded, a dark cloud seemed to drift over them, deepening the shadows that already filled the room's corners. Delaney was frightened, although he wasn't sure why. She spoke again, and the strange premonition of trouble took a face.

"I've got to go see him, Bard. I'm not sure why. Something pulls me. The past, possibly. The things left unsaid. But, Bard . . . don't tell Chance. He would never understand."

Delaney released the air he'd unconsciously been holding. It was not for him to be knowing what had gone on between her and Lee those many years ago, but he was not daft enough to think he could keep her from going to Coeur d'Alene to see him. It was love he must trust. But, oh! Mighty well it was to put the faith in love, but could a man as simple as he hold her heart over the charm of the rich and powerful Solomon Lee, no matter the man's faults?

He held her tighter, praying to the Mother Saint herself that the embrace would not be the last. "Go if you must then, darlin' Lily. Me blessin's 'r' fer a fair trip. And when you return, I'll be here as always, just waitin' to see what he said."

Solomon snorted with irritation and fidgeted with the covers. He'd been in this damned bed so long he was getting bedsores. "I should have known he'd hold you up for every last thing he could get. Fifty percent of the Bitterroot Railroad Company! It's preposterous! It's highway robbery!"

"Quit trying to bellow, Grandpa." Jenna watched as his face turned red and he nearly ran out of breath before he'd finished. "You just came out of your fever a couple of days ago. I'm sure you don't have to go along with such absurdity, but you said get him no matter the cost. So I did. I'm sorry if I went too far, but I'm sure he'd be more than happy to hear that the deal is off."

Suddenly, he waved a hand in the air, carelessly

dismissing the entire subject. "Not on your life. Besides, who cares if he gets fifty percent? I only want to build the damned thing, not make a fortune from it. You did what I asked, and I'll stick by the deal you made."

He smiled wanly at her and Jenna gripped his hand. He was looking tired and she knew it was time to leave so he could rest, but his grip tightened, as though he sensed her thoughts and wasn't ready for her to go.

She was thankful that his fever had broken while she was in Bayard. The doctor said that he was an extremely strong man for his age, which was no surprise to her, but the illness had left him terribly weak, and it might be difficult for his body to fully recover from the infection. It could strike again in the future, and it could be brought on by something as simple as a cold.

"What really made him decide to consider the offer, Jenna? It's kind of you to try and protect my feelings, but even though I might look like parchment, my shell won't crack. I don't believe Killeen would have considered even fifty percent if it meant being a partner with me."

She had known this part was coming, but she had hoped to put it off for as long as possible because she didn't want to repeat Killeen's unkind words. But her grandfather was a wise old man and he would pull the truth from her with the same unrelenting determination that a dentist takes when after one's aching tooth.

"Very well," she capitulated. "He said he would take this deal only if he worked with me. I'm to be your liaison."

Solomon sighed and looked away. So the years had changed nothing. But had he honestly expected them to?

"Well, don't let his attitude toward me trouble you, Jenna. I'm just pleased that he put some trust in you."

"I hope he won't go back on his word. The way he was acting, I wouldn't be surprised if he did."

"For all Killeen is, he's a man of honor. Use your judgment when you meet with him, but don't let him get away from us because of something petty and inconsequential. And, Jenna . . . don't mention this to Henry or the others until the deal is sealed. They think they can handle the engineering, but I'd end up in lawsuits up to my neck if the tracks fall out from under a train or some damn thing. If they know about Killeen, they'll be on my back like a pack of angry dogs. Right now I can't hold a stick big enough to fend them off."

Keeping secrets from their longtime employees, especially Henry, bothered Jenna. But what her grandfather said was true, and she wanted to protect him from undue stress.

Her gaze lovingly encompassed him. She noticed precious little things about him that she'd always seen, but which tugged at her heart more now than ever: the age spots on his hands; the thinning white hair neatly combed and smelling of hairdressing; his overlarge ears; his weathered skin, dry and brittle; and the nose that had grown large as old mens' noses tended to do.

"Tell me, Grandpa," she said hesitantly, sensing she was treading on secrets he preferred to keep. After all, if she wasn't, he would have explained his association with Killeen from the beginning. "Why did you want *him*—at all costs? Especially when there is obviously so much hostility in him toward you?"

Solomon wondered if his loyal young granddaughter would still love him if he told her what he'd done . . . how he'd ruined a family's lives with careless disregard, simply for the sake of his own desires.

He couldn't meet her gaze, and Solomon wondered if he was strong enough to take the risk of her reaction to his unethical deeds. He decided he wasn't.

"I'll tell you someday, Jenna . . . when I'm better. Now, go. Killeen will be here in a few days. You need to make sure the lawyer has everything prepared."

With a snap, Chance closed the cover of his pocket watch and irritably dropped it back into his vest pocket. She was late.

He poured himself a glass of whiskey and drank it. He poured another, then paced the floor of the private cabin he'd rented aboard the steamer. Once again he went to the window and looked out over the buildings of Coeur d'Alene City, hugging the curve of the lake's shore. It was relatively quiet on this April day, except for the men in the bars making the usual amount of noise that seemed to be required in order to spend money.

He'd been plagued with reservations for the full ten days since he'd seen Jenna Lee. He had half a notion to take another steamer back to Bayard before she arrived with the papers that would bring him in partnership to a man he had absolutely no respect for . . . a man he wouldn't trust as far as he could throw him. He would never be able to turn his back on Solomon Lee or become too complacent. Lee knew how to take things away from people, even things safeguarded with contracts.

God, he felt like he'd just sold his soul to the devil, and for what? To save the Wapiti? Was it worth it? He supposed it was, when that was all he had.

He couldn't deny the enticement he'd felt at having the opportunity to be involved with engineering again. In truth, he wanted more than anything to be the man to engineer the line through these mountains. He hadn't been this excited about anything for years. But he'd put the price up so high he never dreamed she'd go along with it. When she had, he would have been even more foolish to turn down the deal.

The mining would be profitable some day, but he hated being under the ground where the sun never shone, and consequently his heart was never truly in it. The mine had seemed to serve only one purpose— to keep him so busy he didn't have time to think of himself or his life, of where he was going or not going. He lived each day as it came, digging out more ore and hauling it away, keeping his mind on the portion of the lode that would be removed the next day . . . and the next. He would have taken a wife somewhere in the course of his life and had a family to ease the loneliness, but he had never met the woman to turn his head.

Until now.

Angrily, he tossed the whiskey down his throat. It troubled him that even the thought of marriage should enter his mind where Jenna Lee was concerned, but it seemed it had been there from the first moment he'd set eyes on her. But he could never court her. He could not become involved with her in any way, or with the empire that had been his father's ruination and ultimately his death. If he did, he would be no better than a traitor to his family, to himself, and to his principles.

A flash of color caught his eye and drew his attention to the woman hurrying toward the steamer on the boardwalk that led to the lake. It was Jenna. He'd expected her to bring a lawyer, or even Henry Paterson, but she was alone. In one hand he saw the contract, rolled up unimportantly. He would have thought she'd have put it under lock and key after what she'd gone through to get it.

He watched her advancement, fascinated despite

himself by the graceful way she moved. She'd given him no reason to be rude and yet he'd been unforgivably so. He simply wasn't sure which was harder—remembering who she was or forgetting.

He sat his shot glass aside, left the small cabin, and trotted down the steps to the main deck. The passengers who had come downriver from the inland had all disembarked twenty minutes ago, and the steamer wouldn't be making another run for a few hours. They had plenty of time to discuss the contract.

Jenna stood on the boardwalk, not knowing quite how to span the two feet of water between the dock and the boat. With the yards of petticoats and skirt, she was sure to fall in. The gangplank had been drawn up when the last of the passengers had departed and would not be lowered until it was time for the next excursion upriver. The boat dipped and swayed with the gentle movement of the lapping water. Jenna shivered at the thought of going for a plunge into the icy mountain waters.

She saw Killeen then, coming toward her. He was dressed casually, wearing no suit coat. A black vest fit snugly over his white shirt. The brim of his black hat concealed his green eyes and any clue to his mood, but his stride suggested irritability and a vague distaste for what he was about to do.

He lowered the chain that stretched across the main deck's entrance and held out a hand to help her. "Come on," he said. "I won't let you fall in."

The sardonic glitter in his eyes made her think of a schoolboy about to put frogs in his teacher's desk. But two could play the game. She would hold on so tight to him that if she fell, he would, too.

She laid her gloved hand in his and lifted the hem

99

of her dress past her ankles. She mustered a leap, he pulled, and she sailed easily to the other side. His arm went around her automatically to keep her from falling backward. The heat of his body made an indelible impression against hers before he released her and pointed to the stairs that led to the upper deck.

"After you, Miss Lee. Second cabin on your right."

Jenna would have liked to pause on the deck to look at the lake on this calm spring day. There were over one hundred miles of shoreline encircled by the forested mountains, most of which was beyond her view. Unfortunately, the trace of lightheartedness he'd displayed had turned to an impatient black scowl and he suddenly seemed in an intense hurry to get on with business.

She led the way up the stairs and to the cabin. The narrow room appeared spacious due to the illusion created by white paneled walls and sunlight streaming in through a band of windows bordering the ceiling. An oil chandelier over the table shimmered in the sunlight but, because of the daylight hour, remained unlit. Color came from the deep jade-green of the upholstery and drapes that separated the small table from another compartment housing a cabin-style bunk bed and rolltop desk.

Chance pulled out a chair at the table for her. "Can I get you a drink?"

"No, thank you, Mr. Killeen. Let's get this settled." She unrolled the duplicate contracts, trying to make them lie flat on the table.

From behind her, Chance took up his whiskey glass again and studied her rigid back and square shoulders. She gave the impression of regal grace and confidence. Her blue-gray dress of sateen and velvet conformed perfectly to her breasts and tiny waist. Lace and bows lavished it in all the right places. The colors and fabrics were reinstated in her small felt hat, cluttered with jewels and feathers.

Stepping closer, the scent of her perfume wafted to his nostrils. The sun's rays slanted through the windows, laying hot kisses of light upon her face and running glistening fingers through wayward strands of hair that rivaled the color of the mountain's gold. He noticed the way stray tendrils of her golden hair curled provocatively at the nape of her neck. The memory of her soft, satiny lips beneath his distracted him from the purpose of this meeting, and Chance quickly forced himself to dismiss further curiosities about her. She was Solomon Lee's flesh and blood, and he must not forget it.

"If there's anything you don't agree to," she said, "we can have it changed. You're welcome to take it to your lawyer and have him approve it, but it doesn't have anything in it that we didn't discuss."

"Changes take time, Jenna. I thought you wanted me to get to work right away."

She turned in the chair and looked over her shoulder at him. "I *do* want you in the field right away. I really can't wait for another week hassling over petty details. There are several miners on the South Fork who won't let the graders proceed, and we can't seem to obtain a right-of-way on their claims. But we're flexible about this agreement with you."

Chance leaned over her and picked up the contract on the top. He moved a safe distance from her in order to keep his mind clear. He read the legal jargon slowly while she sat quietly, pretending to go over the other copy. Satisfied that it was in order, he sauntered back to the table.

"Would you mind telling me which lawyer in town drew it up?"

"Not at all. It was Jonathan Quentin."

Chance nodded approvingly. "Good. He's a friend of mine. I'm sure he wouldn't put anything in here that could hurt me."

"You don't trust my grandfather at all, do you?"

They took measure of each other for a few moments. Finally, Chance said, "No, I don't trust him—and I'm not sure whether to trust you, either. This contract poses as an alliance. But for me it's an uneasy alliance with a man I don't care to be associated with. I'm doing this only for the survival of the Wapiti, so son't let it be misconstrued as anything else—namely, a truce. My opinion of Solomon Lee hasn't changed in the least."

Jenna would have liked to ask him to be more specific about why he hated her grandfather, but his mood seemed volatile and she sensed that pursuing the truth about the past would not be wise at this time.

She reached for the pen on the table with a shaking hand, realizing his animosity had upset her more than she cared to admit. "I have my grandfather's power of attorney. I'll sign first."

His hand came over hers suddenly. Her eyes snapped up to meet his and fell into the troubled green depths that burned alarmingly.

Jenna's heart pounded madly. His hand lay hot upon hers, disturbingly masculine, a quality that seemed to scatter her thoughts to the four corners of the room. His face was too close as he leaned toward her in a demanding stance, his broad shoulders too intimidating but attractive just the same.

"Not so quick, Jenna. I believe we should have someone witness our signing, don't you?"

Crimson color rose to her face. She had forgotten the important necessity of a witness.

"I'll get the captain," he offered, coming to her rescue.

"All right," she agreed. "But before I sign this, Chance, there's something I'd like to ask of you."

He raised a brow inquiringly. Not from her request, but because she had called him by his first name, and the sound of it on her petal-like lips sent peculiar but pleasant flutters throughout his body.

"I would like to go on site with you," she continued. "I want to know everything that goes on. You know what you're doing, but I want you to teach me what you know. Grandpa isn't well and I may have to take over permanently for him."

Chance hadn't bargained for this and immediately rebelled at the idea of her out on the line with hundreds of tracklayers and graders, not to mention being with her constantly himself. She was too beautiful; she would be too much of a distraction.

"It's no place for you. I can't agree to it."

"I won't hold you up. Don't worry."

"We'll be on horseback all day, every day."

"I can ride."

Yes, he knew that. He'd left the mine that day after she'd gone and he'd watched her ride down the mountain without so much as a slip in the saddle.

"I won't take orders from you, Jenna," he warned, realizing he was capitulating to her again and wondering why he seemed to be pure putty in her hands. "As I said, my decisions will be final. I won't have you or your grandfather questioning what I decide to do."

"He wanted you because he was confident in your ability. So am I. You'll get no interference from either one of us. Besides, he's on the mend from pneumonia. He won't be on his feet for weeks, maybe a couple of months."

Chance was surprised to hear that not only had the old man had to recover from a bullet wound, but from pneumonia, too. He was a tough old buzzard, or

103

possibly stubbornness was what kept him going—that and the desire to keep on conquering and ruling the entire railroad world.

"Believe me, I won't get in your way. I'm good at tagging along. Just ask Grandpa." She stood up hastily, picking up the contracts. She hadn't meant to reveal the frustrations of her life to *him*—of all people. "Will you agree to my request?"

His reluctant gaze met hers, slightly pleading. Those eyes . . . just like they had been that night sixteen years ago in the cold, frosty carriage. Sad and alone, and a little frightened.

He nodded toward the contract. "All right. Write it down if you like."

"No, I'll take your word for it."

He opened the door for her. "Then let's find the captain."

Chance led the way up the last flight of stairs to the wheelhouse. The captain was more than obliging, as though he acted as a witness to business agreements every day. When they were once again on the main deck and each had a copy of the agreement, she held out her hand to him.

"Will you shake on the deal this time?"

Chance wondered how much of Solomon Lee's business she had been involved with. Had she only claimed virtual ignorance in order to go everywhere with him and make sure he was doing what her grandfather wanted? He grudgingly admitted, though, that she had gained his respect thus far.

His hand enveloped hers, all soft and feminine, but strong.

"I'll meet you here at the steamer when it pulls out in the morning," she said. "Don't worry, I'll be ready to work."

He released her hand; the deal was sealed. But he still wasn't happy about her coming along. She was going to be in for a big surprise when she found out what it was all about out there in the mountains, and he wasn't sure he could cope with a crying woman. Maybe he ought to at least give her a hint of what to expect.

He helped her back onto the dock. "Don't forget your derringer. You might just need it."

The concern on her face was satisfying. Maybe if she stopped to think about how dangerous it was going to be out there, she'd keep her pretty little fanny parked right here in Coeur d'Alene City.

what it was all about. ... ...
....
... ...

... ...

... ...
... ...
... ...
... ...

Chapter Eight

When Chance saw Jenna hurrying down the boardwalk the next morning, he straightened from his relaxed position against one of the steamer's support beams and tossed his cigarette into the water. If she wasn't a sight for sore eyes, he'd never seen one.

She was trying to straighten her flat-brimmed riding hat over the thick bundle of hair pinned atop her head, and she was leading a sorrel mare that looked as if it had a bloodline as long as its legs.

She herself certainly didn't look like a wealthy heiress this morning. Her blouse was white and lacy enough, but she wore a plain brown skirt cinched at the waist with a plain brown belt. He guessed there were no petticoats beneath the skirt to slow her purposeful stride. She had not only come prepared to work, but she'd replaced her derringer with a revolver, complete with holster. The new getup strapped onto her curvaceous hips didn't detract from her femininity; it just made her look like a woman that a man had better be prepared to reckon with.

She had replaced her sidesaddle with a western one, and had her bedroll and some saddlebags behind the cantle. As she maneuvered her horse up the gangplank and onto the boat, he saw an extremely determined set to her jaw.

Heaven help him. She was taking this whole thing seriously.

He moved through the crowd toward her. She was talking to her mare, calming her for the ride across the lake and upriver.

"You shouldn't have brought that skinny-legged horse into this country," he said. "You might have gotten by with it once, but I'll bet you a twenty-dollar gold piece she breaks a leg."

Jenna patted the horse's nose affectionately, not looking at Chance. "For your information, Tia's Fortune is a blooded American saddle horse and very surefooted. Her lines can be traced back to colonial stock. She's an accomplished five-gaited show horse and an excellent pleasure horse. And she goes nearly everywhere with us in the stock car."

"Yeah, but can she avoid a badger hole on a full gallop?"

Jenna's lips quirked irritably. "I can see you don't understand good horseflesh, Mr. Killeen."

"Oh, I understand it well enough. And I know what's good for this country. And that horse isn't."

"Well, we'll see."

His scrutinizing eyes left the horse and took in Jenna. "And who'd you rob to get those clothes?"

"I found them in my closet, Mr. Killeen," she said, undaunted. "The skirt is from one of my riding habits, but I see very few of the women out here bother with all that yardage, so I cut it off a few inches and hemmed it up. I bought the hat at the general store. My silk one seemed a trifle out of place, don't you think? Now, is there anything else about me you'd care to criticize before we get started?"

She was being plainly facetious this morning, which was a side of her he hadn't seen before but didn't mind. "You'd know more about what's proper than I would, and I guess I've said all I need to. By the

107

way, your trunks have been loaded. Do you have anything else you'd like to bring? Maybe a bed, dining set, some draperies . . ."

Amused by his bantering words, she gave him a saucy smile but no rejoinder. She appeared in good spirits. He just hoped she'd be able to face the reality of the job with as much humor.

His gaze slid again to the gun on her shapely hip. It was an older model Colt Peacemaker .45. The ivory handle jutted out of an embossed holster. He supposed some style-conscious gunslinger had been the previous owner. It probably had a hair trigger, too, which she knew nothing about.

"I hope you know how to use that gun," he said. "You could wind up dead if you don't."

Jenna placed a hand on the ivory handle, remembering all the leering men she'd encountered on the trip upriver with Ritchy, but she didn't want to tell Chance how frightened they'd made her.

"I thought you said you couldn't find anything else to criticize."

"I spoke too soon."

"Well, rest assured. If I don't know how to do something, I'll learn. So don't worry about me. *And,* don't try to frighten or intimidate or belittle me into going back to the hotel, because I won't do it. That *is* what you're trying to do, isn't it?"

He ran an admiring glance over her and nodded his head. "It was worth a try. But I expect you're the sort who can adjust to anything you choose to adjust to. You might even be able to adjust to a first-name basis. I feel like I should be wearing a suit and tie when you call me Mister."

She smiled. "Are you suggesting that we bury the hatchet?"

A cataclysm of emotions surged through Chance. It wouldn't be wise to get too friendly or familiar with her, but he heard himself say, "Yes, I'd like to call a truce with you, but don't think that it includes your grandfather."

Her expression lit with mock disbelief. "Why, whatever would give you that idea, Chance? Things would get much too dull if you were to do that."

The grading crew moved east from the Old Mission Station to their destination, Silver Bend, despite the snow in many places that hadn't yet melted in many places.

Jenna had seen many railroads built, but she had always been fascinated by the task that seemed so monumental but which was completed with amazing swiftness. Construction in the mountains, especially mountains as steep and rugged as these, was dangerous. It required strong men, those most physically fit. It was a sweaty, backbreaking, brawling job.

Like tiny ants crawling over the slopes, the men hacked away by hand and by dynamite, until they literally moved the mountains. Meanwhile, horses and mules hauled the thousands of wagon loads of earth and rock from one place to another to make the roadbed. With only one shovelful at a time, it seemed nothing could be accomplished, but progress was made in astonishing leaps and bounds.

She felt a great deal of excitement as well as apprehension as she watched the workers. She was here filling the shoes of Solomon Lee, and there was a reasonable amount of fear that because she was a woman her instructions might not be obeyed. But Chance Killeen was her co-partner and they would not question him. One look in his steely-green eyes would make any man think twice about crossing him. He might be the enemy in private, but he was her partner in public. She was glad now that he owned part of the railroad. He would fight for it, and they needed that kind of loyalty.

The crew's tents were pitched in a small meadow some distance from the actual work. Jenna and Chance rode silently into the camp looking for Ives and Henry, since neither one had been seen with the grading crew.

Jenna had told Chance that his appointment was not going to be happily received by the three men who didn't believe the BRC needed an engineer. To learn the decision had been made without their knowledge or approval could very well lead to further resentment.

They saw Paterson lounging in the shade of a canvas porch attached to his tent. He glanced at Chance, plainly curious as to why he was there, but his first concern was for Jenna. He helped her dismount and kissed her lightly on the cheek. She greeted him with a happy smile that lit her face in a way Chance hadn't seen before. The two began to exchange little pleasantries, mainly inquiring after each other's health. And of course Paterson finally had to comment about the gun on her hip.

"I never thought I'd see the day you'd take the role of a lady gunslinger, Jenna. Or are you simply enjoying the creature comforts of the West?"

She gave him a saucy grin. "Now, how did you guess, Henry?"

"Be serious, Jenna. Why the sidearm?"

"Oh, just a little precaution. I decided to have better protection than my derringer this time out."

"From the looks of him, I would think that your traveling partner could give you adequate protection," Paterson said, then spoke directly to Chance. "If I'm not mistaken, you're the man who hauled Solomon out of the river. Killeen, isn't it?"

Chance nodded. "That's right. Chance Killeen."

"You must have been heading upriver to your mine when you ran into Jenna. I'm glad you decided

110

to travel with her. It's not a good idea for a woman to be without protection in this country."

Henry turned back to Jenna. "How long will you be staying?"

It wasn't going to be easy to tell her old friend that his authority—albeit self-appointed—had been side-stepped. She didn't like being the one to wound his pride, but she had to agree with her grandfather; they really did need a skilled engineer if the Bitterroot Railroad was to be successful.

"I'm not just visiting, Henry," she said. "And I didn't run into Mr. Killeen accidentally. We're both going to be staying with the construction crew."

He was first surprised and then wary. Jenna rushed into the explanation. "As you know, Mr. Killeen is part owner of the Wapiti. What you don't know is that he's also a highly qualified railroad engineer. Naturally, when Grandpa found out, he hired him to replace Westbrook. And, as for myself, Grandpa has asked me to act as his liaison until he recovers."

Jenna knew she ought to tell him that Chance also owned part of the road, but that would be like touching a match to dynamite. It was something that could be brought up later.

In all the years she'd known Henry, she could only attribute one fault to him. He had a temper that flashed like fire in a pan. Such was the case now.

His blue eyes flared. "It's comforting to know Solomon hasn't been sitting idle up in that hotel room. I surmise Killeen's the reason you took that trip upriver."

She ignored the accusatory tone to his voice. "Yes, as a matter of fact."

"Why wasn't I told about it?"

"Because Grandpa knew you wouldn't agree with him on the decision. And he didn't feel up to dealing with opposition in his present condition."

Henry's gaze locked with Chance's; this time there

111

was no trace of friendliness. "I suppose it'll be interesting to see how a hard-rock miner engineers a railroad. For your sake, Killeen, I hope you really are an engineer. Come inside, I'll introduce you to our grading foreman."

Jenna led the way and Chance followed. The tent was sparsely furnished, as construction tents usually were: an ancient table that was long and narrow; several wooden chairs; three cots with wool blankets and some boxes that served as stands for everything from tools to clothes. Maps were spread out on the table and held down at the corners by coffee cups and ashtrays. Papers with handwritten figures were intermixed with the maps.

Leaman wasn't present, but Ives sat at the table drinking coffee, silently digesting the explanation Henry gave him about Jenna and Chance with nothing more than a raised eyebrow and a slight narrowing of his black eyes.

Neither man welcomed Chance or offered so much as a handshake. Jenna hadn't expected them to treat him warmly, but she hadn't expected rudeness, either, at least not from Henry. He must be more upset at not being able to engineer the road than her grandfather thought he would be. She felt guilty for not thinking more of his feelings in the matter. After all, she was his friend, and friends were supposed to look out for each other.

Feeling the need to break the uncomfortable silence, Jenna took a position by the table and pretended interest in the maps.

Henry stalked toward her, suddenly blowing his composure. "Dammit, Jenna, this whole thing is ludicrous! Forgive me, but I can't agree with Solomon's decision to have you out here. This is a construction camp! It's no place for a woman. It's rough and dirty, and it's mens' work. He's put you in a very dangerous position and there's absolutely no need for it. We'll

112

find someone else who can ferry his messages back and forth." He gave Chance a scathing glance. "And with a new chief engineer, Solomon need do nothing but sit back and wait for the completion of the road. Doesn't he think we can handle it? Or did he send you to spy on us . . . to make sure we do things his way?"

As usual, Ives kept his opinion to himself, but from the look in his eyes, he agreed with Henry. Jenna had never liked Ives because of his cool indifference to everything. Her grandfather didn't particularly like him, either, but he did his bidding and danced to his tunes, so Solomon had kept him around.

She suddenly felt like Daniel tossed into the lion's den, and it was with blessed relief that she was saved by Chance.

"She isn't here to spy," he said calmly, but all the while his eyes glittered dangerously. "She's here not only as a liaison for Solomon, but as the first half of a partnership. I'm here as the second half. I own that much of the Bitterroot Railroad Company as of yesterday. Whatever your feelings are about that, I don't care to know. Now, let's get down to business. We can start by looking at Westbrook's maps."

It was clear that this development held less favor with them than the first. "I'd congratulate you, Killeen," Paterson finally said, "but I think condolences are more in order. You obviously don't know how hard it is to work for—or with—Solomon Lee."

"I'm doing neither," Chance said, getting tired of the two men's animosities. "I'm working with Miss Lee. Now, if you don't mind, I'd like to get down to business."

They moved to the table like recalcitrant children. If they wanted to question that arrangement, Chance made it clear they'd have to do it later. He took a position next to Jenna. Ives and Paterson stood opposite them. With careful consideration, he went

113

over Westbrook's maps, his notations about land contours and elevations, curvature and grades, his comments on fill and gravel requirements, as well as his decisions on where trestles and tunnels would be needed, and his recommendations for length, width, depth, etc.

Ives pointed to a place on the map. "The survey done this winter proved that the course Westbrook wanted to take through here would not only be longer, but more expensive because of the huge amount of fill required along the river. By taking the road this way"—he followed another line with his finger—"we can cut off a quarter of a mile and save weeks of time."

Chance knew the spot they spoke of, but he immediately saw problems with it. "Weeks of time moving dirt maybe, but the snow lays heavy in that ravine. In order to keep the tracks clear in the winter, you'd have to build a snowshed over that stretch, but that area is known for avalanches, and you'd probably lose snowshed, trestle, tracks, and all at least once a year. You wouldn't save time or money in the long run."

"The easiest way through the mountains is not always the best place to lay track, Killeen," Ives said arrogantly. "Henry and I have been at this business a long time. Regardless of what Solomon thinks, we can handle this without you."

Chance straightened from his position over the map, bringing himself to his full height, a good six inches over Ives. "Maybe so, but I'm here to do a job. And I intend to do it my way—not yours. Not Paterson's. And not Westbrook's. Let's just say I know these mountains so well I can wind this damned track all around you and then tie it in a knot right in the middle."

Ives held himself in check, but it was difficult. Paterson stepped forward. "Let him do it his way,

114

Ives. Some people only learn the hard way. We won't be laying track through there anyway if we can't get old man Whitman to give us right-of-way over what he says is his claim."

Chance ignored Paterson's little gibe. "I've heard of Whitman," he said. "He's been here since '83. Does he have legal claim?"

"No," Henry replied. "We've checked it out at the land office and confronted him with it, but he still claims somebody made a mistake and lost the records. He won't budge."

"All right. I'll go up and talk to him."

Chance left the tent. Jenna followed him to the horses. "I'm sorry for the way they treated you," she said. "I'm sure things will improve once they've accepted the situation."

"You're not responsible for them, Jenna. I don't expect you to apologize for their behavior. They were just challenging my experience as I expected them to."

"Testing you?"

"Yes, and not only my knowledge, but my authority as well. Ives knows good and well that the other route through that ravine would be a disaster." He swung into the saddle. "Thanks for your concern, but don't worry about me. You'd best be trying to sweet talk someone into giving up his tent to you."

Jenna suddenly laid her hand on his leg to stop his departure. "Where are you going?" she asked, alarmed. "It's too late to be going to Prospect."

His leg muscles bunched beneath her hand and instantly she pulled away, wondering why she had felt that peculiar flash of life clear to her toes, like a flash of lightning or wildfire.

"I'm heading across the river to talk to Durfey. He's the next order of business to get out of the way."

"What do you need to discuss with him?"

"Nothing. Just wanted to introduce myself. Give

him my howdy-do and let him know who his new rival is."

"You're apt to get yourself killed," she said, with no concealment of how stupid she thought his idea was.

He folded his hands across the saddle horn and grinned at her. "Is it my life you're concerned about, Jenna? Or are you just afraid that if I get myself killed, you're going to have your hands full with those old boys in that tent?"

She straightened with indignant defiance. "I suppose you'll want your body taken to Bayard then?"

He laughed. "Yeah, unless he dumps it in the river."

"Very well. We'll see you get a decent burial, or at least a memorial service. Oh, and by the way, give him my regards."

She turned on her heel and strutted away, her Peacemaker bobbing on her pretty little hip. Maybe he didn't like her grandfather, but she'd inherited some strong points from him. He was glad she had spirit, because he sure as hell didn't want to be shackled to a spineless partner.

Lily Killeen's steps slowed upon the new carpet in the hotel hallway. Up ahead was the door that led to Solomon's room. Would she have been wiser not to come? To have left the past alone and not drag it into the present? Or was the past even over? Would she have to deal with the pain of it again?

It was ironic that her son was working with Solomon, but desperate men did desperate things, and Chance couldn't afford to lose the Wapiti and start over again somewhere else. He had always taken care of her, and much of her motivation for coming

116

out here was to free him of that responsibility. She knew he didn't mind taking care of her, but she felt she was keeping him from a life of his own.

It had been her idea, at the first rumor of gold in the Coeur d'Alenes, to join all the others and "strike it rich." Gold fever had been an easy malady to contract, especially for two people who had no ties to bind them except possibly their loyalty to each other. With her other sons married and scattered about the country, the two of them had nobody to worry about but themselves.

It was a new and hopeful beginning here, one that seemed sure to erase—or at least to blur—the heart-aches and the struggles of the past that they had shared since Duke's death. But it seemed a low blow, a hard lesson to learn, that one can never run far enough or fast enough to outdistance yesterday's ghosts.

Now she had to do what she could to see that Chance's future was not destroyed the way Duke's had been, and by the same man.

Her knock was answered by a maid dressed in a crisp black dress and a stiffly starched white pina-fore. With a British accent, she invited Lily into a small sitting area. While Lily waited, she went into an adjoining room and spoke in muffled tones to Solomon. Lily's heart thudded apprehensively as she wondered what she would say after all these years. Then the maid opened the door and motioned her inside.

Even with the sun shining through white cotton curtains, the small confines seemed dark and gray, as brooding as the keen blue eyes of the old man who watched her.

The old man. Solomon.

He'd certainly aged. Or possibly the tired, ashen face was due in part to the ordeal he'd been through

117

recently. But he was still handsome, the lines of his face still rugged and strong, his presence still eminent.

These qualities had attracted her to him all those years ago, as they had almost every woman who had ever set eyes on him. She had loved Duke, but she had been awed by Solomon. He had wanted her. And he took what he wanted, in whatever way he could. She wasn't sure when the moment had occurred that she had realized he was just a man.

Was he still the same old Solomon with the driving ambitions, the arrogant supremacy, the man who had intimidating bouts of attempted autocracy and the assumption that the world would do and behave as he wished? His presence stirred something elusively unattainable and eternally painful deep inside her, just as it had all those years ago. She wasn't sure if it was love, but if it was, then it was different from the love she had felt for Duke.

"Lily." His voice was an enamored whisper. "I didn't believe Charlotte when she said it was you. Please sit down. What a pleasant surprise to find you here with Chance."

She took the proffered seat, which put her close enough to touch his weathered hand. It was hot in the room, even though a refreshing breeze blew through a raised window.

"I suspect you knew I was here all along, Sol. Nothing goes past you."

For a moment Lily felt as though she were in a dream, saying the things she had imagined she would say if she ever saw him again. But she had never pictured him being old and gray, withered and sad. The ravages of time were not supposed to touch a man as impervious as Sol.

His eyes roamed over her. "So you know me too well. Yes, I knew you were here. I wanted to see you again, Lily, and I'm glad I had the opportunity. I must say, you haven't changed."

She looked away self-consciously. "I hardly believe that, Sol. We all change. More lines, more wisdom."

Silence stretched between them for a span of time. Then, "Is something wrong to have brought you here?" he queried almost reluctantly.

"No, nothing's wrong. I wanted to see how you were. I'd heard that you were nearly killed."

His smile took years from his haggard face, and in that moment she remembered his lips. Oh, he'd been masterful with his kisses, and he'd wanted her so badly. She should never have allowed him to touch her, but she'd craved him for some reason she'd never fully understood. She'd needed him to satisfy a longing, a desire she'd had above and beyond what her loving Duke had given her. She shouldn't have allowed it. He had been a surprisingly gentle man in private, but he had also been demanding. He had assumed that she would leave Duke after that. But when she didn't, he had thought that if Duke was put into bankruptcy and was left in poverty, she would feel no obligation to stay with him and would leave him. Sol had believed it because he willed it, because it was what he wanted.

"Yes, I was nearly killed," he said. "I suppose if I'd died, it would have made a lot of people celebrate, but I've always been too selfish to accommodate others. I thought you might have been satisfied, though."

Her gaze locked with his. The years were easily erased. They could have been back in her tiny apartment that last cold, wintry night. Nothing had changed. But did it ever?

"I wish no man dead, Sol."

"Not even me?"

"Years ago, perhaps. But what would it accomplish today? Solomon . . ." She looked at her hands in her lap and couldn't stop her fingers from fidgeting with the strings on her small bag. "I'm not sure

119

that what Chance agreed to do for you and your granddaughter was wise."

"So that's why you came. I thought as much."

He didn't seem to hold it against her. He only seemed to regret that her meeting hadn't been solely to see him.

She continued. "I don't want you to do to him what you did to Duke. I want you to deal fairly with him—for my sake, Sol."

The clock ticked in the silence. The wind gently lifted the curtain and made nervous little whisperings as it sneaked into the room through the narrow opening. Lily found Solomon's gaze trained on the distance. Or was it the past he watched, miraculously placed before him?

He sounded very tired when he spoke. "I have no intentions of hurting Chance. I need him, Lily, and I believe he needs me. That's all there is to it."

"Are you doing this for atonement?"

His eyes held a deep hurt. "One can never truly make up for foolishness."

She stood up, preparing to leave. He considered taking her hand in his to delay her departure, but strangely enough he didn't want to get too close to the dream for fear he might wake up and find he was clutching nothing more than the bedclothes.

Instead, he tried to memorize what she looked like so that, like a photograph, he could carry the memory with him for the rest of his life. He had meant it when he'd said she hadn't changed. She was older, yes. There were more lines in her face. But there was a maturity that made her more attractive than she had been even when younger. He wanted to touch her, to pull her into his arms. Yet she was as ethereal as she'd always been.

She glided to the door, as graceful as a gazelle. God, why hadn't he ever met another woman that stirred his blood the way she did?

"Don't worry about Chance," he said. "I wouldn't do anything to hurt either one of you again. Please believe me."

Her eyes were full of pain, as when memories came haunting on dark, lonely nights. He knew she didn't trust him, but she nodded anyway, then slipped out of his room as easily as she had once slipped out of his life.

Chapter Nine

Taking this job was the equivalent of advertising for a bullet, but Chance had weighed the risks and now he had to accept them. He stepped down from his horse and wrapped the reins around a bush. Durfey's men were lounging around the camp. Their work was done for the day and they were disinterested in him. He tossed his cigarette to the ground and crushed it out with the toe of his boot. With a hand on the butt of his revolver, he lifted the flap of Durfey's tent and stepped inside.

It was common knowledge in the Coeur d'Alenes that Ted Durfey never got far from a watering hole. Now was no exception. He had constructed his own right here. The table was strewn with maps and papers, but it would have been impossible for anyone to read them for the scores of whiskey bottles scattered on top of them. The place even smelled like a saloon—stale, smoky, and sweaty.

Durfey was stretched out on a cot, his lips locked onto the mouth of a whiskey bottle. He struggled to a sitting position when he saw Chance. "Who the hell are you, mister? And who let you in?"

Chance moved to the center of the tent where he didn't have to stoop. He helped himself to a chair. "I let myself in. Your men didn't seem to care."

Durfey put the bottle to his lips again, downed a good slug, then wiped his mouth with the back of his hand, scraping it across several days' growth of beard. "If it's work you want, I can use you. I need somebody that can handle a team of mules and haul this rock out of here. My mule skinner—if you want to call him that—went and got himself trampled to death this morning. 'Course, if he'd knowed what he was doing, he wouldn't be dead."

"I'm not looking for a job," Chance said. "My name is Chance Killeen and I'm the new engineer of the Bitterroot Railroad. I'm also the co-owner."

Durfey's chest hollowed, as if someone had laid a good punch to his paunchy stomach. He managed to close his gaping mouth with a hastily drawn swig of whiskey. It seemed to give him the necessary strength to continue.

"Co-owner? But I thought—"

"Well, things have changed, Durfey. Seems they always do."

Durfey's eyes darted about nervously. "So what are you doin' here, seeing me?"

Chance leaned back on the wooden chair, lifting its front legs off the floor, and folded his arms across his chest. Durfey took another drink, but Chance could tell he hadn't enjoyed the swallow. He probably hadn't even tasted it. He was scared now that he knew who Chance was. If he was behind the murders and the attempted murder on Solomon, then he had a damned good reason to be sweating.

Chance let the chair drop. Durfey jumped.

"What's wrong, Durfey? You seem a little upset. I only came to introduce myself and see if we could work in harmony. Things have been a little hostile so far and I don't want it to continue."

"Don't lie to me. I know why you're here," he replied vehemently. "You think you can intimidate me into quitting the road the same way Lee tried to

123

do. He used words and money, and now you're trying to scare me with your muscle and your gun."

"My gun has never left my holster," Chance said innocently.

"You're just like everybody. You think I killed those guys on your crew and tried to kill the old man. Well, I didn't."

Chance stood up and sauntered to the door. "I haven't accused you of anything, but I'm beginning to think maybe you are guilty just from the way you're acting." All benevolence left his face. "Just remember one thing, Durfey. If anybody else on my crew turns up dead, you can be sure the law will be right here. You'd better make damn sure you have an alibi for every second of your life until this road is done. Now . . . you have a good day. Hear?"

The sun slid behind the mountains, casting the sky crimson, sapphire, and gold. Jenna moved about the tent by the light of the kerosene lantern, arranging the simple furnishings to her taste and laying her bedroll out on the cot. The men had found an extra tent among the supplies and had gladly put it up for her and donated a few basic furnishings. They had all been kind. Most of them hadn't seemed troubled that she was remaining on-site. There were a few, of course, who seemed to resent her presence, as though she might put limitations on them that they wouldn't have had otherwise. But she planned to stay out of their activities as much as possible.

Of course, the site was only temporary. The tents would be moved often as the tracks progressed eastward. It wouldn't be feasible to bring in heavy items of furniture to make her stay more comfortable. The only item she would request would be a tub of some sort. She would make do with everything else.

"Knock, knock. Dinner is served, Miss Lee."

Jenna smiled, recognizing Henry's voice, and she hurried to untie the tent flap. He ducked inside, balancing a large metal tray that contained two plates of food, silverware, glasses, and a bottle of wine.

"What's all this?" she exclaimed delightedly. "And how did you manage to get wine out here in the middle of nowhere?"

He laid the tray on the small square table. "Money speaks, Jenna. You ought to know that."

"I could have eaten with everyone else," she protested.

He pulled out a chair and motioned for her to be seated. "Yes, that's what I was afraid of. I don't believe you have any idea just what a bunch of uncouth roughnecks those men are out there. Hardly proper company for a lady."

He took the chair opposite her. "It's not as good as what Charlotte would prepare, and can in no way compare to what you'd get at Delmonico's."

Jenna picked up her fork and sampled the stew. Henry said it was venison. It was the first time she'd eaten venison and it tasted good. She took a bite of the sourdough roll. "It's all very tasty, actually."

"You're probably just hungry or trying to be polite," he bantered. "Of course the cook, Moody, is pretty good. If he wasn't, the men would run him off."

He poured the wine. Jenna was amused by the absurdity of his efforts just to protect her. "I daresay you can't keep this up for three meals a day for the next six months, Henry."

"No, maybe not, but it might be a good idea if you took your meals in here, or at least away from the men."

Jenna ate while considering his suggestion, which didn't really sit well with her. Of course, Henry was only worried about her. He was only looking out

125

after her, as he had done from the time she was five and had gone to live with her grandfather in his Great House in New York City. But he was essentially telling her she wasn't to associate with anyone but him for the next six months. Regardless of his good intentions, she simply couldn't abide by that.

She laid a hand over his. "I certainly appreciate your concern for me, Henry, but I don't feel threatened by any of the men at this point, and I think they'll accept me better if I move freely among them and accept them.

"Being here is such a new experience for me. Being involved in something firsthand is an adventure. And these mountains are so beautiful. . . . I just can't wait to saddle Tia and ride and ride. Oh, it'll be wonderful! Try to understand. And don't ruin it for me. Please."

His scowl softened. He brought her hand to his lips and kissed it lightly. "Why can I never say no to you?"

She grinned impishly, happy to have softened his position. "I guess it's just some power I have over you."

He sighed and stood up as if very much defeated. "Yes, a power called love. If I didn't love you, I surely could win a few more battles than I do. Now, I'd better go."

She came to her feet. "But you haven't finished your meal. Don't be angry with me."

He took her hands in his and stood facing her for several moments, wherein he seemed to contemplate exactly what she was comprised of. "Jenna," he said at last, "I'm just afraid life would be awfully empty without you. And this thing you're doing scares the hell out of me."

"I wish you'd stop talking like that. You're beginning to frighten me with all this nonsense."

"Honestly, Jenna, does it mean that much to you to stay out here?"

"Yes. As a matter of fact, it does."

He sighed. "Well, maybe you'll change your mind after a week or two. One can always pray for miracles." He kissed her on the corner of the mouth, then reluctantly released her. "I don't understand this passion that has possessed you, and I doubt I ever will. But if you need anything, my tent isn't far away."

Chance leaned indolently against a tree and watched Paterson leave Jenna's tent. It was pitched in the shelter of some trees, far enough away from the others to allow privacy, but close enough for safety's sake. And he wasn't the only one who had his eyes on it. The men sitting around the campfires seemed glued to her shapely silhouette.

He picked up his bedroll and found a spot farther back in the trees. He was not a man who needed company, and he had the feeling he wouldn't be welcome in the main tent with Paterson, Ives, and Leaman. He would pitch a tent of his own later, but it was getting too dark to start that task tonight.

He stretched out on his blankets and listened to the sounds of the night—the men talking, the night birds calling, the small insects in the foliage. But his mind wouldn't rest.

What exactly was between Jenna and Paterson? For some reason, Jenna's easy familiarity with Paterson annoyed him. And the kiss he'd witnessed bristled the hair on the back of his neck, like an angry old boar that's been confronted out in the woods. Was Paterson her lover? Had she come out here to be with him? And what difference did it make to him if she had?

He looked over at her tent again. She seemed to be

127

sitting at the table, writing something. Probably recording the day's events for Solomon. She reached one hand behind her head. In a moment, he saw her long hair tumble to her shoulders. Even in silhouette, the movement was sensual.

He came to his feet and weaved back through the trees to her tent. He paused at the entrance, asking himself why he was there. What should he care if she was foolish enough to undress with the light burning? Why did he feel he must warn her?

"Jenna." His voice was a hoarse, demanding whisper.

"Yes?" she responded warily, but with that distinct songlike quality to her voice. "Who is it?"

"Chance. I'd like to talk to you."

In seconds she had the tent's flap untied and he stepped inside.

"Would you care to sit down?" she asked pleasantly. "I'll get you some coffee."

He took a chair at the table, while she busied herself with the coffee and a cup of tea for herself.

"Have you ever camped in a tent before, Jenna?"

"Why no, I haven't," she replied conversationally. "But I think it's going to be quite an experience."

"Yes, and I expect it's going to be a memorable one for the men, too."

She looked up, bemused by his comment.

"You see, Jenna," he explained, "when it's dark outside and the light is on inside, everyone out there can see everything you're doing in here. Our voices are probably carrying quite well in the calmness of the evening, too."

Her creamy complexion turned as red as a rose. Chance had intended to be all business, but he couldn't help but be amused by her discomfiture.

"Oh . . . dear." Her hand went to her mouth.

"I doubt anyone is going to believe that Henry's just your friend. After all—dinner, wine, kisses . . ."

She turned back to the coffee on the small stove, hiding her expression. "A kiss on the cheek is hardly what I'd expect from a lover, but believe what you will. All I'll say is that Henry is my dearest and best friend. Actually, he's still very adamant about not wanting me here."

From the silhouette, Chance had thought Paterson had kissed her on the lips. Apparently, he'd been mistaken. Regardless, the man was still being too friendly to be a friend.

"I'd say he has a peculiar way of showing it," Chance said. "I was beginning to think that maybe he was the reason you insisted on coming."

For a moment, Jenna found herself comparing Chance's fiery kiss to Henry's gentle one. There was no good reason to do so, and the fact that she had found Chance's exciting made her angry at herself and frustrated. "He isn't the reason I'm here, but it's none of your business one way or the other."

"It could be—if your amorous adventures keep his mind from his work."

"You needn't worry. That won't happen."

"Maybe I'd better inform Paterson. He could be playing by a different set of rules than you are. And if I were you, I'd be careful of him. He might just be after your money," he gibed.

"I know all about fortune hunters, Chance," she scoffed mildly. "I was married to one. And every man I've ever met since has been after my money. Maybe that's why Henry has been my friend for so long. I know he isn't one of them."

"There's only one thing in this life you can be sure of, Jenna, and *that* is that you can never be too sure of what motivates anyone, including yourself. Maybe Paterson thinks he'll woo you with kindness and trust. I've seen that kind."

Jenna was irritated that he would try to put doubts in her mind about Henry. "So you don't care for

Henry any more than you do Grandpa? I'm beginning to think you don't care for anyone."

"Let's just say I'm selective about who I place my trust in. And you should be, too."

Jenna set the cups on the table and took the chair across from him. Their knees bumped beneath the small table and they both sat up a little straighter.

"If you've satisfied your curiosity about me and Henry," she said, sipping at her tea, "then would you mind telling me how your meeting with Durfey went?"

Chance had tried to ruffle her feathers, but he could see he wasn't going to change her opinion of Paterson. He wasn't sure why he had the overpowering urge to do so. He surely couldn't involve himself with her any more than he already was. But there was something about old Paterson's eyes that reminded him a hell of a lot of a snake in the grass, just waiting to strike.

"It served its purpose," he replied offhandedly. "I believe he'll think twice before he does anything foolish, but he's the prime suspect if anyone else on our crew turns up dead."

Jenna's shapely brows rose speculatively. "I get the feeling your visit to him was actually intended to be a threat?"

His lips curved wryly. "Does that bother you?"

Jenna gave him a thorough appraisal, noting both his physical and mental attributes. From a female standpoint, it was easy to appreciate his strong, muscular physique and to know instinctively that if he made love to a woman, he would surely make her feel like a woman, not simply a nonentity.

But what motivated him was a bit more complex. He wasn't as hostile as he'd been in the mine, but handling him seemed about as risky as handling a stick of dynamite. She sensed she must meet him face to face, on his own ground. He might fall into bed with a woman who was coy or coquettish, but she doubted his respect would be won by such tactics. He was a serious man, and life was no petty game to him. He needed a woman as strong and as bold as he was. If she couldn't be his equal, then he would most certainly dismiss her opinions and overpower her individuality.

No matter how stern he appeared, though, a softness in his eyes told of tenderness. He might not like the comparison, but in that respect, he was much like her grandfather. Tough on the outside; gentle on the inside.

"You don't think much of me, do you, Chance?" she asked suddenly, surprising even herself. But she felt the need to continue, to break down a few of the barriers that had been between them from the very beginning. "You think I'm just a silly rich girl with no backbone. A woman who can't think beyond what sort of fabric she'll need for her next gown. You hope your behavior will shock my sensibilities."

In Chance's opinion, she was a woman born to satin, silk, and fur. Yet she was willing to lay beneath a scratchy wool blanket in a tent with a dirt floor and mutter no words of complaint. Was it her nature to accept these inconveniences so casually, or was there merely no end to what she would do, what she would sacrifice, for Solomon Lee? Whichever it might be, he had to offer her a grudging admiration, although he wasn't totally convinced of her merit.

"Yes, I suppose that's what I think of you. Maybe before this road is finished, you can prove me wrong."

"I was only asking a simple question," she said. "Trying to prove you wrong is not a crusade I intend to take up. People will invariably hear what they want to hear and believe what they want to believe. I won't deny I've been fortunate in my life. I was born with a silver spoon in my mouth—I'll make no apologies for that. I do thank my grandfather, though, for providing a home for me, even if that home has been on the rails a great deal of the time. He's worked for what he has. It wasn't dropped in his lap."

Jenna had not intended to anger him, but she was chilled by his sudden icy attitude. Gone was the friendly battle of wits.

"Worked for it?" he countered bitterly. "Yes, I suppose you could call it that. But it was with little regard for the men he left destitute from his manipulations of the stock market and of peoples' lives. My father was one of those he ruined because he had something your grandfather wanted. But my father's dead now. A product of your grandfather's *hard* work."

He left the table and stalked to the door.

"What happened, Chance? I want to know."

His eyes filled with anger, sadness, and memories so vivid Jenna could almost feel the pain of them.

"Ask your grandfather. You'll probably like his version of the story better than mine. As you said, people believe what they want to believe."

He was so angry he could only fumble with the tent flap. He cursed it for holding him an unwilling prisoner and cursed it again when he felt her hand on his arm, unnerving him with a touch that held some strange magic over him.

"I think you're the one with the double standard, Chance Killeen," she said, all lightness gone from her mood. "You're the one believing what you want to believe. I was not the one who ruined your father or caused his death. Don't hold me accountable for what was between your father and my grandfather. It could very well be that you don't know the whole story, anyway. Don't judge him—or me—until you do."

He pulled free of her restraining hand. "I *do* know

132

the whole story. I saw my father crushed to death between two freight cars. I was there the night Solomon proposed to my mother. I believe you were there, too, Jenna. You were waiting outside that shabby tenement house in your expensive carriage, on a cold December night."

He watched her grope into the past, trying to remember.

"Does it shock you that your dear old grandfather lusted after another man's wife? The mother of three young sons? Did you know he set out to have her, whatever the cost, no matter who it hurt?"

He ignored her anguished cry of denial.

"Your grandfather wanted my mother so badly that he financially ruined my father, having no doubt—in his arrogance—that she would leave a poor man for a rich one. He didn't bargain for the love and loyalty she felt for my father—two things I'm sure he's never experienced. He didn't kill my father with his own hands, but he might as well have. He brought him to his knees, and he had no choice but to take the job that killed him. A job as a brakeman that should have been intended for a younger, more agile man."

She recovered from her shock quickly, but since he'd spared her nothing, she gave him no quarter either in her defense of her grandfather. "I'm sorry about what happened to your father, but you fail to realize something about my grandfather. He's like any other man, Chance. He's human, and he needs and wants love. Yes, perhaps he even lusts for it, the same as I'm sure you do at times! He's not a saint and I won't apologize for him. Maybe what he did was wrong, but he must have loved your mother very much or he wouldn't have done it."

In all the years past, it had never occurred to Chance that Solomon Lee might have loved his mother, possibly even as much as his own father had.

Suddenly, the giant took on the vulnerable proportions of a man. And all because of his own mother. Why had he never visualized her passion? Or a man's passion for her? She was a beautiful woman. It was understandable that men would want her. It was hard to believe Solomon Lee could love anything or anybody, but maybe he had.

And here stood Jenna Lee, lecturing him on love and lust. He knew all about the latter. Very little about the former.

It surprised him when his hand cupped her chin, but he proceeded on an instinctive course of action. He brushed his thumb across the petal-soft lips he'd tasted only once. He'd wanted to scare her that first time in the mine, make her leave and take her idiotic proposition with her. Now he just wanted to kiss her, the way a man kisses a woman he is sexually attracted to. He wondered if this was how Solomon Lee had felt about his mother. Out of control. Burning up inside. Driven to have her and the world be damned. If so, then he had something in common with the old bastard after all.

"You speak easily of lust, Jenna Lee." His voice was a husky whisper. "Is that what lies between you and me?"

Jenna was hypnotized by his eyes, his touch, and the wanton desire within her to have him. It was a primitive desire she'd never felt before but likened to that which motivates wild animals to mate. It could be nothing more, for there was no love between them . . . and little of anything else. Only a powerful electricity that could light their lives or destroy them if not handled with caution.

"Nothing lies between us," she denied. "Nothing but a strained alliance."

Chance saw the thumping of her heart beneath the thin fabric of her cotton blouse, saw the way her eyes held to his lips just as his did hers, and he knew she was lying. She was like a sweet pot of honey, and he a bear who had been in hibernation much too long. He wanted to drain her pot, all at one sitting.

He lowered his hand to his side with a great deal of effort. "I'm glad to discover that you—and your grandfather, too—are human. I'm sure it'll give me a whole new perspective on my new partners. Now, before I go, I'd advise you to sleep with that Peace-maker of yours. Whoever didn't want your grandfather in the Coeur d'Alenes may not want you here, either."

Chance escaped her powerful, invisible hold and stepped into the cool of the night. He ignored the glances of the men and went back to his bedroll. With no forethought, he gathered it up and moved to a spot closer to her tent. He was making life miserable for himself by sleeping so close to her, but maybe in the process he could make any clandestine meetings for Paterson a little miserable, too.

135

Chapter Ten

Jenna stepped out of her tent at sunrise with her bedroll in hand. Henry glowered at her from his tent's porch. They'd already exchanged words over breakfast in a tone they'd never used with each other in the past. He was genuinely angry at her. He'd let her know that he hadn't cared for Killeen being admitted into her tent last night. He'd also tried to dissuade her from going with Chance to talk to Vestal Whitman. But she was determined to go and to learn what she could. Henry would simply have to accept it.

The aroma of bacon and eggs and hot biscuits drifted from the mess tent. The men moved through a line, filled their plates, then found places beneath the trees to sit down and eat.

She got her first good look at the crew. They consisted of almost every nationality, but the railroad jobs particularly attracted the Chinese and the Irish. There were always a big percentage of boomers—itinerant railmen who wandered from one road to another, wherever the work was. They were men from all walks of life. It was difficult to keep a boomer on the job for more than a few weeks. After a few paychecks, they were in search of another railroad and a change of scenery. Many used assumed names for various reasons. Their real name might be blacklisted, or they might be wanted by the law. Some traveled about to avoid the consequences of long-term involvements stemming from romantic relationships. Others had abandoned their wives and children and wanted no one to find them. They were bred of wanderlust, wars, strikes, depressions, and bad luck. But there were also those who seemed to use the bad luck as an excuse for their transient way of life, and they never tried too hard to change their situation.

She saw Chance on the other side of the line, saddling his horse. To her surprise, he had already saddled Tia's Fortune. After his visit last night, she had had difficulty sleeping. She'd lain awake until well past midnight, thinking of the things they'd said. But the memory indelible in her mind this morning was not the words spoken in anger and bitterness, but rather his gentle touch upon her lips, which had miraculously banished all the words that had gone before and after.

She understood now why he felt the way he did about her grandfather, and she could even agree that what Solomon had done was wrong. He had altered one life too many, and his mistake was having a far-reaching effect.

She joined Chance and smiled, pretending last night hadn't happened, in hopes of not starting the day off with tensions. She slung her bedroll behind the cantle and tied it down. "Thank you for saddling my horse, but I told you I'd carry my own weight around here."

He didn't look up, just finished tightening the cinch on his own horse. "Daylight's wasting. I'll have to buy you an alarm clock so you can get up earlier, I guess."

She wouldn't have had to pretend that those tender moments last night hadn't happened because he was

137

back to his old self, purely businesslike and seeming to have forgotten all but the bad parts of their conversation.

He swung into the saddle and waited for her. From habit, whenever she hadn't saddled her horse herself, she lifted the fender to check the tightness of the girth.

"I just tightened it," he said. "Don't you trust me?"

"I'm afraid I don't trust you any more than you trust me." She dropped the fender and smiled up at him. "Now, let's get going. As you said, daylight's wasting."

> *"Oh . . . Sally Martin was a friend of mine*
> *I kissed her twice in the warm sunshine.*
> *She said she loved me with all her soul,*
> *But I left her cold for a pot of gold.*
>
> *A pot of gold, a pot of gold,*
> *'Twas the sweetest story ever told,*
> *I found it here where the mountains are high*
> *And I told old Sally Martin good-bye."*

Evening shadows had lengthened across the mountain valley of Prospect when they neared Vestal Whitman's claim. Long before they could see a soul, an unmelodious voice cranked out the words of a poorly composed song.

A sluice box and piles of dirt and rock strewn on either side of the creek were evidence that he'd been working the river in search of gold, although very little had yet been found on the South Fork of the Coeur d'Alene River. The major gold discoveries had thus far been on the North Fork. There was some evidence that he'd been dynamiting on the nearby hills, which suggested that he was looking for a silver lode, too.

138

A wisp of smoke drew their attention to the small shack tucked far back into a box canyon. Pine-clad mountains rose to the right and left of the cabin and were connected by one long low-slung mountain in the rear. This middle section was wooded toward the bottom, but its low, curving top resembled the seat of an English saddle, or possibly the back of a sway-backed horse. It was covered with loose rock, a maze of deadfall, and scrub brush. Behind it rose more mountains.

When they were within two hundred feet of the shack, a cur dog came from around the corner of the house, barking. The singing inside the cabin stopped, and before Chance and Jenna could take cover, a fusillade of bullets pelted the ground at their horses' feet.

The frightened animals tried to bolt and run. Chance leaped from his buckskin. "Take cover behind those rocks!"

Before Jenna could react, he had pulled her from the saddle and was hauling her along behind him, using the horses as cover. Whitman's bullets came faster and closer. Chance and Jenna dove behind the pile of rocks, turning the horses loose.

"You try to come any closer and the next bullet will get you dead center!" Whitman hollered.

Chance leaned back against the pile of dirt, breathing hard. "Why in the hell didn't Paterson warn us Whitman was going to meet us with a gun?" Worry and concern darkened his eyes as he met Jenna's gaze. "I shouldn't have let you come. This isn't any place for you."

Jenna nodded numbly, unable to muster a rebuttal. But then she saw the blood on his sleeve and her heart leaped into her throat. "Chance, you've been hit!"

He glanced at his shoulder. "Yeah, I know. But I don't think it's too bad."

Blood dripped from the shoulder wound, seeping out beneath the cuff on his shirt and onto his hand. "Maybe it isn't, but the bleeding needs to be stopped."

She went into action. Chance sat quietly while she tore a strip of cloth from her petticoat for a bandage.

His chuckle brought her head up with a jerk. "What's so funny?"

"I would have thought a rich girl like you would never dream of tearing up her petticoat for any purpose, let alone one as tasteless as this."

She couldn't help but be amused by his misconceptions about her. "Money will buy a lot of petticoats, Chance. Now, let's get you bandaged."

She tore the sleeve of his shirt away, exposing the ragged, ugly wound in his muscled arm. She made a thick pad to go over it, then tied it in place, gently but securely, with two more wide strips of cloth from her petticoat.

All the while she worked, she felt his eyes trained on her every move and often on her face. His bold examination made her even more aware of the alluringly smooth heat of his flesh against her fingertips, scattering sexual awareness throughout her body like sparks blown by the gentle breath of the wind. And the dark glow in his eyes made her wonder if these feelings were hers alone, or if they might be shared by him.

"Hey, you two!" Whitman hollered from the cabin. "You'd better not be tryin' nothin' funny out there! You state your business and I might just let you leave here alive!"

Chance tilted his head back so his voice would carry better over the pile of dirt and rocks. "My name's Killeen, Whitman! We don't mean you any harm. I'm the new engineer for the Bitterroot Railroad Company and I'm here to talk to you about this piece of ground we need the right-of-way for."

Three more bullets zinged from the house and thudded into the barricade, sending pieces of dirt and rock into their faces.

"I ain't movin' and that's final!" came Whitman's reply. "My claim's legal and I don't want no damned trains running over it! This here's going to be a mother lode and your friggin' railroad ain't gettin' it!"

"Your claim isn't legal, Whitman, and you know it!" Chance hollered back. "Don't force me to get the sheriff out here with a warrant for your arrest."

There was no response and no more gunshots.

"Do you think he's out of ammunition?" Jenna queried.

"I doubt it. I'd be more inclined to think he's trying to get out the back way. I'd better go around there and make sure he doesn't. I might be able to get him into a position where he'll be forced to drop his weapon."

He scanned the surroundings, looking for sufficient cover that would enable him to sprint to the rear of the cabin without taking another bullet.

Jenna detained him with a hand on his forearm. "No, Chance. It's not worth it to try something so risky. He could kill you. Besides," she added flippantly, "with you dead, I'd have to face Whitman by myself."

Chance grinned. "Now I know why you were so determined to get me to take this job. You just wanted somebody to fight your battles. Well, don't worry. I won't get myself into a fatal situation. I'm not real keen on dying, either."

She held her breath as she watched him zigzag through the trees. Whitman saw him and fired a couple of shots, but Chance vanished from view behind heavy brush and timber. Her heart raced. Whitman knew Chance was circling the house now. What if he set up an ambush?

141

The minutes dragged. All was quiet. A creaking sound drew her attention. It sounded like a door being opened. Surely Whitman wouldn't have the courage to come out the front, right past her? Maybe it was a trick.

She went to her stomach and peered cautiously around the side of the dirt pile. It was no trick. Whitman was making a run for the horses.

The buckskin shied away from him but he managed to grab Tia's reins. Outraged that he would take her horse, Jenna pulled her revolver from the holster on her hip. She'd never fired at a man before. She didn't want to kill him, just scare him. But what if she did kill him? Or what if she hit Tia instead?

Chance burst from around the corner of the house and fired two warning shots over Whitman's head, but the old man forced the mare into the trees and up the slope toward the rim of the saddle mountain. It was the only way out of the box canyon other than past Jenna.

She ran from cover and joined Chance. "He's being a fool! We only want to talk to him."

"Makes me wonder if he's wanted by the law or something. I'm going after him and see if I can get him to talk reason, and at least give the horse back."

He leaped astride the buckskin and was soon only a blur in the trees.

Jenna ran to the back of the house to get a better view of their flight, praying Chance wouldn't be killed. She caught only glimpses of the men through the trees and saw the buckskin was having a difficult time catching up to Tia's long-legged strides. A white rage enveloped her when she saw Whitman beating Tia with a dry, thick tree limb. With no thought to the consequences or even the practicality of it, she started up the rocky saddle slope on foot, determined that if she got a shot at Whitman, she would not hesitate a second time.

Whitman veered from the trees and started across the slope's upper regions, exposing himself to view as he made a break for the ridge and what lay beyond on the other side.

Jenna aimed the Peacemaker and fired. The bullet fell short of Whitman by a considerable distance, but it was close enough to scare him. He urged Tia harder. The mare fought him. She was not used to such abusive treatment, the gunshots, and rough terrain. She refused to go into the loose rock and deadfall. Whitman beat her until her shrill scream of fear and pain echoed back down the canyon. Jenna's outrage soared and her heart cried for the confused animal. She knew that if she were in the saddle, she could have coaxed Tia across anything, but the mare responded to gentleness, not cruelty.

Jenna heard Whitman's cursing, and she saw the limb come down again and again on Tia's neck and rump. She surged up the hill with a power she didn't know she had and with only one thought in her mind: She would use that club on Whitman until she collapsed from exhaustion or until he was dead.

Chance closed in on Whitman and the mare, who was finally making a fearful lunge into the deadfall. Then, in a horror that seemed to come in dreamlike slow motion, Tia reared. Whitman pulled back on the bridle. The action threw the mare off balance and she fell over backward down the steep rocky incline. Her painful scream echoed in Jenna's ears, and then all was silent. In a terrible tangle, neither horse nor rider moved in the maze of deadfall that trapped them.

Jenna didn't recall covering the remaining distance to Tia, but when she collapsed next to the mare, she could barely breathe from the exertion. Chance was already at work trying to move some of the obstruction in order to free the horse. Whitman was on the ground almost beneath the animal and barely

143

breathing. The mare's eyes were wild with fear. Jenna ran to her head and tried to calm her, speaking soothing words and assuring her that they would get her out.

One of the trees was too big for Chance to move, but he managed to lift aside two small ones. He and Jenna were able to get Tia to her side and the mare tried to rise, but she couldn't.

Whitman's eyes fluttered open but didn't seem to focus. He coughed and blood splattered out onto his lips and chin.

"Get up, Tia. Please get up. You've got to get up." Jenna pushed and pushed at the horse's neck and body while tears suddenly streamed from her eyes and down her face.

"It's no use, Jenna." Chance's words were little more than a whisper. "Her leg is broken."

Any sense of reality left Jenna's mind as her gaze raced over Tia's glistening, beautiful body. Her stomach lurched at the sight of the bone protruding from the torn, bloody skin on her right front leg.

"She'll have to be killed," Chance said quietly.

"No!" But even as she cried the word in denial, she knew it was true.

Chance stood helplessly watching Jenna sob against the animal. Whitman's eyes fluttered open again and he tried to speak. Chance dropped down next to him. "We'll get you to a doctor. Just hold on."

Whitman persisted in trying to talk. Chance had to put his ear next to the man's lips to catch the words. "He . . . told me . . . to hold out . . . he'd pay me good . . . he said."

"Who?" Chance's eyebrows knitted together. "Who told you this?"

Whitman's lips came together as if he were going to speak, then abruptly he died.

Chance sat back on his heels, puzzling over Whit-

144

man's last words. So someone had paid him to hold out against the railroad. But who? Durfey? Or maybe some of the freighters who wanted to hold onto business for just as long as they could?

He was disturbed by the transgression of a meeting that had been intended only as a discussion. Now a man was dead who had taken vital information to the grave with him, and Jenna was in devastation.

Gently, he took her by the arm. "There's nothing you can do about the horse. Go back to the cabin. I'll meet you down there."

Still crying, Jenna allowed Chance to help her to her feet. She stared at Tia's big, frightened eyes watching her, trusting her, depending on her to do something to help her. She was letting her friend down, breaking that last and largest trust of all.

"You're going to shoot her?"

Chance's grip tightened on Jenna's shoulders. "There's no other way."

Jenna ran her hand one last time along Tia's graceful neck and down the perfect conformation of her face. She began to cry convulsively. She ran then, stumbling blindly down the rocky hill, never looking back.

Chance waited until she was on the other side of the cabin in the little valley below, and then he reluctantly pulled his Colt from the holster.

Jenna sat rigidly on the ground, her knees drawn up to her chest and her arms encircling them. The gunshot jolted her, echoing against the evening hills again and again, until silence throbbed in her ears. She slumped and laid her head upon her knees.

Damn Vestal Whitman. She was glad he was dead.

145

Chapter Eleven

Henry called a meeting with his partners and Ives got the word to Durfey. They met at midnight in a secluded spot by the river a mile from either camp. They sat huddled together, talking in whispers, only the moonlight allowing them to see each other's faces.

"What are we going to do about Killeen?" Ives asked.

"Maybe if we're lucky, Whitman will kill him," Durfey put in dryly.

That hope had already crossed Henry's mind, but he didn't want the same fate to befall Jenna. He wished he could have talked her out of going. The others didn't care if she perished alongside Solomon, but he had his plans and didn't want them ruined. God knows, Solomon had already complicated things on the railroad. If anything happened to Jenna, his plans of getting Solomon Enterprises would be gone.

Just thinking of Killeen made him angry. Why had Solomon taken a partner, and why had he chosen Killeen over him? He'd known Solomon for years, had been his friend, his trusted employee. But Solomon had undercut him and betrayed him by not asking him to be his partner and by not trusting him enough to let him engineer the road. Maybe he didn't have the formal training that Killeen had, but he had the on-the-job experience that was every bit as good—maybe better.

"We've failed in our attempt to drive Solomon out," he said. "Now that Killeen's here, it changes things considerably. He could find out about us the way Westbrook did. We can't draw any more attention to Durfey by killing anybody else. Nor can we afford to quit this project. We've got too much invested and too much to gain by getting this road through. And if we're careful, he'll never need to know we're the owners of the CDAC, even after it's built. Once we're established, it won't matter."

"Well, I know one thing for sure," Durfey said. "Killing wasn't part of the bargain when I joined up with you guys. I think we'd better find another way for the time being."

A lengthy silence filled the darkness as each man considered the situation that was rapidly becoming a dilemma simply because Solomon was determined to continue. It seemed no matter how they looked at it, they were doomed sooner or later by the baron's power.

In a voice as wispy as his body, and yet one that commanded attention, James Leaman finally spoke. "It *is* too dangerous to keep killing our opponents, gentlemen," he said. "Perhaps we should be more like Solomon. Outsmart them and then hit them where it hurts the most—in their pocketbooks.

"My suggestion at this point is to let Killeen and Solomon build their road," he continued. "But we, the actual builders, can make sure that it costs more than it normally would—at least the figures they see will reflect such. In actuality, we'll overcharge Solomon for everything, cause delays by various methods, then take the excess money to pay for our own road."

147

He paused to allow his partners to ponder the first part of his plan, then he proceeded with the second part.

"When the road is complete, we can then kill Solomon and Killeen. At that point, there wouldn't be any reason to finger us as the murderers. Everyone knows Solomon has a lot of enemies. And with him dead, Jenna should be easy to deal with. In her grief, she'd just want to be rid of it. Since we're her employees, she'll feel loyalty to us and sell it to us for peanuts just to have if off her hands. She's generous and she'll think that it's being placed in good hands. She'll hurry back to her horse farm in Connecticut and will never want to see these mountains again. And, if Killeen finds out about us before the road is finished, he'll just have to meet with a little construction accident."

"What about Killeen's share?" Ives asked. "Who'll we be dealing with after he's dead?"

Leaman had done his homework. "His only relative in this area is his mother. She runs a boarding house in Bayard, and I seriously doubt she'd be interested in having a railroad dumped on her, complicating her life. My guess is that she'll go for the money if the price is right. Women just like the money, gentlemen. They don't like the headaches that go along with it. How many women do you know who could run a railroad, anyway?"

They were all amused except Ives. "It seems to me that Jenna might decide she likes it in Solomon's shoes."

"Possibly, but not to the point of holding onto a railroad that's out in the middle of nowhere, and one she might consider as being the cause of her grandfather's death."

No one could think of any more arguments. It seemed the perfect solution. Henry pondered it deeper than the others, but he couldn't see where it would hurt his relationship with Jenna in any way. If they handled it properly, she would never discover the truth of any of it.

"All right," he said at last. "Does anyone object?"

Ives grunted, which was an indication that he was agreeable. Durfey added his usual whining reluctance. "You're still going to have to pay for *one* railroad, one way or the other."

"Yes," Leaman replied confidently, "but we'll have them both this way, almost for the price of one, and we'll have trains coming and going through these mountains, up one side of the river and down the other. We'll make millions with no competition. With tracks laid on either side of the river, there would be no incentive for any other companies to try to build. Construction other than near the river would exceed profitability, especially in the face of several competitors."

"All right," Durfey finally conceded. "I just hope to hell you all know what you're doing."

When Chance rode down off the mountain, Jenna was in front of Whitman's shack and didn't seem to hear his approach. He had reservations about disrupting her private moment of grief. The horse had obviously meant a great deal to her, more than he had imagined.

He dismounted the buckskin. "We've got to go, Jenna," he said gently. "It's getting dark."

When she made no move or response, he took her hand and drew her to her feet. She seemed to have no strength to do her own bidding. He looked upon her tear-stained face, then tilted her chin upward.

"I'm sorry, Jenna. I should never have allowed you to come. I'll get you another horse."

149

"I guess I owe you a twenty-dollar gold piece. You said she'd break a leg."

Suddenly, she began to cry in wrenching sobs. He drew her into his arms. She laid her head against his chest and clung to him tightly. He wished he could think of the right words to soothe her, but he knew it would take time for Jenna to get over the senseless loss of the animal.

Chance stroked her hair and ran a comforting hand over her back. He became much too aware of her soft curves conforming to the hard lines of his own body. It was only with strict discipline that he kept his lips from the fragrant blond tresses touching his neck like strands of silk.

She was the last woman in the world he should want to hold and make love to, but something besides desire stirred inside him. He found he wanted to protect her from pain, from everything and everybody that might hurt her.

He gently put her away from him. To follow his momentary desires could only create problems for the morrow. Her crying had stopped. Only moisture remained in her overbright eyes; only trails from tears were left on her face. He wiped the wetness away with the tips of his fingers.

"I tied your bag to my saddle and I'll send someone back for your saddle. Now we'd better get going so we can reach Milo Gulch before it gets too late."

He swung into the saddle and lifted his foot from the stirrup, holding out a hand to her. "Come on, Blondie. Ride up behind me."

The sound of his favorite sobriquet jarred Jenna from her state of numbness. He had said the word kindly, not derogatorily. She looked up at him, sitting so tall and handsome in the saddle. Her gaze slid over his broad shoulders, taking in the blood-soaked pad on his arm and the understanding expression on his face. Something was different between them, although she didn't know exactly what it was.

She placed her hand in his and, with his help, swung up behind him. There was nothing to hold onto but him, so she tentatively put her hands along his trim waist. He nudged the buckskin into an easy, swinging walk. By the time they had reached Milo Gulch, she had fallen asleep with her head against his shoulder blade, her arms around him fully.

Wardner Junction was the small town at Milo Gulch. Across the river was its bigger and noisier sister, Wardner. When the rocking motion of the horse ceased, Jenna came awake with a start. Her mind cleared swiftly as she saw the hotel in front of them and heard the tinny sound of a nickelodeon playing somewhere in the distant darkness.

Chance swung a leg over the saddle horn and slid off the buckskin.

"I'm sorry about falling asleep," she said, self-consciously straightening her blouse and skirt and brushing errant strands of hair from her face. "I was more tired than I thought."

"Think nothing of it." He encircled her waist with his hands and helped her to the ground. "That's all the more reason to get you a room."

The hotel was a small two-story structure and, like many things in the mountains, had recently been constructed and still smelled of freshly milled lumber.

There was no one at the registry when they entered. Chance rang the bell on the counter, and in seconds they heard scurrying feet along an upper hallway, then down the stairs. The clerk burst into the room and hurried to his position behind the desk.

"Good evening." His thin face tensed. "I'm sorry,

151

but didn't you see the sign in the window? We have no vacancies."

They both looked over their shoulders at the sign he indicated. Chance lowered Jenna's bags and his saddlebags to the floor, taking the weight from his shoulder. His arm was hurting, and Jenna looked as tired and as drawn as he felt.

The clerk ran a worried gaze over Chance's bloody arm and torn sleeve. "I see you need medical assistance, sir. We have a doctor in Wardner, across the river. There might be a hotel there, too, with some vacancies, although things are filling up fast now that everyone is moving back into the mountains for the summer. A lot of men are hoping to find work on the new railroad coming in. You and the missus wouldn't be, too, would you?"

The innocently spoken words jolted both of them. Jenna straightened perceptibly. For a moment, green eyes locked with blue in total surprise that someone might think they were married. Chance fought the inexplicable urge to let this man think they were, but he wasn't sure why. Was it because any man would be proud to have such a beauty as his wife?

"We're not married," he said quietly. "I'm Chance Killeen, engineer for the Bitterroot Railroad. This is Jenna Lee, Solomon Lee's granddaughter."

The man gasped. "Solomon Lee's granddaughter?" He was equally horrified and then awed. When the shock had worn off, he immediately whirled the heavy registry around and traced the names with his slender white finger. "Such an honor to have you here in Wardner Junction at my hotel, Miss Lee. I'm sure a couple of these men wouldn't mind sleeping in the livery for the night to accommodate a lady."

Alarmed at the man's drastic choice of action, Jenna objected kindly but firmly, leaning forward and placing her hand over the names on the registry.

152

"You are so very kind," she said, "but I won't allow you to put anyone out of his room. Mr. Killeen and I will be the ones to find lodging elsewhere."

"Oh, I won't hear of it, Miss Lee. No, indeed. You are welcome to stay in my home even. It's not fancy, but it's clean and comfortable. My wife is an excellent cook and housekeeper." He started around the desk, grabbing a jacket to ward off the evening chill. "It's right next to the river. Come on, I'll show you the way. Of course, there won't be room for Mr. Killeen, but I'm sure he won't mind staying at the livery."

Jenna halted the man by laying a hand on his arm. She gave him her most gracious smile. "Thank you ever so much, but I wouldn't think of dropping in on your wife so unexpectedly and at such a late hour. I'm sure we'll find a room at Wardner."

Before the man could say more, Jenna had hurried from the hotel. Her long legs took her swiftly down the boardwalk and toward the bridge that led into Wardner. Chance thanked the clerk for his efforts, untied the buckskin, and hastened down the street after her.

She had handled the clerk with smooth expertise. A smile, a gentle hand. She'd never raised her voice, never appeared to be irritated. But Chance knew she was. He respected her anew for refusing to take someone's room and to inconvenience the clerk's wife—and for not leaving him to sleep in the livery.

When her feet came down off the boardwalk and hit the soft dirt of the road to Wardner, she was practically running. Chance finally came alongside her, amused by her haste. "You can slow down now, Blondie. He isn't coming after you."

"He was a very kind man," she replied flatly, looking straight ahead. "His generosity was laudable, but I could just see him and his wife keeping me up until all hours wanting to talk about Grandpa or

153

something, or simply trying to wait on me hand and foot as though I couldn't do a thing for myself. Besides, he wasn't going to let you stay."

She surveyed the small junction at the river and the considerable distance to the larger town of Wardner on the other side. The sounds of town life disturbed the otherwise gentle murmur of the South Fork of the Coeur d'Alene River. A cold edge came into her voice as she gazed about the primitive encampment of civilization. "I remember one time we came into a town and there were no rooms available. My grandfather paid an exorbitant price to have the entire upper floor of the town's only hotel cleared so his entourage could use it. I never felt right about that. Who am I to make someone else sleep on the ground?"

She met his gaze with a stubborn set to her jaw. She was a proud woman, determined not to be treated differently from anyone else, despite her and her grandfather's notoriety. Chance knew she wasn't asking for his answer, and he sensed perhaps she had regretted revealing the incident and something personal about herself. She turned on her booted heel and started off on a fast walk toward the bridge.

He kept his long strides even with her quick, shorter ones. Not only was she upset at the hotel clerk, but Chance knew she was still grieving over losing Tia's Fortune. Despite it, she carried herself with a rigid determination to put the incident behind her.

In Wardner, they were faced with the same situation of overcrowding. Even the liveries were filling up with wayward men. At the last hotel, they once again were sent back out into the street.

Chance pushed his hat to the back of his head and his gaze wandered to the bend in the river where the trees and brush grew thick. It wasn't wise at all, what he was thinking. He should take her right to the hotel

154

clerk's house and insist she accept his hospitality. Instead, he found himself wanting to be alone with her down on the river, with just the stars overhead, the campfire at their feet, and the river murmuring in the darkness.

"How are you at sleeping on the ground, Jenna? It looks as though we have no choice."

Jenna met his gaze and saw something there like a smoldering fire, an ember ready to burst into flame. Her heartbeat quickened and danger signals washed over her body in waves. But caution didn't seem strong enough to linger.

She looked up at the pinpoints of stars in the black mantle of the night; it was safer than looking in his eyes. If she did that, he might recognize the lambent flame of desire in her own. On the horizon, the moon was peeking its head over the mountains. It was going to be a nice night.

"Well, your horse needs to rest," she said, "and so do we. But most of all, you need to see a doctor about your arm."

"I take it, then, that you're in favor of finding a place to camp?"

She nodded.

Chance's gaze slid over the tight-fitting, waist-length jacket she wore. It conformed so perfectly to her curves. Did she have any idea how sensual she was—even with her blond hair falling from its pins and her clothes a bit dusty from the trip? She'd been so soft in his arms, so warm lying against his back in innocent sleep. He wanted to hold her again but knew he shouldn't. He must remember that getting too deeply involved with her could only lead to trouble for both of them.

It was going to be difficult to sleep right next to her all night and not want to take her to him. Why had he even suggested putting himself to such a test of strength and willpower? He had lived long enough to know that the edge of desire did not always border on prudence.

The moon finally popped up over the jagged line of the mountains, casting a sheen that turned her blond hair almost silver. The silky softness of it beckoned a man's touch, a man's lips. He should *make* her go stay at the hotel clerk's house. Yet the words to do it were stuck in his throat.

"All right," he managed. "We'll eat, and I'll see a doctor. Then we'll go down to the river."

Chapter Twelve

Chance chose a secluded spot about thirty feet from the river. Even though they couldn't see the river for the brush, they could hear the rushing sound of it not far away. Trees and bushes formed a thick, protective circle around the small clearing, creating a natural shelter from the wind and from unwanted eyes. With only the light of the moon to work by, he prepared the ground for the fire, clearing it down to the dirt.

When the blaze was self-sustaining, Chance laid out his bedroll on one side of it. Jenna copied his every move, right down to removing all the rocks and twigs from her spot on the opposite side. She uttered no words of complaint, but was as wide-eyed over the entire procedure as a child full of curiosity and enthusiasm, and the quest for adventure and new experiences. She might never suggest sleeping on the ground again when she woke up with sore muscles and cold bones, but at least she could say she'd had the experience.

For a moment, Chance wondered what would she do when her adventure in the Bitterroots was over and the trains were running smoothly, hauling the ore. Even as the question came, so did the answer. She would return to her world. She might even find another adventure. But he would stay behind.

The thought annoyed him. He shouldn't care if she left. He should be looking forward to the moment when Solomon Lee was out of his life.

Solomon Lee, yes . . . but what about her?

She sat on her bed, her legs tucked beneath her, looking nervous and self-conscious. Chance decided it was best to put all the thoughts from his mind that he'd had about her earlier. It wouldn't be wise to try and hold her in his arms the way his desires had urged him to do. He took off his gun belt and set it nearby. Next came his boots. He got beneath his blankets and just before he lay back, Chance pulled his hat off. When he was prone, he covered his face with it.

"We'll be up at daybreak," he said. "Get some sleep."

Jenna watched the play of the firelight over his body. She was disappointed that he hadn't elected to have a little conversation with her, and she wondered about the look that had been in his eyes earlier. She must have been wrong in thinking that he might have had a romantic interest in her.

She removed what pins were still in her hair and tucked them inside her bag. She brushed the long tresses until they crackled with electricity. All the while, Chance didn't stir.

The sound of the rushing river was inviting and she wanted to wash the grit from her face. She took her bag in hand and stood up. "Chance?" she whispered. "Are you asleep?"

"No," came his muffled response from beneath the Stetson.

"I'm going down to the river to wash."

There was a moment of silence. "All right. Be careful."

The spot he'd found for camp was so secluded that Jenna had a difficult time finding a path to the river through the tangle of brush. At least the moon was full, casting a light over the land that rendered it nearly as bright as day. She walked along the edge of the river for a short distance, finding a spot where the water was easily accessible and the bank had a gradual slope.

The moon laid a silver shawl upon the dark, hypnotizing current. She inhaled of the fresh scent of the air, of the pines, of the new shoots of grass and the fresh dirt just free of winter's heavy burden. The sky seemed close and big and full of stars. The mountains that formed Milo Gulch serrated the horizons and invaded the sky in all directions with their impenetrable bulk. Imagination could lead her to believe that she was inside the mighty, uplifted jaws of some mythological monster.

It was getting cold, but it was a crisp, clean cold. The water looked exceptionally inviting, for it had been a long, hard day. A day Jenna would never forget.

Suddenly, the horrible memory of Tia's broken leg came flooding back. She clenched her jaw and fought the oncoming tears. She must be strong. She must not dwell on losing Tia's Fortune. She had wanted to come here; now she must be brave enough to face the consequences of her decisions.

She bolstered herself against the pain, even though it would be much easier to give in to the tears. She'd come to the river to bathe, not to wallow in grief. Jenna took her soap, washcloth, and towel from her bag and set them on a log. She followed with her discarded clothing.

She dipped a toe in the water. The icy shock not only sent her tears scurrying, but made her decide the water was too cold to immerse in. Jenna went in only up to her ankles and the cold immediately rose up into her legs, making them ache. She completed her toilette quickly, then briskly toweled herself dry. Shivering, teeth chattering, and with goose bumps covering her entire body, she hastily redressed in fresh underthings and cotton nightgown. She didn't know if it was customary to sleep in one's clothing while camping out, but she couldn't imagine it being very comfortable. It was getting colder, though, so she slipped her jacket on over her nightgown.

Not quite ready to sleep, Jenna sat on the log near the edge of the river and watched the water's shimmering movement. The moment was peaceful, the noises of the town distant. Closer was the sound of night birds whose names she didn't know.

She closed her eyes and tried to allow the river to carry away her sorrow, just as it carried away winter's melted snow. But unbidden, the tears returned. They poured forth in a rush, hot against her cool skin, overwhelming her and racking her body with sobs she couldn't contain.

She didn't hear the rustle of the bushes as they parted. She didn't see Chance halt there in the silver wash of the moon, pondering whether to step forward and comfort her, or to leave her alone with her grief. The sight of her, huddled and crying, touched a spot in him no decent man could deny.

He stepped forward. In six strides he had covered the distance separating them. He dropped to one knee next to her. She was startled by his appearance and turned her head away, ashamed that he had caught her crying.

"Please leave me alone, Chance. Just for a while."

"I don't believe that's what you need, Jenna," he replied gently, brushing the golden hair back that had fallen like a curtain across her face.

There was a moment's hesitation as her glittering, tear-filled eyes met his, then she turned willingly into his embrace.

He held her for several moments, feeling her body, but especially her unbound breasts, pressed against him with nothing but the thin cotton gown concealing them. His body responded to the feminine stimulus, but as before there seemed to be more than desire that made him want her. Always when with her, he felt a touch of need that centered too alarmingly in his heart, not just in his loins.

"I could always . . . depend on her," Jenna said falteringly as she tried to get control.

Chance knew she spoke of Tia's Fortune.

She pulled a long, sustaining breath, and after some moments the tears and the sobs stopped. "She was my friend. I know that probably sounds silly, but she really was. She was almost human, so intelligent. She came running when I'd step out into the pasture. She looked forward to going through her paces. Oh, she was a beautiful pacer. You should have seen her."

She removed her head from his shoulder and looked away into the distance. Her eyes were still teary but a partial smile brightened her face as she remembered. Chance sat back on his haunches, releasing her reluctantly. He was captivated by her lovely, animated face as she spoke—the strength of its structure, the determination in her eyes, and the set to her lips, even though they still quivered a bit. Her blond hair cascaded over her shoulders and the moonlight bejeweled her eyes. His chest shallowed as the air seemed pushed from him by some invisible hand. He wanted her so desperately it was difficult to think of anything else.

"She was one of the best," Jenna continued in that dreamy, reminiscent way. "She was so easy to sit, it was like resting in a rocking chair. She was like a small child whose only goal was to please. And she judged me on how I treated her. She loved me for myself. She didn't care about Grandpa's money."

The bitter truth of human nature pained her deeply, and it stabbed Chance with a double dose of guilt. He suddenly felt self-reproach, for his behavior toward her had hinged on the very thing she was

161

speaking of. He had judged her because of who she was rather than trying to accept her on her own merit.

"Why don't you go to the person you bought her from and try to get another," he suggested quietly. "I know it wouldn't be the same, but—"

He was surprised to hear her soft laughter. "I *am* the owner, Chance. I raised her from a colt. She came from one of my brood mares on my horse farm in Connecticut. I have many more horses, but Tia was my favorite. She had one colt. A filly. So, perhaps I can at least preserve her bloodline."

Chance was surprised by the information, but he had to admit that running a horse farm actually suited her. She was a vivacious woman, a restless one. She would not be content to sit around in a parlor all day, taking tea with visitors.

"Tell me about your farm, Jenna."

She lifted her gaze from the river and decided he was genuinely interested. Chance Killeen was not a man to tolerate something that bored him, nor was he a man to encourage that boredom with politeness.

"It's my own enterprise," she told him. "When I was twenty-two, I used some of my trust money which my parents had left for me and I bought the farm. Grandpa has nothing to do with it, except that he comes there on weekends when he can. It's a lovely country estate. Of course, the countryside is not so rugged as this, but the peacefulness of this place reminds me of the farm. I stay there as much as I can. I really don't like Grandpa's Great House in the city."

She laughed lightly. "You should see that place. It looks like someone's nightmare. I don't know who decorated it. Of course, it was the vogue at the time and he's never redecorated, finding no interest in that sort of thing. It isn't a restful place at all. It's big and dark, full of all sorts of statues, massive furniture—

162

and ghosts." She grinned impishly at him. "I'm convinced of that. When I was little and first went to live there, I was afraid. I was only five and my room was huge. The light never reached to the corners and left questionable shadows everywhere. I imagined a ghoul behind every stick of furniture, preparing to eat me as soon as the light was doused. Grandpa took pity on me and insisted the servants leave a light burning in my room and one sconce lit in the hall that led to his room.

"My ghosts were not just your typical ghosts, either. I had other fears. I awoke many times in the night from nightmares about the train wreck that took my parents and brothers and grandmother. My grandfather and I were in the wreck, but Grandpa got me out. He couldn't get anyone else out. There was fire everywhere."

She paused for a moment, remembering, then quickly went on. "So it was just him and me after the wreck, and he seemed to understand how frightened I was to be alone. He slept with his door open so he could hear me if I needed him. And if I had a bad dream, he would come and sit with me until I had fallen back to sleep."

It troubled Chance that she'd been left alone to cope with the loss and the pain of losing her family while not being old enough to understand why. He'd lost his father at sixteen, and it had been hard enough to deal with then.

More than these thoughts, though, he was troubled by the image of Solomon Lee that she presented. She made him appear benevolent, normal. She honestly never saw him for what he was—one of the ghouls in that monstrosity of a house.

He came to his feet abruptly. "I'd better go back. I'll need to add more wood to the fire."

Jenna watched him go, feeling regret for having shared those bits of her life with him. He had seemed genuinely interested at first, and she wondered why he'd left so suddenly.

She gathered her things and went back to camp. He was lying on top of his bedroll, smoking a cigarette, one hand tucked behind his head and his legs crossed at the ankle. He hadn't removed his boots a second time. His gaze was caught on the stars, but she sensed his mind outdistanced them. Her arrival pulled him from those faraway thoughts, and he watched her as she hung the wet towel and washcloth on the bushes. He was still watching when she drew back the blankets and slid beneath the covers.

She felt self-conscious again, knowing his eyes roamed the curves of her body beneath the blankets. She only wished she knew if it was with approval or disapproval. One way or the other, it was disconcerting.

Restlessly, he came to his feet and laid more sticks on the fire that didn't really need them. He dropped his cigarette and smashed it into the ground with the twisting motion of his boot toe. It dawned on her then that his pleasantness had vanished at the mention of her grandfather. He still clung so tenaciously to his resentment that it was about to eat him alive.

"Why don't you just forget about him?" she snapped. "It would make our association much easier. At least we could get some sleep."

His head jerked up at her harsh words and he saw the angry sparks in her blue eyes. "Forget about who?"

She sat up. "You know who. My grandfather. You're beside yourself with hatred for him. So much so that you can't even stand the sight of me. Well, you might as well get used to me, Chance Killeen, because I'll be around for at least six months. Every day, day in and day out. Every night. Just being here to remind you of him and to torture you—if you let it."

To her surprise, he stepped across the fire, towering over her ominously with eyes as dark and as dangerous as a keg of black powder. Wariness leaped inside her when he dropped to his knees in front of her and cupped her chin roughly in his hand.

"Yes, you torture me, Jenna Lee," he growled. "But do you know why and just how much?"

Only inches away now, his pupils dilated wider and blacker until all green vanished from their depths. He watched her the way a hawk watches a field mouse, waiting for just the right moment to devour it.

The chill of the night faded as a rush of heat raced over her. Her heart thudded madly and she nearly stopped breathing. He leaned closer to her, until she could feel his hot breath upon her lips and detect the tobacco scent from the cigarette he'd just smoked. His chest rose and fell just inches from her breasts, a solid wall seemingly as massive as the distant mountains, but the warmth from it was disturbingly human, erotically male, unlike the impassive hardness of the Bitterroots.

"I'll show you how much you torture me," he said huskily, sliding his fingers into her hair. "I'll show you why you should have stayed in Coeur d'Alene where it was safe."

With celerity, his mouth closed over hers. The firm line of his lips softened miraculously and moved against hers with moist, demanding heat. Artfully, the movement of his lips against hers persuaded hers to part, to open her more fully to the bold invasion of his tongue determined to explore the sweet darkness within.

The hunger of his lust was evident as he forced her back onto the blankets. His lips left hers to scatter kisses along her face and neck and into her hair, where his hands still held the tangled mass. But she had no power to stop him, realizing she wanted his

165

touch, *had* wanted it since the first time she'd seen him. She slid her arms around him, feeling the play of his muscled back beneath her fingertips. Through the thin cotton of her gown, she felt his sinewed body so right against her own, and she felt, too, with a woman's appreciation, the hard length of his manhood eager to invade her secret softness. He moved against her with yearning and her body matched his with wanton desire, in a dance of fire swiftly spreading out of control.

As if by magic, the buttons on her gown came loose beneath his fingers, and in seconds he laid aside the flimsy barrier. The rosebud peaks of her breasts stiffened, betraying her desire for his touch. In seconds, his hot caress warmed the creamy mounds. A tiny moan of pleasure escaped her throat but she fought it, only because her conscience told her she should. She gripped his shoulders and made a feeble attempt to push him away. "No, Chance. Stop. This . . . isn't right."

He seemed not to hear, or simply chose to ignore. His lips followed the course of his hands, laying soft kisses on her breasts. She buried her fingers in his black hair and lifted toward the fiery ecstasy he imparted upon her. At her encouraging movement, his tongue flicked over the pert nipples, his mouth closed and suckled gently in a drawing motion that pulled all resistance from her body and made her whimper as she tried to deny her need, but all the while wanting him in a way that simply couldn't be denied. His mouth left her breasts and he rained kisses across the swell of her bosom, up to her collarbone, and then all the way down the opening of the gown to the flat of her abdomen. His kiss lingered there, stilling any further debate from her about his lovemaking.

She knew she should make him stop, but the strength and the willpower were gone. She was being driven by a devil who knew no shame nor pride, only an overpowering desire to satisfy the demanding need consuming her. Oh, she knew now what he meant by torture!

She moaned softly beneath his ravaging kisses, responding to his fiery tongue with her own. His hand moved tenderly over her breasts, heating the slow burn in her loins to a raging wildfire, hot and uncontrollable.

"I want you, Jenna," he whispered fiercely between kisses. "Do you want me? Tell me."

She couldn't answer, so confused was she by ambivalent feelings.

Again his mouth traveled from hers, leaving her in a strange limbo until his lips closed over the rigid peaks of her breasts again. With languid deliberation, his tongue taunted and teased. Her hands slid from his head to his strong shoulders, then down until her fingers found the buttons on his shirt, undid them, and slipped inside to touch the scorching heat of his body and the thick mat of black hair on his chest.

The words tumbled from her throat, coming—it would seem—not from the conscious mind but from her desirous body. "Yes, Chance . . . yes, I want you."

The whispered sound of his name upon her lips pulled the fragile strand of restraint to the snapping point. In seconds, they would both be plunged into the swirling depths of a passion that would either hold them forever as loving prisoners or turn them into bitter enemies at dawn's first light. Whichever it might be, it was a place of no return.

Chance felt the answering response of her entire body clinging to his. The circling caress of her hands upon his back heated him as no fire could, for the fire of her touch went all the way to his soul. She was willing and eager. He craved the satisfaction of being inside her, but something told him that action alone might not be enough. There seemed a cavern in him so deep and empty that he wondered if it could ever be filled by a few moments of ecstasy. There seemed something more that he wanted from her, something over and above the joining of her body with his. He knew that if he took her, he would be satisfied for a fleeting moment, but he feared he would be left empty by morning, still craving, still yearning for more. And yet he took the chance.

He lifted slightly, tracing the swell of her hip, the valley of her waist, sliding his hand to the mound of her womanhood beneath the thin cotton gown. His lips closed over hers with hard passion. A moan of desire slid from her throat and into his, a stimulus that went to the core of him.

She arched against him. He pushed her cotton gown upward and slid his hand onto the hot flesh of her inner thigh, then farther, until his exploring fingers found her intimate, velvety folds. Her breath caught at his hot, tender touch but she didn't push his hand away, for to do so would end the perfect pleasure he incited within her. She gripped his back and began a slow rhythmic motion beneath him that he soon matched with his own body.

"Oh, Chance . . . Chance . . . I want you. Now."

In unremembered seconds, his clothes were tossed aside and hers as well. His mind blocked out all but the sound of his name tumbling from her lips and the need for the arms that drew him back into her soft, hungry embrace.

She lifted her silky legs around him, holding him a willing captive, and with urgent hands guided his narrow hips to her. The moist heat of her encircled him, making him shudder with exquisite pleasure and need. He found his way into her with a need that abandoned gentleness, and they moved in instinctive rhythm, clinging to each other, their kisses demanding, deep, as the mounting tremors of pleasure drove them higher and higher to the limits of the sky itself. He heard her cries of passion mix with his own, and she thrust with him in equal fervor.

Like an eagle that soars as high as the wind will allow, everything suddenly and momentarily seemed suspended inside him. In a flash of gold and silver light, the hot trail of fire spread throughout his body, and he felt the molten heat consume Jenna as well. She reached that pinnacle with him. With driving need, they rode out the wild moment of ecstasy as one would ride out a voyage upon a storm-tossed sea.

Gasping for breath but in utter satisfaction, they floated together back to earth, quiet as circling hawks, down and down, rocking back and forth through the last faint tremors of satisfaction until they were laid gently back upon the ground and back into the world.

Suddenly, it was too quiet. Every sound seemed intensified tenfold. The crackling fire, the forest's night creatures, the flow of the river; the pounding of their hearts against each other; the wetness of their sated bodies clinging together; the feel of himself inside her. Glorious, but wrong.

For the love of God, what had he done?

She tensed beneath him, and he knew in that moment she felt it, too. They'd been carried away by passion and need. Now they must pay the fiddler.

He came away from her, reaching for his clothes, keeping his back to her. They weren't even in love. They didn't even care about each other. It was true that something seemed to draw them inexorably to each other, but it wasn't love. It went no deeper than lust. Surely, no deeper.

He heard her movements behind him, and he glanced over his shoulder. She was sitting up, frantically securing the buttons on her gown. Her hair fell across her face, blocking her expression, but her hands were shaking. She looked and acted ashamed, humiliated. He hadn't wanted to make her feel that way. He simply hadn't intended for this to happen. Only in a distant dream had he ever set out to seduce her so completely. No, in actuality, he'd only intended to kiss her.

"I'm sorry, Jenna. I—" He couldn't say more. He had never felt so confused or helpless, so contemptible of himself, in his entire life. He didn't hold anything against her. She had reacted out of need, the same as he had. Their bodies had seemed like dynamite and fire, igniting when coming together.

But still a degree of doubt nudged at him as he watched her for another moment. Could she have possibly made love out of more than need? Surely, she didn't care for him? He hadn't even been kind to her.

Jenna nodded, as if understanding his lame attempt at an explanation. She kept her head down and continued to try to button her gown. She didn't seem to be able to speak, either.

The feeling that surged through him at that moment confused him even more, for instead of wanting to run away from her, as he knew he should, he only wanted to take her into his arms again and make this miserable moment right.

God, he was crazy, and she was making him that way. She, who was Solomon Lee's granddaughter.

Not knowing what else to do, he left camp . . . slinking out, like a weasel who has just raided the henhouse.

Chapter Thirteen

Henry knew immediately that something was wrong when he saw Jenna and Chance riding double on the buckskin. Jenna's expression was glum and weary, Chance's tense.

He rushed to Jenna and helped her from the horse. "What's happened, Jenna? Where's Tia?"

But Jenna couldn't seem to find the words to explain what had happened and Killeen interceded. "Whitman's dead, Paterson, and so is Tia's Fortune. But you've got a clear right-of-way now, so that should make you happy."

Henry put an arm on Jenna's shoulder and ushered her into the tent, leaving Killeen to tend to the horses. He sat her down and pulled up a chair next to her. "Now, tell me what happened up there, Jenna."

It had been a long ride back. There had been no horses available to rent at Milo Gulch or Wardner, and they'd been forced to ride double. It had been terribly difficult to be so close to Chance after what had happened by the river. They had spoken no more than the situation demanded.

Jenna felt used and ashamed by his reaction to their intimacy. She couldn't understand why, after twelve years of being courted and wooed by scores of

171

men, it had been Chance who had so completely and easily unwound her tightly knotted ball of restraint. She had known nothing good could come out of their union because of his animosity toward her grandfather, and yet she had allowed it to happen just the same.

At last she told him what had happened at Vestal Whitman's. When the story was complete and Henry was making his angry comments about "that crazy Whitman," her mind drifted away again.

It was easy to still feel Chance's lips scorching her naked flesh, bringing her alive again after all these years of existing in bland limbo. He had put the thoughts of desire back into her head—not only physical desire, but also the desire for a husband and children. It was ironic that he had revived her dreams, for he would never be the one to fulfill them.

At that moment he stepped into the tent. Jenna couldn't bear the tension between them that suddenly became palpable and she stood up, moving toward the door. "Excuse me. I'll leave you men to talk. I'm going to my tent to freshen up and rest." She hurried past Chance, giving him only a cursory nod.

Henry watched her departure, realizing something was amiss. She and Killeen had been quite companionable before the trip. Now she would barely look at him. But *he* was watching *her*—intently.

From the beginning, Henry hadn't wanted Jenna associating with Killeen. He admitted he was a little jealous of Killeen and felt his own position with Jenna was threatened by the other man's presence. To him, Killeen was just another Philip Dresden. A man with a pretty face and the charm to talk a woman into anything. He couldn't afford to have that sort of a man stepping onto the scene, now of all times.

"What else happened up there at Whitman's, Killeen?" he demanded, riding on his suspicions and his

172

dislike for Chance. "She doesn't seem to be herself. I hope for your sake that you didn't take advantage of her. If you did, I'll see you dead."

Paterson's perception was irritating. Chance decided he must know Jenna well. *Too* well. But for the sake of Jenna's reputation, he kept his thoughts and feelings tightly inside. What had happened between them was best forgotten, anyway, and the less said about it, the better.

"I don't really think a man could take advantage of Jenna, Paterson. She's a woman who lives by her own rules and her own desires."

He turned to leave, seeing no point in staying. "By the way," he added, "it might interest you to know that just before Whitman died, he said somebody was paying him to delay the railroad for as long as possible."

Henry's scowl lifted with surprise. "He did? Well, did he say who?"

Chance couldn't help but believe that Paterson had known from the very beginning that Whitman would give them trouble, but hadn't warned them. Maybe that was why he'd tried so hard to get Jenna not to go. And it probably would have suited him fine if another engineer had fallen by the wayside. But that was an awful risk to Jenna's life just the same.

"No, I'm afraid he didn't," he replied. "But rest assured, Paterson. I intend to find out."

Chance was on the steamer when it left Old Mission Landing the next day. He leaned over the rail, pondering the moments he'd spent in Jenna's arms. They'd been wrong, perhaps. But, God, they'd been good.

He couldn't help but wonder if she and Paterson

173

would meet in his absence for dinner again, or possibly for a late night rendezvous after the camp was quiet.

He took the last draw on his cigarette and tossed the stub into the water. What she did wasn't his business, but he couldn't stop the rearing up of jealousy. This desire between them had a power all its own. Or was it his imagination? Was it something only he felt? Maybe she displayed the same passion for Paterson as she had for him.

Damn, it had to be stopped! He couldn't work with her around. He couldn't think. He wasn't looking forward to seeing Solomon Lee again, but he was the only man who could make her return to Coeur d'Alene.

Chance spent the entire trip across the lake with these and similar troublesome thoughts. When he stepped onto the dock at Coeur d'Alene, he was in a foul, bitter mood. He led his buckskin down the ramp and, once clear of the crowd, stepped into the saddle.

Like a man who has no choice but to go handcuffed to the gallows, he rode the short distance to the hotel where Solomon Lee was staying—if he hadn't by now executed the construction of a mansion somewhere back in the trees. That would be so like him, Chance thought cynically. Buy the hotel, even the town . . . buy anything in the Coeur d'Alenes that would make his stay more comfortable. Or better yet, just filch it from the people.

Chance sent the desk clerk with a message that he wanted to see Solomon. He was surprised when the clerk returned with the approval. He'd thought that if Solomon was well enough to actually receive visitors, he would be difficult enough to insist on an appointment at some future date.

Solomon's servant, Malcolm Reed, led Chance up

174

the stairs and down the hall to the rooms Solomon occupied.

The old feelings of sixteen years ago returned with vengeful bitterness. By the time Chance came to the door of Solomon's rooms, his hands had curled into fists.

He wasn't sure what he'd expected, but it surely wasn't a skinny old man sitting up to his chest in a tub full of water, looking extremely common. Where had the years gone? Where was the Solomon Lee he remembered? Without his impressive silk hats and cashmere coats, he looked like anybody—an old miner, a stoved-up old cowboy, a man worn out from digging too many ditches. That is, until one looked into his blue eyes. The eyes hadn't changed. He was still the power of Wall Street, of the rails, a ruler of men. Still the alert and shrewd robber baron. And he still had enough arrogance to take company while he bathed.

For a few moments they assessed each other in silence, like male dogs circling before tearing into each other.

"So we meet again," Solomon said in a gravelly whisper, which sounded as if the words had been dragged across sandpaper. "Sit down, Killeen."

Chance refused to be intimidated by the hawklike eyes that glinted with the thrill of confrontation and followed him to the only chair in the small room.

"You've changed in sixteen years," Solomon croaked in that weak voice. "You've become a man."

Chance settled into the chair and crossed an ankle over the opposite knee. He met the cunning entrepreneur with cool appraisal. "You've changed, too, Solomon. You've become an old man whose reign of power is almost over."

Solomon was amused. "I like a man who doesn't gloss the truth, Killeen."

Chance pushed his hat to the back of his head, wondering if the tension inside him was evident. If it was, Solomon would take advantage of it. "I could have waited until your bath was over," he said sardonically.

Solomon draped his arms over the sides of the tub and displayed his bony white shoulders. The water rippled against a sagging chest that had once been muscled.

"Perhaps *you* could have waited," he replied. "But I couldn't. Curiosity would have killed me first. Why *are* you here? I'm sure you're not concerned over my health, unless you wanted to come and see with your own eyes how many toes I have in the grave. I have a few, but I don't have a foot there yet, so the world will just have to tolerate me a bit longer. By the way, I never thanked you for dragging me out of that river."

"I wouldn't have, if I'd known it was you."

Solomon hadn't expected kindness. "I thought as much, but things have turned out to your advantage. You're now part owner of the Bitterroot Railroad Company. I must say, you drive a hard bargain."

Chance's gaze pierced Solomon. "Yes, I do. And you'd better not cross me or double-cross me. If you had some ulterior motive in mind to ruin me, you'll regret it."

"My only motive was to get a good man to engineer the railroad and I needed one immediately. I may not have been as generous as Jenna, but I'll stand by her agreement. Now," he continued, "do you have a problem with the railroad?"

"The only problem I have at the moment is with your granddaughter. I'll be blunt, Solomon. I want her off site."

Solomon's bushy white eyebrows lifted. "Jenna? What problems could she possibly be causing?"

From the way Solomon's gleaming eyes bore into

him, Chance wondered if the old man could see into his head and see all the confusing thoughts about Jenna . . . even see the night by the river. Solomon waited, anticipatory, but he seemed to already know what Chance was going to say. That perpetual shrewd smile on his lips deepened.

"A beautiful woman in the presence of hundreds of men, Solomon. I don't need to spell it out. It's dangerous in more ways than one. She could have been killed when we went to Vestal Whitman's this week."

All trace of amusement fled Solomon's expression. He leaned forward in the tub anxiously. "What happened? Is she all right?"

Chance told him about the confrontation with Whitman and the death of Jenna's horse.

Solomon released a regretful sigh. "I am sorry to hear that. She truly loved Tia's Fortune. But what about Jenna? Does she want to stay?"

"I believe so." Chance hesitated, wondering if he should voice his concerns and observations. He also wondered if Solomon could shed light on Jenna's relationship with Henry, which his curiosity couldn't seem to leave alone. "I think she may be staying because of Paterson. He seems to be interested in her in a romantic way. He might even be thinking of marrying her."

Solomon nearly came out of the tub, and a good deal of water did. "By God, he'd better not be! I won't have it!"

Solomon's chest labored. His eyes blazed and his face went livid. His knuckles turned white from gripping the tub too tightly. Chance was suddenly afraid the old geezer might die, and he didn't want him to—at least not just yet. There were still things to discuss. But at least his curiosity had been appeased by learning that Jenna and Henry weren't commonly acknowledged as a couple.

177

Still leaning forward in the tub, Solomon's eyes narrowed almost fearfully. "Has Jenna given any indication of how she feels about Henry?"

"She insists they're friends," Chance said, lifting his shoulders in a halfhearted shrug. "But they don't kiss like friends."

Solomon leaned back against the support of the tub, staring at the ceiling as if drawing his last breath. He looked terribly weak and Chance wondered if he should get the servant to put the old man back to bed.

"Why are you against such a marriage?" Chance tried to sound indifferent.

Solomon's chest rose and fell rapidly. "I could die—today, tomorrow," he lamented. "Oh, I've recovered from the pneumonia, but something else could take me. This could be Henry's way of getting back at me for something that happened twenty-five years ago. I've always wondered if he'd try. And more power to him, but damn him for even thinking of getting even by trying to marry my fortune. Doesn't he know how that would hurt Jenna if she found out?"

"It seems that in your old age, Solomon, all your past transgressions are catching up with you."

Solomon opened his eyes. His gaze ripped into Chance like an angry cougar's claws, but at last he submitted to the truth. "You know I broke a lot of men when I was young and ambitious, Chance. Back then I regarded people as obstacles in the way of my goals. Maybe they still are, but now I've learned more acceptable ways of dealing with them."

"And if Paterson loves her?"

"Love?" Solomon scoffed at the mere suggestion. "Perhaps in his way, but not in the way a man should love a woman he plans to marry. Paterson is too self-centered to love anyone that much, except possibly himself. Don't get me wrong. Henry's the best con-

178

struction boss I've ever had, but I know his flaws."

Worry lines creased his already-wrinkled brow, and Chance knew he was trying to think of a way to stop Paterson. Didn't he know that he couldn't live forever? And when he was gone, he wouldn't be there to mold people to his desires or to stop those who came too close to his empire. Or maybe he did know it, and maybe that was what caused him such distress.

As Chance looked at the old man, it came as a sudden realization that he wasn't afraid of him anymore. He was still afraid of what his power could do, but he wasn't afraid of the man himself. As a youth, he'd seen Solomon Lee as a force that could truly hurt him and his mother and brothers. That illusion was gone. A man could fight Solomon Lee if he stayed one step ahead of him.

"If you're so worried about Henry getting your fortune, Solomon, why don't you just arrange your will so that no man can get his hands on Solomon Enterprises except through Jenna's decision."

Solomon chuckled, his blue eyes looking much younger than the man they belonged to. "You're more naive than I thought, Killeen. It's unfortunate you never knew her first husband, Philip Dresden. He could charm a snake right out of a hole. If a man knew he only had to stay on his best behavior for a few years in order to have her turn everything over to him, don't you think a number of them would become excellent actors?"

Chance shrugged. "Perhaps I'm not yet aware of the deviousness in people the way you are, Solomon. Or perhaps it merely takes one to know one."

Solomon wasn't offended by Chance's bluntness. As a matter of fact, he liked him more every time he opened his mouth. He wasn't a man to be fooled. Maybe he had himself to thank for that. Maybe what he'd done to Chance's father had made Chance a little

179

too suspicious of people and their motives. But it was a good way to be, to a certain extent. Gullibility could be a man's ruination, and Killeen had none, at least not where business was concerned.

Something else struck Solomon as a little odd, however. Killeen hated his guts, but he'd set that animosity aside long enough to try and get Jenna off site. He was worried about her safety, he'd said. That was a likely story. If he were indifferent to her, he wouldn't care. He'd just let her fend for herself or let Paterson look out after her. No, it would appear that Killeen himself had a personal interest in her.

One thing was certain about Killeen: If he *was* interested in Jenna, it was not for the Lee fortune. No, that was the last thing he would want; it would be too bitter of a victory for him. But his grudge was big enough to be dangerous, his bitterness vile enough to destroy his own life if he let it—and hurt Jenna if he became involved with her.

Risks had to be taken sometimes, though, when much could be gained from the venture. First and foremost, he refused to make things easier for Killeen. A man had to face his problems, and this was one problem Killeen was definitely trying to have eliminated for him. It was the only weakness Solomon had seen in him so far.

"Fixing my will might be an idea as far as Henry is concerned, Killeen, but how do I know that you wouldn't benefit from such a clause yourself?"

His cunning eyes caught the shift of Chance's body in the chair—that nervous sort of squirming that occurs when the truth has struck too close to home.

"I could care less about your damned money. I sure as hell wouldn't marry for it."

"My point exactly. You may not marry *because* of it, either. Not only would you not want people to think you were a fortune hunter, but you would want nothing to do with me. This clause you suggest would protect you, too. You're quite clever to have dreamed it up."

Chance scowled. "I'm not interested in your granddaughter."

"Oh? You seemed concerned over her welfare. How do I know that you don't want Jenna off site because you're attracted to her yourself and would like to eliminate the temptation? I'm no doddering old fool, Killeen. If it weren't for me, you might just find her attractive. Most men do. Not only is she beautiful, but she's a very pleasant woman to be around. She isn't silly and stupid the way some of them are. Some men *like* fluff, because it doesn't threaten their masculinity, but some of us prefer substance and intelligence. I think you and I are similar in that respect, Killeen. You're not the sort of man who could tolerate fluff for any longer than a one-night stand."

Chance was tight-lipped, but Solomon saw the tempest brewing in his expression and the eyes that were growing dark, closing, as if someone were pulling shutters over windows to keep out an impending storm.

Chance stood up. "I believe your age has brought on some delusions, Solomon. She's your granddaughter. If you're not concerned about her welfare, then I won't be, either. Just remember that out on-site, she's more susceptible to Paterson's sweet talk."

He started for the door.

"I always stick to my word, Killeen. That is one thing you can count on me for. And I expect you to stick to yours."

Chance turned. "What do you mean?"

"You made an agreement with Jenna that you would let her go with you and learn more about the business. I was in favor of that. Jenna needs to know what's going on, or people will take advantage of her. But if she wants to quit and come back, then that

181

decision will be hers. I'm sorry, but I won't call her in. Thank you for warning me about Paterson. And yourself."

Chance's gaze locked with Solomon's in a sort of battle stance, a challenge of two men who refused to back down to each other. If he didn't hate Solomon so much, he might even like him. He couldn't condone the things he'd done in his life and the people he'd hurt, but Solomon had made the world obey his commands. He didn't care what others thought of him—or if he did, he had long ago become immune to it. He could have been a ruler of nations, but he had controlled the nation's strings and shaped the way of the future from his own little pulpit just as effectively.

"Remember one thing," Solomon added before Chance could get out the door. "Jenna isn't responsible for what I've done, so don't hold her accountable. And don't make her suffer for your one-sided hatred."

His words were almost identical to those Jenna had spoken. In the doorway, Chance paused and looked over his shoulder at the old man. The eyes the same color as Jenna's gleamed with the challenge. So he knew that there was something between him and Jenna, but surely he had to be smart enough to know that because of him it could never be allowed to grow.

"I'll do this job because I need this railroad," he said. "I'll show Jenna what she needs and wants to know. But make her suffer? I'm afraid that if she suffers from knowing me, you can take the blame yourself."

Solomon made no attempt to respond. They were two stubborn men who would not concede, or even admit to their own weaknesses and their own mistakes. Chance left the room, turning his back once again on the man who haunted his life. But Solomon Lee had expected no quarter.

Chapter Fourteen

Delaney easily lifted Lily over the fallen log, then twirled her around twice before setting her to her feet. She gripped his broad shoulders tightly and laughed, a sound as pleasant in the still forest as the melodious notes of the songbirds. It should have put him at ease, but he felt very much like a nervous youth, courting a girl for the first time.

He scooped up the picnic basket with one hand and pulled her along behind him with the other. "Come now, darlin'. The spot where I'm takin' you is just ahead."

He tried hard to act normal. He didn't want her to see his secret, consuming fear. She'd come back from Solomon in a pensive mood that had lasted for days. His heart had ached during that time, until he thought it might stop entirely. He was so afraid he might be losing her to Solomon Lee, her old flame. Now, he had to be sure that wouldn't happen.

"The spot is just up ahead," he assured her. "I wouldn't be tellin' a yarn to say that it's shoorly made fer lovers."

At last the thick trees opened onto a clearing. Before them lay a wide, grassy meadow with a stream running down the center. Overhead, the azure dome was uncluttered by clouds.

"Oh, it's perfect, Bard," she said. "How did you know it was here?"

"There's many a one like me comes here to hunt," he said. "But, ours i' tis today."

They found a place in the center of the meadow and Delaney spread the red wool blanket on the grass. Lily settled herself into a comfortable position, arranging her cotton skirt about her ankles, and then she slipped an arm through his.

"It really is a lovely spot." She sighed contentedly. "Thank you for taking time from the mine to bring me here."

"Oh, it's here I'd bring you every day if I could. But if we don't get some spring rain soon, I'm thinkin' the lovely place will all but be withered up. See there, Lily," he pointed, "the stream isn't rushin' like it should be fer so early in the year."

Lily's brow furrowed. "If we don't get rain, it could mean fires. If that happens, it could mean a holdup on the railroad."

"Aye," Delaney agreed. "And I'd hate to see it. I'd like Keely to come back and help me. It's tired I am o' haulin' the ore to Thompson Falls alone. To be sartin, Keely's company makes it a wee bit more appealing."

He feasted his eyes upon her. Just looking at Lily made his heart skip a beat and turn over with a love so intense he could barely contain it. Ah, she scared him in a peculiar way, but she also made him happier than he had ever been in his life.

He studied the face that reminded him of a fine china doll his mother had had once upon a time—fragile, delicate, with a face all creamy smooth. There was a little gray in her black hair, and some lines around her green eyes and a few on her forehead, but to him she hardly looked fifty-five. She was still shapely and slender. Her eyes held a perpetual youthfulness that kept her young in heart and mind. She was older than he by a few years, but he didn't care, nor did she, and no one who looked at them would know, anyway.

She caressed his cheek, absently stroking his recently trimmed beard. He'd thought of shaving it off for her, but he was afraid she wouldn't like his face if she were to see it without the hair. He'd decided years ago that Delaney without his beard was not really Delaney. There would be no sense in setting off on some foolish tangent to change himself at this late date. Besides, without it, he felt as naked as if his drawers were down.

He took her hand and laid a loving kiss right in the center of the palm. Then he sampled her lips. Immediately, the ever-present desire for her came alive and he pressed her back upon the blanket.

They would make love here. He'd planned it. But it was here he had brought her because he had something to say. His heart thudded much harder and faster than it ever had. He was afraid, but he couldn't be a coward and let what was on his mind go unsaid. He couldn't let Solomon Lee take her from his life.

Stretched out on his side, he propped himself on one elbow and continued holding her hand. "Fer years I've searched fer me fortune," he said. "But did you know that at last I've found it? By me word, it wasn't here in these mountains that I found it, nor there in the stream." He looked deeply into her eyes, drawing her hand to his lips. "It was in you, me darlin' Lily. That was where I found it."

She remained lying on the blanket, looking up at him. Moisture collected in her eyes and gradually slid from the corners into her hair. Did she cry out of pity for his foolish heart? No matter. He had to finish what he had started.

"It's a handsome man I'm not," he said. "Me riches could barely fill yer pocket. And, Lily, another Duke I can niver be. . . ."

Suddenly, a huge wave of disgust surged up from inside Bard and completely overwhelmed him. He couldn't expect her to marry him! Cracked mad he was to even think it!

He started to rise, but she caught his hand and pulled him back down. "What in the name of Heaven is wrong with you, Bard Delaney?" She smiled, bemused. "Is there a point to this confession you're making?"

She was stronger physically than he thought, or perhaps he was simply weak and under her spell. But one way or the other, he was totally unable to move away from her.

"Tell me why you're demeaning yourself," she prodded. "If you're really as bad as you're trying to make me believe, then I might be wise to end our love affair."

Her eyes glittered with mischievousness, but such a threat was enough to make any man confess anything—even someone else's sins.

"Aye, 'tis a hard bargain you drive. I wouldn't be so sartin ye're not a she-divil." He took a deep breath, knowing that he might as well die today if she ended their relationship. "But even if y' are, I'm givin' me heart to you and askin' fer yers in return. What I'm askin' is fer you to marry me, Lily."

The smile that surfaced on her face was the most beautiful thing he'd ever seen. She threw her arms around his neck and laughed into his ear, kissing him upon the cheek and drawing him back down into her embrace. "It's about time you decided to make an honest woman of me."

His heavy brows rose skeptically. "Then, I'm thinkin' yer answer is yes?"

Her lips touched the corner of his mouth. She whispered seductively, "I can think of nary a reason to say no."

"Oh, Lily," he moaned in utter relief as he

enveloped her in his strong arms. "Ye're the body an' bones o' me. You know I couldn't live without you."

She looked deep into his eyes in a searching sort of way. "I love you, Bard. Let me show you just how much."

She pulled his shirt free from his pants and slid her hands up under it to caress his naked flesh.

"Ah, the saints he praised," he moaned. "You c'n show me anytime, darlin' Lily. I wouldn't be fer mindin'."

The setting sun painted the thin strands of clouds a vivid pink and swept the sky with a wide stroke of sapphire. Darkness settled into the corners of the timbered canyons. Dusk's fanciful magic wand swept over the meadows, diffusing everything until all that was left were shades of light and dark that held no certain shape or color. Even the tents in the meadow that had at first appeared as hundreds of large white mushrooms now seemed just a lumpy river of curdled cream.

Chance hesitated on the Mullan Road and looked down at the encampment. He saw Jenna's tent near the edge of the trees. A light came on inside, turning the canvas a golden color. Immediately, it seemed that an invisible, paralyzing hand closed around everything vital to life—his heart, his breath, even his mind. He was too far away to see anything except the occasional movement of a shadow inside the tent, but his mind filled in the details of the woman inside.

He hadn't succeeded in removing her from his life. On the trip here, he had vowed to stay away from her, though, to let what had happened slip away as all yesterdays inevitably did. But at the mere sight of her tent, all his good and worthy intentions vanished. She was like unfinished business that couldn't be put off. He could think only of holding her in his arms

187

and experiencing again the satisfying ambience of being a part of her. All sensibleness slipped farther and farther into a grayness as obscure as the dusk. Even the face of Solomon Lee became a mere shadow of yesterday, resting hazily and harmless upon a horizon so distant it was almost unnoticeable.

He focused his attention on the black gelding he'd bought for her in Coeur d'Alene. The horse wasn't the classic beauty that Tia's Fortune had been, but being a mountain-bred animal, it was surefooted, with plenty of stamina. It would be easy for her to handle, too, because its disposition was even and calm. He'd ridden it, and its gaits were smooth and easy.

He didn't know what had induced him to buy it. Without a horse, she wouldn't have been able to keep riding with him. Granted, she would have bought another soon enough to replace Tia, but she might have been so depressed that she'd have gone back to Coeur d'Alene just as he'd hoped for all along. By buying the horse, he was only encouraging her to stay, and that didn't make a lick of sense at all.

He nudged the buckskin forward. Leading the black, they meandered down into the meadow. One by one the lights in the tents came on, as did the darkness. Many of the men had already gone to bed, but others talked or played cards while lounging in the grass. Some watched his advance with quiet interest. One called out, "Hey, Killeen. Good-looking black you've got there. Is he for sale?"

Chance gave the man a pleasant grin. "Sorry, Bazil. I bought it for Miss Lee."

The other man's jovial smile faded to a sad look. "Yeah, we heard about you having to shoot that horse of hers. Well, she ought to like that black. Leastwise, he won't be fallin' down gettin' his legs broke."

"No, I doubt it. He's pure cayuse."

Outside Jenna's tent, Chance dismounted and tied the two geldings to a nearby tree. He started for the canvas door, then stopped dead in his tracks. From inside came Paterson's voice. A heavy wad, like a ball of writhing snakes, seemed to settle in his stomach.

"I had it brought in from New York," Paterson was saying.

"It's very good, Henry—for champagne." Jenna's teasing tone was pleasant to the ear but caused the knot in Chance's stomach to cinch down even tighter, making it feel impossible to disentangle. She had spoken to him that way a few times, too. In their lighter moments.

Paterson chuckled. "I guess I'll never get you to acquire a taste for champagne, will I?"

"I doubt it. You've been trying now for years."

So they were having dinner again. Had they been together every night since he'd been gone? How many nights had it been? Only two? It seemed like ten. Had she made love to Paterson the way she had him?

His foolish thoughts tormented him, but from the sound of her voice, Jenna was untroubled. Perhaps she was in the habit of making love to men and then dismissing them. Could it be possible she was one of those women who couldn't be satisfied with just one man? Is that why she didn't marry?

The breeze caught the tent flap and Chance realized it wasn't tied down from the inside. Deciding to put a little dent in Paterson's shenanigans, he lifted the flap and entered. The smile faded from both of their lips, but for a fleeting moment, Chance saw in Jenna's eyes everything they'd shared by the river, both the good and the bad.

"So you're back from Coeur d'Alene, Killeen," Henry said dryly. "Do you have something to tell us?"

Chance found it hard to concentrate, because his

189

peripheral vision allowed him to see Jenna. She wore a dress of a pale salmon shade, trimmed with beige lace, rosettes, and darker velvet ribbons. He wondered if she'd dressed so elaborately to please Paterson.

"Yes, I need to have a few words with Jenna. Would you come outside?" He motioned for her to lead the way from the tent.

She was surprised and then clearly wary, but Jenna couldn't conceal her curiosity so she rose. Chance held the tent flap back for her, and as she passed in front of him, she tried to ease the tension between them.

"How were things in Coeur d'Alene?"

"Oh, just fine," he replied. "I saw your grandfather."

Dismayed, she looked over her shoulder at him. "*You* went to see *him?*"

Chance nodded, taking her by the arm and leading her across the rough ground to the two horses. He was surprised she didn't pull away from him, but with only thin-soled slippers on, she seemed to appreciate his assistance.

"I figured you'd want a report on his health," he said in explanation.

"And?"

"He's fine." He smiled at the memory of the brazen old man. "Actually, he took his bath while we visited."

She laughed. "Are you joking?"

"No, ma'am. But he didn't seem to mind."

All jest gone from her eyes, she said, "Why did you really go to see him? After what's been between the two of you."

Chance kept his hand on her elbow and his eyes pinned to their feet and the uneven terrain. He couldn't tell her he'd gone to try to get her removed from the site. Now he was glad he hadn't succeeded,

190

because even these few moments with her seemed special.

He was aware of Paterson tagging along behind them, listening to every word. He lowered his voice. "It was time, Jenna, that's all. Now"—he stopped her next to the horses—"I want your expert opinion on this horse I bought. What do you think? Is he sound?"

Jenna didn't hesitate in going right up to the black horse and immediately crooning to it. She ran a hand along its back.

The soft lantern light from the tent spilled out, barely reaching them, but there was enough so that it fell upon her like a golden sunset, illuminating her hair and cheeks, shimmering off the salmon-colored dress. Only the sides of her hair were drawn back with tortoiseshell combs; the remainder fell loose down her back. It would be easy to pluck the combs out and allow the entire mass to tumble like strands of spun gold into his hands.

At the thought, Chance rammed his hands into his back pockets. It was safer to have them there. It would be more difficult for them to reach out, of their own volition, and touch her. In his pockets they couldn't tremble and reveal the strange desperate need for her that was leaving him confused. If only he had not been so weak that night by the river, he might be able to be stronger now.

Jenna had walked all the way around the horse and was back again at its head. There wasn't a trace of white on the animal, not even a star on its forehead, nor one white stocking. He was as black as the night. She spoke to him and stroked his face. His ears twitched at the sound of her voice, approving of its soothing quality.

"Chance, he's a beautiful horse. But you know horses. You don't need my opinion." Her eyes met his as she continued to stroke the inky black neck.

"Maybe not, but I wanted it. So you like him?"

"Of course." She laughed lightly and straightened the horse's coarse forelock until it lay in a nice little twist down the center of his face.

"I bought him for you, Jenna. I know he can't replace Tia, but—"

Jenna squealed despite herself and flung her arms around him, kissing his cheek before she even knew what she'd done, gushing what seemed to be a multitude of thank-yous. When her heels settled back on the ground, his arms came around her tightly. Immediately, she was captivated by the burning embers leaping in his eyes, reminding her of the passion he was capable of. The length of his body branded hers, renewing the exquisite torture of being so near to him. He splayed his long fingers across the width of her back, each tip making a penetrating impression upon her skin.

With alarming swiftness, desire compelled her closer to him, or perhaps it was merely his arms that drew her there more snugly against his chest. Her gaze found his lips, just as his did hers. In that moment she thought he might kiss her, and she yearned for it again, no matter the foolishness. She felt the eyes of some of the men upon them, but she was irresistibly drawn to him, unable to move.

"Thank you, Chance," she murmured. "He's a very fine animal."

"What will you name him?" His eyes remained transfixed on her lips.

She thought for only a second. "Well, he reminds me of a bandit all dressed in black. A thief in the night. I think I'll call him Desperado."

Paterson spoke up from his position not far away. "Tell us how much you paid for the horse, Killeen, and I'll have Leaman write you out a bank draft from the company's construction fund."

At the sound of Henry's voice, Jenna and Chance

separated. They had both forgotten his presence while he stood silently by, watching them in the darkness. Chance put his hands into his back pockets again, realizing it hadn't been a foolproof place after all.

"Jenna lost Tia's Fortune because I chose to confront Whitman," Chance said. "The horse is a gift from me, Paterson. It has nothing to do with you or the BRC."

"So it's gifts now, is it?" he said sarcastically, then turned to Jenna. "Are you going to come in and finish dinner?"

Jenna wondered why Henry was being so demanding of her, so possessive. Surely he wasn't jealous of Chance? Didn't he realize that no one, not even a lover, could take his place in her heart as her loyal friend?

Before she could answer, Chance intervened. "I'll take care of the horses, Jenna. You finish your meal." He looked back over his shoulder at Paterson. "Did anybody go back and get Jenna's saddle at Whitman's?"

Henry nodded. "Yeah, I sent a couple of guys."

Chance untied the horses and turned them away from the tree. "By the way, Paterson, I want you to nudge the crew into a faster pace. Durfey's quite a ways ahead of us. At this rate, we'll never have a chance of getting to Silver Bend first."

Henry was coolly indifferent to the order. "There's no race going on here, Killeen."

"I beg to differ with you," Chance replied just as coolly. "The men at Fatty Carroll's Saloon were laying down their bets, and word has it that they favor Durfey to win."

Henry shrugged. "Even if we lose—we don't lose."

"I'd like to know how you figure."

With arrogance born of age and experience, he said, "You've got a lot to learn before the tracks are

193

down, Killeen. Why don't you just cool your heels."

Both Chance and Jenna watched his cocky departure back to her tent. Chance fought the urge to follow him and plant a fist right in the center of his insolent face.

"You know, I don't believe he likes you," Jenna said.

"Then I guess we're about even."

Chance left her side, leading the horses into the encroaching darkness.

Part II

The Requital

Chapter Fifteen

July 1886

The mountains were a place where civilization could dwell but which man could never fully conquer. The mountains had given birth to the miners' towns, and men had made roads and trails through the thick timber, but their mark upon the land was as insignificant as the labors of a worker ant in a giant's kingdom.

Until now.

The haze of the afternoon sun slanted over the huge "S" bridge that spanned Wolverine Canyon—the widest, steepest, and most difficult to engineer on the entire line. Like an intricate and cleverly designed spider's web, the latticework of lumber rose one hundred feet into the air and over eight hundred feet in length.

In a moment of awed silence, Chance, Jenna and the crew stood on an overlooking hill and marveled at the sheer magnitude of the structure created by human hands. Suddenly, someone let out an earsplitting hoot, followed by a raucous mayhem of backslapping and hat tossing, whistling and shouting.

Chance grabbed Jenna by the waist, lifted her off her feet, and whirled her around. "What do you

197

think, pardner?" His grin rivaled the width of the bridge itself. "Do you think it'll hold a train?"

Her laughter bubbled forth as he set her back on the ground. "For your sake, Mr. Engineer, I surely do hope so."

He threw his head back and laughed, then leaped into the back of a wagon. Cupping his hands around his mouth, he hollered above the din, "The work crew is officially off until noon tomorrow! The guards will get relieved when you get back! Now, all of you—get to town and celebrate!"

Another whoop resounded in the canyon. In seconds, the ground rumbled beneath the stampede of feet as the men climbed into wagons, mounted horses, and took of for town on a mad dash.

Still laughing, Chance jumped out of the wagon. Jenna had never seen him so delighted, so animated. He grabbed her hand and started running for the tents. Laughing, she tried to keep up. "What in the world, Chance Killeen . . ."

"We're not going to settle for Moody's jackass stew tonight! No, sir! That bridge calls for a real celebration. So you run into that tent of yours and pack the prettiest dress you've got. We're going to Blackshere House in Wallace."

They were still laughing when they brought their horses to a halt in front of the Blackshere an hour later, and Chance tossed some coins to a boy to take care of the two geldings. They hurried inside, dusty and out of breath.

The opulence of the Blackshere subdued them momentarily as they stepped up to the register. While Chance signed them in, Jenna glanced happily about her surroundings, for she had heard much about the place but had never been inside.

Blackshere House exquisitely reflected the wealth of the Coeur d'Alenes probably better than any establishment she'd seen thus far. The lobby gleamed with

198

walnut wainscoting and glittered with wallpaper in the colors of money—gold, green, and silver. Imported plush rugs muffled footsteps and followed the curving staircase to the second floor. A wide mahogany balustrade displayed intricately carved designs and a shine that was almost reflective. Huge full-length mirrors in several locations doubled and tripled the opulence. Through an arched doorway, glass chandeliers cast golden light on white-draped dining room tables, where fine silver and china winked like hundreds of stars in the muted glow.

Chance and Jenna were given rooms across the hall from each other, and two hours later, after a warm bath, Jenna stood before her mirror styling her hair into a simple coiffure atop her head.

The maid returned with her freshly pressed dress of midnight-blue silk. Of the two she'd brought from Coeur d'Alene, it was Jenna's favorite. The neck was moderately low, designed for a necklace or velvet choker, and the sleeves were three-quarter and adorned with lace and bows just below the elbow. It fit tightly through the bodice and waistline. Tiers of white lace draped across the skirt front from the waist to the floor. More white lace, along with ribbons in lighter blue, bedecked the creation in all the appropriate places. After placing some jeweled combs in her hair and draping her matching bag over her wrist, Jenna was ready to go.

"You look very lovely, Miss Lee," the maid said. "I'll remove your tub and wet towels while you're at dinner. If there is anything else I can do for you, please don't hesitate to let me know."

Jenna thanked her, gave her a generous tip, then left the room. Even though her spirits were still soaring high, the closer to the dining room she got, the more trepidation she felt. Out in the field it was easy to play the role of Chance's partner. But tonight, that role was blurred. Still, she must keep up the pretense. She must not humiliate herself by revealing her personal feelings and desires for a man who didn't want her.

A camaraderie had developed between them, but Chance had made no more overtures to her in the weeks that had passed since the night by the river. He had been polite but businesslike. He had apparently put that night from his mind, into the past where it was to be forgotten, excused as an error, a weakness of the body and mind. It seemed he had easily vowed to never commit the cardinal sin again. For her, it hadn't been so easy to dismiss what had happened.

Even though they hadn't been close physically for two months, they had grown close in other ways. They had acquired mutual trust and respect. Each day they had ridden together, discussed the railroad, and watched the progress of the work. They had spoken to members of the thousand-man crew scattered the length of the line, ensuring that all was proceeding as it should be. Chance had explained details of the construction to her, and each night she had gone back to her tent and written in her journal the things she'd learned from him.

But it was this very closeness that inflicted a new and deeper pain in her heart. For while she had gained his friendship, she knew she would never have his love, and the reason hadn't changed and never would: She was Solomon Lee's flesh and blood, and he refused to forget it.

She saw Chance at a corner table, waiting for her. Hatless, his freshly washed black hair gleamed beneath the chandeliers. He seemed adverse to suit coats and never wore one, but his shoulders looked exceptionally broad in the stiffly starched white shirt and black silk vest that hugged his chest. Black pants conformed to his muscled thighs and legs in an exacting way. A black string tie adorned his neck. Like nearly all the men in the West who were accustomed to a sidearm, he went nowhere without his, and it hung on his hip in savage contrast to his dinner attire.

He rose when he saw her and weaved through the tables to escort her. The earlier delight still danced in his eyes, but as his gaze swept over her approvingly, a sultry glow crept into the depths. "You look lovely tonight, Jenna," he said, holding out his arm for her. "Shall we?"

She slipped her hand into the crook of his elbow. With all eyes in the dining room on them, he escorted her back to the table. Immediately the head waiter appeared, bringing the wine list and suggesting the scalloped fillet of chicken from the menu. They gave their nod of approval, and Chance selected a white wine. After the ritual of sampling it, the waiter at last left them alone.

His exuberance returned. He shook his napkin out over his lap. "It's too bad your grandfather couldn't be with us tonight to celebrate the successful completion of the "S" bridge. Do you know when the doctor will give him a release to go back to work?"

Jenna had caught the steamer every Friday afternoon and gone to Coeur d'Alene with her news and reports on the railroad. And every Sunday night she had returned to camp with instructions from her grandfather for Henry, Ives, Leaman, and Chance. She was surprised that Chance would want her grandfather to share this moment with them. It seemed rather uncharacteristic of his feelings toward Solomon Lee.

"None too soon, I'm afraid," she said. "He sits in that hotel room and stares out the window at the lake, chomping at the bit like a horse that wants to run. He can't wait to be part of the action again. Idleness is about to kill him."

"How does he feel about us being behind? Has he said?"

"It's upsetting him. It's all the more reason he wants to get out here."

"You know, I think we could get ahead of Durfey if Henry and Ives weren't dragging their feet. If I didn't know better, I'd think they wanted him to reach Silver Bend first."

The problem hadn't gone unnoticed by Jenna. Henry had never been so complacent in all the years she'd known him. He had always seemed to have a fire under him when it came to building a railroad, and it had been a personal satisfaction of his to complete a job as quickly as possible.

"Henry has been against this road from the beginning." Jenna sipped at her wine. "I thought it was because he was worried about Grandpa's safety and about mine, but that shouldn't stop him from doing the sort of job he's always done."

"Well, he's an angry man, Jenna." Chance refilled her glass. "He's angry with me, you . . . your grandfather. All of us."

"I understand how he feels about losing his opportunity to engineer the line, and I believe he does blame both you and Grandpa for it, but why should he be angry with me?"

Chance lifted his broad shoulders in a shrug. "Because you're with me every day, and he's so jealous he's about to turn green."

Jenna's back stiffened. "Henry has no reason to be jealous of you, at least not any—" The word rose, but then caught in her throat.

A scorching heat replaced the bantering light in Chance's eyes. It was the same look Jenna had seen that night by the river, just before he had pressed her back upon her bedroll.

"Not anymore?" Chance finished for her.

She lifted her wine glass to her lips, hoping it wouldn't slip from her quivering grasp. "Yes, that's right," she replied, almost defiantly. "It was two months ago, Chance. It's over. And in your opinion, it was a mistake anyway."

"And was it a mistake in your opinion?" he asked softly.

No matter how angry she tried to be, she just ended up confused where her feelings for him were concerned. "It must have been. After all, no good came from it."

He drained his glass, filled it, then drained it again. A sudden surliness hardened his expression. "Drink up, Jenna," he waved a hand toward her glass. "I believe we're supposed to be celebrating."

She didn't know what brought it on. But the pain inside her heart was suddenly too great to bear. She leaned across the small table toward him, finding it difficult to keep her voice in control. "I don't know what you want from me, Chance Killeen. I don't know why you asked me to have dinner with you. Why don't you just go celebrate with the men! I'm sure you'll have a better time. Now, if you'll excuse me . . ."

She tossed her napkin down and pushed back her chair. With tears threatening, she hoisted her skirt above her ankles and nearly ran from the dining room.

Chance uttered an expletive under his breath and started after her. Damn the woman, she kept his mind in constant turmoil and his body in constant pain. No woman had ever done that before and he didn't know quite what to do about it.

She was at the top of the stairs when he hit the bottom one, taking three at a time. Her long legs carried her down the hall in a flash, but he caught her fumbling with the key in the lock. She saw him coming and tried harder to get inside before he reached her, but she was barely through the door when he stuck his foot in it and pushed it back out of his way with the palm of his hand.

203

He stood on the threshold, staring down at the tears on her face that she angrily and defiantly wiped away. He was breathing hard, but not out of exertion as much as out of distress. In frustration, he ran a hand through his hair, not knowing what to do, only knowing what he wanted to do.

"Damn it, Jenna. What got into you? All I wanted was for us to have dinner together. To celebrate the bridge. As partners and friends."

"Friends! How ludicrous! Why don't you leave?" She tried to close the door in his face but he pushed himself more firmly into the room.

He didn't know why, but he couldn't leave. His feet seemed rooted to the floor and his eyes glued to the regal back she promptly turned toward him. She was a queen in her own right, heiress to one of the richest fortunes in the country, but she had never treated him as an inferior. He almost wished she had; it would make his association with her so much easier. He had tried for weeks to find some completely unacceptable flaw in her. Anything. But he had found nothing.

"I don't want to leave tonight, Jenna." The words fell from his tongue, surprising him, but then they continued, coming in a rush he seemed to have no control over. "For two months I've wanted nothing but to go into your tent every night."

He sank into the fathomless depths of her eyes, so angry they were almost as dark as the midnight-blue of her dress. Moved by desire beyond control, he reached for her and hauled her into his arms. There was the thought that someone would come down the hall and see them, but when his lips closed over hers, the reality of the world was not powerful enough to compete with the rush of need controlling him, surging hot and wicked to his loins. It was a single-minded devil that beckoned him to follow the glorious but dangerous trail to loving her.

He dragged his lips from hers, his breathing hard and ragged as he laid his head against hers. "Oh, Jenna, I want you. Being without you has been pure hell. I—"

Her lips silenced any further words with another drugging kiss. He brought her hips closer to his, but that action only intensified his need and did nothing to satisfy it.

He didn't understand how it happened, but in moments he was kicking the door closed behind him, then reaching back and turning the lock. In the next instant, he had scooped her into his arms, strode to the bed, and laid her gently upon it. He came down over her, holding her his captive with the weight of his body.

It all seemed part of a wonderful dream he'd had many times over the past weeks. He didn't know if he imagined it, but it appeared the depths of her eyes revealed a sultry passion, as if she waited, anticipatory, for him to make love to her.

Part of his conscience managed to surface. "I should go, Jenna. *Make* me go. I can't offer you a future or a tomorrow. My God, you know that. We shouldn't let this happen again."

As a woman touches that which she loves, Jenna drew his head down and lifted her face to his, kissing his lips to silence the doubts she didn't want to hear. Nor did she want anything to remind her of what lay ahead at the coming of the dawn.

"Tomorrow will take its course, Chance. Let this night be ours."

She caressingly traced a finger along his cheek, and the tenderness of the action, coupled with the warm glow in her eyes, was his undoing. With a moan deep in his throat, his lips hungrily enveloped hers, none too gently. He wanted all of her at once, so strong were his needs, and yet he knew he must make the moment right for her as well.

He slid his hand up her ribs, protected by what he considered too many layers of cloth and lace, thwarting his intentions. And the yards and yards of skirt, gathered here and tucked there, hindered his ability to slide his leg between hers, allowing him the closeness to her he needed and wanted as desperately as a thirsting man wants water.

While he scattered kisses over her face and neck, he deftly undid the tiny buttons on the front of the dress until at last all that stood in his way were the stiff bones of her corset and corset cover. He undid more buttons and a ribbon. At last her firm, full breasts spilled free above the corset and rested hot and firm in his hands, so soft they demanded tasting, taunting.

But ultimately, the garments still stood in his way.

Breathing raggedly, he came to a sitting position, bringing her up with him. A growl of impatience rumbled in his throat, followed by an uttered oath. "The designer of your clothing was definitely not a man—or at least not one with any sense."

Her laughter loosened him, lightened him, and his lips followed the falling of the gown as his calloused hands slid the fabric off her shoulders, down her arms, until it lay in lacy folds at her waist and around her wrists. His lips found the graceful column of her neck and the golden tendrils that had escaped the pins and drifted down to tickle the velvety smooth skin of her shoulders.

Now only the corset hindered further exploration of the soft flesh he wished to know again. "Take this damned thing off," he whispered against her neck, splaying his fingers over the rigid contraption. "I want to touch you."

Shortly, the remaining pieces of her attire fell in a disregarded pile on the floor along with his. Soon she was back against the pillows and he was poised above her. He was now able to take the creamy mounds of her breasts fully into his hands and the nipples fully in his mouth, exciting both himself and her with the contact.

"Oh, God, woman," he murmured low and husky against her naked flesh. "You don't know what you do to me."

His words were spoken so emotionally, his touch placed so tenderly, that Jenna's need quadrupled. "But I do know what you're feeling, Chance. And it's glorious."

But she wanted the splendor of it to last for as long as possible. She eased Chance onto his back and moved over him, taking her turn at feathering kisses from his hair to his toes over muscles as rigid as steel, then turning him over to place more kisses up his thighs, his buttocks, and on the sensitive spots along his spine.

At last, however, he turned enough to reach back and catch her in the circle of one arm, drawing her onto her side to face him and holding her possessively in his embrace. When his kisses and the play of his hands over her body had finally made her move in a seductive dance of heightened passion, he took a position beneath her and lifted her over him, this time sliding his shaft deep inside her.

In perfect unison, they climbed to a pinnacle as high as the Bitterroots. They crested the peak together, and as Jenna cried out in sweet ecstasy, Chance emptied his hot seed deep inside her.

They lay, spent, against the pillows, out of breath, tangled in each other's arms. The night breeze ambled in through the open window, cooling their hot, damp bodies. But, in a warm embrace, sleep and contentment soon found them without difficulty. A bond had formed between them, and this time Chance felt no need to leave.

Chapter Sixteen

The walls of the room became the boundaries of the world, and beyond them nothing existed in the dark hours that followed except the glorious wonder of their togetherness. The darkness provided a haven where they could dwell away from reality at least until dawn.

Jenna had expected Chance to leave as he had done before, but he held her tightly in his embrace. They dozed between lovemaking, and in those calm interludes he drew her up against him possessively. Very few words were spoken, as if words might destroy the illusion of the perfect state.

She needed no light to see him. Her sight came through her fingertips, exploring and memorizing his body, and through her own body conforming to his. She felt the life of him through his hot kisses, felt the thudding of his heart against hers. She had committed to memory the feel of his silky black hair against her cheek; the contrasting coarse black hair on his chest against her bosom; the way his calloused hands felt slightly rough against her skin but immeasurably gentle. These things were tangible, even though time was not; and these memories would be with her forever, even though time would run out.

She felt a change in him, felt the rightness of their union. Perhaps dawn would bring the dark shadows from his past once again and she would lose him. But for now she had him, and she would not think beyond these moments.

The explosion rocked the town of Wallace and brought residents from their sleep. Chance threw back the covers and leaped up, fumbling for a match to light the lamp. A second explosion shook the ground and made the hotel tremble.

Jenna sat up, too, drawing the covers over her naked body. In the weak glow of the kerosene lamp, she saw Chance jerking on his clothes. "What is it?" she asked. "What's wrong?"

He heard the fear in her voice even above the hammering of his own heart, pumping out a foreboding feeling to every part of his body. "A series of explosions. That's all I know."

"I'm going with you."

Two more blasts rent the predawn darkness. He yanked on his socks and boots, strapped his gun on, and checked the load. Meanwhile, Jenna was haphazardly throwing on her riding clothes.

He opened the door.

"Wait for me, damn it!" She grabbed her jacket and pulled it on over a blouse that was not tucked in. Her blond hair tumbled down over her shoulders. Her blouse gaped and revealed her creamy breasts.

Chance momentarily forgot the explosions as his mind wandered to the wondrous hours they'd shared, unlike anything he'd ever experienced with any woman in his life. She was beautiful. Always, so beautiful. And special.

"Stay here where it's safe, Jenna," he said, suddenly fearful that something might happen to her if she came with him.

She pulled her holster and gun from the top drawer of the bureau and slung it around her hips as she headed for the door. "Something's wrong. I'm not one for sitting and wringing my hands and wondering."

Chance knew there was no point in arguing with her when her mind was made up. They raced down the stairs together as other people from the hotel popped their heads out of doors and asked what was happening. In the street, Chance recognized members of the bridge crew who had stayed in town. They spotted him and gathered around. Others soon appeared and joined them.

Chance leaped up into the back of a wagon bed so they could hear him. On the horizon to the east, they saw the black sky burning from the bottom up, or so it seemed. Chance's stomach knotted as his fears surged.

"The fire is in the vicinity of the "S" bridge. Let's get our horses and go out there!"

Soon the thunder of hooves and the rumble of heavy wagons shook the town as they stampeded down the Mullan Road toward the "S" bridge as swiftly as they had left it only hours before.

Chance's worst fears came true. All the guards were dead, and the once-intricate latticework of the "S" bridge had been reduced to piles of shattered timbers aflame at the bottom of the canyon. Only one end of the structure remained standing. Then, as if on cue, a fifth charge of dynamite shook the earth and sent everyone diving for the ground. They watched helplessly as the force of the charge flung the last remaining gigantic timbers into the darkness like mere matchsticks. The burning timbers sailed back to the canyon floor, setting the rain-starved grass on fire.

They heard numerous more explosions to the west, but because of the distance separating them, they sounded like firecrackers on the Fourth of July.

Chance feared other trestles had also been blown up. The men stared in shock at the devastation, not knowing what to do. Tears streamed from Jenna's eyes and ran down her face, glistening red from the fire's reflection.

"Jacobson!" Chance hollered at the foreman of the bridge-building crew. "Take half the men to the other side of the canyon. I'll keep the rest here. Let's try to make a firebreak to keep that fire from spreading into the forest. Moody!" He looked over the heads of the men and saw the cook wave an arm. "Moody, you stay here in camp and keep the food and coffee coming. We're going to need it."

"What about those other explosions!" one man hollered above the crowd.

"We can only hope the other crews scattered out along the line will take care of them."

"Could be Durfey's bridges are blown, same as ours!" somebody shouted.

"That bastard Durfey probably did this!" came another voice and a chorus of agreement.

Chance felt the stirrings of a riot. He palmed his Colt and fired a shot into the air to silence them. "If he did, we'll find out about it—later. Now, get to working on those fires before the whole goddamned country goes up in flame!"

The men hurried off to gather shovels and axes. Chance turned to Jenna. His angry, commanding features softened. He laid a hand along her neck, his thumb stroking the curve of soft flesh beneath her chin. In that one action, every emotion they'd shared during the night returned. And every emotion they had shared during the past few months was intensified. They were indeed partners on this railroad, in both the joy and the futility.

"You stay here with Moody and help him, will you?" Chance asked softly. "Fighting the fire is no

211

place for you. I don't want you to get hurt."

She gripped his arm, concern etched deeply in her expression. *"Do* you think Durfey is behind this?"

A muscle jerked along his clenched jaw. Fire leaped into his eyes, more than the mere reflection of the huge blaze before them. "In my opinion, he'd be a damned fool to do something like this when he would obviously be the prime suspect."

"Whoever did it can't be far away."

"No, but far enough away that we could never find him or link him to this in any way. I would imagine the culprit is clever enough to cover his tracks. I'm going to load the guards' bodies into a wagon, then I'll go help fight the fire."

Jenna watched until he had vanished into the night with the rest of the crew. She stared at the blazing timbers, at the red flames against the night sky, and at the men, like tiny ants, frantically but valiantly trying to keep it from spreading. All the work was lost. The money. The time. She knew from experience that those things could be overcome. But how would they ever overcome the despair?

When the men had done all they could and the fire was under control, the sun was high in the sky of a new day, making the incident seem little more than a nightmare. The only fragments of reality were the black and smoking bridge timbers sullying the bottom of Wolverine Canyon. Exhausted, the men dragged themselves into camp and formed weary lines to accept the coffee and food Moody had fixed with Jenna's help.

While they ate, curious people came down the road to see what had awakened them from their sleep. A newspaper reporter was there and spoke to Chance, then rushed back to Wallace to put it all into print. A couple of hours later, the first men from Ives's main

212

body of graders came to report that three other smaller trestles had been dynamited and fired.

The men lay in the grass or sat slumped on tree stumps in exhausted and discouraged silence. So much sweat and blood had been put into the bridges, and it would have to be done over. And of course the question lingering in everyone's mind was, "If we rebuild, will it happen again?"

Around noon, Paterson, Ives, and Leaman rode into camp, confirming what the first messengers had said. Chance's ire rose at the complacent acceptance on their faces as they surveyed the smoking ruins of the once-fabulous "S" bridge as if its destruction was inconsequential.

"Nothing can be salvaged here, either," Ives said, matter-of-factly.

Henry nodded and turned to Leaman. "How much did this bridge alone set us back?"

Leaman had the figures in his head and answered quickly. "This bridge took six-hundred-thousand board feet of lumber at a cost of thirty-thousand dollars."

Henry turned to Chance, his gray-blue eyes piercing him. Dead silence washed over the crew as they craned to hear the exchange. "I guess you know this entire thing is your fault, Killeen. You should have had at least ten guards on this bridge alone. I foresaw this happening, but you're in charge here—you and Jenna. I wasn't about to tell you how to run things."

Chance barely batted an eye at Henry's accusation, but once again he squelched the urge to put his fist into the man's arrogant face. Ives and Leaman, too, stood by in smug agreement.

The three turned away and went to the coffeepot. Jenna laid her hand on Chance's arm, feeling his muscles bunched and tense beneath her fingers. "What's gotten into him?" she asked as she watched Henry's retreat. "I can't believe the man I'm seeing."

213

"Power for the powerless, Jenna. That's what this is all about. Henry sees the prime opportunity to be in charge again, and he's not about to pass it up."

With food in their stomachs and a few hours of sleep in the hot July sun, the men awoke with their weariness giving way to anger. Whispering among them soon turned to elevated, angry exchanges of their displeasure over what had happened and their personal views on retaliation.

The noise brought Chance and Jenna from their respective tents. They were followed by Henry and his two cronies. The men gathered in a mob, a group of ugly, belligerent faces still carrying the soot and dirt from the fires.

"We think it's time we got even with Durfey!" Blake Barlow shouted. "We'll play by his rules, and go over there and blow up his trestles and dynamite his tunnels!"

Chance moved to a position in front of them. Like a shadow gone unnoticed by everyone but him, Jenna walked to his saddle near his tent and slipped the Winchester from the scabbard. She drifted to his side. In a movement hardly noticeable, the rifle went from her hand into his.

He became keenly aware of the heat of a riot about to break loose. He appreciated Jenna's loyalty but wanted to tell her to get inside. The least wrong move, the least indication of fear or concern, however, could be the catalyst that broke the mens' restraint. It was fortunate none of them had guns. Their firearms were all locked up to keep peace among them, for large groups of men who came together from different backgrounds and different nationalities often thought the only way to settle arguments was with a bullet. They could still take up

214

clubs and rocks, though. He was not concerned about himself, but he was worried about Jenna. Still, the best course was to act as though nothing were amiss.

Off to the side, he saw Ives, Paterson, and Leaman waiting with closed expressions to see what would happen.

"What you gonna do, Killeen?" Barlow shouted mockingly. Echoes from the crowd backed him up. "We won't build those damned trestles just to have them fired again! We want Durfey's goddamned neck and we want it now!"

In a smooth downward motion of his right hand, Chance pulled the .44-.40's lever action and ejected a bullet into the chamber. His green eyes had turned a threatening black, and the mountain meadow suddenly became very hushed. "We don't play by those rules, Barlow. This is a matter for the law, not a bunch of graders turned vigilante. Everything that was destroyed last night *will* be rebuilt. If you don't want to participate, then draw your pay. And do it now."

Barlow folded his arms across his scrawny chest. A thin man of average height, he was hardly one to be threatening anybody, but he was known throughout the camp for his cocky self-assurance. "If you want us to rebuild that friggin' bridge and risk our lives like those guards did, then you're gonna have to give us more money or go find a new crew."

A shout of angry agreement rose up behind him. Chance noticed that not all of the men were rallying for higher wages. Some remained silent and waited nervously to see who would win out. Most of them needed the job and weren't willing to walk away from it. Some had even separated themselves from the mob and had formed smaller groups on the perimeters, not wanting to be associated with the rebel rousers.

215

"You signed to do a job, Barlow, for a set amount of money. There won't be a raise because of some setbacks."

Henry Paterson sauntered forward. "You know, Killeen, I think Barlow is right. I think we ought to offer these men more money considering what has happened, and then weighing the dangers of what Durfey might pull tomorrow. How can any of us sleep nights from here on out, wondering if Durfey might kill us all in our sleep? These men can't take chances like that without some compensation."

Those on Barlow's side cheered Henry's support. Those men who had dissented moved in closer again, swaying like willows in the wind with the hope of more money sweetening the pot.

Paterson turned to Leaman. "You're in charge of the payroll money, James. Do you think it's feasible to give these men a raise, considering of course that Killeen's lack of judgment has cost the company thousands and thousands of dollars?"

Leaman had eyes of steel, quite contradictory to the image he presented. "I'll have to talk to Solomon to be sure he even wants to proceed after what's happened, but I feel we can handle a payroll raise."

Satisfaction was evident on Henry's and his cohorts' faces. Chance knew they were trying to get the men against him, and what better way than to start a fight over money, the universal weakness of men.

"We need a decision now." Henry turned to Jenna. "We can't wait to talk to Solomon or we could lose our crew. You're going to have to stand for your grandfather on this one, Jenna."

"You son of a bitch, Paterson," Chance interceded. "Don't put her in that position."

"Why not, Killeen? She's acting as Solomon's mediator. She knows better than anybody what he

216

would do. And we can't make the decision on only one half of the partnership."

Jenna sensed by the confidence in Henry's eyes that he expected her to side with him, and it angered her that he would use their friendship in that way. She absolutely didn't agree with him, but if she went along with Henry to salvage their friendship, then Chance would lose the mens' respect. His position would become one of impotence.

She glanced at Chance, who waited with a clenched jaw. He might not appreciate it, but at the moment he reminded her a lot of her grandfather—a man who wouldn't be taken advantage of and who wouldn't back down to anyone.

"You're right, Henry," she said levelly. "I am Grandpa's mediator, and I'll stand by the decision of the man he trusted enough to put in charge of this railroad. I'll stand by Chance Killeen."

Henry was stunned at first, but then he was filled with a sense of betrayal. Jenna looked at him sadly and explained her position. "A payroll raise would only leave us open to future blackmail. You know that."

"We want the money!" Barlow yelled, trying to keep the discontentment alive. "That woman don't know nothing!"

Chance's expression remained threatening, but he was secretly pleased with Jenna's astuteness. More than anything, he was touched by her support.

"There won't be a raise just because those trestles were destroyed, Barlow," he replied, still holding his rigid position. "You hired on to do a job no matter the obstacles and setbacks encountered. You're getting paid fifty cents more a day than Durfey's crew, and he's paying standard wage. You can't get more than what you're getting with the BRC. As I said before, the job is yours if you want it."

217

Chance stood with the Winchester across his chest and Jenna stood next to him, ready to use her Peacemaker. But it was more than the weapons in their hands that deterred a riot. It was clear by the determined set to their expressions that the two of them would go up against the entire crew if need be, regardless of the odds.

Finally, a man who was not part of Barlow's dissension stepped forward. "Most of us don't want no fight, Mr. Killeen . . . Miss Lee. I think I can speak for a good many of us. We're happy with our wages and happy to have work. We've got families we're sending our paychecks to. We don't blame you for what happened last night. I personally figure that if Miss Lee has the courage to go on after what happened, then we all ought to be men enough to do the same thing."

A low rumble of agreement spread throughout the group. Barlow's men made another attempt to fire them up, but slowly those who wanted to work dispersed and went back to their previous stations. Barlow and about fifty followers promptly gathered up their belongings and demanded their pay from Leaman. They collected their weapons from Ives, their belongings from their tents, and headed up the road to Mission Station and the next steamer bound for Coeur d'Alene City.

Chance went to his tent and Jenna to hers.

She had been there only moments when Henry came in, his eyes shooting sparks. She was still upset from the harrowing incident, but what she had to say to him wasn't going to be any easier. She felt the threads of their friendship unraveling and hoped it was only a temporary thing.

"You nearly caused a riot out there, Henry." Jenna tried to remain calm, but inside she was very agitated by his foolishness. "Somebody could have been killed. If I didn't know better, I'd think you wanted that 'somebody' to be Chance."

"I was trying to keep them from killing us, for God's sake. And *especially* him, because he was standing in the way of what they thought they wanted. They were mad at the whole mess and they were venting that anger in the only way they could. I never dreamed you'd go against me."

Suddenly, her temper got the best of her. "If you hadn't sided with Barlow, the whole matter would have ended. Going along with them only gave them fuel for their fire. Don't you *ever* put me—or Chance—in a position like that again!"

"And what if I do?" he snapped. "Will you go to Solomon and have my job? I thought friends stuck together."

That sad, regretful look entered her eyes again. "They do, Henry. When they can. But don't take me lightly. I'll do what I have to do as long as I'm in Grandpa's shoes."

"I was only trying to solve a problem and I thought you were the one to break the deadlock."

"You were *creating* a problem, Henry. You were trying to ruin Chance's authority over the men."

"And you just ruined mine! I'm beginning to think you're in love with Killeen. God, Jenna, don't you see him for what he is—a bastard and a beggar? Another fortune hunter?"

"Oh, everyone's a fortune hunter in your eyes!"

"He'll only hurt you," he warned. "Believe me."

"We're copartners on this road, Henry. Nothing more."

"I'm not sure I believe that. I see the way you look at each other. He's coming between us, Jenna. Do you *want* him to do that?"

Before she could reply, the tent flap lifted and Chance stepped inside, appearing tall and ominous.

But Jenna was relieved to see him. She'd had enough of the argument with Henry that seemed to be accomplishing nothing. And she didn't like what he was saying about Chance.

Henry's cool blue eyes met Chance insolently. "Your habit of breaking in on private conversations is annoying, Killeen."

"Don't give Jenna trouble over her decision, Paterson," he replied. "After all, you're the one who forced her to make it."

Henry was disturbed about Killeen in a new way. If he and Jenna did get serious about each other, then his chances to marry her would be gone.

"This is none of your concern," he said. "You've got fifty men to replace. I suggest you get on your horse and start looking."

Chance leaned on one hip, his hand resting on the butt of his gun. "You don't give orders to me, Paterson. I suggest you remember that."

"You made a big mistake today by not giving those men more money. You'll be left building this road yourself before it's all said and done if you don't wise up. I'm going to talk to Solomon. I believe he'd like to know how his new partner is handling his affairs."

Chance countered in a deadly calm voice. "I made no mistakes today, Paterson, unless it was by not putting a bullet in you. Jenna was right—and you know it—that once you give in to a bunch of men like Barlow, they'll be blackmailing us right and left for an increase in wages every time they don't like the way Moody stirs the beans. If I didn't know better, I'd think you were *trying* to sabotage this project. As for Solomon, you go right ahead and talk to him, but watch what you say. You might just be collecting your own walking papers."

Henry shouldered his way past Chance in his usual arrogant manner. "We'll see who gets ousted, Killeen."

Jenna was shaking and blamed it more on the argument with Henry than on the confrontation with the men. After Henry had gone, she turned to Chance. "I don't know what's happening," she said. "Henry and I never fight."

Her sad, confused eyes stirred Chance's compassion. He pulled her into his embrace. "Don't brood about him, Jenna. He's just temporarily on fire. And I expect Solomon's got a cold bucket of water that will take care of that."

Chapter Seventeen

Jenna left her tent and pulled her shawl tighter around her shoulders to ward off the night chill. Here in the mountains it didn't seem to matter how hot and dry the days were, how stagnant the air, for when the sun finally set and its golden warmth vanished from the land, a chill quickly set in. It was a welcome relief from the hot, dusty, rainless days they had experienced since the onset of spring.

It was late, but many of the men were still sitting on their bedrolls, smoking or talking or just staring up at the broad, star-filled sky.

Jenna didn't see Chance's familiar profile in the red glow of the small camp fires or in the bright light of the full moon. He must have already gone to the ridge where they'd agreed to meet.

She strolled back to her small tent, bypassed it, and moved up the hill toward a ridge that overlooked Wolverine Canyon, where the "S" bridge had stood in all its magnificence. It was darker in the shelter of the trees and eerie at night. Away from the human noises of the camp she heard the small rustlings of the forest animals and insects, but she was beginning to feel more at ease in these mountains and wasn't really afraid.

Near the ridge, she saw a small round point of red

glowing light. Soon she separated the dark shape of the tamarack tree from the man leaning against it, smoking a cigarette and looking out across the destroyed bridge. The slump to Chance's shoulders was evident, even in the dark.

A twig snapped beneath her foot. He didn't turn around but spoke in a low voice. "I was beginning to think you wouldn't come."

She came up behind him and put her arms around him, pressing herself against his muscled back and firm buttocks. He smiled at her from over his shoulder but it didn't succeed in removing the deep disappointment from his eyes.

"You can't blame yourself for this, Chance," she said. "It was unforeseeable."

"Paterson was right. I should have had more guards posted on that bridge. And I should never have left."

"We'll rebuild. We've already determined that."

He released a weary sigh that deepened the crow's feet around his eyes. "Your grandfather has the money to redo this, Jenna. But what if he didn't? It's a tremendous loss, even to a rich man. I can't help but feel responsible."

Wolverine Canyon was black. She could see nothing in its depths, but she could smell the timbers still smoldering some one hundred feet below. The bridge had been fantastic and they'd all been so proud of it. It was one of those instances where getting up from a fall was harder than the fall itself.

"Is there any way we can retaliate against Durfey?"

He drew her around in front of him and she rested her head on his chest. She felt the steady thump of his heart against her bosom and her ear, and when he spoke his chest vibrated with the force of his whispered, venomous words.

"I'd like nothing better than to cross the river," he said, "find Durfey, and tear him apart with my own bare hands, then blow up every damn thing he's constructed. But we can't prove it was him, and nothing would be accomplished by starting a war. This railroad isn't worth the lives of any more men."

"Someone thinks it is."

"Yes, but we need absolute proof before we can do anything. We already know the law here in the Coeur d'Alenes isn't very determined to help us, or even very capable for that matter. What we need is a spy . . . an investigator."

Excitement suddenly glittered in her eyes as she tilted her head back to meet his gaze. "I know just the man, Chance. His name is Jethro Ritchy. He escorted me to your mine. He's a hard man, but he's loyal to the person who's paying his salary."

Chance had heard of Ritchy, an ex-private investigator for the railroad and a spy for the Union during the war. "Then I'll talk to him. But, Jenna . . . let's not tell Henry and the others. I don't want his opposition on this. And I don't want anything leaking out that could tip the guilty party off to what we're doing. The fewer people who know about it, the better."

"All right, but there's no need for you to talk to Ritchy. I'm going to Coeur d'Alene this weekend to see Grandpa. I'll contact Ritchy. I'm sure he won't turn me down."

Chance's arms tightened about her; his tone grew husky. "Any man would be insane to turn you down."

His kiss cut off the little chuckle of delight in her throat and moved over her lips without haste, slowly stirring her senses to a heated pitch. The buckle of his gun belt pressed against her stomach, along with the hard length of his manhood. Her fingers found the belt buckle and in seconds had it free. It slid off his narrow hips and to the grass with hardly a sound.

"You're disarming me, woman," he whispered,

his hands moving from her face into her loose blond tresses.

"Oh, but I intend to," she purred.

She slowly removed his vest and followed it with his shirt, scattering kisses over the thick mat of black hair on his chest, while his lips in turn roamed along her neck, starting their own little fires of arousal deep inside her.

The buttons on her cotton blouse were more to his liking than those on the gown she'd worn last night. He soon had them open, and both the blouse and the camisole pulled free of her skirt band. There was no corset.

"You should dress like this more often," he bantered, his white-toothed smile flashing in the faint light from the sky.

He sucked in a sudden ragged breath when her nimble fingers found and released the buttons on his pants. Before she could go any farther with her attentions, he took her by the hand and led her deeper into the trees, to a secluded spot where the ground formed a small hollow and the tall pines and tamaracks towered above it, protecting them from anyone's sight and insulating the sound of their murmured exchanges. Here, too, the starlight dropped its faint silvery light, as if prepared just for them and for this moment.

With no preliminaries, they shed the remainder of their clothing and laid the articles out on the grass to form a sort of blanket. Chance drew Jenna down next to him. His hands, rough but masculinely sensual, moved over her body, exploring and once again easily kindling a blaze of passion she seemed to feel only with him. And as his hands roamed, taking liberty with what they silently claimed as theirs, so did his lips.

She made a halfhearted attempt to stop him as his kisses slid down past her breasts to her stomach, past

225

the taut skin of her flat abdomen, and even on to the delicate and sensitive recesses of her womanhood. As his hands spread her thighs, she gripped his shoulders, arching toward him, thinking she might die of the wondrous feeling if he didn't stop, and yet thinking she would surely die if he *did* stop.

"Chance, no. Stop. . . ."

But he must have known her words—so obviously spoken without conviction—were merely grounded on ignorance or modesty, and were not her real desire. Soon he had her crying out for more, tossing her head back and forth on the rumpled clothing beneath her, feeling a splendor she could not deny.

She would have asked him to take her to him, but she didn't know which pleasure she sought the most—this new one he gave so unselfishly to her, or the one they had shared together before. But he seemed to know these thoughts of hers, and at the precise moment she felt as if she would burst inside, he rose above her and joined their bodies in one plunging stroke. His thrusts were hard and deep, but she wanted them and took his buttocks in her hands, urging him not to stop. Together they rode the storm, they the sole creators of it. A cry of release rose in her throat. But fearful the sound would carry back to camp, she bit it off, muffling it until it sounded more a cry of agony than of ecstasy. Simultaneously, she felt him shudder and felt his release deep inside her.

They sank together, sated, into the darkness of the little hollow, mindless of the knot of clothing beneath them. His caresses continued and seemed so right. She had never experienced lovemaking with her husband that had been so utterly complete, and once again she refused to think beyond the wonder of the moment, not wanting to know what the morrow would bring.

She nestled against him, kissing his throat and

murmuring, "We should just stay out here all night. If only we had some blankets."

Chance didn't know for sure what brought it on—definitely not her lovemaking, for no other woman he'd ever known compared to her—but possibly it was the sweet innocence of her words that suggested nothing would change between them tomorrow. Whatever it was, something triggered an overwhelming tide of guilt that came crashing down on him with such force that he felt as if he might drown in it. A flash of heat covered his body but quickly changed to a cold sweat, and his arms around her loosened while troubling thoughts tightened around his heart.

Why did she seemingly trust him so implicitly that she handed not only her body to him, but her soul as well? Didn't she know that in the end he would have no choice but to tell her good-bye? Or did she know and not care? Maybe she wasn't interested in long-term commitment.

If that was the case, then there might be no reason for him to feel guilty. But the bond he felt with her was a powerful one, which both pleased and frightened him. Beyond this moment was the future and the past, intermeshed in an ugly tangle created by Solomon Lee, in which the baron reigned from the center point. If he could separate Jenna from her grandfather, it would make things easier, but she was completely devoted to the old man. She would never turn her back on him or believe he'd done anything wrong. Besides, it was not his intention to alienate her from the only family she had. That would only create a bigger chasm between them.

It was in utter confusion that he released her. "You'd better go back to camp alone, Jenna," he said. "I'll follow later."

The moment of total physical and mental abandonment was past. They came apart, reaching for the clothing scattered beneath them and around them.

Jenna tucked in her blouse and buttoned her skirt, misunderstanding the sudden distance he'd put between them. "Don't think about the bridge, Chance. Not now. And don't worry about Grandpa, either. I know he won't hold you responsible."

A wave of belligerence surged through him. "I wouldn't care if he did. I don't answer to him. Both of you had better keep that in mind."

The words were no sooner out of his mouth than he regretted having lashed out at her, but in that moment he also realized what life would be like if he was married to her. They would never have a moment's peace. Solomon Lee would always be standing there between them until the day he died— and knowing that old geezer, he'd probably live to be a hundred. Even in death, his shadow would haunt them, his fortune hanging over Chance's shoulders like a yoke never to be forgotten or removed.

Jenna drew her shawl over her shoulders. Her movements were not the usual fluid, graceful ones. Chance looked closer and saw the moonlight catching on soundless tears gliding down her face.

Guilt flooded over him again like a suffocating sea of water. She started past him, but he caught her arm. "Jenna . . . I'm sorry. You've got to understand that I can't help the way I feel about him. I won't let him rule me, nor will I live my life to satisfy him the way you have."

Her back stiffened at that remark and her blue eyes flashed, even in the pale light. He continued, not giving her a chance to admit or deny the truth of the statement. "There can never be true reconciliation between him and me. The wounds are too deep. Can't you understand that?"

She tossed her head in that defiant way. She was so proud; damned if she would be considered weak or wrong. "He isn't what you think."

"Damn it! What do you want from me, Jenna? I can't erase what happened."

"No, but you might try understanding why Grandpa did what he did and try to forgive him."

"Let God do that. I'm afraid I can't."

"And who will forgive you your bitterness, Chance Killeen? I'm not at all certain yours is the lesser sin."

He released her, the words driving home the truth. Chance watched her stumble in her haste along the ridge, until the distance and the moonlight no longer offered illumination.

But what did one do about hatred and bitterness pent up for sixteen years? It ran deep and cold within him, containing underlying currents strong enough to destroy not only him, but others around him as well—namely Jenna. It would be easy to marry her but impossible to stay separate from the world of Solomon Lee. If he became a part of the very thing that had laid waste to his family, he would be no better than a traitor.

Chapter Eighteen

Like an ant clinging to the mountainside, the Chinese coolie called Shang was lowered by rope from a granite ridge by a force of men and mules. Around his thin waist was a heavy leather belt that contained charges of dynamite, hand drills, and the sledge hammer he would need to bore blasting holes into the rock.

Chance sat astride his buckskin in the canyon below. He was alone again today. Jenna was still in Coeur d'Alene, having sent word that she was going to stay another week, making for a total of two. He surmised the harsh words they'd exchanged had been a factor in her decision. And in all honesty, he missed her terribly. He had grown comfortable having her by his side, and he was too much aware of the empty space she had once filled.

Henry's visit to Solomon had brought no changes, and he'd returned thwarted in his attempt to make Chance look incompetent. Solomon had stood by Chance and Jenna's actions and with their decision to rebuild, apparently refusing to lay the blame of the bridge loss on Chance.

Chance had been busy seeking replacements for those who'd quit with Barlow. He'd left notices in the saloons and oftentimes came out with several men who were ready to work. His quota was only short a few men now, and two dozen had been hired as guards; the latter were men better suited to the gun than to the pickax. Contrary to what Henry had warned, there was no end to the men filtering into the Coeur d'Alenes seeking their fortune, whether it be in gold, silver, or in the steel rails of the railroad.

He'd had no luck finding out who had promised to pay Vestal Whitman for holding out against the railroad. The man had been a hermit, had apparently had no close friends, and was afraid that everybody who appeared at his door was out to jump his claim. He had taken his secret to his grave, and it would not likely be revealed unless Jethro Ritchy could uncover who was behind the scheme to ruin the Bitterroot Railroad.

Word had also reached them that Barlow's body had turned up on the shore of Lake Coeur d'Alene. From the looks of the mutilated body, authorities believed he'd either fallen overboard into a paddle wheel or been thrown. And Chance couldn't help but wonder if it had something to do with the incident in camp.

Shang's sledge resounded through the canyon with a steady rhythm. Chance focused his attention again on the man swinging like a puppet over the side of the mountain. Shang was the best man they had with dynamite. How he'd gotten to be a blaster nobody really knew, but he had the respect of most of the men, except for those who insisted on maintaining their prejudice because of his nationality.

His job would keep him on the mountainside for a considerable time, since he had seven holes to drill and dynamite to place. Chance decided everything was going fine and a cup of coffee would just about hit the spot, so he nudged his horse and rode down the canyon toward the main camp. Several bridge and grading crews were also scattered up and down the line. These sub-camps allowed the men working on the outreaches of the line to get back and forth to their jobs without so much distance to cover each day.

The main camp was quiet, except for Moody who was working on supper. Ives and Paterson were gone, and Leaman was still in Spokane buying lumber for the bridge and trestles. The order had been so large that Louis Wood had been unable to supply it in the length of time that they needed it.

Chance stepped from the buckskin and walked over to pass some time with Moody and get a cup of coffee. They had barely exchanged the pleasantries of the day when the rattle of a wagon drew their attention.

In minutes, a heavily loaded freight wagon creaked into view. "Looks like Baker from town," he said to Moody, setting his coffee cup aside. "He must have something Leaman ordered." Leaving Moody to his cooking, Chance walked to the edge of the road to meet the driver.

Baker leaned out over the wagon seat and spat a glob of chewing tobacco onto the ground. "Hello, Killeen. I got a shipment of dynamite for you."

"Leaman's in Spokane. I'll sign for it."

The driver handed him a smooth board and slapped the bill on it. "Sign right there on the bottom line, Killeen. Press hard. I got that fancy newfangled carbon paper in between, so's you can have a copy of that there bill. It's so's you can't tell me later that you didn't get the dynamite.

"You know, Killeen," Baker continued. "I can't figure out why you need all this here dynamite—less'n you're blowin' up your own damned bridges." He let out a hoot of laughter at his own cleverness. "You ain't doin' that, now, are you? I've heard of the sort. Trying to milk the company any way they can."

Coldness swept over Chance despite the heat of the

232

late July day. He hadn't kept tabs on what Leaman had ordered, but he knew for certain that there had been a recent shipment of dynamite that had been large. It should have lasted longer, come to think of it.

Chance took the proffered pencil and scratched his signature in the proper place.

"Yeah," the driver added, glancing at the construction camp and the new roadbed for the tracks. "Guess my days here in the Coeur d'Alenes are near ended. Liked it here, too. But it figures. I've been all over the West, hauling freight from California to Montana, from Texas to Washington. I was always there when the miners and the settlers needed goods. Then along comes the railroad and drives us out of business. Always happens. Probably always will 'til they don't need wagons no more for nothing."

Chance handed him back the board and the bill. The thought crossed his mind that a man like this one might have enough resentment to blow up the bridges, but if he really didn't want to see the road go through, he would have done the same destruction to Durfey. No, all fingers still pointed to Durfey. If Jenna had talked to Ritchy, as she'd said she would, then he might already be out in the field investigating.

Baker took the bill, painstakingly separated the precious carbon from between the sheets, and handed Chance the copy on the bottom. While Chance folded it and tucked it in his vest pocket, Baker put his copy in a metal box next to him on the seat.

Chance helped him unload the dynamite and carry it to the supply tent, listening all the while to his incessant talk. "Yes sir, I've been loyal to the miners and this is what I get from the lot of them, but you can bet if I started charging you more for that freight, you'd be squawking to high heaven. No sir, freighting with me is the best deal you'll get, and just 'cause

233

you're running me out of business, I still won't raise the price on you."

The driver leaped back onto the wagon seat and gathered up his reins. "Well, good day to you, Killeen. I'll see you on the next run." He spoke to his mules, then headed off down the Mullan Road to deliver the rest of his shipment.

Chance waited until he was out of sight, then making sure no one was returning to camp, he lifted the flap on Paterson's tent and went inside. He dropped the bill onto the table, glancing over the figures more closely now—the quantity, the amount. The driver's words kept going round and round in his mind: *trying to milk the company . . .*

He glanced about the tent. Everything was neat and orderly, but he knew it wasn't because of Ives and Paterson. It was the meticulous James Leaman who kept everything in straight-column order, just as he did his record books. Chance thought about Ives and Paterson and how they had sided with Barlow on that pay raise to the point of nearly causing a riot. He'd thought it was a ploy to crush his authority, and maybe it had been, but there might have been more to it, too. And now Barlow was dead.

Paterson's construction company had contracted to do nearly every aspect of the railroad for Solomon, just as he had for years and for scores of railroads. Could it be possible that Paterson was skimming money off the top, padding his own pocket? If he was, it didn't make sense. According to Jenna, he had been adamantly against building this line, especially after the attacks on Solomon's life.

Chance cocked his head and listened for sounds that might signal the return of one of the three. He heard only Moody's clatter of pots and pans.

He quickly went to the bed that was Leaman's and dragged out the metal box beneath it, where the pur-

234

chasing agent kept his accounting books and materials.

The record books contained the usual—prices, dates, amounts ordered. Leaman was thorough. Nothing had been left out—except for the copies of the invoices. They weren't in the metal box, and he wondered where Leaman kept them. The last shipment of dynamite had been just before the bombings of the bridges. He agreed with the driver of the wagon that it looked as though they were going through the dynamite at an unhealthy speed. He also noticed that the price for the dynamite Leaman had recorded in the book was considerably higher than what was on the invoice Chance had received today— and from the same company. That was irregular, since the driver had said he wouldn't raise prices . . . even if they were running him out of business.

Chance glanced at some of the other figures, checking lumber costs, equipment, even the men's wages. He wrote some of the information down in the little black book he kept in his shirt pocket. He checked to see how much money had been drawn from Solomon Enterprises for Paterson's construction expenses. Finally, he put the books back in the same order he had found them. After sliding the box beneath the bed, he glanced about to make sure everything looked the same as before. James Leaman was so meticulous that he would most certainly notice if one particle of dust had been disturbed.

Satisfied that he'd covered his tracks well enough, Chance left the tent—and ran face to face with none other than James Leaman.

Leaman's gaze narrowed and Chance smiled, inwardly cursing Moody for making so damned much noise with his pots and pans that he hadn't heard Leaman ride up. He'd come about five seconds from getting caught red-handed.

"Got your shipment of dynamite," he said off-handedly as he walked casually to the buckskin. "Bill's in on the table." He swung into the saddle and pretended to be unaware of Leaman's cold, assessing eyes. "How did things go in Spokane? Did you get the lumber?"

"Yes. We'll have it in good time."

"Good." Chance wheeled his horse from the tent and trotted back up the road toward the "S" bridge camp, glancing back once to see Leaman hurrying to his tent.

The noise in the camp hushed as the buckboard transporting Solomon Lee and Jenna pulled up in front of her tent.

Chance wasn't happy to have to associate with Solomon again. He automatically went on the defensive, wondering what warranted the visit. He stayed where he was and forked the last of Moody's stew into his mouth, watching with outward detachment as Henry handed Jenna to the ground.

With curious disdain, he noticed that the entrepreneur hadn't completely recovered to his former robust self, but it was the tall woman next to him that drew Chance's deepest emotion and demanded his full attention. As her gaze found his, a mixture of joy and agony battled inside him. It was all he could do to keep from greeting her with open arms.

Solomon wasted no time with greetings, however. He saw Chance and strode toward him purposefully. Chance didn't move from the tree stump where he sat sipping coffee.

"We need to talk, Chance," Solomon said. "Will you join me in Jenna's tent?" Not waiting for a yea or a nay, he headed to the tent.

Chance had a notion to ignore him. He didn't like being treated like a lackey, especially by the imper-

236

ious robber baron, but he rose and sauntered after the old man. He braced himself for battle; it seemed a typical frame of mind when he was in Solomon's presence.

Inside, he pulled out the chair across from Jenna. Their eyes locked again for a moment, and he wondered if she was still upset over their last meeting and if she might have missed him the way he had her. The distinct fragrance of flowers, uniquely her own, aroused again the familiar aching desire to pull her into his arms and kiss her. But the old man was watching him with shrewd blue eyes, as if he knew his every thought.

Solomon positioned himself between the two of them. He pulled a cigar from his pocket and Jenna immediately scolded him.

"The doctor said no smoking, Grandpa."

He sighed and handed the cigar to Chance. "You might as well have this, Killeen." He reached into his pocket and removed five more. "These, too. I must say it's been a pleasure having her out here with you. When I'm by myself, I can indulge in anything I please."

"And I'm sure you do, Grandpa," she objected to his sulkiness. "But you know I'm only concerned about your health."

He nodded with a degree of submission. "Yes, dear, I know. And I'm glad you are." He then patted her hand, forgiving her completely. "You're right, of course, but I've never had any willpower when it came to something I wanted."

How true, Chance thought bitterly as he watched the two, doting over each other. Perhaps Jenna was not aware of it, but she obviously held the ultimate power over Solomon and he over her. Their loyalty toward each other would keep them forever inseparable.

Chance put the cigars in his pocket, deciding he'd

give them to the men. He wanted nothing that had belonged to Solomon, but he wouldn't voice his feelings in front of Jenna. Instead he said, "I hope you're not intending to go back on your agreement, Solomon. Even though you're here, I still work with your granddaughter."

"Oh, I won't interfere. Actually, I came out just because I was tired of being cooped up. As for the bridge, we'll rebuild, of course, regardless of Henry's attempts to talk me out of it."

He continued, "Jenna tells me she hired a private investigator to find out who blew up the bridges. I just wanted to say that you have my complete approval."

Chance debated whether to tell Solomon about the dynamite orders and his niggling suspicion that Leaman might be up to something. He decided against it until he had definite proof of illegal actions. He would contact Ritchy, or leave a message for him in Coeur d'Alene, and have him investigate Leaman as well, since he really didn't have the time to do it himself.

Solomon slid his chair back, and both Chance and Jenna came to their feet with him. "I'm heading up the road first thing in the morning to check the line, Chance. Jenna says she's going with me, so you'll have to do without her for a day or two. She's afraid I'll smoke a cigar or get too lively with the ladies," he jested, giving her a wink.

At Solomon's dismissal, Chance left the tent, but with an uneasy feeling. Bayard was "up the road." And his mother was in Bayard.

He had been outside only a few minutes when Solomon came out, too, and strolled over to Moody's coffeepot. He poured himself a cup and found the shade of a tree. No one came forward to speak to him, but he seemed not to mind. His gaze encompassed the mountains, impressed as everyone was by their lofty heights.

Leading the buckskin behind him, Chance walked toward Solomon, deciding now was as good a time as any to say what was on his mind. Jenna was out of earshot, and so was everyone else.

The friendly glow in Solomon's wise old eyes grew until expectant lights flickered across their cool blue surface like tiny fires upon a sea of oil. He was always ready for battle. It was apparently a way of life for him. He saw in every man an adversary. But in his position, it was probably true.

"I'm sure you didn't come to tell me to enjoy my stay, Chance. What's on your mind?"

"Your trip to Bayard tomorrow. I'm not naive, Solomon. You've hurt my mother enough. Why don't you stay away from her?"

Solomon sipped at his coffee, unmoved by Chance's emotional declaration. "I'm staying out of your love affairs, Chance. I suggest you be the same sort of gentleman and stay out of mine. Besides, your mother is a big girl. She doesn't need her son making her decisions for her."

"She wants nothing to do with you anymore."

"I'm not so sure of that. After all, she came to see me when I was ill. I thought perhaps she still might care. One way or the other, I felt it only courteous to return her visit."

Chance felt as if someone had laid a punch to his stomach and knocked the wind out of him. In the name of God, why would his mother want to see Solomon after she'd told him to leave her life forever? And what did that do to all the struggles, all the years of trying to protect her from hurt, to cushion her life—and all because of this man? Everything he'd done all these years he'd done for her. He had even carried her vendetta and made it his. Now he

239

suddenly wondered if hers had been a vendetta at all, and he felt mildly betrayed.

He recovered from the shock of Solomon's words and swung into the saddle. "I'll say only one thing to you, Solomon. If you hurt her again, you'll live to regret it."

Myriad emotions moved across Solomon's face, but none indicated concern over Chance's threat. At last he looked away to the mountains again, appearing extremely weary. His words drifted back to Chance on a solemn, sad whisper, which may or may not have been intended to be heard.

"I have already lived to regret it, Chance. Every day of my life for sixteen years."

Chapter Nineteen

Word had reached Coeur d'Alene that a forest fire was in progress on the other side of the mountains, and already hundreds of men had been dispatched to fight it. If rain didn't come soon, the entire area could be in extreme jeopardy. But the men from the Bitter-root Railroad crew rose on this particular day with restless anticipation. Not even the balloon of gray-white smoke rising above the southern band of mountains could mar the beauty of payday. Most of them would be going into Coeur d'Alene or nearby Wallace to spend their money on whiskey and women, as their consciences would allow.

The rumble of a wagon coming fast drew the attention of everyone in camp. In moments, Leaman's buckboard burst into view, careening out of control down the tree-lined Mullan Road.

Men came running, prepared to stop the runaway horse if necessary, but just before Leaman reached them, he stood up in the seat and hauled back on the reins for all his wispy body was worth, bringing the horse to a halt in front of the main tent.

He'd lost his hat and his gray-white hair stuck up everywhere, making him appear a madman. He collapsed back on the spring seat, shaking, his eyes large and frightened.

Everyone gathered around the wagon, throwing questions at him, but Leaman was out of breath and couldn't respond. They saw the dirt on his clothing, and the streaks of it on his face and in his beard, which was usually always neatly combed but was now all roughed up. There were even a few tears in his suit coat.

The men were still trying to get answers from him, when Chance, Jenna, and Solomon pushed their way through the crowd.

"Leaman, for God's sake, what's happened?" Solomon demanded, as concerned about the frail man as everyone else was.

"I—I've been robbed," he managed, gasping for breath and holding his chest. "Some road agents jumped me . . . a couple miles back. I thought they were . . . going to kill me. It was the payroll. I was . . . hauling the payroll."

A roar of anger and anguish went up among the men. Immediately, they wanted to know why he was hauling their money when the wagon with armed guards usually transported it.

They shot their questions at him thick and fast, on the verge of an angry riot again. Chance, Jenna, and Solomon also wondered why a change had been made and they hadn't been informed.

Chance shoved his way past the men and climbed into the back of the wagon to get their attention. "Don't worry. You'll get your money as soon as arrangements can be made to replace it."

"That damned Durfey is behind this again!" one hollered.

"We have no way of being certain. But why don't we hear what Leaman has to say."

With all eyes on him, Leaman began his dissertation. "There were four of them. And they wore

242

bandanas over their faces, so I couldn't tell who they were. Henry and I got word of a robbery being planned that was going to involve some big money. We didn't know if it was our payroll or not, but we couldn't take any chances. We spoke to the guards who usually haul it and decided we'd better take it out because no one would suspect us of having it. The guards were agreeable. They proceeded as planned, making it look as though they were carrying it. The only way anybody could have known Henry and I had it was if one of those guards was the informer for the road agents."

The men were angry enough to go down the road, meet the guards, and threaten to kill them all unless one confessed, but Chance silenced them again.

"All of you go back to work! You'll have an extra day off to go into town when we get this straightened out."

They grumbled about having to work when they'd had their hearts set on a day and night in town, but they did as Chance ordered. When they were well on their way, tools in hand and wagons rolling, Chance leaped down from the buckboard.

Leaman barely had the strength to alight from the wagon. Gripping the sideboard, he turned to Solomon. "The decision Henry and I made was obviously the wrong one. We tried to get your advice on a course of action to take while we were in Coeur d'Alene, but the desk clerk told us you'd gone. Apparently, we just missed each other."

"Where *is* Henry?" Solomon asked gruffly. "Don't tell me the damned road agents killed him?"

"No. Everything appeared to be going along with no problem, so he left me when we reached Prospect. He wanted to talk to Ives, who was there looking over one of those trestles that's being rebuilt."

Solomon nodded, his thoughts racing. He wasn't

243

happy at all at what had happened, but he couldn't do anything about it now. "Go on in and get a belt of whiskey, Leaman. And don't worry. We'll get this straightened out."

After Leaman had gone, Solomon started in on a personal tirade directed at Jenna and Chance. "If that sniveling Durfey—or whoever is behind this—thinks he can hurt me by hitting my bank account, he's used the wrong tactic. But we've got to start anticipating the treachery of this person better than we have been, if we're to stay ahead of him. Whoever it is will stop at nothing. Therefore, neither must we."

Solomon turned directly to Chance, who was lifting the harness from Leaman's horse. "I want you and Jenna to go to Coeur d'Alene and make the transaction for a second payroll. Two signatures are required, and I'm not up to returning to Coeur d'Alene and then coming back here. Besides, I want to take that jaunt upriver."

"But Grandpa," Jenna objected, "you shouldn't go alone. The doctor said—"

"I'll be fine, Jenna. Just fine."

"That wouldn't be very safe for Jenna, Solomon," Chance interceded. "Not after what happened to Leaman."

"She can sign for the money and return here at a later date, and you and the guards can bring the payroll back. Take six or eight of the best men off our bridge guards with you. The crew can keep an eye on things until they get back. The guards who were supposed to haul the shipment will have to undergo questioning when they get back. I can't believe Henry and Leaman did such a boneheaded thing, but the damage has been done, so there's no sense crying over it."

Chance found his mind straying from Solomon's words, until he wasn't listening at all. As he ran his

244

hand along the neck of Leaman's horse, he noticed that the animal was barely lathered. Even altering paces, a horse that was in top shape would show more fatigue after two miles of being pushed hard. This animal was not accustomed to running, and yet it barely acted winded. It appeared as though it might not have been whipped into a run until just before it had reached camp.

Chance's gaze lifted contemplatively to the tent where Leaman had disappeared. The little man had arrived in camp frightened and out of breath, almost wild-eyed. But for Leaman, just holding on to that galloping horse for a hundred yards would have been enough to put him in that condition.

Yes, indeed, it looked as though he had a couple more tidbits for Jethro Ritchy to inspect.

"I'll get the men to bring the payroll in, Solomon," he said, then added sardonically, "But something tells me lightning won't strike twice."

Jenna still objected to the entire thing. She was concerned for her grandfather, but she also knew that sooner or later the topic of her and Chance's last disagreement would have to be aired again, and it would more than likely happen alone with him en route to Coeur d'Alene. She didn't want to discuss her grandfather with Chance any more. It hurt too much to listen to Chance's unkind opinion of him. Maybe Solomon Lee wasn't perfect, but he was all she had. She didn't want her belief in him shattered or even cast in doubtful light. He'd been her strength, her anchor, and she didn't want that only bit of stability destroyed.

She was torn between the two of them, and Chance was putting her in the position of choosing one or the other. But she couldn't turn her back on her grandfather and she wouldn't—not for love, not for anything.

"The doctor doesn't want you traveling alone, Grandpa."

"Humph," he snorted. "I know how I feel. He doesn't. Now, you'd be helping me more by going with Chance and getting that payroll. The trip back to Coeur d'Alene will be more tiring for me than a leisurely drive upriver."

"At least stay here at camp and rest, Grandpa. We can send someone else upriver to check on things for you."

"Let him go, Jenna," Chance said quietly. "A trip upriver might be just what he needs to set his mind straight."

The two men exchanged a glance whose meaning they seemed to share, but which totally alienated Jenna. What was between them that they chose not to tell her? And how odd that the two of them would be siding on anything. Yet, she had the distinct feeling they were.

Her grandfather was certainly anxious to get on his way. He was fairly dancing, waiting for her to say she'd go to Coeur d'Alene and relieve him of the chore. Hadn't she always done what he said? Could she ever not?

"All right," she finally conceded to their wishes. "But stay away from cigars, Grandpa, will you?"

The sun rested on the crest of the peaks hours later when Solomon left his rig at the Bayard livery. After a short nap at the Galena Hotel, he changed into fresh clothing he'd brought with him, then started down the street toward Lily's boarding house.

Mountains rose on either side of Bayard, leaving very little bottom land for the town. It stretched out long and narrow with only two streets, one on either side of Canyon Creek. The steep canyon city held the smoke from the summer's fires that drifted across the mountains, burning Solomon's sensitive lungs and making it painful to breathe.

As his footsteps sounded on the boardwalk, so did his inner voice asking him if it would be wiser not to interfere in Lily's life again. But all the while the thoughts raged, his feet moved steadily closer to her and his heart pumped as eagerly as a young man's.

The boarding house was noisy when he stepped inside. Miners sat around the supper table in the dining room, talking and clattering dishes and silverware. He caught the tempting aromas of fresh baked bread and pot roast and, if he weren't mistaken, cherry pie. It reminded him that he hadn't eaten all day.

No one noticed him standing in the foyer with his hat in his hand. He was glad because he felt like a nervous boy and an old fool all rolled up into one. And surely that was the worst combination there could possibly be.

The house contained the same warmth that Lily herself possessed and had been decorated in soothing, fashionable colors of green and beige. A gleaming hardwood floor stretched from the foyer into a large sitting room and beyond it into the dining room. Handmade rugs added color to the floor's polished surface. Oak wainscoting and wallpaper sporting tiny flowers and birds added interest to the walls. The dining table, where the miners were heartily passing steaming bowls of food, was long and wide and adorned with a lacy white tablecloth and topped with a bouquet of fresh cut flowers. Four horsehair chairs and two matching sofas were obviously the finest pieces of furniture in the sitting room. Their frames of cherry wood matched the china cabinet that sat in one corner, displaying behind its glass doors an assortment of figurines and other cherished knick-knacks.

She had done well for herself, and he was happy for

her success. Such a stubborn, prideful woman she had been. If only she had given into that pride, he could have had her as his wife all these years.

A door from the kitchen opened and Lily herself swept into the dining room, carrying a large bowl of mashed potatoes. She wore a simple cotton dress and an apron, but she looked as fresh and as lovely as a spring day. Her pleasant smile filled the room with sunshine and every man's eyes followed her movements.

"Would anyone care for more potatoes?" she queried.

Practically all the men spoke up at once, then immediately started squabbling over whom she should serve first. It was plain that each one wanted the pleasure of a few seconds of her personal attention. Good-naturedly, she obliged, even innocently flirting with each one a little, which they seemed to eat up with as much relish as they did her food.

She heaped some potatoes on one man's plate. He was so fresh-faced, he didn't look as if he could be over nineteen. He gazed up at her with eyes full of adoration. "Your cooking makes me think of my Mama," he said. "I swear you've outdone yourself tonight, Miss Lily."

Lily laughed a happy, trilling sound and rumpled his hair as if he were her own boy. "You're just hungry, Sam. Anything tastes good when you're hungry. Even potatoes."

"Yeah, and Sam's always hungry," another man said. "He reminds me of this dog we used to have whose teeth fell out from lack of use 'cause he just swallowed everything whole."

Sam scowled at the man but smiled sheepishly when he looked up at Lily again. Her smile made all the mens' teasing bearable.

"Don't pay Zeke any mind, Sam," she said, then

248

left his side to circle the table. She stopped by one older miner and, before giving him a second portion, laid a hand on his thick shoulder. "Have you heard from your wife, Riley? Is she doing any better?"

He hastily swallowed a mouthful of food and looked up at her respectfully, if not a bit starry-eyed. "Yes, ma'am. She's doing better now. But I just can't get her to come out here."

Zeke spoke up again. "Don't reckon you've been trying very hard. You bein' sweet on Miss Lily and all."

A chorus of laughter filled the room and Riley's face turned red, but Lily just laughed. It appeared she might have heard such comments before.

It was plain to Solomon that she was the darling of the men, but the scene brought back another in his mind. It was the first time he'd ever seen her.

They had been at a ball that scores of railroad men had attended. No one had ever seen her before and she had every man in the room standing in line waiting to dance with her. It didn't even matter to any of them that she was married. While she danced, she had flirted a bit with her many admirers, but her gaze had constantly betrayed her heart. Solomon might have been the only one to notice, but she had eyes for only her husband.

Duke Killeen was blind to the furor her beauty and charm had caused. He'd been so wrapped up in some new railroad deal that he seemed to have completely forgotten about her. Maybe he just thought she was having a good time, but Solomon had seen the anxiety and disappointment in her eyes. He'd used it to his advantage. Little did he know he was going to fall in love with her.

"Well, Delaney ought to be back from Thompson Falls real soon, Miss Lily. Don't you fret none about him. Now, do you have any more of that hot bread?"

The words brought Solomon back to the present.

Lily laughed again and turned to go into the kitchen. It was then that she saw Solomon and an audible gasp escaped her. All the men turned to see what had startled her.

There were things Solomon wanted to say, but not in front of a roomful of strangers. If he hadn't been seen, he might even have considered leaving unnoticed. Seeing how happy she was only made him sad.

"Solomon," she said disbelievingly. Then suddenly fear crept into her eyes. "Has something happened to Chance?"

"No," he quickly eased her concerns. "I just came to check on the branch line to his mine. I decided to stop in and see your boarding house while I was here."

She breathed a sigh of relief, but her hands were shaking when she nervously wiped them on her apron. She introduced him to the men, and at learning who he was, they all became very reserved. Sensing he wanted to speak to her alone, she said, "I need to go back to the kitchen. Could you join me in there?"

Lily led the way. The kitchen was hot, and the only thing coming through the open windows was the smoke from the fires.

She pulled the oven door down and, with thick hot pads, removed more bread and laid it on the counter. Standing self-consciously on the threshold, Solomon watched as she spread butter over the golden loaves with hands as graceful as butterfly wings. He remembered her hands . . . touching him. . . .

"I imagine everyone in Bayard enjoys the smell of your food drifting through the air. I smelled the cherry pie even from down the street." He stretched the truth but made her laugh.

250

"You wouldn't be hinting for a piece, now, would you?" Her green eyes danced for him just as they had for the miners she took care of.

Solomon *was* hungry, and it would give him an excuse to linger. "I don't believe I've ever tasted your cooking, Lily. It would surely be a treat." Without further prodding, he pulled out a chair at the table next to the window and seated himself.

She cut a serving for Solomon and set it before him, then filled two cups with coffee and took the chair opposite him.

With every bite, Solomon exclaimed how wonderful the pie was. Laughing, Lily cut him a second piece. "If I didn't know better, I'd think you hadn't eaten all day."

"The truth of the matter is, I haven't. Our payroll was stolen first thing this morning and I wanted to get here before dark, so I drove steadily. When I arrived, I collapsed onto the bed like a typical old man and fell asleep."

At the twinkle in his eyes, Lily's heart slipped a bit from its stable position. She remembered all too well the way he had been able to simply look at her and charm her in an irresistible fashion. She wasn't sure why, but she was glad Bard wasn't back from Thompson Falls yet. She didn't want him to witness this meeting, although he was bound to hear about it from the men.

"Maybe you're driving yourself too hard, Sol," she said, genuinely concerned. "You went through quite an ordeal."

He shrugged, working steadily on the pie. "My days are numbered, Lily. Therefore, I intend not to waste them. Now, tell me. How is your business doing?"

Lily loved to talk of the thing she had worked so diligently to make successful. "I have all my rooms

251

rented. All the boarders work at the mines. I have a woman helping me cook and clean, but today is her day off."

Watching her animated actions was pure pleasure for Solomon. Even in a cotton dress and apron she was that beautiful goddess of his dreams that he could never quite seem to capture.

"I'm glad to hear you're doing well, Lily," he said with true sincerity. "Now"—he reached into his pocket—"I've brought you something."

He handed her the small package tied with white paper and a red string. Lily took it hesitantly. "You shouldn't be buying me gifts, Sol. It really isn't necessary."

"I seldom do anything necessary anymore. I try to do only those things which bring me pleasure."

Lily thought of Bard again and wondered if it was proper to take a gift from an old lover now that she was betrothed. But Solomon eagerly awaited her reaction. She couldn't hurt him. He was a heartless millionaire to the world, but he had shown her only love and compassion.

She undid the simple bow that tied the small package. The paper slipped off easily, as did the box's lid. Before her in a rumpled bed of sapphire blue velvet lay a gold locket in the shape of a heart, attached to a solid gold chain. Two sapphires and three diamonds clustered together in the left-hand corner of the heart.

Murmuring her astonishment at its exquisiteness, she lifted the necklace from the velvet bed. The puffed shape of the heart rolled over naturally in her hand. Engraved on the back were the words "To Lily with love, Sol." A choking feeling rose in her throat and she fought to hide sentimental tears.

Solomon stood up and took the necklace from her hand. "Let me help you with it."

"It's so beautiful, Sol. I really should save it to wear

252

with something special."

He chuckled as he stepped behind her and draped the necklace around her neck. "Wear it anytime, Lily. There's no sense in putting it away to be worn only a few times in life. I gave it to you to enjoy."

"And to remember?"

There was a pensive quality to her voice. Solomon finished clasping it, struggling against the urge to lay his lips against the soft, graceful curve of her neck. Little did it matter to him that strands of her black hair had fallen during the course of her busy day, or that her apron was stained with flour and cherries. He would take her into his arms this moment and make love to her, except that something told him it would not be so easy to erase the years of hardship and painful memories, and return to the darkness wherein they had shared love in a few idyllic, stolen moments. He might never have her again in that capacity, but he could not be hasty in this new relationship, either. There was much wrong to be undone.

She fingered the necklace with one hand, but the other he enclosed in his. "I gave the locket to you so you would remember me, Lily. I gave it to you, too, because I have never given you anything but sorrow. It's my heart. It was yours back then. It belongs to you still. And you will have it until the day I die."

He lifted her hand to his lips in a gallant gesture, but it was with reluctance that he released it and gathered his hat from the table. "I must be going now."

She followed him to the back door. He paused on the threshold with the same love showing in his eyes that had been in his words. He cupped her chin in his hand—a hand that had seen the years, but one that was also very gentle with ageless masculine assurance. He tilted her chin and kissed her cheek.

"Until the next time, Lily."

She watched him go, wanting to call him back but all the while knowing nothing could be gained by it. When he had disappeared inside the Galena Hotel, she folded her fingers around the gold heart. She didn't know if the tears that came in a sudden rush were for Duke or for Sol. The past could not be revived nor relived—surely not—with one keeping the best parts and tossing away the worst. It could only be remembered.

And she must remember that.

Chapter Twenty

Chance and Jenna took the trip to Coeur d'Alene with minimal discussion, just as they had the entire day. Jenna was grateful for the guards' presence, to ease the strain between her and Chance. It was ironic indeed how two people could be lovers one day and virtual strangers the next.

When the steamer docked, the sun was sinking behind the mountains. "We'll meet in front of the bank at nine o'clock sharp in the morning," Chance told the guards. "And stay away from the saloons tonight. I want you alert in the morning."

While he gave orders to the men, Jenna saw her opportunity to slip away. She made her way to the hotel, where her grandfather had retained their rooms. At the desk, she requested water for a bath. It came shortly after she was in her room.

She had barely settled into the tub when footsteps sounded in the hall. Even on the carpeted floor the rhythm of the walk was all-too familiar, and her heart began to thud rapidly. A knock followed shortly, and with it Chance's deep voice held to a low pitch. "We need to talk, Jenna. Can I come in?"

For seconds she debated her response, ambivalently wanting to see him and not wanting to see him. "I can't right now," she replied in a tone she hoped sounded adamant. "I'm bathing."

"Are you going to be bathing all night?" he grumbled.

"Maybe."

The floor creaked near her door. She visualized him shifting his weight impatiently, and she visualized the frown deepening on his face. There was a long pause before he strode away, retracing his steps down the hall. She was mildly disappointed that he'd given up so easily. But what had she expected him to do? Break down the door?

After completing her bath, she leaned her head against the tub's high back and closed her eyes. She would soak for a while, until the water became cold. Outside her door more people passed, but in the quiet confines of her room, her clock ticked away with a soothing, restful sound that tempted to lull her to sleep.

"You make a pretty picture, Jenna Lee."

Her eyes popped open and she grabbed for the nearby towel, putting it hastily over her while sinking deeper into the water.

"How did you get in here?" she demanded.

He leaned indolently against the door frame that separated her room from her grandfather's, dangling a key from his forefinger and wearing a boyish, mischievous grin. "I needed to get something for Solomon out of his room. It helps that everybody knows I'm his partner. The clerk didn't even question me."

"You could have knocked."

"The door was open. And you were so lovely, I was too tongue-tied to announce my presence for several seconds."

His soft-spoken flattery had its appeal, as well as the hint of seduction in his probing green eyes. "No one likes to be spied on," she said. "What do you want, anyway, that I couldn't have gotten for you?"

256

He stepped into the room and deposited the key on the dresser. "Darn, I forgot what it was I wanted. I do remember, though, that I wanted to talk to you and you wouldn't let me in."

He sauntered across the space of the small room and positioned himself behind her. She tensed, anticipating his touch, and shivered when he began massaging her shoulders. He leaned closer and nuzzled her neck, leaving a string of fiery kisses in a curving path along its slender length.

She tried to speak, to tell him to stop, but his hands glided over her shoulders and down into the water, moving gently across her breasts and weakening all willpower she might have had to fight him with. She was like potter's clay in his hands, and she would always be ready to be molded by him into any shape he desired.

"Get out," she said only halfheartedly as his masterful touch ignited the passion she tried to deny. "I don't want to hear any more of your remarks against my grandfather."

"I didn't come ... to make any," he said between kisses. Then, whispering fervently against her cheek, "I missed you, Jenna. Why did you stay away so long?"

The battle that raged within her was the hardest she'd ever fought. She knew she shouldn't continue to succumb to her desire for him; it could only hurt her in the end. But, after all, it was she who had encouraged their love affair in the beginning. He had been the one to fight against their becoming involved. She remembered her own words to him: "Don't worry about tomorrow." Such foolishness, but she'd said the words in hopes that his love for her would be stronger than his hatred for her grandfather. It couldn't be denied she had wanted to make love to him in a way that defied common sense, even though it seemed a hopeless situation.

"I won't turn my back on Grandpa for you," she declared.

"I won't ask you to."

He straightened away from her. Without the heat of his body, she felt a sudden chill, an unmistakable emptiness. She glanced over her shoulder, oddly afraid he was going to leave. But he had flung off his vest and was peeling out of his wet shirt. In the next instant he was back to his former position, with his hand down in the tub, groping around for the bar of rose-scented soap.

"Get your hands out of this tub, Chance Killeen! I don't need your assistance!" She tried to rise out of the tub, but he pressed her back into the water.

"Relax, Jenna. I'll wash your back. You know it gets as dirty as the rest of the body and is usually the part that gets the least attention."

"You can't have it both ways, Chance."

There was a considerable pause as his soapy hand made circular movements on her back. "Neither can you, Jenna," he said quietly. "So which way do you want it?"

"Things can't work out between us, Chance, because you won't let bygones be bygones. I can't continue to . . . I mean it would be best if we . . . well, maybe it would be best if we don't . . ."

"Don't what? Make love anymore?"

She nodded, the lump in her throat too big to speak around because it was the last thing she truly wanted. But he couldn't just keep coming to her, expecting her to give him sexual pleasure with no promises of the future or words of love. She had tried to make it work out between them, had hoped and prayed it would, but with each advancing day she only felt as if she were being used.

"All right," he said. "That sounds like a simple solution. Now, be quiet and let me wash your back."

"I can wash it myself! I've *already* washed it! Give

258

me that soap!" Suddenly angry with his easy agreement, she reached around and grabbed for the soap, but he held it beyond her grasp.

"Be an obedient girl, for just once in your life."

Something in the way he was looking at her assured Jenna that he had no intentions of abiding by the agreement that they quit making love. Quite to the contrary; he would still try to seduce her if he could.

She put her back to him again, feeling very recalcitrant. She could never seem to get the upper hand with him. If she tried to get out of the tub, she'd more than likely be in a more vulnerable position to his charms than if she stayed put.

With stubborn determination, Jenna folded her arms over her breasts and decided she would steel herself against his touch, something she should have learned to do long ago. If he thought he could lure her to bed again and have all forgotten, he was sadly mistaken.

He soaped her back and shoulders in a soothing, circular motion that had a hypnotic effect upon her troubled mind and tense nerves. Soon her eyes closed of their own volition and her entire body became limber under his ministerings. Their argument, their differences, vanished as if they had never been. Her resolution was quickly forgotten.

His hands slid from her shoulders down the front of her, over her breasts and to the flat of her stomach. She lost herself in the sensation of his touch and his kisses as they worked their magic. As if in a dream, time slipped away, until eventually he drew her to her feet. Entranced and once again full of fire for him, she allowed him to dry her. It seemed too long indeed before he lifted her into his arms, leaving her to wonder if she would ever get enough of him and of his lovemaking, which made her feel so much a woman.

And once again, vows forgotten, she lifted her long, slender legs around his muscular, lean hips and pulled him deep inside her. She surrendered wholly to him and he to her. They gave not of just their bodies but of their souls, too. If nothing else existed between them, this desire for each other did. It changed nothing beyond it, but it was complete unto itself. It spoke when words seemed insufficient. It built the bridge over waters too stormy to cross. And when it had succeeded in once again breaking down the barriers that held them apart, they lay beneath the covers in each other's arms in quiet moments when holding and touching are enough.

It was some time later that Jenna listened to Chance's steady, even breathing and knew he'd fallen asleep. She closed her eyes and put her mind only on his nearness, on the warmth and strength of her body against his. And while she did this, she tried to tuck away every sensation and every memory as deep into her mind as possible, so that she might never forget it. Only time could tell where their passion for each other would lead, and until then there was no use fighting it. It was, in a way, like a special, beautiful gown that a girl simply could not part with until it hung threadbare and tattered and could no longer be worn.

It's so damned slick out here, I can't stand up, and I can't remember when my hands and toes have ever been colder. I'd like to know how he does it. He walks along, swinging that lantern like it was a hot day in July. How can anybody be so tough?

"Son, being a brakeman is easy to learn, if you can stay alive long enough to get through your apprenticeship. Most accidents are from coupling freight cars. Night work in the yards is the most dangerous."

"I'll get that coupling pin, Dad. Let me do it. I've

got to learn."

"No, not this time, Chance. Everything's slick with this damn black ice and it's darker than hell. I'll do this one. You just stand back and be ready to signal the engineer."

Damn, it's cold. This freezing rain's going right through my coat and into my shoulders. I wish Ma wouldn't have been so determined to make me wait until Christmas morning to open that sweater she knitted for me. But Dad doesn't act like he even notices the cold. I wish I could be like him.

What! What's that?

"Dad! Slack running! Get out of there! DAD!"

Chance came awake with a start and saw all too clearly in his memory his father's body crushed between the two freight cars—the broken rib protruding from his strong chest, the blood, the last breath of air as the life left his eyes. And for long, frightening moments he suffered the anguish of his father's death all over again, as if it had just happened.

But slowly, like ebb tide, he put it behind him and found his place in the dark room of the present.

Jenna sat up behind him and laid a hand on his back, asking sleepily, "Chance, what's wrong?"

"Oh, nothing . . . just a dream."

He felt exhausted, but the dream—the remembrance—always had that effect on him. He leaned away from her only long enough to light the lamp by the bed. The weak yellow glow didn't obliterate the dark nightmarish image of his father's mangled body, but it did serve to dim it.

Jenna came up on her knees behind him, enfolding him in her embrace. "Care to tell me about it?"

He felt as silly as a little kid having nightmares about monsters, but she was there offering comfort and understanding. It was so like Jenna to put other's concerns over her own. He slid his arm around her, feeling so much a part of her, feeling so much in need of her. Together they lay back, still cradled in each other's embrace.

"I was dreaming of the night my dad was killed. I guess I've been thinking of him a lot lately."

Jenna laid her head on his chest, fingering the thick mat of black hair growing there. "Tell me about him, Chance," she whispered. "Was he like you?"

Chance's contemplative gaze drifted to the ceiling. "I'm told I look like he did. I don't know if I'm actually like he was. I guess you'd have to ask my mother that."

"And where is your mother?"

"She's here in the Coeur d'Alenes. She runs a boarding house in Bayard."

It was only a slight movement on her part, but he felt her tense. "Bayard?"

"Yes."

The only sound in the room was the ticking of the clock.

"Then Grandpa went there because of your mother. And you knew it."

"I suppose he thinks he can find something he lost. But I saw no reason to tell you."

"What is it all about?" Jenna asked. "This love affair of theirs. Tell me. Tell me the whole story, Chance. I know how your father was killed, but why were you there? How did you fit into it?"

He had never told the intimate details of his father's death to anyone other than his mother and Delaney, mainly because those details were so horrible. But the incident was so fresh in his mind, almost as if needing to be told, and at last he succumbed to her wish and related to her exactly what had happened that tragic night . . . how he'd been

262

working at the rail yards as a brakeman under his father's tutelage, and how in one second his family's lives had been changed forever.

"I've always felt Dad's death was my fault," he said quietly. "Maybe if I'd been paying closer attention, I'd have seen that loose car coming back at him sooner."

"From what you've told me, you can hardly blame yourself. But, Chance, why do you blame Grandpa? He wasn't there, was he?"

"No, but Dad was working at the yard because of your grandfather. Perhaps I'd better start at the beginning.

"You see, my parents left Ireland as newlyweds," he began the story. "They were like the others from that country at the time, running from the oppression, the famine, and seeking the fortune America offered. Dad was independent, a fierce man in his beliefs and his loyalties. His biggest dream was being his own boss and doing good by my mother. He started out working for the railroads and through some wise investments finally got enough to form a small railroad company of his own. It consisted of just a couple of short lines, but they were profitable.

"I remember the first decent house we lived in. It was far from being a mansion, but we thought it was."

"Was that when your father met Grandpa?"

Chance nodded. "Solomon never really had anything to do with my dad, but my folks started attending some of the social functions, and I would surmise that's where my mother caught his eye. I remember this one ball my folks went to. My mother worked as a seamstress, so naturally she made her own gown. It was the most beautiful thing we boys had ever seen. It was a shimmery green satin, cut low across the bosom. We were stunned to see any part of our mother exposed," he chuckled as he remembered.

"We stared at her, our eyes as bugged out as three little toads. And Dad was just as incredible in his black suit that made him look like somebody's butler. He cut a striking figure and we were awed by them, proud of them. We couldn't believe they were our parents all decked out in satin and lace and fine milled wool. Mama was afraid she wouldn't fit into that elite crowd. Dad didn't care if he fit in or not. He just hated being all cooped up in that suit. I never figured he'd make it through the night without taking it off, but I guess he did."

He paused, considering those happy moments with fondness. Then he continued. "The company did good for a few years. My dad bought Mama some nice things she'd been wanting, and he bought me a horse. It was just an old plug he'd rescued from the bone factory, but I thought it was the greatest thing alive.

"Then one day we were out on the street again. Just like that. All I knew was that it had something to do with some big baron manipulating the stock market. And Dad was back to being a brakeman, a job he was really too old to do safely. It was a dangerous job, even for someone young and agile. Little by little, we lost the few things we'd acquired. We had to sell them to pay rent and buy food and clothing.

"We settled back into poverty easily enough. I guess we'd never quite gotten it out of our minds." He glanced at her again, his mood lightening and his eyes suddenly twinkling. "I've eaten a lot of potatoes in my life. My mother cooked them every way you could think of. Fried, baked, boiled, stewed, hashed. She's a master chef when it comes to potatoes."

They shared a few strains of laughter, but as quickly as it had come, the humor faded. Jenna thought perhaps the memories might become too disturbing for him to relate, but after a contemplative moment, he went on.

264

"It was a couple of years before I was old enough to take a job at the rail yard. All they had available were brakeman jobs. They were always available because they lost somebody about every week. Dad didn't want me to do it but I just insisted. I said, 'Well, if you can do it, I don't see why I can't.' I didn't leave him much room for argument, and I was at an awfully independent age. Sixteen. Besides, we needed the money desperately.

"Dad wanted to start over again and I wanted to help him, because losing what he'd worked so hard for had embittered him. It seemed he lost a lot of his drive and his dreams when he lost his company. I think he figured he had failed my mother. He was never the same after that, and I wanted things to be the same. I wanted to see him and Mama happy again. Back then, I didn't know there was more to it than just losing the business."

The storytelling stopped abruptly. Chance turned the wick down in the lamp until the room was dark again.

Jenna had questions such as, "Did your mother love my grandfather?" But she didn't ask because she felt the dark brooding going on inside of him, even though she could see no expressions and could only feel his body next to hers. He released her, as she had expected him to, for the story had ended on an unhappy note that had brought them full circle back to the uneasy topic of her grandfather.

She understood now how Chance had felt as a boy seeing his father brought to his knees and then killed before his eyes . . . seeing his mother devastated and his brothers and himself thrust into hardship with no anchor to hold onto. He'd felt guilt that he hadn't been able to save his father from death. To compensate, he'd tried to take his place. He'd been forced to grow up fast. A boy would naturally turn bitter toward the source of such anguish, no matter what he

265

perceived that source to be; and he would not soon, nor easily, release that strongest of all emotions.

Jenna realized her presence might very well be causing him more anguish by serving as a reminder. She considered returning to New York. It might be the best course, except that tomorrow she had to sign for the payroll. Neither could she forget the contract she had signed, agreeing to be the one he worked with rather than her grandfather. If she backed out, she would lose his faith just as her grandfather had. It would prove his belief that Solomon Lee and any blood kin of his could not be trusted.

His feelings ran so deep. And she understood them now. It was very true that there might be no hope for their relationship beyond the building of the railroad. Could she honestly blame him for not wanting to become a part of the dynasty that had had such a far-reaching effect on his life?

She turned her head upon the pillow. His eyes were closed, but she knew he wasn't asleep. She wondered at the silent thoughts he chose not to share with her.

Suddenly tears sprang to her eyes, soundlessly, futilely. Was she being selfish in holding on to him? Would it be best for *him* to let him go? And yet, how could she release him? After twelve years of emptiness, he had entered her life and made her feel alive again. It was a sacrifice she wasn't sure she wanted to make.

Oh, Grandpa! Why did you try to take what wasn't yours? I don't fault you for wanting love, but now your love is costing me mine.

Delaney entered the boarding house through the parlor. Another trip to Thompson Falls was over and it was good to be home. Lily was in the kitchen preparing supper, and from the aroma filling the house, he knew she was baking his favorite—gingersnap cookies. No doubt a little "welcome back" surprise.

It was his custom each evening to come in from work and snitch a taste of whatever she was cooking. Then when she scolded him, he would regain her favor by giving her a monstrously sweet hug and kiss before hurrying to his room to bathe and change before supper.

Therefore, it took great effort for him to bypass the kitchen and the dual temptation awaiting there. He skipped lightly up the carpeted stairs to Lily's room, going directly to the dresser and pulling the top drawer open. He removed from his shirt pocket the tiny bottle of French perfume, wrapped and beribboned in its own box.

Delaney didn't know the meaning of the fancy French name on the bottle, but he knew she'd be delighted and so would he when she wore it, for it smelled all soft and powdery, enticingly silky, like Lily herself.

He was about to set the box atop her lacy white underthings, when he saw something else lying there. The golden flicker of a heart locket caught his eye, along with the winking of three diamonds embedded in its surface. He'd never seen her wear the locket. Yet it appeared to have been worn just recently to have been resting right on top of everything else.

It was surely the devil that took hold of him then. Delaney knew he shouldn't be going through her personal things and he hated himself for it, but he couldn't help himself from reaching into the drawer and taking the gleaming locket into his hand. The diamonds sparkled brightly, expensively, paling the little bottle of perfume by comparison and making it appear cheap and worthless in his eyes. He turned the locket over and the light caught on an inscription. He lifted it to the light coming through the window and saw in finely etched words: *To Lily with love, Sol.*

If he'd not had the muscle that he did, he might have collapsed. As if the locket were on fire, he dropped it back into the little dent in the lingerie where it had nestled before. In nearly the same movement, he whisked the beribboned box back into his shirt pocket.

He closed the drawer as quietly as he'd opened it, then left her room. In his own room, he sat on the bed and clenched his fist around the perfume box.

What did the locket mean? Had she made love to Solomon Lee while he'd been gone?

Oh, murther! You're all that matters to me, Lily.

To be certain, if he lost her he'd have no reason to even go on. He wasn't sure how he'd lived all those years without her, but there was no denying that he would never be able to live without her now.

He buried his face in his hands. "Ye're doin' the divil's own handiwork, Solomon Lee. By the Murther Saint herself, I swear if y' steal me darlin' Lily, I'll see y' in yer grave."

Chance turned to his side and reached for Jenna. He found only an empty bed. He came awake suddenly, almost alarmed, thinking that maybe he had dreamed her being there with him. But he couldn't have, for the smell of her perfume lingered on the sheets and the pillow he'd pulled up under his arm. Rolling to his back, he felt peculiarly alone.

Morning light spilled through the window, an indication he'd slept longer than he should have. From outside a stagecoach driver hollered at his team to "Get up!" as they started their morning run between Coeur d'Alene and Rathdrum.

He forced himself up and pulled his clothes on,

deciding she must have woke early and gone into the adjoining room to have coffee and read a book or the paper. He sauntered to the open door and was relieved to see her standing by the window. She was beautiful in the morning light and desirable as ever, in a walking dress of blue-gray Sicilienne. It was most unfortunate that she wouldn't be making the return trip with him upriver.

"There you are," he said. "You should have woke me."

He gathered her into his arms, but she gently extricated herself and went to the mirror to pin her hat on. He was puzzled by her distant, cold attitude.

"Is something troubling you this morning, Jenna?"

She evaded his direct gaze. "No. I'm just worried about getting the payroll back to camp with no one getting hurt."

"We'll be all right," he tried to assure her.

"I hope so," she replied. "Now, we'd better eat breakfast and get over to the bank."

It was ten o'clock by the time the guards had the strongbox loaded into the wagon from the bank's back door. One man would drive; the others would guard it on horseback.

Chance and Jenna emerged on the boardwalk. Nothing looked amiss in the bright light of the early morning, but if anyone had gotten word of the shipment, the danger wouldn't be here, anyway. It would be somewhere along the Mullan Road.

Chance untied his buckskin from the hitching rail. Jenna remained on the boardwalk, watching him swing into the saddle. A troubled look was in her eyes, and he guessed she was worried about him getting the shipment back without incident.

He sidled the buckskin alongside the boardwalk and, leaning down toward her from the saddle, stroked her cheek with his fingertips. "Don't worry.

The BRC won't lose any more money. Just promise me you'll be careful returning to camp day after tomorrow."

"The BRC is the least of my worries, Chance. Take care of yourself. Now go. The guards are waiting."

Jenna turned and hurried away, quickly blending in with the morning's bustling crowd. She vanished around the corner and he reluctantly turned the buckskin toward the dock. While she'd seemed concerned about his safety, there was something more about her demeanor this morning that bothered him. He couldn't quite put his finger on what it was, but he had the uneasy feeling that the distance between them had suddenly become more than physical.

Chapter Twenty-One

"This had better be good, Durfey," Henry said, stepping from the saddle. "You know how dangerous a meeting this close to camp could be."

In the distance they heard the discordant sounds of hammering, of dynamite shattering segments of mountains, of wagons groaning beneath their loads of dirt and rock and ballast.

Durfey jerked his hat off and revealed a long, ugly gash along the side of his head. "Somebody busted into my tent night before last and was going through my record books when I woke up, and he hit me in the head with something. I didn't see who it was, but I'll stake my life it was Killeen. He seemed to know right from the beginning I was involved with this."

The others exchanged glances, wondering if it could be true. Killeen had been in Leaman's tent—albeit to leave a purchase receipt—but Leaman had felt some of his things had been moved.

"Maybe the law's got somebody investigating you," Ives commented, leaning indolently against a tree.

"Have you been keeping your record books the way Leaman told you to?" Henry questioned. He didn't like any of this. They had to keep things going smoothly, and if anybody could mess them up, it would be Durfey.

"You don't need to worry. There's nothing in there that can finger us one way or the other, even on that payroll heist."

The three said nothing, but Durfey saw the doubt written all over their faces. His voice rose in anger and a degree of panic. "Somebody's on to us, I tell you! I could have been killed just as easily as I was hit over the head. Your damned plans are falling apart, it appears to me."

Henry didn't like having doubt cast on his plans, especially by an idiot like Durfey, who'd been chosen only as a scapegoat, anyway. When his usefulness was over, they'd get rid of him just as they had Barlow, but they couldn't afford for him to be killed until the line was finished.

Durfey continued his whining. "Maybe blowing up those bridges was too drastic. One would probably have been enough. I'm being blamed for it all because I haven't had equal damage. Maybe we ought to blow up one of our own to make it look good."

Ives was amused. "Then the money we made from the BRC would be for nothing, Durfey. Why don't you quit worrying so damn much and put your energy into getting that track laid."

Leaman, who had found a seat on a large boulder, cleared his throat. "Maybe it's time to get rid of Killeen and end our problem," he said in his whispery voice. "If it was him snooping around, we can't take any more chances waiting until the road's done. It won't take long to put the tracks down now that most of the grading is done. Solomon might not think it's necessary to bring in another engineer at this point if Killeen were to show up dead."

Ives gathered his horse's reins. With arrogant ease, he settled into the saddle. "If it was Killeen, then he's getting too nosy for his own good. We'll watch for the first opportunity to put an end to his excessive inquisitiveness."

"Make it good," Durfey said as they all mounted, preparing to leave. "I don't want the blame for no more killings."

Durfey led the way from the ravine. Henry brought up the rear, troubled that things weren't going the way he'd planned. Killeen was not only a threat to their plans, but he was also a threat to Henry's plans where Jenna was concerned.

Killeen had even put ideas in Solomon's head. The day Henry had gone to Coeur d'Alene to talk to him about Killeen, the old man's fingers had curled around his wrist like the sharp claws of a hawk.

"Killeen seems to think you're after Jenna for my money," Solomon had said. "Let me tell you, Henry. You won't have Solomon Enterprises."

"Killeen doesn't know what he's talking about," Henry had responded. "If anything, he's after it himself. I've noticed the way he looks at Jenna."

"Killeen is no stranger to me, Henry. I can't guarantee that he isn't interested in Jenna, but I know for a fact he wants my fortune about as badly as he wants a bullet in the head. But I *have* known for years that you think you have some claim to Solomon Enterprises because you believe I'm the one who destroyed your fortune. But you lost it because of greed and stupidity, Henry. I did nothing but pull you up out of the gutter . . . and don't you forget that I can drop you back into it just as easily. If the thought has even crossed your mind to marry Jenna for my money, you'd better do some rethinking."

Solomon's words had cut too close to the truth, and Henry didn't want to hear the truth. It was easier to blame broken fortune on the likes of the baron. Solomon *had* pulled him up out of the gutter, but he had made damned sure he'd never walk on the board-walk again.

As for Jenna, no matter how she might deny it, he felt there was an attraction between her and Killeen. If he was going to propose to her, he'd better do it soon. He might be risking her friendship, but it was either that or risk losing Solomon Enterprises forever—and he would have it, because after Solomon was dead, he couldn't do anything to prevent it. With Jenna as his wife, she'd give him anything.

Killeen was the most immediate problem, however, and he was definitely going to have to be eliminated as soon as possible.

Excitement increased when the first shipment of railroad ties was dumped off the steamboat at Old Mission Landing three weeks later. Along with them came steel rails, spikes, and hammers. The next day several hundred experienced tracklayers disembarked from the steamer, ready to go to work.

There were no onlookers, no applauders, except for the members of the grading and bridge crews. This momentous step toward the Bitterroot Railroad's completion was downplayed because Durfey had already completed a mile of track and had hosted a party over a week ago for that occasion, which had drawn a large assemblage to see the first spike driven on his line. There had been banners, a bandbox, political figures, speeches, music, food brought by the local ladies, and photographers capturing Durfey driving that first spike. Durfey was being applauded as the man to bring the first railroad through the Coeur d'Alenes and the man to reach Silver Bend first, subsequently winning the contracts to haul the thousands of pounds of stockpiled ore in every mine from the Bunker Hill to the Gold Hunter.

When Henry had questioned Solomon about holding their own assemblage, Solomon had simply snorted and said, "Get on with the damned track,

274

Henry, and if we ever arrive at Silver Bend, I'll host the biggest party the Coeur d'Alenes has ever seen."

The tracklayers started tossing down the ties and the rails with no fanfare. From the steamer came flatcars that could be pulled along the newly laid track by horses. One car held nothing but the railroad ties, which were black from their soaking in creosote, a solution that prevented rot. Another flatcar held the rails and spikes. Still another had miscellaneous supplies.

There were five ties to every twenty-eight feet of rail. Soon the men were working in an unbroken rhythm. Five men hefted the steel rails from a flatcar and, on command, dropped them in perfect alignment, four feet eight and a half inches apart, the distance of standard gauge. Behind the tracklayers came the spikers and bolters. In a musical rhythm, the klink of the hammers drove the spikes.

The steel rails hummed with energy and the men worked them proudly. Soon their labors brought sweat to their brawny bodies, and their muscled torsos gleamed in the hot sun as if oiled. They lifted the hammers and let them fall; three strokes to the spike, ten spikes to the rail, four hundred rails to the mile.

The spike drivers developed a grunting exaltation of breath to accompany the rhythmic ring of their sledgehammers. Toward the end of the day when the men began to tire, they also began to sing, as though song were a secret remedy that would take their minds from their work and sustain them until they could lay down their hammers at the day's end. From up and down the river, they could be heard singing the well-known song:

> *"Yonder comes the train, comin' down the track,*
> *Carry me away but ain't gonna carry me back,*
> *My honey babe, my blue-eyed babe."*

275

At sundown the men turned in, but excitement was still high, for they'd made good progress that first day. By the end of the week, the crew was catching up to Durfey's men. The closer they got to his men across the river, the faster they worked, determined among themselves—for the sake of their manly pride—that they were going to beat the other crew of tracklayers even though they'd started second. Before long it was known throughout the Coeur d'Alenes that there was, indeed, a race.

It didn't take Durfey long to retaliate against the sudden advancement of the BRC's crew. At the end of the third week of laying rails, word reached the Bitterroot crew that a portion of the track back by Old Mission Landing had been torn up.

Chance rode up the line to see the damage, accompanied by Solomon in a buckboard. Jenna, as had often been the case over the last two weeks, had elected not to accompany them. Since her grandfather was present, she had taken a back seat and remained virtually out of sight and completely unavailable to anything but evening conversation, and only then in the company of her grandfather. When they had been together, she'd been distant, as she had been in Coeur d'Alene, and Chance wondered what could have happened that last night they'd shared together to bring about the change in her.

While she hadn't completely broken her agreement to work with Chance, she was nonetheless forcing him to work with Solomon. He wondered if she was doing it on purpose, trying to make him see the side of her grandfather that she insisted existed. Indeed, that side did exist, but so did the other. And it was that which he couldn't bring himself to forgive or forget.

He and Solomon reached the site where the tracks had been torn up. The guards were found tied, gagged, and blindfolded. After they were released they volunteered what information they could, but no one had seen anything.

Chance and Solomon started back to camp. Scowling, Chance said, "I've half a notion to turn the men loose on the other side of the river and give Durfey a taste of his own medicine. I might not have proof that he's behind it, but I'd stake the Wapiti he is."

"Yes," Solomon replied, "but if we're wrong about him and get caught, then we'll be the ones in jail instead of him. We'd better give Ritchy a chance to collect some good solid evidence first. The last time I met with him, he hadn't come up with anything."

"This road is costing you a lot," Chance said. "Do you think it'll be worth it in the end?"

Solomon shrugged. "It's my last hurrah." His gaze followed the length of the winding road ahead, almost as though he saw the end of his own life around the tree-shaded bend. "It'll be that much more money that some fortune hunter won't be getting. And after having talked with Henry, I tend to agree with you. I think he *is* interested in marrying Jenna. I just hope he isn't merely trying to get even with me through her. I know he cares for her, but who knows the extent of a man's motivations?"

Chance wasn't content to believe that Henry might be honorable. There wasn't much about the man he was content with. As a matter of fact, he wasn't content about Leaman and Ives, either, but he hadn't mentioned his suspicions about the former because Solomon seemed to think so highly of the man. He needed proof before he said anything. And hopefully Ritchy was finding it.

"Well, it wouldn't bother me if Paterson *did* get all your money," Chance replied. "It would serve him right to carry a burden like that around for the rest of his life."

Solomon chuckled. "It's only a burden if you let it

be, Chance. Now, ride on ahead. I know you've got things to do. I'll be along, but at a slower pace."

Chance didn't argue, he just kicked his buckskin into a lope. He was anxious to see Jenna for a few minutes without the old man around.

The camp was quiet except for Moody rattling his pans in preparation for supper. The aroma of the food made Jenna's stomach turn. Deciding some fresh air might help, she left the tent and found a shady spot beneath a giant conifer tree.

She drew her knees up and circled them with her arms. Almost immediately she put her legs back down, having the fleeting concern that the position might put undue pressure on the baby growing inside her.

Jenna placed her hand on her flat stomach. There was no outward evidence of its existence, but she had missed her menses two weeks ago and had begun getting ill shortly after. She'd seen enough pregnant women to know the signs.

She envisioned holding the tiny soft bundle as she had other women's babies. She would cherish it whether it was a girl or a boy. It would most certainly have Chance's complexion and black hair, his green flashing eyes that openly expressed every mood.

But in truth, what was she to do? She'd longed for a child for years, but she'd wanted love and marriage to be part of it, a husband who would want the baby as much as she did. A husband who would want her, first and foremost. She doubted Chance would be pleased about it. He would feel obligated to marry her, and then he would never forgive her for forcing him to become part of the empire that had hurt his family so much. She wanted him, but only if he willingly wanted her.

She would have to tell her grandfather sooner or later, too. He had her up on a pedestal, his little girl who could do no wrong, make no mistakes. He didn't even consider Philip *her* mistake, but rather his own for not seeing the man's true character. What would he think of her now? And of course the press would have a heyday with it.

Possibly the best thing to do to save her grandfather the shame would be to go to Europe or California or someplace far from New York and have the child, raise it there, and start a new life under an assumed name. If she could never have a man's love in this life, then she would give what she had to a child.

The sound of hoofbeats coming down the road interrupted her thoughts. Jenna recognized Henry as the rider. She was admittedly disappointed that it wasn't Chance. Even though she'd been careful not to be alone with him for fear he would somehow sense her condition, she still yearned to be near him, to see him at the end of the day, to have supper with him and her grandfather. She could still hope he would put the past behind him and decide to face the future anew . . . and with her.

Henry saw her and drew rein a few feet away. Folding his arms over the saddle horn, he smiled down at her. "Now, don't you look as pretty as a mountain meadow."

She returned his smile. "Thank you for the compliment. How are things going on the line?"

He swung to the ground and sat next to her, holding the ends of his horse's reins so it could crop the grass at their feet.

"The work is made much more bearable knowing I can return to camp and find your lovely smile awaiting me." He lifted her hand to his lips, kissing it gallantly.

"Aren't we full of flattery today?"

279

He looked away from her, almost self-consciously, and focused on the toe of his boot. Seriousness replaced his smile. "It wasn't just flattery, Jenna. I really do care for you. As a matter of fact . . . I love you."

She ran a hand up his back in a soothing gesture. "And I love you, Henry. But why the glum expression?"

She saw something akin to agony in his eyes. He wanted to speak but seemed to be having a hard time getting the words out. Still holding her hand, he continued, "Yes, Jenna, you love me—as a friend. God, I don't see how I can hide it much longer. It's been torture as it is."

"Henry, whatever are you talking about?"

"I'm talking about love, Jenna." He looked deep into her eyes. "And not just the love of friends. But love the way a man loves a woman. I want to marry you, Jenna. I have for several years, but I was afraid you'd turn me down. And then I decided I had to quit being a coward and just bare my soul to you. I wasn't exactly planning on doing it at this moment, but—"

The seriousness in his eyes dispelled any notion that he might be joking. He must have seen her inclination to bolt, for his grip tightened on her hand.

"Hear me out, Jenna. In all honesty, is there anything wrong with our friendship turning to love?"

Jenna's first thoughts were of Chance. She loved him. She didn't love Henry—in that way. She'd experienced a passion with Chance that she seriously doubted she would ever feel again with any other man.

She found it difficult, almost embarrassing, to meet Henry's solemn gaze. She must have been blind not to see his love for her. Even Chance had accused her of having a love affair with him. Had Chance—and everybody else—seen how Henry felt? But how could she respond now . . . now that she was pregnant with Chance's child?

The contents of her stomach suddenly threatened to come up as they had so often here lately. "This is so sudden, Henry."

"For you, but not for me. Think about it, Jenna. Maybe you'll allow your feelings for me to change as mine have for you. I'll wait for however long it takes you to get Killeen out of your system—yes, I know you're attracted to him. But we both know he'll be gone when this road is finished and you'll never see him again."

His words cut too painfully close to the truth. She might agree with him, might even believe what he said, but if the thoughts were only in her mind and left unsaid, then there was still hope that something would change.

He laid his hand on her cheek. "You've got to put him behind you just as you did Dresden. He'll only hurt you, too."

"All this talk of Chance . . . I really don't think you know him, Henry. He's not like Philip at all. He's a good man."

Even as she spoke, it occurred to her that if she were to accept Henry's proposal, it would save both her and her grandfather from the shame of what she'd done. But Henry would have to know the truth about her pregnancy, and she doubted he'd want her then. He hated Chance—she saw it in his eyes—and he wouldn't want to have anything to do with Chance's child, let alone raise it as his own.

"Henry, I need to go now. I need to think."

He came to his feet with her, and before she could turn away, he drew her into his arms. Weak and confused, she couldn't seem to break away.

"Think about what I've said, Jenna. Believe me, Killeen is only an interlude in your life. I'll be here forever."

He tilted her chin up and kissed her lips gently,

much in the same way he had always kissed her cheek or her forehead. But it was different now because she knew where his heart was. Yet no sparks of flaming desire came alive within her. Oh, how wonderful it would be if Chance had spoken these words of love!

Above the pounding confusion in her brain, she heard another rider approaching. She tried to break free, but Henry held her tightly. When she finally managed, she found herself staring up into Chance's hurt and angry eyes as he brought his buckskin to a dancing halt in front of them.

She wanted to tell him it wasn't what he thought, but before she could explain, he had galloped on into camp, leaving them in his dust. Something told her that if there had been anything between them, it was lost forever now. She might try to explain to him what she was doing in Henry's arms, but he would never believe her.

She stumbled away from Henry, away from the shade of the tree and into the forest. And she was thankful he didn't follow.

Chapter Twenty-Two

From down the road raced two men riding double on one of the supply mules. The traces dragging in the dirt were an indication that the mule had been unhitched from the wagon in haste; the mens' anxious faces alerted Chance to trouble.

"Mr. Killeen!" the man in front shouted. "Shang was blasting out a tunnel. There was a big explosion! Come quick!"

The tracklaying halted at the distressing news. Solomon Lee was in his buckboard, watching the progress. Jenna sat nearby astride Desperado.

Chance called down to the ganger, "Keep 'em working, O'Callaghan!" He turned to speak to Solomon, but the baron already had the reins in his hands.

"You and Jenna ride on ahead!" he said. "I'll follow!"

Twenty minutes later, Chance and Jenna reached the tunnel. Chance leaped to the ground before his horse had barely come to a halt. He rushed up to Henry, who was standing outside the tunnel with his hands in his pockets.

"What happened, Paterson? Is Shang dead?"

"Yeah. The only thing we can figure is that he was picking out a blast hole that misfired."

283

Ives sauntered over to join them. "There's a weak spot in the ceiling, about two hundred feet from the entrance. A bunch of rock gave way after Shang's last blast. Ain't much left of him. What do you want us to do with the parts?"

Chance cursed inwardly. Shang had been a good man, and he had a family back in China he'd been sending his money to. "All we can do now is say a few words over him, then ship his body back to China."

Solomon arrived in the buckboard and joined Jenna and the others as they gathered around the wagon that would take Shang's remains to Coeur d'Alene and the undertaker. The heat of early September bore down upon the small assemblage. In its stillness, the air was still thick with smoke from distant fires.

Despite the shade of the pines, Jenna felt the nausea coming on again. She avoided meeting Chance's gaze from across the wagon but felt his eyes on her.

The day he'd seen Henry kissing her, she had returned from her walk and found him waiting outside her tent.

"So this is what you've been doing these past weeks," he'd said caustically. "I was wondering why you weren't riding with me anymore."

"It's not what you think, Chance."

"Can you honestly tell me you haven't been making love to him, too?"

She'd slapped his face. Slapped it so hard the imprint of her hand had left a red welt. And then she'd lashed at him verbally. "Believe what you want, Chance Killeen! You have no rights over my life. You've made it clear your bitterness outweighs any love you might feel for me."

A week had passed since then, and the subject hadn't been broached again. They had continued with their duties, almost as if nothing had happened, not even the nights in each other's arms.

His voice moved over the solemn group now like a soothing hand, wiping away her thoughts. "Yea, though I walk through the valley of the shadow of death, I will fear no evil."

When he finished the psalm, everyone mumbled "amen" and gathered in small groups, talking in low whispers.

Jenna started toward Desperado but felt a hand at her elbow. She was startled to see Chance by her side, offering assistance. Not wanting to make a scene in front of the men, she accepted, and he gave her a leg into the saddle. He seemed to want to say something, but the men were still close in, and then Solomon and Henry joined them. Solomon climbed into his buckboard, but Henry just leaned against the wheel.

"Well, Killeen," he said, "what are you going to do about a replacement for Shang? We don't have another man on this crew who can handle dynamite without blowing himself up on the first try. And the other crews can't spare any of their blasters."

Chance was troubled by Shang's death and the problems it was creating, but it was difficult to keep his mind off Jenna. Now he had to deal with Paterson's arrogance, acting as if this setback were Chance's alone.

"We'll have to see if we can find somebody," he snapped. "And if it takes a few days, then so be it."

"It's our last tunnel," Paterson continued, "and the tracklayers are progressing. They'll be caught up to us soon. It could take us a long time to find a reputable blaster."

"I see as we have no choice."

"You've had some experience in your mine," he said challengingly. "Why don't you handle what little is left?"

"Because I'm not a blaster, Paterson. I've helped my partner drill holes and set dynamite, but always under his supervision. He's the expert."

"Is that your Irish friend who helped rescue me from the river?" Solomon queried. At Chance's affirmative nod, he added, "Could you get him?"

"I don't know if he can leave the mine."

Solomon gathered the reins and prepared to leave. "Make it worth his time, Chance. Offer him a bonus or something." He slapped the reins lightly across the horse's rump and headed back to the main camp on a lively clip.

Jenna nudged Desperado into a lope to catch up with him. Chance would have liked her to come with him to Bayard, maybe get things straightened out again between them and meet his mother. Yes, he'd like her to meet his mother.

He pulled his eyes from her retreating figure and turned to his waiting crew. He saw their hopeful anticipation. They wanted to wrap up the tunnel in the worst way. Well, so did he.

"All right. Finish mucking it out, boys. I'll get Delaney."

The heat dissipated as the shadow of night stretched out over Bayard. All that remained of the sunset was a mixture of gold, amethyst, and fuchsia, creating a rubescent glow that fanned upward above the mountains and brushed its color upon gossamer clouds stretched thinly across the sky like strands of colored taffy.

Chance dismounted in front of his mother's boarding house. He didn't hear the clatter of dishes from inside or voices in conversation, so he knew he'd missed the evening meal.

He wrapped the reins around the hitching rail and went inside. The parlor was empty and so was the kitchen. The men from the mine had probably gone to the saloons or brothels. As for his mother, he decided to check out back in her garden.

As he suspected, she was there, pulling weeds. She turned at the sound of his booted feet in the garden rows. "Chance!" A smile burst upon her face. "I was beginning to think you'd wait until that road was finished before you came home for a visit."

They hugged each other and he kissed her cheek. "Sorry, Mama. Everything's been going wrong, and I can't even get away long enough to get drunk and flirt with the girls."

She laughed and went back to pulling weeds. "I don't believe getting drunk is a prerequisite, is it? As for the girls, is all you're ever going to do is flirt?"

If it weren't for his own mother's love affair all those years ago, he might even now have Jenna for his wife. But it wasn't fair to judge her life or the passions she might have had. God knows, he could understand the consequences of passion. Who was to say that his passion might not affect some child of his in the future?

"You're one to talk, Mama," he countered lightly. "You flirt with every miner in town. You've got them all hopelessly in love."

"I do not!" she denied, laughing.

"Ha! And you could take your pick of them, too, if you would. I don't think Dad would have expected you to remain a widow for the rest of your life."

Lily pulled off her gloves. Her smile faded despite her effort to keep it in place. There was no need to tell Chance that she and Bard had planned to marry. She wasn't even sure they were going to now. Bard hadn't been his usual self lately and it appeared as though he might be getting cold feet.

"Speaking of men, Mama," Chance smiled, "why did Solomon come to see you?" He felt the twinge of betrayal again, but he needed answers and Solomon wouldn't give them to him.

"He just came to visit. To see how I was."

287

"You'd like me to absolve him, wouldn't you, Mama? I guess it would make it easier for both of you to pick up where you left off." He hadn't wanted it to sound so bitter, but it had.

Her eyes flashed. "What exactly do you mean by that?"

Being at odds with his mother the minute he stepped foot on the place hadn't been his intention, but there was no use beating around the bush now that the subject had been brought up.

"Listen, I know you and Solomon were lovers," he said, half apologetically, "and I'm not condemning you. But I don't understand how could you forgive him for what he did to all of us, and how you could go to him in Coeur d'Alene as if you still wanted him."

Lily sighed and rubbed her forehead. "I guess it's time to explain it all. I should have years ago. First and foremost, Chance, I want you to know I loved your father. But sometimes in a person's life, someone comes along who is totally fascinating . . . who draws you to them like the proverbial moth to a flame. I couldn't help but respond to the exciting magnetism between Solomon and me. But it didn't diminish my feelings for your father. It merely made me realize just how much I did love him.

"You probably didn't realize how much your father was gone with that damned short line of his," she said angrily in remembrance. "Solomon gave me the attention I needed . . . that your father gave to his new business and his associates. If you want to blame anyone for what happened, you should blame me, not Solomon. Not even your dad. He did what he did to help us, and I allowed my loneliness to rule my better judgment."

"But why did you go see Solomon again in Coeur d'Alene?"

"Because I was afraid he would die, and I wanted to

see him again before he did. And because . . . well, I was afraid he might do to you what he had Duke. I couldn't let that happen again.''

If Chance had hoped to receive fuel from her for his own bitterness, he had been grossly mistaken. "God, Mama, I'm sorry. I had no idea you did it for me. But what is it about him that he always manages to capture the sympathy of women and the contempt of men?''

She shrugged. "I suppose it's because women need and want a strong man. And because men are frightened and jealous of power that rests in anyone's hands but their own. He won't compromise his principles, whether or not anyone else thinks those principles are admirable. He goes after what he wants, where the rest of us let people and things stand in our way. Nobody wants to admire those seemingly greedy traits in an ambitious person when it's so much easier to hate them.''

She turned and walked back to the house. He caught up with her just before she opened the screen door.

"Thank you for talking to me, Mama. I needed to know if I've been holding on to something that doesn't mean anything anymore. And you helped to answer my question.''

He kissed her cheek and started back to his horse.

"I'm glad I helped you with whatever it was," she called after him. "But where are you going? You just got here.''

He ran backward like a kid, grinning, hoping to lighten the mood that had gotten too tense. "I'm going to get drunk and flirt with the girls, what else?''

She waved him away with a smile of understanding. "All right. Go on and enjoy yourself.''

Chance rode to the Widowmaker. To his surprise, he found Delaney sitting alone at a corner table, looking about as sour as a shirt that had been worn for two weeks in the mines. In one hand he had a glass. In the other a bottle. He poured and drank, poured and drank. He was nearing the bottom of the bottle and Chance wondered what it was that was keeping him upright in the chair.

He didn't even look up when Chance stopped in front of the table. His blurry gaze went no farther than Chance's legs. He slurred his words through a brogue that was muddier than usual. "Go to the divil, you thickheaded vagabond. I'm sharin' me whiskey with no one but meself tonight."

Chance pulled out a chair and sat down. Delaney's head came up, then swayed around on his neck before he managed to set it stationary. At the same time, his fist tightened on the whiskey bottle and a snarl sullied his kind face. He finally recognized Chance through a haze thick enough to cut.

"Aye, 'tis me good frind, Keely." He poured himself another drink with an unsteady hand. "What in the world would bring you here, when it's mindin' the railroad you ought to be?"

Chance slipped the bottle from Delaney's hand. "I just came to see how things were at the mine." He took a swig directly from the bottle since he didn't have a glass and at the moment was too indifferent to go get one.

Delaney reached for the bottle again but Chance took another swig, and the Irishman slumped in his chair. "Aye, the mine is fine. 'Tis the one thing I can handle."

"Did a mule kick you in the head or something, Delaney? You never drink alone."

Delaney stared at him through glazed eyes. "I came to this great land o' the mountains in search of a pot o' gold I was told was lyin' somewhere abouts. Here's me word, fresh and fastin'. I niver mit an Irishman

290

who did not want a pot o' gold. But curse me luck, Keely. Why mightn't it be me good fortune to be the man that it was laid out fer to find?"

"I can't understand a damn thing you're saying, Delaney. You and I found the Wapiti and it might be silver, but it's still your pot of gold."

"Aye, to be sartin, but I've spent me life thinkin' gold was gold when, in fact, 'twas love all along." He stared down at the glass and then drained the last drop of amber liquid onto his lips, licking it off with his numb tongue. "'Twould be monstrous sweet indeed if I'd been touched by the faeries, Keely. But who can compete with the divil? Would you be knowin'?"

Chance didn't know what to think of Delaney's ramblings, and this was definitely not a good time to ask him if he'd come with him tomorrow to dynamite the tunnel.

"A snakin' old sinner, he is," Delaney continued. "If the man were a sow, he'd eat his own farrow."

"Who, Delaney? Who are you talking about?"

Delaney lifted his gaze to Chance. His hazel eyes narrowed. "That thievin' rogue King Solomon, ov coorse. He's tryin' to coort yer murther, Keely. And I'll tell you what'll become o' him. By the seven blessed candles, if he hurts her, I'll chop him as small as herbs and put him in a pot o' stew."

If Chance's comprehension was accurate, then it would appear that Delaney was in love with his mother and he knew Solomon had stepped back into the scene.

Against the Irishman's wishes, Chance dragged him from the saloon. He untied the buckskin, gripped Delaney's muscular arm in one hand, and navigated him down the street toward the boarding house. When Delaney saw their direction, he rebelled and tried to break free. But he only managed to stumble and weave. His legs crumbled and twisted as though there was no bone in them. He almost went down.

"I'm going to pour some hot coffee down you, Delaney."

"Ye're a black-hearted traitor, Keely. You won't even let yer frind get drunk."

"You're pretty drunk. Now it's time to sober up."

"God forbid! 'Tis not the likes o' you I'd be wantin' by me sickbed!"

Chance hauled and dragged him up the back steps, which was no easy feat, considering the bulk of the man. He stumbled a few times before he finally reached the kitchen chair and fell into it. His mother had apparently retired to her room, for she was nowhere around. As soon as he caught his breath, he fixed a pot of coffee and stoked up the fire in the cook-stove.

When he turned to Delaney, the man was laid out over the table with his head on his massive arms. In seconds, loud snores rumbled from deep within him. Chance pulled the coffeepot from the stove and sat down next to Delaney at the table.

He sat there for hours. And as he sat, everything unfolded before him as clear as a picture.

What would they all do if his mother married Solomon Lee? The irony of it might have been humorous if it hadn't been so devastating. Here was Delaney, finally finding the woman he loved at the age of fifty. As for himself, he had been ready to sacrifice his own future, his own love, for the foolish past; for his mother's sake, for the sake and the memory of a dead man, and for something that he had never been a part of. He and Jenna had simply been outsiders looking in. And they still were.

The present was shaped by the hands of Solomon Lee and Lily Killeen. The future might very well be, too. The two of them would take what they wanted—

what they could get—now as they had then. They'd had no consideration for what he might think or feel. In reality, they'd had no obligation to. They had their own lives to live, their dreams to fulfill, their hearts to satisfy.

For sixteen years now, he'd been adamantly determined to remain enemies with the dynasty that had temporarily laid waste to his family's lives. He suspected now that one of the reasons was that he hadn't truly *wanted* to give up his hatred for Solomon Lee. It had been a powerful incentive to succeed, to continue where his father had been forced to stop. It had given him a purpose in life. Every man had to be driven by something. If not by love, then by hate. But now he had love.

Yes, he saw it all clearly. Loyalty to a memory could do nothing but ensure his own loneliness. Maybe Henry Paterson had been right all along in wanting Solomon's fortune because he figured it was rightfully his, or at least part of it.

It was time to take some lessons from King Solomon himself. Blood money or not, he would take what he wanted. And Solomon's fortune be damned.

Chapter Twenty-Three

The big ship rocked endlessly, making Delaney green with sickness. What a blessing it would be when it docked in America. If it didn't dock soon, he feared his father would be burying him at sea just as they had his dear mother.

"Wake up, Delaney. Rise and shine."

He managed to pull his eyes open, but they felt as if they were sealed with glue. Through a blur, he saw Chance standing over him, shaking him. Outside, dawn was barely breaking. He was at the table in Lily's kitchen and vaguely remembered Chance bringing him there last night. Then he smelled the coffee.

He lunged to his feet and ran for the door, holding his hand over his mouth. He'd barely reached the step when the sour contents of his stomach were expelled.

Chance came out on the porch behind him and shoved a towel in his hand. "Ready for coffee now?"

Delaney's stomach lurched a second time, but nothing happened, bless the Mother Saint herself. "Curse yer impudence, y' bloody fool," he choked as he wiped his face clean. "No, I wouldn't be wantin' coffee."

He draped the towel over the porch railing, then headed down the wooden steps to the path that led

294

out of the yard. He didn't know where he was going, but Lily would be in the kitchen soon to start breakfast and he was in no condition to be seen by her.

He stopped short at the sight of Chance's buckskin tied to the hitching rail, already saddled. "To be shoor, Keely, I'm losin' me faith in y', leavin' that poor crayture tied to the rail all night."

Chance was right behind him, chuckling as he always did whenever Delaney was in misery of some sort. "No," he replied. "I was up early. I've got to be going."

Delaney gave him a once-over. "Ye're gettin' to be a scarce item around this mine, Keely. I'm beginnin' to think ye've turned monstrous sweet on old King Solomon."

Chance tightened the cinch, laughing again. "Not hardly. I'm looking for a blaster. I lost my last one."

Delaney sauntered closer, tucking his hands into his front pockets while his Irish eyes failed to conceal his sudden interest. "And how did you lose the man, might I be askin'? Was it in the woods y' lost him? Or did he blow himself up?"

"The latter, unfortunately." Chance dropped the saddle's fender and readjusted his saddlebags behind the cantle. "We're on the last tunnel. We should be wrapping it up pretty soon."

"It's ungrateful y' are, not even stayin' fer breakfast."

"I've got to go. Daylight's wasting."

Delaney licked his lips with a tongue that still felt as thick and dry as an old crust of bread. "I can do the blastin' fer y', Keely. It'll at least keep work progressin' 'til y' find someone else. Y' know all y' had to do was ask."

"Are you sure you want to? It'll take you from the mine for a while. Would the men be able to keep busy?"

"We've got ore by the piles to be hauled to

295

Thompson Falls. It's behind I've gotten without yer help. But there's more I've been meanin' to tell y' about, Keely. That vein we've been workin' on is gettin' as wide and pretty as any I've ever seen. It's rich we'll be, and it won't be long now."

Chance grinned from ear to ear, glad to hear the news. "So lady luck has finally come our way?"

"'Twould seem."

Chance had some reservations. "If that's the case, maybe you really ought to stay here. I can find somebody else."

Delaney glanced back at the boarding house. He'd been so heartbroken since he'd found the locket that he could barely think straight. He'd given Lily the perfume and she'd loved it. He'd waited, hoping she might say something about Solomon's visit, but she never had. As much as he loved her, he knew she would be better off with Solomon. The old man didn't have too many years left, but no man had a guarantee on his life, especially one who worked with dynamite every day as he did.

He'd decided that Lily would be taken care of in the finest fashion by Solomon, and when the old man died he would leave her with enough money to keep her for the rest of her life. He didn't want to give her up, but he was no match for the baron. He was just a simple, hotheaded Irishman who had been born with nothing. Even if he should become rich before he died, he would still be a simple, unsophisticated man. It would be best for his darling Lily if he would step into the background of her life and let Solomon take the foreground.

"I'm goin' with y', Keely," he said stubbornly. "It's only a minute I'll be."

Delaney hurried back into the house through the front door and Chance sauntered back into the kitchen, deciding he'd have another cup of coffee

296

before he left. His mother was there, tying on her apron.

"You're up early," she said, surprised to see him.

He leaned against the pie keeper and watched while she took ingredients from the pantry for the morning meal. He wanted to tell her about Jenna and his decision to marry her, but decided to wait to make sure Jenna would even consent.

"I'm afraid I've got to be going."

"About last night, Chance . . ."

"No, Mama," he interjected before she could say more. "Let's not discuss the past anymore. I've put it behind me where it belongs. I want to apologize to you for what I said and let you know I don't blame you for anything. I never did."

Her green eyes searched his. "And Solomon? Do you still blame him?"

He hesitated. "I'm trying not to, Mama. That's the best I can do." He set his coffee cup on the cupboard when he heard Delaney coming across the parlor. "Delaney's coming with me for a few days."

Her eyes filled with objection. "What do you need him for?"

"I lost my blaster. He's going to take his place."

Delaney stepped into the kitchen and stopped short at the sight of Lily. Chance saw the turmoil and indecision in his eyes. He was so far in love, he was drowning. His mother's expression wasn't quite so easy to read, but he wondered if she cared for Delaney or if it was Solomon who held her heart.

He stalked toward the door, suddenly angry as last night's thoughts came back with crushing intensity. Everything was happening all over again, and it was out of his control now just as it had been then. Only this time it was Bard Delaney who was going to get hurt instead of Duke Killeen.

He got Delaney's horse at the livery and was just

297

tying it to the hitching rail next to his buckskin when the Irishman came out of the house, followed by Lily. Delaney was unusually quiet as he mounted his horse. He gave Lily one last look and loped away. Chance wondered what had happened or been said between them, curious whether Delaney's determination to go with him had anything to do with it.

She handed him a sack. "Since neither of you can take the time to eat breakfast, at least take these rolls left over from supper." Her gaze strayed worriedly to Delaney's retreating figure. "And, son . . . have a safe trip."

When Chance and Delaney arrived at the tunnel, Solomon was taking his shade beneath the drooping boughs of an old pine tree while the men on the crew finished up the last of the bracing that had been destroyed by the blast.

Solomon shook hands with Delaney, although the Irishman acted none too eager to do it. Discussion of the situation commenced. Henry and Ives left the tunnel work to meet Delaney.

Chance's gaze wandered to Jenna's tent, and Henry saw the direction of his interest.

"She's asleep in her tent, Killeen," his top lip curled unamiably. "The heat's been bothering her—that and the smoke from the fires. She asked not to be disturbed."

Chance didn't like Paterson's possessive attitude and started toward the tent anyway. He had to talk to her now before another minute passed to change things.

"I *said* . . . she's sleeping!" Henry grabbed him by the arm.

Chance jerked free, his animosity toward Paterson rising so high it was hard to contain. But others were watching the exchange, waiting for his leadership.

He was torn between duty and desire. Duty won.

"All right. Is everyone ready to get started?"

They all nodded and Ives turned to Delaney. "We could have a couple of men help drill the holes for you, so you could get in there and get a blast off tonight. We can start clearing out the rock first thing in the morning after the dirt and fumes settle."

"I hear that Killeen and you work good together," Henry interjected. "Maybe you could get him to go in and help you. The two of you could get it done quicker."

"I intended on it, Paterson," Chance replied curtly.

"Good. Come on, Delaney. We'll show you where the dynamite is. We've got a couple of holes already started, but we decided last night to stop the men in case they weren't putting the holes in the right place."

The men started into the long tunnel. When completed, it would be nearly seven hundred feet in length, the longest on the line. Chance and Delaney walked side by side, carrying the leather tool pouches in one hand and their lamps in the other. Every man carried a lamp because the light from the entrance didn't reach far into the long tunnel. It merely remained at the end, a large eye watching them getting farther and farther away.

Delaney stopped occasionally to inspect the rock formation and any signs of slabbing.

"The rock's bad only in one place," Henry offered, "but not bad enough to be rock bolted. We've got it braced."

They walked another fifty feet and Henry showed him the spot. Delaney held up his lamp, as did the others, and looked at the area of the weak back, or ceiling. The back was so much higher than he was, to accommodate a train, that his light didn't do much to illuminate it. He could have climbed up the side of the bracing for a ways, but from what he could see, the bracing was good and tight. It was so good, in fact, that he could barely see the rock beneath.

Delaney decided they'd done a good job. He nodded his approval. Four hundred more feet and they came to the blast site. There were more men here finishing mucking out from Shang's last blast. They had only a few piles left to remove.

Delaney went to one knee and started to remove his tools from his pouch. "What's left here isn't bad, Mr. Paterson," he said. "You and the others can leave. We'll be gettin' started."

On command from Paterson, everyone in the tunnel gathered up his tools and retreated to the half-circle of light at the tunnel's entrance. Paterson and Ives waited until all the men were out of the tunnel, then they followed, leaving Chance and Delaney alone.

Chance and Delaney prepared their drills. Delaney examined the two holes that had been started, two feet apart. They were in accordance with the pattern he liked to use. Added to a third, they would form a rough triangle and angle to meet at the apex of a pyramid within the rock.

"We'll drill these out," he said, "then make the edgers."

They simultaneously lifted their compressed-air drills to the two predrilled holes. But Delaney lowered his. "Keely, it's bloody dark in here. Niver have I seen a tunnel so long. Would y' be so kind as to bring me a few more of those lamps and hang them about? If ye'll do that, I'll get started."

Chance nodded, set his drill down, and headed back down the tunnel, mumbling, "Your eyesight must be failing, Delaney. It's damn near as bright as—"

Suddenly, an explosion tore open part of the mountain behind Delaney's drill. The force threw

Chance to the ground. Chunks of rock hit him with vicious force, and he automatically covered his head with his arms to protect himself.

The blast had barely settled when the ground beneath him shook with another explosion farther down the tunnel toward the entrance. He heard a grinding rumble and snapping timbers, and knew the weak back and new braces had gone. Chance lunged up, freeing himself of the rocks and debris that had fallen on him. He sat up, coughing and choking. Dust suffocated him until he could barely breathe. He blinked and blinked again. He didn't know if he was blind or if the explosion had put out all the lamps. He turned his head in the direction he thought was the entrance—the direction he'd been facing when he'd gone down. There was no light there. No light anywhere. The tunnel was like a Cimmerian hell.

"Delaney!"

He weaved and staggered, falling down on the sharp rocks, ignoring the way they tore at his flesh. On his hands and knees he searched the ground. The fumes from the charge were suffocating. He fumbled for his bandana and pulled it over his nose.

"Delaney! Answer me! I can't see a goddamned thing!"

He heard movement and moaning in the rubble, then a raspy fit of coughing. He went forward toward the sound inch by inch, his chest burning from the effort and the fumes. At last he felt a human arm. He thrust the large chunk of rock aside until he could feel hair, a face, a beard.

"Delaney. Hold on. I'll get you out."

By feel alone, he removed rocks and more rocks until Delaney was clear. With strength that came from some super source, he hauled the Irishman into his lap.

"Keely?" He gasped and coughed. "Is that you?"

"I'm here, Delaney. Right here."

"I can't breathe, Keely."

Chance pulled his bandana over his head and positioned it over Delaney's mouth and nose. "This will make it easier."

Delaney groped for him, and Chance circled his hand with his own.

"'Tis darker than death, Keely. Am I blind?"

"If you are, then so am I. I don't know what happened. There were two explosions. One here and one down by the weak back. It blew out the lamps."

"How could there have been an explosion farther down?" Delaney asked in a weak voice.

"All I know is that when you started to drill out that hole, it exploded. There must have been a charge in it that went off when you hit it with the drill."

"Then we're trapped."

"It would seem so."

The dust and the fumes of the nearest charge of dynamite had begun to disperse down the long length of the tunnel. They could only hope the fumes would thin out even more, because the gases could be deadly. As it was, Chance had to put his arm over his nose and mouth to breathe. They both knew, too, that depending on the size of the cave-in that blocked the tunnel's only exit, it could take days to get them out.

The absolute darkness and stillness settled over them. Already the seconds ticking by seemed much too long. Chance suddenly wished he'd told Jenna he loved her.

"I hurt all over, Keely," Delaney said weakly. "And me arm feels bloody odd, it does."

Chance slid his hands around Delaney's face and felt the warm wetness of blood. He examined the massive shoulders and chest, then Delaney's arms.

Everything inside him tightened with raw fear. He felt again and his hand was filled with blood—a lot

302

of blood . . . and a stump of flesh where a forearm and hand should have been.

He went back on his haunches and into action. He undid his gun belt, stripped from his shirt, and by feel alone ripped it in half.

"Keely, what is it? What would you be doin'?"

"You're bleeding, Delaney. I'm going to try and stop it."

Chance emptied the cartridges in his revolver and cast them aside. He found the stump, severed below the elbow. With no sight, his senses came alive. He forced his fingers to be his eyes. Working against time, he knotted the shirt down good and tight on the severed limb, then used the gun barrel to make a tourniquet. Silently, he simultaneously cursed and prayed; cursed because Delaney could very well bleed to death, but prayed that the crew would get them out before that happened. Never in his life had he been so scared. God, if Delaney died . . .

"What're y' doin'?" Delaney asked groggily, turning his head toward the arm Chance was doctoring.

"Fixing you up. Now just lay quiet."

Delaney lifted his right arm across his chest. His fingers fell upon rock where his left forearm should have been. The realization of what had happened came with a gasp of horrified anguish.

"Me arm, Keely! Murther Saint, it's gone!"

He tried to rise, but Chance pressed him back down. "It's going to be all right, Delaney. The less you move, the less you'll bleed."

"The bloody hell! You bastard! Me arm is gone! What do y' mean it'll be all right? Let me up. Find me arm. Get it!"

"No!" Chance wrestled him to the ground. "What in the hell good do you think that will do? They can't sew it back on!"

A stream of cuss words came from Delaney, then

303

suddenly he collapsed. Chance lay on top of him, making sure he wouldn't try to move again.

Silence, heavy and oppressive, hung over them. They heard nothing but the shifting of the rock in the tunnel and the timbers farther away. Delaney lay as still as death, as if he'd passed out, but Chance sensed he was fully awake in the darkness, numb from shock, eyes staring upward. Chance was afraid the shock alone might kill him.

"Let's get out of this rock, Delaney. Come on. Can you walk a ways down the tunnel?"

There was no response.

Sensing Delaney was slipping into unconsciousness or possibly even death, Chance pulled him to his feet and got his shoulder under him. He hauled him carefully over the rocks, then found a place where the tunnel's floor felt relatively clear of debris. Chance sat down against the wall and laid Delaney's head across his thigh. But the Irishman started to shiver and shake. Chance drew Delaney's torso up against his chest and held on to him tightly in an effort to keep him warm, for already it seemed cold in the darkness, even to him.

"They'll be getting through the rock in no time," he said, trying to sound encouraging. "We'll get you to a doctor."

A strange noise came from Delaney. Chance cursed the darkness that kept him from seeing his friend, from seeing what was happening to him. He held him tighter, as if that alone could keep the life from going out of him. "What is it, Delaney? What's wrong?"

The sound continued, but no reply. Chance finally realized the burly man was breaking down, losing a grip on the pain and losing control over his mind. His chest began to heave with frightened sobs, which he was trying desperately to keep inside. His head began to thrash against Chance and he tried to rise

304

again. It took all Chance's strength to hold him down.

"It's going to be all right, Delaney. I'm here with you. We'll get you out."

Delaney released an anguished roar of denial, and then suddenly he started to scream.

Chapter Twenty-Four

The explosions jarred Jenna from her sleep. She came awake, realizing they had started blasting the tunnel again, which meant Chance must have returned with Delaney. She forced herself to a sitting position and sat for a moment to allow the sleep to leave her. She'd been sleeping too much lately, but it seemed she was tired all the time. At least when she was asleep, she wasn't sick.

After rising, she filled the metal basin with tepid water and splashed it on her face. She gradually became aware of the unusually loud commotion outside. She took the basin to the tent opening to empty it. Men were everywhere, racing frantically, grabbing up shovels and pickaxes and running to the tunnel. Others came with wheelbarrows. Some brought the carts and wagons that were used to haul the rock from the tunnel after the blasts. There was an urgency in their actions she'd never seen before. After a normal blasting, the crew always waited until morning to begin hauling out the muck, mainly to allow the fumes to settle.

Her grandfather stood in the center of an un-hitched wagon, shouting orders. On the ground, Henry and Ives were tearing open wooden crates that contained more shovels and pickaxes. She didn't see

Chance and Delaney. And suddenly she knew some-thing was wrong.

With a sudden wave of fear overcoming her, she lifted her skirt past her ankles and ran to the wagon. "Grandpa, what's wrong? Where's Chance and Delaney?"

He stepped down from the wagon and rushed to her, gripping her arms as if to offer support. "I'm sorry, Jenna, but Chance and Delaney were in the tunnel when two explosions went off unexpectedly. Much too soon. The weak back collapsed and blocked off the tunnel."

Physical weakness washed over her and she felt like she might faint. She held on to her grandfather tighter. "If the dynamite went off before planned, it could only mean—"

"They might still be alive, Jenna," he hesitated. "Don't think the worst yet."

She willed herself to be strong. Action would take her mind from the fear threatening to debilitate her. Before her grandfather could say more, she ran toward the shovels and tore one from Ives's extended hand. Ignoring the surprised stares of the men, she ran inside the tunnel to the cave-in. If they were still alive, time was of the essence. With urgent purpose, Jenna began to dig.

Lily was awakened in the middle of the night with word of the explosion. On horseback, she and the miners from the Wapiti raced to the tunnel site. It was barely daybreak when they arrived. The miners went to work immediately, giving some of the other men a break.

Solomon was there to meet her. Silent thoughts and fears passed between them and he pulled her into his arms. "Chance will be all right, Lily."

She wondered if she should tell him about

307

Delaney, but this hardly seemed the appropriate time to go into an explanation of her love for another man. She wiped away tears that began to slide down her face. She'd lost one man. She prayed she wouldn't lose these two who were the very essence of her life.

With Solomon next to her, she went to the tunnel to see the extent of the cave-in. It was then that she saw the blond-haired woman in the golden glow of the lantern light. She was shoveling with the men, helping fill the wheelbarrows and wagons that would take the rocks and dirt out of the tunnel. Her movements were steady and mechanical, like those of a machine. She appeared to be in a tired stupor. She was covered with dirt from head to toe, and her hair hung lose and bedraggled about her face.

Lily turned to Solomon. "That couldn't possibly be your granddaughter?"

Worry deepened the lines on his tired face. "Yes, it's Jenna. She's barely taken a break since the moment this happened yesterday afternoon. I can't make her stop. No one can."

"But why?" Lily asked, bewildered.

Solomon sighed. "If I'm not mistaken, she's in love with your son. And I believe Chance may be in love with her, too. That is, if he would admit it."

Lily was surprised, but it explained why Chance had been so troubled on his visit to Bayard. She had thought it was merely because of being forced to work with him, but now she saw his anxieties went much deeper, and she could well understand why.

It took her only a moment to realize what she had to do. She left Solomon's side and gathered up a shovel from one of the men who had stopped to rest. With the purpose only a woman can have when she sets her mind to something, she marched into the center of the activity and positioned herself by Jenna's side. Without a word, she too started to dig.

308

For the first time in hours, Jenna's movements faltered at the sight of the other woman. Lily's gaze locked with hers, and Jenna knew instantly that the black-haired, green-eyed woman was Chance's mother. The resemblance was strong. Where Chance was handsome, his mother was beautiful. It was no wonder her grandfather had been entranced by her all those years ago and remained so even to this day.

"They're going to be all right," Jenna said, refusing to believe otherwise.

Lily set her face squarely with determination. "Of course they will be, Jenna. We'll have them out in no time."

They worked in almost perfect rhythm. Solomon joined them, shovel in hand. Slowly, as an ant moves a piece of bread crumb by crumb from a picnic cloth, the rock and the dirt came out of the tunnel. More people came from town to help when news reached them of the trapped men. The crews divided into groups to alternate work and rest.

The afternoon sun moved to the mountaintops, marking twenty-four hours since the explosion. To Jenna, time had been forgotten. She focused her mind on a level where weariness didn't exist, a level that went beyond awareness of everything surrounding her, except her ultimate goal. In this way, she could go for hours and not feel the pain of her body. She could block out nearly everything going on around her as she slipped into an almost transcendental state.

At Lily's insistence, Jenna rested for a few hours but she couldn't sleep. She finally went back to her former station. Three hours later, she was lifting large chunks of rock into a wagon when Henry appeared by her side.

"I insist you leave this tunnel, Jenna."

She shrugged him off, staggering a little from the

weight of the rock as she heaved it into the wagon. "I can't stand to pace the floor and wait, Henry. I have never been any good at that. Now, leave me alone."

He forcibly jerked her around. So near exhaustion, she weaved and he had to grab her to keep her from falling. "Jenna, Chance isn't going to be alive. Face it! If the blast didn't kill them, the fumes from the charges would have."

"Let go of me, Henry."

A worker nearby intervened. "She only wants to be here when they get him out, Mr. Paterson. He's her partner. You can't blame her for that."

Henry was about to engage in more discussion of the matter when suddenly a shout went up from the main body of workers near the cave-in.

"We've broken through! Bring the stretchers!"

The mens' weariness disappeared as they scrambled to get an opening large enough to get Chance and Delaney out. Someone ran to get the doctor, who had been on standby in the main tent ever since word of the explosion. Jenna and Lily found themselves shoved to the side of the tunnel's walls as the activity hummed around them and more men came to help. In no time, they had enough dirt moved to get the men through a narrow opening. A number of them, armed with the stretchers and numerous lamps, squeezed through the opening, preceding Ives, Henry, and Solomon.

Jenna started in after them, but Solomon blocked her way. "No, Jenna. The back could still be weak. Stay here."

Now that the moment was here, she was afraid of the final reckoning of the disaster. She fought the tears that threatened to come.

As if reading her thoughts, Lily slipped an arm around her waist. Silent understanding passed between them. With almost deadly grips, they held

310

each other's hands. Jenna's heart pumped so fearfully she could scarcely breathe and she was afraid she was going to faint. A sharp pain pulsed through her, centering in her abdomen, but she forced herself to ignore it.

It seemed an eternity before they heard the men coming back down the tunnel. They weren't speaking. There were no voices of glad reunion and thankfulness at being rescued. The heavy way the rescuers' footsteps sounded against the tunnel's floor indicated that they carried someone.

Henry stepped through the opening. "Everyone back! Give us some room!"

Jenna tried to get over the rubble to be closer when they brought them through, but the workers who had been crowding around the opening surged away to make room, forcing her and Lily back again. She tried to read something from Henry's expression but saw only an angry set to his jaw.

The rescuers brought the first stretcher through the hole. A cry of anguish erupted from Lily's throat as she shoved men aside, rushing to the bloody body of the Irishman and dropping to her knees next to him. At the sight of his still form, his severed arm, and Lily's uncontrollable sudden sobs, fear for Chance's life rose up inside Jenna, threatening to choke her.

Jenna watched numbly as Lily placed her hands alongside Delaney's bushy face as carefully as if he were some fragile thing that might break as easily as a china teacup. Her heart went out to Lily, realizing in that poignant moment that the woman had worked for the lives of *two* men she loved, not just her son.

One of the rescuers tried unsuccessfully to pull Lily away from the stretcher. "We've got to get him to the doctor, ma'am. Please move aside."

Lily's sobs stopped, and she stared incredulously at

the man and then back to Delaney. "My God, he's alive?"

"Yes, ma'am. He's just unconscious."

"Oh, Bard!" Suddenly, she collapsed against his massive chest, weeping with utter relief and joy.

As if Delaney had heard the sweet sound of her voice, his eyelids fluttered and weakly opened. "Lily?" He lifted his hand to her arm.

Henry assumed authority. "All of you, clear out of here! It's over! Let's all go to our tents and get some rest." Angrily, he stalked from the tunnel behind the men carrying Delaney's stretcher.

Everything inside Jenna seemed to die. She glanced after him, feeling completely helpless.

It's over? But where's Chance?

Her strength vanished and her knees began to buckle. A haze descended over her like a suffocating blanket—strange and white, ringed with black. The pain in her body became almost more than she could bear. She was too tired to fight it any longer. Something warm and wet flowed down her legs, but she felt oddly disconnected from the sensations and the sudden pain of her body.

She groped for something to hold on to and found Lily's hand. She didn't want to faint in front of the men and show her weakness. She needed to go back to the tent with the others, with Lily and Delaney. It was over. At least Delaney was alive.

"Jenna."

The voice held a strained note, a note of extreme weariness, but it reached out and encircled her in a warm embrace all its own. She lifted her tear-filled eyes and saw him standing next to her grandfather. Surely she couldn't be dreaming. No dream would conjure up such a pathetic sight so completely covered with blood and dirt. But he was on his own two feet and had both arms.

The fear fled in a wave of overwhelming relief, and

with it the last of her strength. She reached out to him. "Chance, thank God you're—"

"Jenna!"

He rushed forward and caught her just as she crumpled to the ground, unconscious. Dropping to his knees, he gathered her in his arms. And it was then he saw the blood.

Chapter Twenty-Five

Chance shouldered his way through the men, ignoring their questions and curious eyes as he carried Jenna to her tent. Lily and Solomon ran on ahead to get the doctor.

Chance laid Jenna on her cot and covered her with a blanket. The amount of blood staining her skirt was entirely too much for her monthly menses, and she looked as pale as death itself. He'd been able to save Delaney, but this time he didn't have the slightest idea what to do. He only knew something was terribly wrong to bring on so much blood. And while he'd feared for Delaney's life, the fear in him now for Jenna's life cut into a place he'd not been aware existed.

He sat on the edge of the cot and took her hand in his. "Jenna. Wake up. Come on, honey. You've got to wake up."

She stirred at the sound of his voice but she seemed in a place too distant from which to return.

The tent flap lifted and the doctor, Uriah Drummond, entered with Solomon on his heels. One look at the blood and he was barking orders. "Everyone out. I'll summon you if I need you."

"What's wrong?" Chance asked. "Is she going to be all right?"

314

"I don't know the answer to either of those questions yet."

The impact of the news left Chance numb. He didn't want to leave Jenna, but Solomon took him by the arm and directed him toward the tent's door.

"By the way, Killeen," Drummond said as he found the basin and proceeded to scrub, "you did a good job with Delaney. Your mother's in there now, cleaning him for surgery. You might clean yourself up so I can look at your injuries later."

Dazed, Chance stepped outside. Disregarding the doctor's orders, he left Solomon to his own devices and went to join his mother in Delaney's tent. She was busy cutting away the soiled clothing, seemingly unaffected by the gruesome sight of the bloody stump. And he was glad it had been dark in the tunnel, so he hadn't had to look at it through all those torturous hours of trying to keep Delaney from slipping over the edge into either death or insanity.

"How is he, Mama?"

Having not heard him enter, she looked up, surprised. "Oh, Chance! I was so scared!" She rushed into his arms, holding him tightly. "I was so afraid I'd lost you both!"

"I know, Mama. I was scared, too. I never thought he would make it out of there."

Together they moved to his bedside and Lily resumed her duties. "He's drifting in and out of consciousness. How's Jenna?"

"I don't know yet," he replied numbly.

"Go back and be with her," Lily encouraged. "I can take care of Delaney, and she needs you."

"Are you going to be all right, Mama?"

She tried to smile, but exhaustion and the emotional strain of the situation had taken its toll on her lovely face. Her lips quivered, but her tough facade didn't crumble. "Heavens, yes. But you need to have someone look at that cut on your head."

He touched a hand gingerly to the sore spot that was no longer bleeding but covered with caked blood. "I'll be fine."

"At least get cleaned up then. When Jenna wakes up, you don't want to frighten her to death."

He left reluctantly, but sensed his mother needed and wanted time alone with Delaney and with the emotions so frayed and raw and so close to the surface. He felt them himself.

In his tent, he cleaned up the best he could from the basin, washing his hair and the wound, then shaving and changing clothes.

When he stepped outside again, Solomon came from Moody's mess tent with two cups of coffee. "Here, get this down you, Chance," he said, handing him one. "It'll hold you over until you can get some sleep."

Chance was too weary and too worried about Jenna and Delaney to waste energy telling Solomon he really wasn't interested in the coffee. He took it and sat on the ground between the two tents. Solomon joined him.

It was quiet in the narrow river bottom as the sun once again set behind the mountains and cast long shadows across the land. The exhausted men stretched out in the grass to rest and to eat, but tension still hovered in the smoky air that had become commonplace to the mountains.

Solomon and Chance said nothing, but listened to the hushed talk of the others and picked up enough of the conversations to know that the men were conjecturing in whispers as to how and why the explosions had happened.

Henry came from his tent just as Drummond exited Jenna's. The doctor's appearance brought everyone to attention. The mens' talking halted in hopes of hearing what he had to say, either out of concern for Jenna or out of curiosity. Henry stepped

316

forward, surprised to see the doctor in Jenna's tent rather than with Delaney, for he had left the tunnel ahead of them and missed the incident. He pushed his way through the men.

"What's the matter with Jenna, Doctor?" he demanded. "Has she collapsed from exhaustion? I told her she was pushing herself too hard."

Drummond scanned the curious, waiting faces of the crew, but before he could speak, Solomon took him by the arm and led him behind the tent for privacy. Henry and Chance followed. Again, before Drummond could speak, Solomon intervened. "Henry, I believe you should stay with the men."

"All right, but what about Killeen?"

"I'd like him to stay here."

Henry didn't like being excluded if Chance wasn't going to be, too, and suspicion entered his eyes. "What's going on here, Solomon? What are you hiding from me?"

As soon as Solomon had seen the blood, he'd known what was wrong with Jenna. His wife, Marietta, had miscarried a number of times. She had only been able to carry one child to term. His main concern now was that he didn't want this news spread around about his granddaughter and subsequently see her reputation ruined. Many of the men, if any had seen the amount of blood, might very well suspect the truth, anyway.

No one needed to tell him the father of the child was Chance. Jenna had worked too hard to get him out if she hadn't been in love with him. Of course, he hadn't known they'd been having a love affair. But Solomon couldn't fault her for her passionate nature. If Lily came to him now, this very moment, he would let his desire rule his mind and suffer the consequences later. But he'd seen the tears in Lily's eyes when they'd brought the Irishman from the tunnel; he'd seen the way she went to him and stayed with

317

him. Her concern had been more than the mere desire to help a fellow person. Yes, his Lily was once again in love with another man.

"I want some answers, Solomon," Henry demanded.

Solomon relented. "All right, Henry, but for Jenna's sake, keep what Drummond tells you to yourself. Doctor, go ahead."

"All right," Drummond said quietly. "I'm afraid Miss Lee has suffered a miscarriage."

Chance wasn't prepared when Henry plunged a fist into his jaw, sending him reeling backward into a tree.

"You stinking sonovabitch!" Henry lunged at him again. "I should have known how you were using her. I'll kill you!"

Chance staggered away from the tree. Then gathering his wits, he charged Henry like a raging bull. The collision sent Henry stumbling backward with Chance on top of him. The fight took them right into the main body of the camp. The crew scrambled out of the way, but immediately formed a loose mob and began encouraging them on with loud hoots, whistles, and shouted advice.

Henry and Chance broke apart and Henry sprang to his feet, thrusting a boot into Chance's stomach that doubled him over. Chance managed to grab Henry's foot before he could lash at him again. With an upward thrust of his hand, Chance sent Henry onto his back. Leaping to his feet, he waited for his opponent to rise.

Like wolves eager to kill, they circled each other, waiting for the precise moment to attack. Henry swung with his right and Chance dodged it, sending one fist into Henry's nose. A split second later, his other fist bore into Henry's stomach. Henry doubled over, blood spurting from his nose, but Chance sent another punch to his head.

Suddenly, he was grabbed from behind by members of the crew. Others manacled Henry in the same fashion. Chance fought against the restraining arms.

"He's responsible for what happened in that tunnel and for everything else that's happened on this line!" he proclaimed angrily.

Henry tried to get a hand free to wipe the blood dripping from his nose, but the men held him so tightly he could scarcely move. "You're crazy, Killeen," he retaliated. "I had nothing to do with that explosion and you can't prove otherwise!"

Solomon stormed into the center of the fracas, holding his arms out like a referee in a prizefight. "Enough! It's time to find out just who is responsible. Carson, Byers, Smith!" He singled them out from the crowd. "I want you three to go to Coeur d'Alene and get the sheriff. Tell him he'd better get to the bottom of this or we'll take matters into our own hands. Now, the rest of you, go to your tents and get some sleep!"

Cautiously, the men released Chance and Henry, fearing they might tear into each other again. When they were satisfied the fight was over, they returned to their former positions, but their adrenaline was nearly as high as the two who had been fighting. They eyed Henry suspiciously, wondering if what Chance had said was true.

Solomon drew Chance aside. "My God, man! What makes you think Henry's behind this? He might be after Solomon Enterprises, but he's not underhanded enough to attempt murder!"

Chance's chest heaved as he wiped blood from a cut lip. "I didn't expect you to believe it."

"You may be a threat to him where Jenna is concerned, but this . . . I think you'd better cool off. Ritchy will come through with some evidence and prove Durfey's behind this."

"Jesus Christ, Solomon! Don't you think it's a

little late for evidence? Delaney's lost his arm and Jenna's lost our baby." He tore free of Solomon's grip and stalked to Jenna's tent.

Solomon stared after him, grimly hoping his accusations about Henry weren't true.

Chance found Jenna sleeping peacefully. Uriah Drummond was gathering up his bag.

"I've given her a sedative," he said. "It'll allow her to get the rest she needs. I'll be back to check her when I'm done with Delaney."

Chance pulled up a chair next to her cot and gently took her hand in his. "How far along was she, Doctor?"

"About two months. If I'd only known her condition earlier, I could have prevented this. The shoveling, the lack of rest, and the strain on her emotions was simply more than her body could handle. And there's the possibility she could be susceptible to miscarriages, anyway. I'll be around for a few days to keep an eye on both her and Delaney. She'll need a lot of rest, so would you see that she gets it?"

Chance leaned forward on his elbows, closer to her. "Could you tell whether the child was a boy or a girl?"

"No. It was too early for that."

Chance released a ragged sigh, feeling tremendously empty. "This won't prevent her from having more children, will it?"

"No. She's a healthy woman but she's thirty, so I would suggest that if she's going to have a family, she not waste too much time. May I make one suggestion, Killeen?"

Chance waited.

"I don't know what's between the two of you. But if you love her—and I think you do—I'd like you to stay here and take care of her for a few days. Get someone else to do your work. As is often the case with women who have miscarriages, she might be very despondent. She'll need your love and understanding now more than ever."

Chance closed both hands around Jenna's one. "Don't worry. I have no intention of ever leaving this woman."

Drummond left to commence surgery on Delaney's arm. It was getting dark, so Chance lit a lantern and set it on a wooden crate near the bed. He heated water and gently wiped the smudges of dirt from her face and hands, then lifted her head and spread out the tangled golden length of her hair onto the pillow. Tomorrow he would get something more comfortable than the cot for her to sleep on until she could be moved to a hotel.

He took up his vigil again on the hard chair by her bedside. The softness of her hand in his belied the hidden strength, but her palm was blistered from the recent shoveling. He kissed the blisters, as if his love alone could heal them.

Dear God, she'd worked herself nearly to death to get him out of the tunnel. She'd lost their baby. *His* baby.

Suddenly, his chest tightened painfully. Hot tears stung his eyes and he swiped at them angrily, time and again, not wanting anyone to walk in and see his weakness. But still they came. And it was a long time before they stopped.

Amazingly enough, the request for a soft bed for Jenna produced three feather mattresses. The crew pitched in together, and in no time their hammers and nails, saws and ropes, had produced a rough bedstead on which to lay the mattresses. Chance transferred her to the new bed but she barely stirred, then dropped immediately back into a deep sleep.

Nothing was said to the crew about the miscarriage. It had only been stated that she suffered from extreme exhaustion and just needed some time to rest.

Around ten o'clock the second night, Lily came into the tent with a bedroll for Chance, along with a plate of food.

"How's Delaney?" he asked.

Lily set the food on a small table and the bedroll on the cot. She couldn't help but notice the desolation in Chance's red-rimmed, bloodshot eyes.

"The pain medication is keeping him asleep," she said.

"I'm afraid he won't take the loss of his arm very good. It was all I could do while we were trapped in the tunnel to keep him from giving up. He's afraid you won't love him anymore." He looked up at her as she pressed a hand to Jenna's forehead, checking her temperature. "I thought it was Solomon you wanted, Mama."

"I've loved Delaney for a long time," she said simply. "And this won't change my feelings about him."

"That's what I told him."

"Chance . . ." She laid a hand on his shoulder, squeezing it sympathetically. "Don't carry the guilt for what happened. I know you are, because I can see it in your eyes. If anybody is to blame, it's the person who tried to kill you."

He hadn't expected her keen insight into the situation. "Why do you think someone was trying to kill me?"

"You know better than anybody what happened in there. *Was* it dynamite that hadn't blown from a previous charge? *Did* it just accidentally go off as some are saying?"

Chance was almost too weary to think, but the moment of the explosion had recurred so many times

322

in his mind he knew he'd never forget it. "It does happen, Mama. You know Delaney has to check his charges after every blast."

"Yes, I know, but what's your honest opinion?"

"Well, first off, the holes had been predrilled to make our job quicker. Delaney had barely put the drill to one of those holes when it went off. A few seconds later, there was another explosion down by the tunnel's weak back."

"What does that indicate, Chance?"

"It appears that there was some black powder in that hole, buried back deep, and it probably had a cap that exploded at the pressure of Delaney's drill, setting the whole thing off."

"And the other charge down by the weak back?"

"That's not so easily explained. The first explosion could have shifted things enough so that if there *had* been misfired dynamite from an earlier charge, it could have gone off."

"The odds of there being misfired dynamite down there, though, seem rather small to me."

"Yes, but the only other thing that could have happened is that a charge had been set and someone lit the rattails on their way out of the tunnel. They'd have had to estimate how long it would take before the first explosion went off, and then had the tails cut to just the right length. And that's a shaky calculation at best."

"Maybe not for someone who knew about how long it took for those rattails to burn. Besides, after the first explosion, they'd have waited for things to clear before going in, anyway, wouldn't they? A few minutes here or there wouldn't have mattered, and then the second explosion would have gone off and sealed the entrance. Who were the last ones out of the tunnel?"

Chance had already thought all this out during his long hours in the tunnel. It was why he'd so openly accused Paterson in front of everybody. "Ives and Paterson were the last ones out, Mama. They hung around until everybody was out. Then Delaney told them to go."

Lily toyed with his explanation a bit longer, then finally sighed and bent to kiss his cheek. "I'd better go now. The only thing I can say is don't turn your back on those men. The way things are shaping up, you'd better not trust anyone."

"I won't. And, Mama, I'll be over to check on Delaney."

"He'll be fine. You get some rest."

When she was gone, Chance's thoughts wouldn't give him any rest. He'd suspected Leaman of milking the company. Now he figured Paterson was in on it. And if Paterson was in on it, Ives had to be. If that was the case, the explosion would have not only eliminated him permanently, but it would have cost the BRC more money.

Paterson had been the one to suggest Delaney do the blasting, then practically insisted that Chance help him, knowing he'd more than likely be the one to drill out the holes. It hadn't been Delaney they'd wanted dead, but they'd considered him dispensable. The second explosion was merely a precaution; if the first explosion didn't kill him, then the fumes from the blast and the delay in rescue might. Paterson had wanted his death to look like an accident so no questions would be asked. It damned near worked. Now, if he could only prove his hunch.

He picked up the fork next to the plate of stew and forced himself to eat, but he tasted nothing. Like a zombie, he carried the contents to his mouth, chewed, and swallowed. When he was finished, he set the tin plate aside and shifted positions on the hard chair. He ignored the bedroll stretched over the cot.

He remained on the hard-backed chair, watching Jenna sleep while his mind raged in ceaseless, troubling thoughts. It was well after midnight before he finally dozed.

Consciousness returned with a jolt. Chance's dreams had placed him back in the dark tunnel, in a sea of blood and dismembered body parts, while the plaintive cry of a baby echoed somewhere at the end of the tunnel, which was always just out of his reach. He pushed his slumped body into a straighter position on the hard chair.

In the dim light of the lamp left burning, he saw Jenna's head moving fitfully back and forth on the pillows while little whimpering sounds came from her lips. Was it possible that his nightmare was also hers? That she, too, tried in vain to get to the end of the tunnel where the baby was crying?

He brushed the errant strands of hair from her cheek. His touch brought her awake with the suddenness that he himself had been summoned from sleep. Her gaze locked with his for a startled moment.

"Chance," she said weakly, "you're alive. I dreamed—"

Before she could say more, he was on the edge of the bed, drawing her into his arms. He held her tightly, burying his face in her hair and neck. Her embrace was weak, but it satisfied him just to feel the life of her again and to be a part of it. To know he hadn't lost it. He whispered huskily against her ear, "I've been so worried about you, Jenna. Thank God, you're all right."

When he finally laid her back on the pillows, he searched her face anxiously, trying to assure himself she was truly all right. Dark circles beneath her eyes made her skin appear exceptionally pale, and the vibrant blue color lacked its usual luster.

He took her hand and drew it to his lips. Feeling the full extent of emptiness again, he said softly, "I'm sorry about the baby."

What little bit of light there was in her eyes vanished. She turned her head away and stared off into space, withdrawing inside herself in the same fashion as she slowly withdrew her hand from his. He felt himself losing her in both body and mind, drifting away from him like a gentle stream of smoke tugged by the wind. The silence became heavy and his ability to converse vanished.

"I need to be alone, Chance," she murmured. "Please."

The doctor had warned him that she would be like this. It was something he would have to ride out with understanding and patience.

He rose, not wanting to go but seeing no choice. "All right, Jenna, but I'll be just outside if you need me."

There was so much he wanted to tell her, that he'd been waiting to tell her, but it would have to wait a little longer. For now, her wounds needed to heal, both mentally and physically. And later, he would speak of love.

Chapter Twenty-Six

A week later, Jenna sat near the window in the dining room of the Silver Bend Hotel. It wasn't as elaborate as Blackshere House in Wallace, but if it had any shortcomings, she didn't notice. The small square table contained a meal she had no appetite for. Food didn't seem to have any taste ever since she'd lost the baby. The doctor had said it was all a function of her body making its adjustment from the pregnancy back to normalcy.

Two other plates shared the table—her grandfather's and Henry's. The two men were bickering over the railroad, but she was only listening with half an ear as she watched a blond-haired little boy toddling down the boardwalk, his short legs unsteadily rising and falling in exaggerated steps to keep up with his mother's graceful walk. The flat, stiff soles of his shoes were intended to aid his walking, but she wondered if he wouldn't have been better off with his bare feet.

"Come along now, Edward," the mother's musical voice drifted through the open window. The baby teetered precariously and the mother gasped, reaching for him just as he managed to steady himself. Then she laughed and held out her hand. "You'd better hold on to me."

"No!" he stated emphatically, hurrying past her, determined to walk unassisted.

"Jenna, would you like a fresh cup of tea?"

Henry's doting words pulled her away from the scene of the little boy and his mother. She stared at her cup for a moment, finding it most difficult to focus her thoughts. "No, thank you," she said finally. "I believe I've had enough."

"But you've hardly drank any of it and you haven't even touched your meal."

"I'm sorry, but I'm not hungry."

Henry laid a hand over hers. "You've got to put this behind you, Jenna. Put Killeen behind you. Why do you insist on loving men who hurt you?"

Solomon frowned. "Why do you insist on pestering her, Henry? She'll eat when she damn well feels like it. And let her make up her own mind where Chance is concerned."

"Yes, please," Jenna said. "Enough talk about me. Would someone please tell me how Delaney is? I haven't seen him about, and all Lily would say is that his arm is healing normally."

The glow faded from Solomon's eyes at the mention of Lily. Jenna knew he still loved her. It had been hard for him to accept the fact that she loved the Irishman.

"Chance says he isn't taking the loss of his arm in very good spirits—which he can hardly be blamed for," Solomon replied. "Apparently, he thinks it's making him less of a man, and he doesn't want anybody to see him—and especially Lily. He's turning her away, from what Chance says."

"I'm sorry to hear that," Jenna said sincerely. "I believe I'll stop by his room and visit him."

"That wouldn't be wise until you've had another week to recuperate," Henry inserted.

Jenna sighed. Henry had been so kind since the

miscarriage, but she was getting tired of him playing the mother hen role. She sensed she'd fallen from grace with him because of her intimate relationship with Chance, but he still pursued her as if he wanted her hand in marriage. It perplexed her as to why. Surely he knew now she could never love him.

She felt herself drifting away from the conversation again, back to her own private world of thoughts, and dreams, and regrets. It took an effort to force herself from inertia. "Did they question Durfey about what happened?"

Henry leaned back in his chair, chewing on a toothpick. "Yes, but they didn't have anything to hold him on. They're saying it was just an accident."

Solomon snorted with disgust. "That sheriff would have a difficult time finding his way off Main Street without a map. What happened was no accident, and I won't let it rest."

Solomon had done a lot of thinking about Chance's accusation against Henry—he'd said nothing of it to Jenna—and he'd been covertly watching Henry's moves, but he'd seen and heard nothing out of the ordinary. He just wished Jethro Ritchy would report in soon with something substantial so they could get to the bottom of it once and for all.

"The men were upset when the law released him for lack of evidence," Solomon continued. "We had to quickly divert their energy into tracklaying or they would have had their own vigilante trial and hung him from the nearest tree."

"Did you get someone to finish blasting the tunnel?" Jenna asked somberly, still very disturbed by the memory of the entire incident and wondering for the first time if this railroad had indeed been a mistake to pursue. It seemed to have caused so many heartaches for so many people.

"It was a coincidence," Solomon replied. "A miner

appeared one day out of the blue and said he knew Delaney. He wanted to help us by finishing the work."

"Where's Chance?" she asked. "I haven't seen him today."

"Apparently, he prefers engineering over nursemaiding," Henry remarked snidely. "He's back out on the line, regardless of Drummond's orders."

Jenna frowned at him. "What orders? Why would Drummond give Chance orders?"

"When I spoke to Drummond, he said you'd be all right but that you just needed support from the baby's father until you got back on your feet. He said he told Killeen to stay with you and help you over the emotional stress of losing the baby."

Solomon snorted again and came around to Jenna's chair. "I'll take you to your room, my dear. It seems the conversation here is getting so dull that Henry's resorting to storytelling."

If she could have run from the dining room, she would have. As it was, Jenna rose too quickly and immediately felt light-headed. She gladly accepted Solomon's helping hand to her room, and she was relieved when Henry made his excuse to return to work and not join them. She simply didn't want to hear any more of his remarks against Chance.

In her room, she relaxed on the green brocade chaise longue her grandfather had bought in Wallace for her convalescence, and Solomon brought pillows to prop behind her.

"Did Drummond really order Chance to take care of me, Grandpa?"

"Jenna, if foolishness could be minted, Henry would be a millionaire. Of course it's not the truth! He's stayed by your side because he's very concerned with your health. Now, you'd better rest. Going downstairs for dinner was probably more activity than what you should have had so soon."

She took his hand and had him sit next to her. Her gaze roamed his aged face and she studied his eyes, for it was there that his thoughts could be read.

"Are you ashamed of me?" she beseeched softly. "Tell me the truth, Grandpa."

He patted her hand, and for a moment it was as if she were a child again in the Great House, frightened by the shadows, and he had come to reassure her that there were no such things as ghouls.

"Oh, my dear Jenna. How foolish." A sadness entered his eyes. "Let me answer a question with a question. Has it made you love me less knowing that I have loved a woman other than your grandmother?"

"Of course not. If anything, it's made you seem a little more—"

"More what?" His brows shot together as he playfully baited her. "Now you be honest with me and don't spare my feelings. What were you about to say?"

"All right," she conceded with an impish grin. "Knowing about your love affair with Lily has made you more human, more accessible."

He chuckled. "Love happens to the best of us, Jenna. How could I be ashamed of you for falling in love? As for the Lee name, it's been strong enough to hold up to plenty of scandal in the past. I'm sure it will be again. The question is, are you strong enough to hold up?"

She looked away from his caring blue eyes. "The newspapers have had me having so many love affairs, I suppose another one won't matter. Except that this one was real."

Solomon gazed at her sorrowfully, knowing all too well the pain of love and knowing he couldn't do anything to help ease her anxiety. Nor could she do anything to help ease his.

A knock sounded on the door. He gave her a peck

on the cheek and rose. "You have company, and it's time for me to leave, anyway. I'll be back later to check on you."

He left the room and it was Chance who stepped inside, closing the door behind him. She thought of what Henry had said about him, but then she saw the bunch of wildflowers he held in a glass vase in his hand and all else was forgotten.

"Oh, Chance, they're beautiful!"

He moved to her side and bowed from the waist in a mock gesture of gallantry. The water in the vase spilled on the chaise longue. She laughed. He swore and quickly tried to brush it off, but succeeded only in rubbing it in worse.

Finally, he gave up and handed her the vase. "Be careful. It's been known to spill."

Still laughing, she inspected the blossoms of hollyhocks, Indian paintbrush, lilies, and wild roses. Then she became aware of him still standing over her with his hat held rather awkwardly in his hands. She lifted her gaze to his and her smile faded at the look of earnestness on his face. She knew immediately that the flowers had only been an icebreaker. He had something serious on his mind, and she sensed what it was. As a matter of fact, she had sensed it all week, but today she knew he was going to bring it out in the open at last.

He pulled up a chair next to her. "We need to talk about what's happened, Jenna," he said softly. "You know we can't put it off forever."

In the past week, she had come far toward closing the yawning emptiness inside her, but at his words it opened again, so vast and huge she feared it could never be forgotten or filled with anything, not even hope.

She set the flowers on the small table next to the chaise longue, finding it difficult to meet those green eyes that never failed to unsettle her. "What do you want to say to me?"

Chance was sorry the gaiety left her voice, but he'd held this discussion off much longer than he'd wanted, and only out of concern for her ability to deal with it so soon after the miscarriage. He felt her withdraw back into her own thoughts that she had refused to share since losing the baby. Maybe he had spoken too soon, but the pain inside him needed balm, the same as hers did.

"You could have told me about the baby, Jenna," he said in quiet anguish. "I had a right to know . . . to be a part of it."

"It matters little now." Her voice was flat and dull.

"The hell it doesn't!" he said in sudden anger. "It wasn't right of you to exclude me. You probably never intended on telling me, did you?"

He thought he saw only pity for him in her eyes. Hope of crossing this most difficult bridge was fading quickly. She sought the view from the window, as if it were so much easier to look at than him.

"Maybe I was wrong in not telling you," she said distantly, "but I didn't think it would accomplish anything except to force you to marry me." Her tone hardened. "I don't want you or any man to marry me out of obligation. The baby's gone. It's over! You don't have to stay with me. You're free to go."

He moved from his chair and sat next to her on the chaise longue. He gently turned her head, forcing her to look at him. "I don't believe you mean that, Jenna Lee. If you'd wanted me out of your life, you wouldn't have lifted a finger to help me get out of that tunnel, let alone nearly killing yourself doing it and losing our baby. If you think I'm here only out of a sense of duty, then you're wrong. I'm here because I love you . . . and I want to marry you."

Jenna wasn't sure why, but she couldn't respond to him. She felt numb. For all the wonder of his words, they came like salve applied too late to heal a wound. She thought of what Henry had said at dinner, and every emotional doubt and fear, every hurt and anxiety she'd had over the past six months, came forth.

"I find that hard to believe, Chance. Before all this happened, it seemed you were willing to let me go when this road was completed. Don't tell me Grandpa has come after you with a shotgun or a bribe?"

Chance was crushed by her calm, almost vicious reaction to his proclamation of love. He stood up, suddenly unable to be near her. What was she doing to him? All these months he'd tortured himself over a decision that had come to this moment, and now she acted as if she hated him, resented him.

"Your grandfather has said nothing to me," he replied hotly. "When I got back from Bayard with Delaney, I intended then to ask you to be my wife. You were asleep and Paterson refused to let me wake you up. I had to go directly into the tunnel and start blasting. My decision came before any of this."

"Henry was right all along," she said dully.

"What are you talking about?"

"He said you were only staying here because Drummond told you to. You're only asking me to marry you out of guilt."

Chance didn't like being put on the defensive, especially when he was innocent of any wrongdoing. "You'd believe Paterson over me?"

"Did Drummond ask you to stay with me?"

"Well . . . yes, but I'd already intended to stay with you."

She gave his answer a measure of consideration. "I'd like to believe you, but how can I? You tried so hard to make me understand how you felt right from the beginning, but I had the foolish notion I could make you see things as I saw them. After our night in Coeur d'Alene, I realized that what my grandfather did to you and your family was of the magnitude that could never completely be forgotten or forgiven. He still stands between us in your mind and in your past, and he always will, Chance. Even when he's dead, his empire will be there to haunt you, until one day you'll even hate me. How can you have changed your mind so suddenly? You can't tell me it doesn't have to do with guilt over the baby."

He ran a frustrated hand through his hair. "It was hardly sudden, Jenna. And it isn't out of guilt. You don't know the turmoil I've been through since I first discovered who you were. I wanted you from the beginning, but there was your grandfather and the memories."

"Nothing's changed—least of all, the past."

"Nothing's changed in *your* eyes, Jenna. But everything's changed in mine. I've discovered the fine line between saint and sinner, and your grandfather walks it. When I was sixteen, I saw him as a man who ruthlessly took what he wanted and knocked aside anybody in his path. Now I see him merely as a tired old man who can wield power and put fear into people if they'll allow it.

"People change," he continued. "I have, and I know he has. Maybe I'll never forgive him completely for what he did and I will never condone the actions he took, but I understand *why* he did it. He did everything in his power to win my mother's love, and I believe he did. But in the end, he couldn't win *her*. My family all lost in his quest for love, but he lost even more."

He tried to calm himself. "I can't change the past, but call it wisdom, truth, or weariness—whichever it is—I don't care about your grandfather and what he did anymore. I have *my* life to live."

Her contemplative gaze told him that his words had definitely had an impact on her, but she still seemed unconvinced of his true motives. Tears came to her eyes. "How can you expect me not to doubt this change of heart? To not think this isn't some sort of requital for damages done, especially now, coming on the heels of having lost the baby. Maybe you should think about it awhile. Maybe we *both* should. It may be best for you if I let you go."

Chance felt the ground being pulled out from under him. A man had only so much pride. He'd bared his soul, his heart, and it hadn't been easy for him to do it. Now she was dashing it all as if it were nothing. *Think about it a while.* As if he hadn't.

Angrily, he went to the bed and picked up his hat. "You question my feelings, Jenna. Now I question yours. I'm beginning to think that you never wanted me. You were always saying to let tomorrow take its course. Maybe you planned all along to go back home and make our love affair just a part of your summer holiday. For all I know, maybe you did all that shoveling so you *would* lose the baby and not have to face your Eastern friends in shame."

"That's not true, damn you! The baby meant everything to me!"

His compassion was overruled by his wounded pride. "It hurts, doesn't it, not to be believed? I won't beg you to marry me, Jenna. I won't beg for your love. You have no way of knowing whether I'm telling the truth except to believe me. And if you can't do that, then I guess we never had anything, anyway. Now, if you'll excuse me. I have a railroad to build."

Chapter Twenty-Seven

In the days to follow, the heat slowed the workers almost to a standstill. Thirsty trees drooped and forest grass was green only in the deep canyons where the sun's rays were unable to reach. The river level dropped, and many of the streams had been dry since July. Rain at this late date couldn't help the foliage, but if a rain was heavy enough and sustained, it might douse some of the forest fires and help the fire-fighters in their vigil to keep the canyon towns from being destroyed.

When the locomotive was finally brought in from across the lake and placed on the tracks at Old Mission Landing, Chance saw Jenna for the first time since their last disastrous meeting. She arrived with Solomon in a polished slat-bottom road wagon. Extremely light and springy, he knew it had been acquired for her comfort. From a distance, she looked as if she had fully recuperated from the miscarriage.

Jenna was given the honor of christening the new engine. Staying well back in the crowd, he watched her do the honors with laughter and delight, her blue eyes as bubbly as the bottle of champagne she smashed against the engine, dubbing the Silverado. Everyone cheered as the gleaming machine chugged along the newly laid track with passenger cars in tow, replete with their cargo of curious visitors.

Chance fought ambivalent feelings of wanting and not wanting to talk to her. In the end, he left unnoticed in the midst of the celebration and rode back down the Mullan Road to work.

As the track inched onward, the locomotive moved with it, carrying supplies and tools on its flatcars, thus making things easier for the workers. Reporters followed the road's progress daily now, adding excitement to the final days. Residents of Silver Bend made plans for dancing and celebrating upon the road's completion. Dignitaries arrived, along with hundreds of people not wanting to miss the momentous occasion. At Silver Bend, visitors cheerfully disembarked from the train and boarded vehicles that escorted them the remaining distance into town, where the track had not yet been laid.

On the eve of the final day, Chance gave his crew orders to be on the job at six in the morning. "Durfey won't be wasting daylight," he said. "And if he gets so much as a fifteen-minute head start on us, we won't reach Silver Bend first. So we'll keep watch on his camp and start when they do."

He rode into town, wondering as he went what had happened to Jethro Ritchy. Not only had he not reported in recently, but no one around Coeur d'Alene had even seen him for over a month. Chance was beginning to fear that maybe he'd unearthed his information, been discovered, and killed. He didn't care what Solomon and Jenna thought about Henry, but in his own mind, Paterson was still under suspicion for sabotage of the line, and time was running out to prove it.

At the Silver Bend Hotel, he took the stairs two at a time to the second story. He strode down the carpeted hall, slowing at Jenna's door. He'd wanted to talk to her a hundred times, and each time it had been harder for him to resist. But there was a dance tomorrow night and something inside him kept nudging to ask her to go with him. If they were together again, maybe they could straighten things out between them. He'd said a lot of things he regretted, and he wondered if, perchance, she had, too.

He lifted his hand to knock, but voices inside stopped him. The tones were too low to decipher words but loud enough for him to realize she was talking to Paterson.

Always Paterson. He'd been there from the beginning, lurking in the shadows. For all Chance knew, the baby Jenna had lost might not have even been his but the other man's, and maybe Henry had only jumped him to take the heat off himself.

He felt as if time had gotten lost en route to this moment and had somehow double-backed to the beginning. But how could he erase everything that had happened in the interim? How could he erase the fact that he still loved her and always would?

He was angry enough to go inside and tell her about how he suspected Henry of wrongdoing, but he was also afraid to open the door for fear he might find her in Paterson's arms. That would kill him, and it would be exactly what Paterson would like to see happen. If they were going to be lovers, let them do it without his knowledge. Suspicion was bad enough to live with. The truth was worse.

He forced himself to continue down the hall to the room he shared with Delaney. It was locked. Damn Delaney for locking everybody out! He'd even locked out Chance's mother, and Chance knew how much she was hurting. Well, the Irishman was going to have to answer to that before he was through with him. He fished in his vest pocket until he found his key.

Delaney heard the key in the lock and hollered out in a drunken slur, "Go away, whoever y' be. I'm in no mood fer yer bloody company."

Chance stepped inside the dim room. Delaney was stretched out on the bed with a whiskey bottle as his bed partner. His clothes were a rumpled mess. His sleeve was pinned up over his missing arm and he lifted the stump in a sort of greeting, but he was so drunk his tongue would barely operate.

"So it's me frind . . . Keely. And what would y' be wantin' this morrow? I hope 'tis not whiskey, fer it's not in me plans to be generous."

Lily had warned Chance that Delaney was sinking deeper and deeper into a depression despite her efforts to draw him back into the world, but the last time Chance had been here he'd seemed in control of things. He wondered where she was tonight. Maybe Delaney had chased her right into the arms of Solomon Lee. He couldn't say as he'd blame her. A body could put up with only so much abuse.

"A lot of good you are, you one-armed Irishman. I was looking for a drinking partner, but I see you don't need one."

Delaney shot him a dirty look, but Chance couldn't even seem to get him riled. If he was interested at all in Chance's reason for wanting to drink, he feigned indifference and tipped the bottle to his lips. When he pulled it away, he said. "Well, where would be yer bottle, Keely? I see ye're empty-handed. 'Twould be monstrous sweet indeed if you'd been so kind as to bring me a new bottle—and maybe even a new hand to hold it with. Aye, I could truly use the one I lost in yer bloody train tunnel."

Chance grabbed the bottle from Delaney's hand and thrust his arm in his friend's face. "Here, you son of a bitch! Cut mine off and take it if it'll make you feel better!"

Delaney lunged at him, hurtling his burly weight on top of Chance. They crashed to the floor. The whiskey bottle flew from Chance's hand and shattered, spilling the precious amber contents all over the hardwood floor. Delaney roared like an angry bull at the sight of it and held Chance down with his stump, which had amazing strength. With his good arm, he swung at Chance's face, but he was so drunk Chance dodged the swing and Delaney hit the floor with his fist, cursing and yelling.

Chance rolled him off and pinned him to the floor. "What in the hell's got into you, you crazy bastard?"

Delaney struggled against him but the liquor had made him weak. He finally gave up, panting for breath. "So I'm a bastard now? Well, so are you! And you'll pay fer that bottle o' whiskey, I swear!"

Chance stared into the familiar bushy face twisted with agony, knowing the real agony went much deeper than spilled whiskey, and knowing his own agony went much deeper, too, than simple anger and frustration at Delaney's behavior. No, here they were ready to kill each other, when the truth was that they were both in love with women they were on the verge of losing.

He sat back on Delaney's burly chest. "God, would you look at us, Delaney? I guess you know we'd be miles ahead if we'd never jumped that train."

Delaney tried to move but couldn't. "What in bloody hell 'r' you talkin' about, Keely? And git yer lard ass off me. Ye're cuttin' me wind off."

Chance came to his feet and helped Delaney to his. "Come on, Delaney. Let's head down to the saloon. Remember what you told me about drinking by yourself."

Delaney turned with some effort to keep his balance. He stared at Chance blankly, as if nothing he said had made a lick of sense. "And what is it about jumpin' the train, Keely? I hope you wouldn't be askin' me to do it agin, b'cause with only one arm it would be much harder than the last time."

Chance steered Delaney to the door. "No, we're not going to jump any more trains. We're going to buy you another bottle of whiskey. Good whiskey. Not that rotgut you've been trying to kill yourself with."

"The saints be praised, Keely. Ye're as generous a man as I've ever known, but I'd best be fer tellin' y' I'm just a wee bit drunk already."

Chance closed the door behind him, glancing grimly down the hall toward Jenna's room. "Yeah, I know you are . . . but I'm not."

"No, Henry. I've put a lot into this railroad, and I have no intention of leaving Silver Bend until everyone else does. We may lose, but I'm strong enough to stay here and watch the defeat—if that's what it turns out to be."

"Jenna, you've had enough disappointment lately without adding to it."

"Why do you keep insisting we're going to lose? We have as good a chance as Durfey to win."

Henry held his patience and looked to the window, where he saw the great billows of smoke rising above the mountains like huge white mushrooms into the azure sky. A worried frown creased his forehead. "Rumors have it that the fires are boxing us in," he said. "Just two days ago, Durfey's crew had to stop work to fight an outbreak just over the ridge from here. Some of our best workers quit after that because they were afraid. We could be trapped here before it's all over."

"I've heard the rumors. Everyone has. But the big fires aren't close. If they were, I'm sure Chance and Grandpa would have said something and would be pulling the men out."

"Killeen won't do that. He doesn't want to pull anybody out because he wants to win that damned race."

Jenna wasn't sure she believed anything Henry

said anymore, especially where Chance was concerned. She'd had a lot of time to consider her error in believing his last disparaging comment about Chance. She'd since spoken with Drummond and he had verified having asked Chance to stay with her during her recovery, but then he'd smiled and said, "Of course, I couldn't have dragged him away with a team of mules. You're lucky to have someone who cares that much."

She realized then that she'd let Henry influence her too much. That, coupled with her own nagging doubts and the depression from losing the baby, had caused her to turn Chance away when they had both needed each other the most. She had essentially called him a liar, and she knew she'd hurt him deeply. But how could she ever get him to forgive her now?

It was kind of Henry to worry about the encroaching fires and her safety, and it was kind of him to worry about her state of mind if they lost tomorrow. But she was in control of her emotions now; the depression was lifting.

"I'm afraid I have to disagree with you, Henry. Chance *is* worried about the crew's welfare. Just last week Grandpa said that he gave the men the opportunity to leave and they voted unanimously to stay. They want to win, and all the setbacks have only made them more determined to be the victors."

"Even after what he's done to you, you still see Killeen as that knight in shining armor, don't you?" he said disgustedly.

She looked away, saying nothing.

He sighed and took her hand in his. "If nothing else, Jenna, let's be friends again. I can wait until you get over Killeen. But just don't turn your back on me. And why don't you be on the train tonight to Coeur d'Alene? I would feel so much better if you were. You may not think that losing will throw you into another depression, but I'm afraid it could. And what with the fires . . . well, I'm really worried about you."

"I don't believe you're truly worried about my depression or my health, Henry," she replied with a smile. "You just want to get me away from Chance, don't you?"

He was exasperated. "Well, you can't blame me, can you?"

"I'm staying, Henry. And that's final."

She was the epitome of stubbornness, but at least he'd tried. "All right, Jenna. Have it your way. God knows you always have."

He departed her room and left her staring at the closed door, wondering sadly if he was right. And wondering, too, if hope and fools go hand in hand.

The noise outside made it impossible to sleep. Jenna glanced at the clock by the bed and saw it was nearing midnight. She tossed the covers back and went to the window. Below, Main Street was lit with lanterns hung on poles and couples twirled beneath the lights to the tune of a square dance. Tomorrow night was supposed to be the real celebration, but apparently all the people who had come to town for it were too excited to wait.

Farther down the street the temporary police force, assembled for the celebration, were in the process of breaking up a gang fight. It was probably the two factions of the railroad finally getting their opportunity to release the animosities that had built up over the preceding months.

The men were pulled apart, and three of them were hauled away by the scruff of the neck to the jailhouse at the end of the street.

It was then that a strange noise, much closer, caught her ear. She cocked her head to listen, finally recognizing it as singing—drunken singing.

"Oh-h-h-h, in eighteen hundred and seventy-eight
The ladies begged us to stay out late.

They still love us, yes they do,
But we've given our hearts to someone true.

Whiskey! Whiskey. You're so true and blue.
Whiskey! Whiskey. We'll never cheat on you."

The horrible bellowing sound came closer. She heard the thud of heavy footsteps stumbling up the stairs to the hotel's second floor. The singing stopped in the midst of a loud clatter that sounded as though the singers had missed a stair and fallen down two.

"It's not you I'd be wantin' by me sickbed, you black-hearted traitor!"

She recognized the Irish brogue as well as the deep roll of laughter from the other man. It was none other than Chance and Delaney, drunk to the gills.

The raucous tune started all over again, same verse. It was bad enough to make goose bumps of displeasure jump out all over her skin. She feared a complaint would bring the sheriff and they'd be tossed in jail. She decided it wouldn't do to have the engineer of the BRC thrown behind bars, so she pulled her cotton wrapper on and stepped out into the sconce-lit hall.

Another door opened and Lily peeked her head out. She saw Jenna. "What in the name of God is that horrible noise?"

"I hate to admit it, but I think it's Chance and Delaney."

Soon the two men reached the top of the stairs and

literally fell onto the hall floor in a tangled mass of limp limbs.

"You niver could hold yer liquor, Keely. To be shoor."

"You're one to talk. Whose on the floor? You or me?"

Delaney moved his head from side to side. "'Twould appear we both are."

Chance staggered to his feet first, then weaved around like a top that's on its last few spins. He finally righted himself and reached a hand down to Delaney. The Irishman stuck up his stump, stared at it through glazed eyes, then offered the other arm. "Here's me hand, Keely. I'd fergotten which side it was on. Grab hold, and I'll pull y' up."

Delaney came to his feet, and the two draped themselves over each other again for support and started down the hall.

"If you two don't make a fine impression," Jenna declared.

The two staggered to a stop and, with extreme effort, focused on Jenna and Lily.

"Well, if it isn't the darlin's," Delaney remarked, his head rolling on his neck as if he'd not been given a spine to offer support. "And dressed all in their nightclothes, too. Have y' been waitin' up fer us, darlin's?"

Lily took Delaney by the arm, pulling him away from Chance, only to discover that her tiny frame was hardly adequate to support the weight of the burly Irishman. She staggered under the strain, but managed to push and steer him toward his room.

"Come and sleep it off, Bard. I'll talk to you when you're making sense."

He offered no resistance, and when the door closed behind them, Jenna faced Chance. He was watching her intently through glassy, bloodshot eyes. Neither seemed to have anything to say, but finally Chance mumbled, "I think they . . . went into my room. And I think . . . she's staying. I could use hers . . . I guess."

The floor seemed to be uneven for him, like the deck of a ship on a stormy sea. He finally put a shoulder against the wall, as if to stop the upheaval, and put a hand to his head. "God, I drank too much . . . I think."

"And why did you, Chance? It isn't like you."

"Paterson . . . and you. You were . . . with him. I hear-r-r-d you . . . talking."

Jenna's lips pursed. "Yes, and that's all we did. *Talk*. He wanted me to leave Silver Bend."

So he'd heard her talking to Henry in her room and had probably thought they'd been making love. She smiled. His jealousy lifted her spirits higher than anything had for weeks.

"Come on. I'll help you to bed."

She put an arm around his waist and got her shoulder beneath his. He didn't seem to notice that she took him to *her* room. He collapsed on the bed and she removed his boots. In only seconds, he was asleep.

She sat down next to him, automatically pushing back a lock of black hair that had fallen onto his forehead. As she gazed at his handsome face in repose, she understood clearly the agony of the decision he had been faced with in loving her. And loving him had cost her much more than she'd ever bargained for, too. But loving him had also given her ecstasy and pleasure she'd never thought possible. Knowing him had given hope to the future, which would have otherwise stretched out in dismal, never-ending monotony.

She *wanted* to believe his words of love. Now, if only he would speak them again.

Chapter Twenty-Eight

Solomon looked out his window at the people dancing in the street below. Around the weak lanterns' glow that lit their lively steps, smoke swirled from the forest fires, giving the illusion of fog. A makeshift band had been thrown together to supply the music, but their songs clashed with those coming from the many saloons, creating a cacophony that no one seemed to mind but him. While the men partook of the liquor flowing freely both in and out of the saloons, the ladies filled their cups from punch bowls on long, food-laden tables.

He searched the shadowy figures for a glimpse of Lily but saw no sign of her. He wondered if it could be true that she and the Irishman might be breaking up. He would never interfere with her life again, but he would gladly welcome her into his arms if she came to him.

He pulled his handkerchief from his back pocket and mopped the sweat from his brow. The heat had barely dropped a degree even with the setting of the sun. It was too damned hot for merrymaking. Besides, it was time for old men to be in bed. And a toddy sounded good.

A knock came at the door.

Now, who in the hell can that be? I don't want

company. Unless it's Lily.

The sheer possibility of that idea lifted his spirits and he hastened forth to pull open the door, as if his dreams could produce reality. Instead, before him stood Owen Ives, hands resting on his gun belt.

Disappointed, Solomon turned away from him and went back into the room. He reached for his whiskey decanter and glass. "What do you want, Ives? It's late and I want to go to bed."

Ives followed him into the room and closed the door behind him. Solomon heard a scraping sound, like metal against leather. He turned with a faint degree of alarm. Ives's .45 was leveled at his chest. His beady black eyes held the gleam of a man who had no reservations about pulling the trigger.

"If it's sleep you want, Solomon, then maybe I can help."

The heat was suffocating. Jenna awoke to find herself in Chance's arms, but his body was like an oven. She disentangled herself from him and flung off the sheet that was over them. She tried to go back to sleep, but the party was still going strong in the street and her nose stung from the smoke. They'd been contending with smoke for weeks, but there was something vaguely different about the smell tonight. It reminded her of the sharp, distinct smell of burning pine first thing in the morning, when someone starts up a cook fire.

She got out of bed, deciding to close the window. She would suffer the heat over the noise and the smoke. Suddenly, two gunshots sounded from the outskirts of town. Her sleepy mind quickly cleared. The music stopped. The singing and hooting turned to screaming and shouting.

She peered out the window into the darkness. Like a stampede of frightened animals, the remainder of the all-night party ran helter-skelter through the lantern-lit street. From the dry slope of the mountain that rose like a wall on the north side of the town, flames leaped into the black sky and rushed with alarming speed through the dry grass. In the red glow, she saw men running with shovels and axes to try and stop the fire from reaching the town.

She tore herself from the window and shook Chance roughly. "Chance, wake up! There's a fire!"

He sat up with a start, still a little hazy from the liquor but sobering quickly. "Where is it?"

"On the north slope of town."

She lit the lamp and they dressed hastily. Carrying the hurricane lamp, Jenna hurried into the hall behind Chance.

"Wake Solomon," he said. "I'll get Mama and Delaney."

Jenna's knock at her grandfather's door produced no answer. She pounded harder, insistently. From across the hall a door opened. A scowling woman stuck her head out. "This place is beginning to sound like Grand Central Station," she snapped. "There's enough noise outside. For the love of God, do you have to bring it in here, too?"

"Help us wake everyone up," Jenna said as calmly as she could. "There's a fire on the outskirts of town. We need—"

The woman went into hysterics and fled back to her room, screaming, "Luther! Fire! We're all going to die! FIRE!"

Her shrieking reverberated throughout the hotel. A scramble of feet could be heard in every room on the second floor.

The door to Solomon's room was unlocked so Jenna hurried inside, only to find the bed empty. She held her lamp higher to better illuminate the dark corners and the chairs, but he was not there, either.

Back in the hall, she joined Chance. "Grandpa's

not in his room," she announced worriedly. "I wonder where he could have gone to at this hour."

Chance tried to reassure her. "Don't worry. He's probably gone down to see what the commotion was about."

Lily and Delaney came from their room, pulling on clothes. All four were forced to step out of the way as people in nightclothes raced down the hall with lamps and overflowing carpetbags. There was still no sign of Solomon.

"He must have gone down to join the party," Jenna said.

They took the stairs with the others. Word of the fire had reached the first floor. While occupants rushed outside, others pushed their way in, returning to their rooms to collect the things they didn't believe they could leave behind.

Outside on the boardwalk, the four searched the mass of people but didn't see Solomon among them. The town, lit now by the fire's red-orange glow, was in complete pandemonium, and a wind made things worse by tossing the gigantic flames into an even greater frenzy.

Men spilled from every building and every side street. In minutes, they formed bucket brigades from the river. Others with shovels, axes, and crosscut saws started working on a firebreak on the town's north side—something that should have been done long ago. Those who didn't seem to know what to do simply turned in circles, looking for loved ones in the crowded streets while dodging people, horses, and wagons.

On the mountainside, the flames climbed the tree trunks with lightning speed and engulfed the dry branches, spiraling with ferocity into the sky for incredible distances. Elsewhere, the fire roared through the grass and brush, destroying acres in awesome swiftness, all the while edging toward town and the first row of buildings on the back street. It moved in every direction where fuel existed. And Silver Bend was a tinder town, its buildings made of logs and unmilled clapboards sawn from pitch-filled native pine. The town was completely devoid of fire-fighting facilities, helpless against a fire of this magnitude.

A man forced his way through the crowded street on horseback, shouting, "Women and children! Evacuate! Head for the trains!"

Chance took in the situation and made a rapid decision. "Let's get the horses from the livery. We'll have a better chance of getting out of here."

Jenna grabbed his hand, beseeching him. "I can't leave without Grandpa. Please let me look for him."

"I won't leave without him, Jenna, but I want to make sure you and Mama get out."

"But what about you? It isn't wise to get separated and possibly leave anybody behind."

Chance forgot the raging fire as he fell into the depths of her eyes filled with concern for him. She held his hand tightly. Was it possible she did love him?

In that moment, it was all he could do to keep from pulling her into his arms and kissing her, hoping that in some way he would know by her embrace and the feel of her lips against his whether the answer to his question was yes. But Delaney and his mother stood by, anxiously watching and waiting. And the fire raged, not waiting at all.

"I'll be fine. Now, let's get you and Mama to the train."

They formed a human chain, with Chance in the lead and Delaney bringing up the rear. They shoved their way along the boardwalk, gripping each other's hands to keep from getting separated in the crowd of terrified people.

The livery was only a short distance away, but by

the time they got there, they were exhausted from the jostling of the frantic crowd. The situation was no better here. Horses, sensing the danger, kicked their stalls and fought their ropes. Some managed to escape and galloped from the livery into the street, sending the people screaming and scattering even worse. The horses in the corral circled and pushed at the pine poles, to find a way out or to make one.

The hostler was as frenzied as his animals. He trotted back and forth, not knowing whether to turn the animals loose or to hold them in case the owners came for them.

He recognized Chance. "Better get out of here, Killeen. Word has it that another fire's broke out 'tween here and Mullan. We don't know how bad it is, but could be we're trapped, less'n we go east over Lookout Pass. And you know that road is a killer at night."

"Can the trains get back to the lake?"

"Don't know. All I know is that there's more damn people than both yours and Durfey's trains ought to haul in one load."

"Has Solomon Lee come by for a horse or a buggy?"

"Ain't seen nary a sign of him."

Grimly, they led their horses from the stalls and hastily saddled them. The wavering orange tentacles of the fire towered over the town like monstrous hands, reaching out menacingly with heat so hot it made a blacksmith's forge cool by comparison.

"Delaney," Chance said, pulling his eyes from the roaring inferno, "go with the women. If you get down to the tracks and find out the train can't get through, then get them to safety somewhere. I'll find you later."

Delaney nodded, helped Lily into the saddle, then mounted his own horse.

Chance turned to Jenna. Her eyes were oval with

fear, reflecting the orange flames of the fire in their depths. Unspoken words hung between them, needing to be said, and in those final moments before separation they both realized there might never be another time.

Jenna suddenly flung herself into his arms. "Oh, Chance! I love you! All those things I said . . . I was so confused and hurt. And after losing the baby, I . . . oh, I shouldn't have listened to Henry!"

If Chance could have accomplished the act, he would have drawn her inside him and kept her safe next to his heart forever. He whispered fiercely against her ear, "Oh, God, Jenna. And I love you. When this is all over, tell me you'll marry me."

She tilted her head back to meet his anxious gaze. She had barely whispered "Yes!" when his lips came down hard on hers in a kiss as tumultuous as the fire. Much too soon he was forced to set her away from him and help her mount Desperado.

"You'd better be going," he said, still holding her hand. "But don't worry. I'll find your grandfather. Just don't waste any time getting out of this canyon. If the fire spreads across the entrance, the only way out will be over the south side—and it won't be a pleasant ride down that rocky embankment."

She touched his cheek as though she might never be able to again. "Be careful, Chance."

"I will, Jenna. I'll come back to you. I promise."

With tears welling in her eyes, she rode away with Lily and Delaney. Chance watched them work their way into the flow of people, praying they'd be all right. Then he turned to the hostler.

"I'll need another horse if I find Solomon."

The hostler turned on his heel toward the corral. "I've got one you can take. Follow me."

A few minutes later, Chance rode the buckskin out into the street, leading the other horse, a big sorrel gelding. With nearly everyone on their way out of town, he was moving against traffic. He saw right away that the men had given up the bucket brigade and were attempting to tear down the houses on the back street closest to the encroaching fire, but many of the buildings were already ablaze. The fire was quickly spreading out along the entire north side of the town. It was simply too big to fight with the lack of equipment and for as fast as it was moving.

Chance scanned the crowd in vain for Solomon. He worked his way back to the hotel, thinking the baron might have gone there looking for them. As he approached the large two-story building, he noticed a house behind the hotel on the back street had already gone up in flames. Cinders and sparks floated down through the air, settling on his clothing and on the roof of the hotel. He knew the hotel's dry shingles would ignite any second.

He leaped to the ground and tied the two horses securely to the hitching post, hoping they wouldn't panic and break loose or that someone wouldn't steal them. He ran inside and up the stairs with no interference, because everyone was gone.

He burst into Solomon's room. The red glow of the fire from the building behind the hotel cast its eerie light into the room, making it easy to see that the baron still wasn't there.

"Goddamn it, Solomon! Where are you?"

In total frustration and desperation, he stared at the belongings in the room, thinking there might be some clue as to where Solomon had gone. But there was nothing.

He ran down the hall. "Solomon! Solomon, answer me!"

On the main floor of the hotel he did the same, pausing to listen for an answer.

Nothing.

Chance started for the door. Suddenly, a large form loomed in the doorway. With the back light of the fire, he easily recognized Owen Ives. The grading foreman was a calm man by nature, almost too calm. Even now, the fire seemed to have about as much impact on him as a lighted match.

"Looking for Solomon?" he asked idly.

Chance suddenly felt like a deer that has been stalked by a cougar for miles and is just now aware of it. "You know I am, you bastard."

Ives's lips lifted in an evil smile.

Something hard and round pressed into Chance's side from behind him. He easily recognized it as a gun barrel. At the same time, a hand jerked his Colt from the holster.

"We figured you'd come looking for him," came Paterson's voice from behind him. "And we'd be more than happy to show you where he's at."

Chapter Twenty-Nine

The sheriff turned the keys in the lock and flung open the door to the jailhouse. "You three trouble-makers, get the hell out of here before you burn to death!"

Thanking him profusely, they tore after the last of the people leaving town. They made it to the end of the street in record time. The sheriff was just turning to his horse when the impact of a bullet flung him to the ground. The burst of the report was lost to the roaring fire.

Ives, Paterson, Leaman, and Durfey emerged from the shadows on horseback, with Chance and Solomon in tow at the end of two lariat ropes wrapped around their chests and arms.

Ives stared impassively down at the dead sheriff and shoved his gun back into his holster. "Durfey, get the keys and toss him in the building with these two."

They shoved Chance and Solomon to the jail-house at the end of their gun barrels. The building was constructed like a fortress, with a heavy wooden door and only one small window covered by iron bars. There was little hope of escape and no one was left in town to hear any calls for help.

Solomon had to hand it to Henry. He'd had a good

plan that would have worked to make him rich again if Solomon hadn't come along to interfere. The milking of the company had been a clever alternative to defeat, but he was more shocked by Leaman's betrayal than by that of the other two. Through all the years, he'd never dreamed Leaman had held a grudge of any sort. That they would resort to murder was the biggest shock of all. They'd killed Barlet, Westbrook, the guards, Barlow, even Shang, making it look like an accident. And just as Chance had said, they'd planned the explosion in the tunnel to try and kill him.

They would be the winners in the end. And if Henry convinced Jenna to marry him some day—and he would continue to try—then even Solomon Enterprises would be lost. If only he could warn her that the Henry Paterson she knew was not the real Henry Paterson at all! But for the first time in his life, he was powerless.

"Why don't you just shoot us, Henry?" he snapped. "Why bother with all this nonsense?"

Henry walked his horse to the open door of the jail and watched idly while Ives took the ropes off the two of them. "Well, Solomon, the way I see it, you've lived a notorious life, and I feel your death should be just as outstanding. A bullet just isn't quite enough. Your death should make the headlines. Something really spectacular, you know? And you, Killeen. It's just your misfortune to have gotten in the way of my plans with Jenna. It's too bad you didn't die in that tunnel."

"So you think she'll marry you after all this?"

"Yeah, I think so. She'll never find out I'm the one who killed you. There's no way we can get charged with anything. As you can see, there's no witnesses." He reined away. "Lock 'em up, Ives. Then let's get moving. We'll take the south ridge so no one will see us, and we'll still get to the trains before they pull out.''

Jenna and Jethro Ritchy forced their unwilling horses back into the blazing town. The fire was close to the canyon's entrance now and could close it off any minute. The last of the fire fighters fled on the trail of the women and children. Three men on foot passed them on a high run.

Ritchy had met Jenna on the way to the train, with all the information needed to put Henry and his friends away for life, as well as having overheard a conversation that they planned to kill Chance and her grandfather. Jenna hadn't wanted to believe the incriminating evidence, but as her heart denied it, her mind couldn't. She knew now that Henry had tried to get her out of town not for the reasons he stated, but because he had planned this fire as a distraction to cover his tracks while he and the others committed murder.

Darkness was lifting as daylight neared. The street was cast in black shadows and a red glow from the fire that now consumed the entire north slope of the mountain. The wind roared like a tornado and whipped the flames into towering columns, with orange smoke billowing above the trees as high as a hundred feet into the sky. Trees snapped and popped, exploding under the intense heat. Sparks fell like millions of burning stars. If it weren't for Chance and her grandfather, Jenna would never have had the courage to venture into it.

The back street, as well as the north side of Main Street, was ablaze. The hard-packed street and the distance across it, even though not great, served to keep the fire from the one row of buildings that hugged the river on the south side.

Ritchy was obviously impressed by it all but wasn't keen on staying around. "They've probably already been killed, Missy. I hate to say it, but we'd better be for hightailin' it out of here ourselves. This is more than I bargained for."

Jenna grabbed the reins, afraid he might very well leave her alone here. "We've got to look for them. Please stay and help me. I've got to find them!"

"Missy, unless they're dead or tied up, there'd be no damned good reason for them to be here. Maybe they've already gone."

"But we would have seen them."

"Not if they went over the south ridge."

Angrily, she put her heels into Desperado's flanks. "I'm not leaving until I'm forced out. Go if you want, but if they're still alive, I can't leave them to die."

Jethro Ritchy couldn't be shown up by a mere slip of a woman. After all, he didn't want her thinking he was a coward. Against his better judgment, he followed.

The horses refused to go down the main street. The fire rose up on the north side much too close. The roar nearly deafened them, the heat was insufferable, and buildings were collapsing all around them. If Chance and Solomon were in any of them, it was too late to save them.

They turned to their one last hope—the street that was next to the river and not yet touched by flames. They checked every building. Most had the doors hanging open. Some were only one- or two-room shacks, and they could see inside without getting out of the saddle. Others required a more thorough search and they held each other's mounts while they alternated the task.

After the last building had been searched, Jenna swung back into the saddle. Her gaze reluctantly drifted to those buildings ablaze on the other side of the street.

Ritchy was sympathetic. "I'm sorry, Missy, but they ain't here, and if they're in any of those other buildings, then they're already dead."

The hope Jenna had carried with her crumbled like the burning timbers, but she had to keep searching. She couldn't give up. She couldn't! Chance and her grandfather were all she had. And yet Ritchy was right. There was no place left to look.

Hot tears scalded her face as her eyes took in the fire-lit town and the dawn-gray perimeters. And then she saw it. "Ritchy! The jail! We haven't searched the jail!"

On a gallop they raced toward the structure, set off by itself and nearly unnoticeable next to the underbrush that lined the river. Jenna set Desperado back on his heels in front of the building as she leaped from the saddle. A horse's nicker from the river bottom drew her attention. From the brush trotted Chance's buckskin, an unknown sorrel wearing only headgear, and a third horse, completely saddled.

"It's their horses!" She ran to the jailhouse door, pulling and pounding on it. "Chance! Grandpa! Are you in there?"

"Jenna!" came Chance's glad reply. "We're glad to see you, but you won't be able to get the door off. It's locked and solid as a barge. You'll have to try and pull the bars out of the window."

"Okay. I'm here with Ritchy. We'll get you out."

"And hurry," Solomon inserted impatiently. "It's hot enough in here to roast a side of beef."

With nimble fingers made even more deft by the threat of the onrushing fire, Ritchy looped his lariat and Jenna's around the iron bars. They remounted and he handed her the rope. "Okay, Missy. Wrap a dally around that saddle horn and make it a good one. When I say go, you kick that black pony for all he's worth."

Jenna watched how Jethro made his dally and then

copied him. On the count of three, the two horses lunged ahead simultaneously. Jenna felt the resistane on the saddle and feared it would be pulled right off the horse's back and her with it. The two horses bowed their necks and put their weight into the pull. To her amazement, wood started to splinter from beneath the bars.

"Pull, Missy! Pull! We've almost got it!"

With the shattering of wood, the bars came free, along with part of the wall. It was enough for Chance and Solomon to get through. Ritchy flung the ropes aside. His attention shot to the wall of fire closing off the canyon's entrance. "We'll have to take the south ridge."

Chance mounted the buckskin and Solomon took the sheriff's horse because it had a saddle. They turned the sorrel loose to follow. On a lunging lope, Chance led the way up the south side through the trees. The horses soon slowed, for it was a steep climb. The forest near the town had been logged heavily, but the stumps posed an even worse danger than the trees. The first gray cast of dawn helped to light their way, but once over the ridge and into the next canyon, they were flung into darkness again and had only the backwash of red from the fire to guide them. In the distance, they heard two long-drawn whistles from one of the trains—the signal for departure.

They tried to hold their speed down as they descended the south ridge, but the animals gained momentum on the steep incline. Their front legs dug into the slope with bone-jarring intensity. In places they hit loose rock, causing the horses to slide worse. Jenna gave Desperado his head, knowing his mountain instincts would enable him to find the best course down. She felt blinded by the half-light and the eerie red cast of the fire. Dark shapes loomed up, then rushed past. Limbs slapped her in the face,

362

stinging and cutting her, but the black kept his footing and she kept her seat.

At last they came to the canyon floor and hit the wagon road used by the lumbermen. They pulled rein to rest their horses.

"We're safe now," Ritchy said. "The only other fire close by is the one between here and Mullan. It was heading for the tracks when I came through earlier. I wouldn't be surprised if the trains have to turn back."

"They can't go anywhere but back to Silver Bend," Chance said. "They could be trapped between the two fires."

"It's possible. I suggest we head over to Dorsey or even the pass 'til we see what's going to happen."

The sheriff's horse already seemed winded. Sweat stained its neck. Chance wondered if the animal could make it the distance to the train.

"My mother and best friend are on that train," he said. "I need to be there if something happens that they can't get through. Besides, I have a hunch Paterson and the others are headed for the train, too. I've got a score to settle and I don't intend on waiting."

"You'll be riding hard, Killeen. I can't go with you," Ritchy replied. "I pushed my horse hard to get to Silver Bend. He hasn't got much left in him."

"That's fine. I'll go alone, but I'd better get moving. That train's still a mile away and getting farther."

"You might need a weapon," Ritchy said, unstrapping his gun belt and handing it to Chance. "That bunch means business."

Solomon spoke up while Chance buckled on the gun belt. "I'd go with you, but I'm afraid I'd only slow you down."

Chance could tell the rough ride had been hard on the baron and he nodded understandably.

Jenna nudged Desperado up alongside him. "I'll

go with you. I may be able to help," she said flatly. But her eyes said, *I don't want us to be separated again.*

Chance read her feelings clearly, for they were his own. But there was a practical side he had to consider. "It's too dangerous, Jenna. You know Ives won't hesitate at murder."

She sat her saddle with a rigid, stubborn posture and her chin elevated defiantly. "I'll take the chance—same as you."

He looked to Solomon for support, but the baron said nothing. They both knew that to argue with Jenna Lee when her mind was set was a fruitless endeavor that could only take up more of the precious seconds ticking away.

The train wailed two more times in the distance. "All right," he capitulated. "Let's go."

Chapter Thirty

The sky was considerably lighter when they galloped into view of the Silverado. The Coeur d'Alene Central was already out of sight.

"There's Henry and the others!" Jenna cried, pointing toward the train. "They're getting on!"

They watched as the four men in turn left their saddles and scaled the ladder at the rear of the caboose, quickly dispersing themselves along the top of the train. The last one up was Henry. He saw them and in haste hurried after the others.

"Damn! He's seen us," Chance said. "Now they'll probably jump off the first chance they get. If they manage to get to Canada, we've lost them. We've got to catch the train before it takes that grade. Our horses are just about done and we won't be able to catch it when it picks up speed."

The train wasn't moving fast yet and it was overloaded. Hysterical women and crying children filled its three passenger cars. The two freight cars and caboose were packed with men. A number had even found a place on top of the cars for lack of room elsewhere.

Delaney and Lily came out onto the caboose's platform and waved them on with encouragement. Galloping alongside the train, Chance leaned out and easily swung from his horse onto the platform.

He hurried to the other side and held out a hand for Jenna. "Come on! Grab my hand and jump!"

The urgency and worry in his eyes didn't help Jenna's fear. She urged Desperado on at what seemed a breakneck speed, leaning out over his neck until his black mane was whipping in her face. She could only pray he wouldn't stumble. At first she gained on the caboose, then suddenly it started pulling away.

Panicky, she urged the horse faster and he obeyed, stride after ground-eating stride. She reached for the rail. Closer it came, until at last her fingers touched it. With her heart in her throat, she kicked free of the stirrups, grabbed for it with both hands, and lunged from the saddle. The movement of the train yanked her body forward, then flung it back, but she clung to the rail and felt Chance's arm snake out to catch her. Her feet hit the platform stairs and safety.

Out of breath, they watched the horses veer away from the tracks. Along with those turned loose from Silver Bend, they would have to find their own way clear of the fire.

"The engineer held the train as long as he could," Delaney shouted about the rumble, "but the passengers were threatenin' to riot if he tarried a moment longer."

Furrows appeared in Lily's brow as she clasped Chance and Jenna's hands. "What about Solomon? Is he—?"

"He's alive," Jenna managed between breaths. "He and Ritchy are headed for Dorsey."

Lily breathed a sigh of relief and stepped back into the comforting circle of Delaney's embrace.

Chance pulled his hat down tight on his forehead and surveyed the ladder that went up onto the caboose. "I guess Ritchy told you that Paterson, Ives, and Leaman were in on the sabotage of the BRC with Durfey?"

"Aye," Delaney responded. "And does that mean they were also behind the explosion in the tunnel?"

Chance nodded.

"Well, then, get movin', me frind, and I'll be right behind you. I've got me own score to be settlin' with that bunch o' black-hearted traitors."

Chance was afraid Delaney wouldn't be able to make the ladder with only one hand, but he didn't want to say so. "I could use your help in a different way, Delaney, other than coming up here."

Delaney peered up at him from beneath the brim of his hat. "Yer will is me pleasure."

"I need you to send word up to the front to that police force that manned Silver Bend. If any of them can get into the wood car, they might be able to stop them up ahead."

Delaney nodded. Chance ran up the ladder and disappeared over the top. Lily hurried after Delaney. And that left Jenna free to follow Chance.

Shunning the consequences of her actions, she climbed out over the platform as she'd seen Chance do. The train had gathered considerable speed on the downgrade and wound swiftly along the curving track. Somewhere up ahead was the fire that Ritchy had told them about, but Jenna kept that in the back of her mind. She forced herself to concentrate on the ladder and refused to look down at the ground rushing past on either side of her. The bottoms of her boots were slick and her riding skirt continually got in the way with each new rung she took.

With utter determination, though, she reached the top rung. Men were perched on the cupola. She recognized a couple of them from the tracklaying crew. When they saw her, they hastened to help her to the top.

"Miss Lee! What's going on? Killeen just rushed by with no explanation."

Quickly, she explained the situation. The men

found it hard to believe that their own employers had been the culprits all along. With a fire of their own to see justice enforced, they set out behind Chance, gathering more men along the way. With arms outstretched for balance, Jenna followed behind two of the men who had taken the lead. Behind her, the numbers increased.

The wind beat at her hair, whipping it into her face and obscuring her view, but as the train rounded a bend, she was able to see Chance one car ahead. Paterson and the others were hurrying toward the front of the train, having some difficulty getting over the men blocking their way.

The men in front of her easily leaped the distance between the caboose and the rear passenger car. It looked to be a yawning span she wasn't sure she wanted to attempt.

"Come on, Miss Lee!" the two in front hollered. "You can do it! We'll catch you!"

They held out their hands. Jenna backed up a few feet and took a running leap. She sailed over to the other side easily but was thankful for the hands ready to catch her.

"Look!" hollered a man behind her. "There's the fire they warned us about!"

In front of them flames thirty feet high reached out over the tracks nearly filling the narrow gorge ahead, reminding Jenna of a fiery hoop at the circus that the lion tamer expected his unwilling subjects to jump through.

The engineer blew his whistle, a succession of short sounds to alert everyone to the danger. It was apparent he was going to make a run through it. If the stretch wasn't too long, they'd be all right, but those on top of the car could be burned.

Chance saw the men following him with Jenna in their midst. He motioned for them to get down, then dropped to his own knees. The engineer pushed the throttle forward. The train picked up speed, moving faster and faster toward the fiery walls. From inside the cars, the women and children whimpered and cried. Some screamed out hysterically.

Ives and Durfey moved ever closer to the wood car. Henry and Leaman tried to catch up, but Leaman couldn't seem to maintain his balance. Jenna and the others went down and covered their heads. Jenna closed her eyes and felt the intense heat envelop her. If the flames reached their clothing, it would be disastrous.

The seconds ticked by. Was it only ten before the heat vanished? It felt an eternity. At last the train slid through the fiery walls and reached safety on the other side. The people came to their feet again, but were too shaken and subdued to count their blessings or shout for joy.

From between the first passenger car and the wood car, the first sign of the police force materialized, cutting Ives and Durfey off. They turned to go back and saw the scores of others blocking that exit, too. Like trapped animals, the four had no way to escape.

Chance advanced on Henry, gun drawn. "There's no way out for you this time, Paterson. Toss your gun down."

Paterson seemed to consider his alternatives and finally drew his pistol from its holster. As it cleared leather, though, a venomous expression burst onto his face, giving away his thoughts. Chance dropped to his stomach just as Henry jerked the gun up and fired. Henry's bullet hit the roof of the car just mere inches from Chance's leg, but Killeen's returning bullet found its mark. Henry's gun flew from his hand, clattering over the side of the train and to the ground. He clutched at his bleeding arm, gritting his teeth in pain.

His gun aimed at Paterson's head, Chance stood up and walked to within a few feet of his adversary.

He found it extremely difficult to keep from squeezing the trigger a second time. Before him was the man who had caused Delaney to lose his arm and Jenna to lose their baby . . . the man who had nearly succeeded in killing both him and Solomon. Perhaps Ives was the cold-blooded murderer, but in Chance's eyes, his accomplice was no less an animal.

"Go ahead and kill me, Killeen." Paterson's lips curled contemptuously. "I *dare* you."

"Sorry, Paterson. I want you to face the world— and Jenna—with your humiliation, especially after what you've done to her."

"I did nothing but care for her."

"You did nothing but try to take advantage of her. But you've built your last railroad. I'm just sorry it had to be mine."

"You bastard. I may go down, but you'll go with me!"

He lunged at Chance, hitting him in the chest with his head and shoulders. They fell backward in the center of the roof. Paterson grabbed Chance's wrist and tried to get the gun, his fingers clawing to reach the hammer and trigger. He was strong, even with his wounded arm, and he slowly succeeded in turning the gun toward Chance's head. With untapped strength, Chance thrust his body upward, throwing Paterson over onto his back. Pain streaked across the older man's face but still he tried to hold on to the gun. Chance slammed his wounded arm against the edge of the raised roof until Paterson finally screamed in pain and released his grip from Killeen's wrist.

Chance shoved the gun up against the throbbing vein in Paterson's throat. "Don't tempt me again," he said with cold decisiveness.

The men in front of Jenna hurried to intervene. They hauled Henry to his feet and nudged him toward Leaman, who was gathering himself up from the prone position he'd taken when the gunfire broke out. Chance stepped around them and Jenna ran into his arms. The police force, guns ready, stood up in the wood car and gave Ives and Durfey instructions to throw down their guns. They had no alternative but to comply.

Unexpectedly, the engineer let up on the throttle again, throwing everyone forward. Leaman was flung back down. The others managed to keep their footing but quickly went to their hands and knees for better balance. The only ones remaining standing were Ives and Durfey, up on the freight car.

Everyone craned their necks to see why the engineer had slowed down. They saw Durfey clutch at Ives with one hand while pointing with the other and screaming, "No! He can't go over that trestle. He's a fool! Somebody stop him!"

As the fore part of the train emerged from the gorge, they saw with sinking hearts that the fire had also made its way into the ravine, devouring the dry foliage as well as the center part of the spidery frame of a one-hundred-foot high trestle.

Before them was fire. Behind them was fire. Only on the other side of the ravine was the forest untouched. If the train could reach it, they would be safe. But in order to reach it, they had to cross the blazing trestle.

The train slowed even more as the engineer assessed the fire and his alternatives. If they reversed, they would face the licking flames in the narrow gorge from which they'd barely escaped just moments before. Not to mention that retreating could leave them trapped between this fire and the one at Silver Bend, with absolutely no way out but on foot through the burning mountains.

Chance looked out over the trestle, silently making

his own assessment of the fire consuming the lower part of it. The way he saw it, they had only one choice.

As if the engineer had read his mind, he thrust the throttle forward.

"Get down!" Chance yelled. "He's going to take the trestle!"

Durfey screamed again, clutching like a madman to Ives. "No! It'll collapse! He can't go across! Somebody stop him!"

The train rumbled out onto the trestle. Absolute silence engulfed the passengers. The screaming ceased as prayers took precedence. The massive structure gave no indication of weakness until the train reached the burning center. Then far below came groans and snapping timbers. The trestle dipped and quivered beneath its heavily loaded burden. Gasps and muffled cries, sobs and quiet cursing, rose up from the passengers. Then all was silent again. Frozen in terror, they barely breathed as the Silverado inched closer and closer to the other side. Black smoke poured back over the cars, but it kept its speed without faltering. It clung to the rails with the tenacity of a clawed beast rather than a machine, with nothing more secure than smooth metal against metal.

The engine finally rumbled onto the solid end of the trestle, and with it the first three cars. But suddenly a mighty crack came from the center of the trestle. It dipped beneath the last three cars, sinking out from under them. The passengers' screams roared above the straining growl of the Silverado with bloodcurdling intensity.

Chance and Jenna lay side by side, facedown on the roof, their fingers dug into whatever handhold they could find. In those seconds, agonizing and amazingly long, they felt the trestle sinking. Their gazes locked in those moments that might very well be their last. Almost simultaneously, they each released a handhold. Their two hands met and caught, fingers entwining as they clung tightly to each other.

The engineer shoved the throttle full speed ahead. The train lunged forward with all the power it had left. Durfey, still standing hypnotized by the scene, teetered precariously and grabbed Ives, who had gone to his hands and knees. Ives tried to shake himself free but Durfey wrapped his arms around the other man's waist and clung to him like a crying baby.

"Let go of me! Let go!" Ives screamed desperately, but Durfey held him with a death grip that pulled them both over the side. They fell into the fiery ravine, their screams mingling with the cracking timbers.

The trestle shuddered and swayed again. The caboose barely reached a solid part of the trestle when the center part collapsed and crashed the one hundred feet to the bottom of the ravine.

At last, like a winded horse, the Silverado panted to a shuddering stop. The only sound now was the stillness of the mountains, the distant roar of the fire, and the weeping of relief from the women and men alike.

It was long minutes before anyone moved, but slowly they all began to rise, to sit up and look around, almost disbelieving the fact that they had survived the ordeal. Chance drew Jenna against him, nearly smothering her in his thankful embrace.

Henry curled into a sitting position, clutching his bleeding arm. His gaze held unconcealed bitterness for the two of them.

Jenna's tear-filled eyes met his. "I never thought you would betray me, Henry. Never."

"I owed Solomon for what he did to me when you were just a child. But I guess nobody ever beats the baron."

Jenna turned away from his hateful eyes and hid her tears in Chance's chest. If only she could hide from the pain.

The train let out several sharp blasts, cheering its victory. The whistle seemed to jar the people from their state of shock, and a few at a time they joined in by cheering, until everyone was shouting with joy and relief.

The police force took Henry and Leaman into custody. Slowly, the train gathered speed, resuming its journey.

Chance and Jenna sat down side by side on top of the passenger car again. Jenna looked ahead into the dawning of the new day that lit the winding tracks through the towering green mountains. Except for the smoke making a haze over them, everything appeared peaceful and calm, fresh and inviting, almost dreamlike in contrast to the nightmarish hours that would eventually dim in memory.

Chance saw Jenna's gaze following Henry's retreat, then noticed how it remained in the far distance long after her old friend was gone from sight. "There's nothing anyone can do for him, Jenna," he said. "You can only put it behind you."

She looked at him with eyes that sought comfort and assurance from the pain of disillusionment, from the pain of all they had suffered. "I was thinking more of what lies ahead, Chance. I hope there are no more fires . . . no more trouble. For our sake. For you and me."

His pulse pounded wildly to see her heart laid open for him without reservation of any kind. But then it had always been that way. He had simply been too prideful to forget the past and to accept what she had offered so willingly.

He curved her body more fully to his. "Everything will be all right, Jenna," he whispered huskily. "I promise you . . . the worst is behind us now."

Epilogue

A drizzling rain quenched the parched land and extinguished the fires in the Bitterroot Mountain Range. Solomon Lee stood under the porch of Rathdrum's railway depot and looked across the grassy plain that stretched south to the Coeur d'Alene Mountains. He was reluctant to leave here. Not only had the place come to have a special meaning for him, but he was leaving behind the only two women he truly loved. Still, it was for the best. His presence would only interfere with their lives.

He heard footsteps on the wooden porch stairs. The familiar sound of the feminine step drew him around. Jenna and Chance approached with arms linked. They'd been newlyweds for several weeks now, and the love glow between them was as noticeable as a gold nugget winking in the noonday sun. Oh, what would it have been like to have shared such bliss with Lily?

Jenna held up a paper in her daintily gloved hand and smiled like a schoolgirl who'd just come home with the best grade in the class.

"Grandpa!" She left Chance's side and rushed forward, linking her arm through his. "We've got the deed! We can start clearing the land and constructing the house. And the property is going to be the perfect

375

place for my horses." The words continued to roll excitedly off her tongue. "We won't be able to see the lake, but we'll be close enough to go there as often as we like. And of course we'll have an excellent view of the mountains. Chance will still be able to run the railroad as well as keep tabs on the Wapiti. Delaney is going to be in charge of the mine now, and he and Lily will stay in Bayard. With the trains running, it'll be easy to visit them often."

Then he saw that pleading look in her eyes he'd always found hard to ignore. "I wish you'd reconsider and stay, Grandpa. You could open up an office here and build a house on the lake."

So she knew he'd be lonely by himself in New York. He seriously doubted he could hide anything from her.

"Perhaps I will some day," he said, patting her hand to alleviate her concerns. "But I've neglected Solomon Enterprises for far too long. As I promised, I'll join you for Christmas. And the spring may find me out this way."

The train chugged down the track toward them, with the *Marietta* and the *Crescent* in tow. Its body glistened black and shiny from a recent polishing as well as from the rain. The two cars had been Jenna's home for so long, and for the first time in years, she wouldn't be on them with her grandfather when they pulled out.

Suddenly, tears sprang to her eyes and she threw her arms around his neck. "Oh, Grandpa! I'm going to miss you!"

He held her tightly. "And I'll miss you," he replied. "But we'll adjust—you and I. We always have."

When the tears had subsided, Jenna set herself away from him. She joined Chance again and slid her hand into the warm assurance of his. She didn't want

376

him to think for a moment that she regretted her decision to stay here with him and make her life in these mountains—for she didn't. How ironic it was, though, that she had once told him she would never choose between him and her grandfather, and yet she had. Taking a mate meant choosing. It meant devotion to one's spouse and to the life you've vowed to share together. But she would never forsake her grandfather. No, never.

Love filled his old blue eyes. "Don't cry, Jenna. I've had my turn at love. Now it's yours."

The train pulled to a stop in front of the depot. The steam puffed out along its mighty wheels and drifted onto the depot porch. The pattering of rain on the depot roof increased. The train whistle blew and the conductor yelled, "All aboard!" reminding them that they must hurry with their good-byes.

"Take care of yourself in New York, Grandpa. Are you sure you don't mind handling the sale of the horse farm for me?"

For a fleeting moment his face looked pinched and strained, but as quickly as the telltale sign of emotion appeared, it was gone. "Don't worry about the farm. I'll get you a handsome profit and ship your horses out here. You'd better get this husband of yours going on some pastures, though."

His gaze lifted to Chance's. There was a quiet moment as they conducted their silent appraisal of each other. Chance had wondered if time would renew the bitterness. He'd feared that Solomon might be too autocratic, but the baron had kept completely out of their lives as if he was all too aware of what his power and his presence could do. Now he was stepping away from them even more. Chance hoped, for Jenna's sake, that he wouldn't alienate himself completely. She needed him. As for himself, he never would have thought he would actually miss the old man, but after having worked alongside him and nearly having died alongside him, he felt a kinship that settled the past in a way nothing else had.

He extended his hand. Solomon gripped it tightly and said, "When will the BRC be open again for travel?"

"The trestle will be done by the end of the week, so probably Monday the trains will start running. It'll be a big day and a lot of fanfare when the first loads of ore start going out. Of course, when that new company that bought Durfey's line finishes it, we'll have us a little competition," he added with a wry smile. "We didn't have a conclusion to our race, but it'll be interesting to see how soon the price wars begin."

Solomon chuckled. "That's the spice of life. I could have bought Durfey's line, I suppose, but I've discovered the only pleasure in monopolies is the difficulty in acquiring them. In this case, there would have been no difficulty at all. Besides, who wants to buy a railroad when he can have the challenge of building one?" His eyes sparkled like a young man's full of mischievousness, then slowly faded back to solemnity. "It's unfortunate, though, that this road had to cause us all so much grief. Who could have known that Henry's desire for revenge would have taken on such magnitude?"

They stood in silent recollection of the quick trial and subsequent prison sentences of Henry and Leaman. Since they hadn't actually murdered anyone themselves, they had been spared the noose, but they would both be old men before they got out of prison—if they didn't die first.

Chance squeezed Jenna's hand, mindful of how talk of Henry always affected her. She still found it very difficult to cope with her friend's betrayal. She preferred to remember him in the years when he had

378

always been there as her friend.

The train whistle blew, giving its last departure warning.

Chance reached into his coat pocket and pulled out an envelope, handing it to Solomon. "It's from my mother."

Solomon stared at Chance for a moment, then at the letter. Finally, he took it in a hand that had begun to tremble. He looked at his name written across the front in Lily's neat, flowing hand. What had she to say to him? What more was there *to* say but good-bye? Did he even want to know what she'd written?

He slipped the envelope into his inside coat pocket and hoped that Chance and Jenna would merely think his hand shook from old age.

"Solomon . . ." Chance began. "There's something I wanted you to know."

Their eyes met again. In that instant Solomon clearly remembered that day, sixteen years ago, when he'd confronted Chance in the hall of that tenement house and had seen the burning hatred that would be the force to fire him in his youth and on into his manhood. But he did not see that hatred now. He saw maturity, understanding, a man at peace with himself and his world. A man in love and comfortable with that love.

"You don't need to tell me, Chance. I believe I know what you're going to say. The past is over. Let's leave it at that, shall we?"

Chance studied Solomon for a moment, then finally nodded in contemplative agreement. "Yes, let's leave it at that."

Solomon turned to Jenna and gave her one last hug. Tears threatened to fall from both their eyes, but Solomon sidestepped his with a chuckle. "I'd better go. The train won't wait forever, and I'm anxious to get to New York. I intend to do some playing that I'm sure Jenna wouldn't approve of."

"Grandpa!" She shot a scolding but loving glance at him.

He laughed and hurried up the steps of the *Marietta* before she could say more. From the platform, he waved at them. The train started to pull away.

Jenna called, "I'll see you at Christmas! And *please* take care of yourself."

"You don't need to worry about me." He grinned for her benefit and cupped his mouth with his hands. "I'll take my toddy every night—right along with my cigars!" Laughing, he hurried into the car.

Jenna stared, slack-jawed, after him. Then she declared, "Cigars! He knows he's not supposed to start smoking again. What am I going to do with him!" Her voice caught and she began to cry. "My God, Chance. What will I ever do *without* him." She turned into his arms. "What if I never see him again? What if . . . something happens to him?"

With gentle fingers, Chance wiped her tears away. "Don't worry about him, Jenna. You know your grandfather is a survivor."

Arm in arm, they stood on the platform, waving good-bye. Solomon Lee stood at the window, waving back. He was still there when Jenna and Chance became small stick figures in the distance. He stood there even after they had left the depot and gone to their buggy, cuddling into it close together and kissing. At last the train took the bend out of Rathdrum and he could no longer see them or the town.

He left the window and wandered down the hall to the dining room. Sitting in his favorite chair, he pulled the letter from his pocket and stared again at his name written across the front. To him, it seemed to have been written with a great deal of care and possibly even love. He debated whether to even open it but curiosity won out and he slid his finger beneath the sealed tab. With hands shaking again, he opened the single sheet of folded stationery. The words blurred before him; words that had been said before; words of love, words of regret, words of good-bye— but not good-bye forever.

He read it several times before putting it back inside the envelope. He felt unusually calm. He would see Lily again at Christmas, and someday they would be grandparents together. It was a small consolation, but it was all he had. It was time to face once again that old demon called reality. Most importantly, though, he had something from her he could cherish. And she had signed it, "With love, Lily."

As the train rumbled north, he rose from his chair and went to the buffet, pulling open the top drawer. There was something he had been thinking about doing now for days.

Malcolm appeared from the kitchen. "Would you care for something to drink, sir?"

Solomon didn't even look up as he rummaged in the buffet for his map. "No. I'll wait until dinner."

Malcolm bowed formally as he always did, then left.

Solomon took the string from the rolled map and laid it out upon the big table, setting some glasses and ashtrays on the edges to hold it down.

It was a weathered map but one he'd had for the greater part of his life. It held special meaning to him. It showed America and the rough lines of the states as they'd been admitted into the Union, as well as the territories. The boundaries had changed many times in his lifetime, but the lines of the railroads he had built had not changed.

With his pen, he made a line through Idaho Territory's panhandle, adding the Bitterroot Railroad. As the train gathered speed, he leaned back in his velvet armchair and focused on the map, looking at all the bare spots where he had no lines and where he knew there were none laid by anyone else, either.

The old feeling returned—the excitement, the challenge. There was more track to be laid, more men and more mountains to conquer. He pressed his finger to a bare spot on the map. With sudden, renewed glee, he traced the course for his next railroad.

AUTHOR'S NOTE

For the purpose of this book, the author has fictionalized the events, as well as the characters, surrounding the first railroads that came to the Coeur d'Alenes of Northern Idaho.

In 1886, there were six plans to build railroads in the area. D. C. Corbin, a young entrepreneur from Montana, finally won the bid by getting the support of the Northern Pacific. He incorporated his Coeur d'Alene Railway and Navigation Company (CR&N) on April 22, 1886.

The first line built left the Northern Pacific main line at Hauser Junction, seven miles west of Rathdrum, and passed through Post Falls on the way to Coeur d'Alene City, coming to its end at the dock. The second line ran from Old Mission to Wallace. Soon other lines followed and other companies stepped in. Eventually there were lines on both sides of the river, and every canyon that had mines also had railroad service. The difficult branch from Wallace, over Lookout Pass, and to Missoula was finally completed in 1890, thus eliminating the need for lake transportation of the ore.

There was an actual "S" bridge built near the town of Mullan in 1889-1890. It was seriously damaged by a snowslide in 1903 and then destroyed during the disastrous fires of 1910. It was rebuilt and used until the NP replaced it with a switchback in 1963.

The desire for the fabulous wealth of the Coeur d'Alenes, and the challenge that the Bitterroot Mountains posed to the miners and railroaders alike, has been portrayed as accurately as possible in this story.